The Castle of Stories

Books by Matt Cain

THE SECRET LIFE OF ALBERT ENTWISTLE

BECOMING TED

ONE LOVE

THE CASTLE OF STORIES

Published by Kensington Publishing Corp.

Outstanding praise for Matt Cain and his novels.

ONE LOVE

"A beautiful, deeply human exploration of the blurred lines between love and friendship that exist in the queer community, with a tender understanding that the most important love of all can be the love and forgiveness we hold for ourselves."
—Steven Rowley, *New York Times* bestselling author of *The Celebrants* and *The Guncle Abroad*

BECOMING TED

"Sweet, detailed, and heartwarming." —*Kirkus Reviews*

"Another charmer." —*Library Journal*

"This is fun, frothy and frivolous; perfect for the gay beach."
—*The Bay Area Reporter*

"*Becoming Ted* is a thoroughly detailed portrait of the fictional small town of St. Lukes-on-Sea and the colorful characters who call it home. It's also a touchingly reflective examination of how much gay identity has changed over time, with queer folks of a certain age or growing up in other parts of the world having to cope with issues—like abuse, imprisonment and internalized homophobia—that are much more dangerous than those with which Ted is contending. In the end, however, most of the story's many strands are tied up neatly in a show-stopping finale that, while perhaps not entirely realistic, is quite satisfying."
—*BookReporter*

Please turn the page for more reviews!

More praise for BECOMING TED!

"*Becoming Ted* is truly a journey for all the characters, and I loved reading about people who are discovering new things about themselves later in life and evolving, which is my favorite part of the book. It truly goes to show you can always start anew at any time!" —*The Southern Bookseller Review*

THE SECRET LIFE OF ALBERT ENTWISTLE

"A heartfelt coming-of-age story—first love and first loss, new friends and new identities, the realization that your parents aren't who you think they are—except that the age Albert is coming-of is retirement. The most remarkable thing about the many wonderful love stories in this novel is how unremarkable they are after all."
—Laurie Frankel, *New York Times* bestselling author

"Wonderful. Written with such a good heart, filled with joy and strength and optimism . . . inventive and fun but most importantly, true." —Russell T. Davies, creator of *It's a Sin*

The Castle of Stories

Matt Cain

JOHN SCOGNAMIGLIO BOOKS
KENSINGTON BOOKS
kensingtonbooks.com

JOHN SCOGNAMIGLIO BOOKS are published by

Kensington Publishing Corp.
900 Third Avenue
New York, NY 10022

ISBN: 978-1-4967-6048-7

ISBN: 978-1-4967-6049-4 (ebook)

First Kensington Trade Paperback Edition: May 2026

10 9 8 7 6 5 4 3 2 1

Printed in the United States of America

The authorized representative in the EU for product safety and compliance
is eucomply OU, Parnu mnt 139b-14, Apt 123
Tallinn, Berlin 11317, hello@eucompliancepartner.com

For Chris Bollinghaus,
the best man at my wedding
and a better man than any I could invent

Prologue

It's beautiful. Much more beautiful than I imagined—or dared let myself imagine.

"Mr. Webb," says the lawyer in his strong Italian accent, "I present you *il Castello Montemagno*!"

Signor Mancini gestures to a ruined castle perched on top of a little hill, a vineyard snaking along its slopes. At the bottom stands the sole remaining wall of a stone chapel, which is painted with a flaking mural of a man he tells us is San Bartolomeo—which I can only assume translates as Saint Bartholomew. We've already driven through an olive grove containing nearly fifty trees and Signor Mancini leads us around the side of a terracotta-tiled garage to reveal a handsome three-story stone farmhouse, with a smaller cottage built onto the side. Both are framed by the magnificent, velvety green Apuan Alps, while in front of the property stands a paved patio covered by a pergola entwined with gnarly—and what look like very old—vines. We cross it and step onto a small lawn, which runs up to the ridge of a hill, along which have been planted bushes, shrubs and trees. From there, Signor Mancini shows us a spectacular view over the Freddana Valley, the Ligurian Sea in the distance. I let out a breath.

"All of this now belongs to you!" Signor Mancini announces, waving his arm with an extravagant flourish.

Theo gives my shoulder a squeeze. "Adam, I can't believe it."

Neither can I.

"But you must believe it!" protests Signor Mancini, a dark-haired, wiry man wearing a fitted navy suit and square spectacles in silver frames. "The *castello* was the property of your great-uncle Wilfred Treadwell, and he named you his heir."

"But that's just it," I say, "I never even met my uncle. I only vaguely knew he existed. Why did he leave it to me?"

The lawyer shrugs. "He did not have a wife or children so I do not think it is unusual."

"But why not leave it to friends?" I lay my hand on the trunk of the vine. "I didn't think he even knew about me."

"He was not in contact with your family?" asks Signor Mancini.

"No, there was some kind of disagreement." I tug at the collar of my polo shirt. "Well, it was more a rift, I suppose. But that was way before I was born. By the time I came along nobody even talked about him. I didn't know he lived in Italy till I got your email."

I think back to the day that email arrived, just over a week ago. I'd been in the office, trying to feign interest in yet another meeting—one of the least enjoyable elements of my job as Head of Human Resources in a big insurance company. As the Chief Operating Officer ran through the latest list of employees who'd applied for voluntary redundancy, I spotted an email pop into my inbox from an Italian address. I couldn't resist lowering my phone under the table and opening it. On reading the first line, I gave a gasp, which I quickly disguised as a coughing fit, excusing myself and ducking outside for some water. Within an hour, I'd called Signor Mancini—who confirmed I was the sole beneficiary of a house, eleventh-century castle and nearly fifty hectares of land just outside the village of Montemagno in the remote hills of Tuscany. I immediately followed this up with a call to my boyfriend, who was even more surprised than I was as he'd never heard me mention a great uncle. As Theo's a headmaster and had just broken up for the Easter holidays, he suggested we fly out to Italy as soon as possible.

We landed in Pisa yesterday, picked up a car rental from the airport and drove to Lucca, which is where Signor Mancini had suggested we stay. It's the provincial capital, fourteen kilometers from Montemagno, and the location of his office. By the time we'd checked into our hotel it was early evening, but we still made time for a quick stroll around what we discovered to be a charming medieval city, before stumbling on the adorable Piazza dell'Anfiteatro. As it was warm, we sat at a table outside and shared one dish of pasta with wild boar and another of risotto with porcini mushrooms, accompanied by a bottle of local wine. We held hands as the sun went down and the lights in the square flickered into life. I told myself how lucky I was to have such a gorgeous man—a man who's over six foot tall, with fair hair, dazzling blue eyes and a physique that can still be described as athletic. It was such a magical evening, I convinced myself it had to be the start of something special—a special adventure for the two of us, together.

This morning we reported to Signor Mancini's office, handed over my identification documents, and listened to him read out a translation of the will. Then we followed his car up here—to the house where Wilfred Treadwell lived for over sixty years. Sixty years during which the rest of his family was in Manchester. But what did they fall out about in the first place? And how did he end up here?

"I am sorry," Signor Mancini says, his forehead creasing. "It is always sad when families do not speak."

"Yeah, it is," I answer. I remember how long it's been since I spoke to my dad. "Can we go inside?"

Signor Mancini takes out a set of keys and inserts a long iron one into a pair of wooden doors that have been painted turquoise. He slowly pushes them open and we step into a stone-floored, wood-beamed kitchen with larder—both of which are probably best described as "basic." The patterned brown ceramic wall tiles look like they date back to the 1960s, the wooden units are rickety—with one of the cupboard doors missing and another hanging off—and what's being used as a sink is just a slab of stone with its middle scooped out. Along the far wall is an open fireplace, the back of which has been stained black and over which hangs a brass cauldron that looks like it belongs to a witch. As a keen cook, I'm more struck by how little counter space there is. I also notice that there's only a small, freestanding oven. Even so, I picture myself zipping around, preparing a risotto or a pasta sauce, the room filling with enticing aromas.

We climb up a stone staircase to the first floor, where we find not one but two lounges, the first of which is snug and cozy, the second double-ceilinged and more like a hall. Both of them are filled with battered old couches and dark wooden furniture, much of it tatty or dilapidated. The floors are paved with terracotta-colored bricks and the walls of irregular-shaped stones have been left exposed, some of them stained with patches of damp. Although Wilfred only died a few months ago, the surfaces are already covered in dust and there are cobwebs trailing from light fittings. Between the lounges there's a study stuffed with old books—their spines faded and their pages yellowed—and a bathroom fitted with a suite that must once have been white but is now streaked with an orange almost as bright as the Aperol Spritz I drank last night. Not just that, but the sink's cracked, the toilet's so old the chain has rusted, and the inside of the bath is spattered with animal droppings. It's a grim sight. But despite this, there's something romantic about the place, something I find enchanting.

But how does Theo feel about it? I turn to see him rushing around, flinging open doors and poking his head in and out of rooms.

"Bloody hell," he booms. "This place is amazing!"

Relief sloshes through me.

We follow Signor Mancini through a connecting door into the little two-story cottage, which has its own—even more run-down and less user-friendly—bathroom and kitchenette. He directs us back into the main house and up another flight of stone stairs to the third floor, which has yet another big lounge, another grimy bathroom, and a couple more rooms that have been left completely empty.

"It's so weird that there are all these rooms but hardly any beds," I comment.

"I'm sure we could get hold of some beds quite cheaply," offers Theo. "The kids could have a bedroom each."

My stomach dips. I was only making an observation: the last thing I wanted was to suggest bringing Theo's children here. It's six months since he introduced me to them but only the youngest has shown me anything other than hostility—a hostility I'm desperate for Theo not to witness. I don't want him to think that in the long term we're only going to be incompatible.

Signor Mancini cocks his head. "I did not know you had children."

"Yeah, three," says Theo, breaking into a grin. "They're fifteen, thirteen and eight."

"In Italy it is very unusual for a gay couple to have children," the lawyer observes.

"They're not mine!" I butt in. "We've only been going out for eighteen months."

Signor Mancini scrunches up his forehead.

"Theo used to be married to a woman," I explain. "He came out as gay when they split up, two years ago."

Theo looks uncomfortable.

I'm annoyed at myself: I need to remember he doesn't like sharing the personal details of his story, especially those that have been the source of intense emotions—that *continue* to be the source of intense emotions, emotions that I know torment him and keep him awake at night.

"Did you say the house is eleventh century?" I quickly toss in. "Or is that just the castle?"

Signor Mancini smiles. "Both. The rooms at that end are the oldest." He points to the section farthest from the castle. "That part was originally a tower. Sorry, I'm not sure how to say it in English: it was where soldiers watched for enemies."

"So it was a lookout post?" says Theo.

"Yes, exactly! Then later it was extended and became a farmhouse. Over the years more and more rooms were added."

"That'll be why there are no corridors and the layout's a bit random," Theo suggests.

"But why's it so run-down?" I ask. "Why haven't the bathrooms been modernized? Did my uncle have no money?"

Signor Mancini throws up his hands. "I'm afraid I know very little about Mr. Treadwell. But he did not leave any savings—just a few hundred euros in a regular bank account."

I'm desperate to know more but there's no point in persisting. "Do you know how he died?"

"Yes: Mr. Treadwell died in his sleep. His neighbors found him—Signor and Signora Fiore. I understand they helped him with jobs on the house and land."

"Well, it's the perfect way to die," Theo remarks. "Isn't that how we all want to go?"

I smile but feel a tug of sadness. I would like to die in my sleep but not on my own.

"Which was his room?" I ask the lawyer. "Do you know?"

Signor Mancini nods and guides us downstairs. On the right he opens a creaky door into a square room that has plastered white walls, a large wooden wardrobe and chest of drawers, and a wrought-iron bed on which lies a bare mattress. Standing next to it I spot a framed photo of two men. It looks like it was taken in the 1970s, as one of them is wearing flared jeans and a paisley shirt with a wide collar. This man's probably around my age—in his mid-forties—but still has a boyish face and caramel-colored hair.

"Is this him?" I ask, picking up the photo. "Is this Wilfred?"

Signor Mancini peers at it. "I believe so, yes."

"Let's have a look," says Theo.

I hand it to him.

"You can see the family resemblance," Theo comments. "He's got the same dimples in his cheeks!"

I lean in to examine it. "Oh, yeah."

"Although he isn't as cute as you, Ads," Theo says, handing back the frame.

I smile my thanks.

"And who's the other bloke?" I ask Signor Mancini. The second man is quite a bit older than Wilfred, with a bald head and five-o'clock shadow, and is dressed more traditionally, in a crisp white shirt with beige chinos and brown leather shoes. The two men look stiff and uncomfortable next to each other. I wonder if they might have had some kind of business relationship. Except it looks like the picture was taken outside the house.

"I'm sorry, I don't know," confesses Signor Mancini. "There was no mention of this man in the will."

I put the photo back on the nightstand and sit down on the mattress. The old coils squeak.

"I must also show you the wine store," says Signor Mancini, exiting the room and trotting downstairs. "It occupies most of the ground floor."

As Theo follows him, I remain sitting on the mattress and run my hands over its surface. So Wilfred died right here on this bed. I wonder what he was thinking before he went to sleep. Did he still think about his family?

I jog downstairs and follow the sound of Signor Mancini's voice—and the smell of his strong aftershave—outside, then back into the house through another big door, entering a cavernous ground-floor chamber that looks like it hasn't been used as a wine store for some time. Although there are a few empty kegs and barrels, it's clearly been repurposed as a dumping ground for all kinds of domestic items, such as broken tables and stools, tins of dried-up paint and varnish, and a storage heater that looks like it hasn't worked for years. There's also an enormous old mustard-yellow boiler, a washing machine that—thankfully—seems to be in working order, and various dustbins for rubbish and recycling. It smells damp, musty and a bit rank.

The lawyer's phone pings and he lifts it out of his briefcase to read a message. "I am sorry," he states, "I must return to Lucca. But I think you have seen most of the important things."

I try not to look disappointed. "But what about the castle?"

Signor Mancini leads us outside and around the wall of the chapel, where he points towards a crude path that zigzags up the side of the hill. "That is the way. But I am afraid the castle is only a pile of stones."

"I'd still like to see it," I say. "If you don't mind."

"Not at all. But it is difficult to climb and I cannot do it like this." He gestures to his smart suit and black leather shoes. "If you like, I can leave you the keys and you two can enjoy more time here?"

We accept his offer and he takes us back to the house and shows us how to lock up.

"Please return the keys to my office in the morning," he says. "And we must start the process to get a *codice fiscale*—that is an Italian social security number. We must also deal with the issue of inheritance tax."

Shit, I didn't think of that. I've never inherited anything before—I'm not from that kind of family, nor are any of my friends.

"What do you mean, inheritance tax?" I ask, aware that the pitch of my voice is rising. "I'm not going to have to pay any money, am I?"

Signor Mancini rakes his fingers through his hair. "Yes: in Italy everyone who inherits property over a certain value has to pay tax."

"But how much?"

He runs his hand up and down the strap of his briefcase. "I do not know for sure but I have done a very rough calculation." He tells me what it is.

I give a yelp. "Where am I supposed to find that kind of money?"

He raises his shoulders. "Most people who do not have the money choose to sell the property."

"Sell it? But I haven't even finished looking at it!"

Theo puts his arm around me. "Ads, let's not worry about that for now. I'm sure you'll have plenty of time to decide what to do before you have to pay."

He thanks Signor Mancini and we shake hands. Once his car has driven up the graveled lane and disappeared around the corner into the olive grove, Theo suggests opening a bottle of wine. "Come on, I spotted some in the larder."

"But can we just take it?" I ask, following him through the turquoise doors. "None of this belongs to me yet. And I don't think I can afford to keep it!"

Theo reassures me it'll be fine, finds a bottle opener in a drawer he has to yank open, and rinses a couple of glasses under a tap that splutters out water. We fetch some chairs and sit on the patio, looking out over the valley.

As it's only April and the trees aren't yet in full leaf, the landscape contains patches of brown as well as green. And there are various grays in the stone of houses, farm buildings and churches, plus splashes of blue in the smattering of swimming pools. The blue of the sky is much lighter and broken up by a strip of little clouds, like puffs of smoke released from a stuttering engine. It's quiet, apart from the odd snatch of birdsong and the sound of the occasional car or motorbike driving through the valley.

"Cheers," I say.

"Wait, how do you say that in Italian?" asks Theo. "Is it *salute*?"

"Something like that." I tap my glass against his. "*Salute!*"

"To the Castello Montemagno!"

"*Prego! Certo! Buonasera!*" I say, affecting an over-the-top Italian accent. "Do we know any other Italian?"

"*Mamma mia!*" joins in Theo.

"*Mamma mia!*" I warble, even louder.

We both laugh.

I gaze out at the sea, which is nestled in the V between two mountains, the diminishing foothills of a third stretching behind it, as if wrapping it in an embrace. The sunlight is reflected on the sea's surface, so it shimmers, almost winking at us.

"It's like something out of a fairy tale," Theo says, rubbing stubble on his chin that—even though he's about to turn forty-seven—is only just flecked with gray.

"I know." I turn to face him. "And it's got so much potential."

"Yeah, but there are loads of jobs that need doing," he points out. "I've already spotted a few rotten window frames and missing roof tiles."

I take a swig of my wine. "And there's the damp."

"And a couple of leaks."

I let out a long sigh.

The sun has started slipping down the sky. Soon it'll be setting. When I was little—and the weather was half-decent, which wasn't guaranteed in Manchester—I used to watch the sunset with my mum. She used to say it was our way of saying goodbye to the day. The two of us would sit on a wooden bench in our back garden and look out over the playing fields. But these have since been turned into a housing estate and Mum's been dead for over thirty years. Thirty-four to be exact: I was eleven at the time.

I stand up. "You know what, if we're going to see the castle, we should probably get up there—it'll be dark soon."

Theo tips back what's left of his wine. "Yeah, come on."

We walk around the chapel, find the path and begin our climb. Well, Signor Mancini called it a climb but if he'd known the word *scramble*, I'm sure he'd have used that. The hill's steep and there's been no attempt to flatten the earth, so we have to cling onto stones, trunks and tree roots to haul ourselves up. When we finally reach the top, we stop to dust ourselves down, then push through the thick overgrowth, taking care not to prick ourselves on the brambles. I'm glad my legs are covered with jeans but wish I was wearing long sleeves. By the time we emerge in a clearing, I've picked up several scratches on my arms.

The land in front of me is stepped and there are thin strips of wall visible between the different levels. But that seems to be all that remains of the castle—which is strange as looking up from below, the walls were several meters high. I realize that the rooms of the castle must have been filled in with earth, which would explain why they have so many bushes and trees growing out of them. I wonder if it would be possible to dig the earth out again and restore the castle's basic structure.

We find a spot on a stone wall, only half of which is intact: the other has fallen away. We sit down and go back to enjoying the view over the valley. It's pretty much the same as it was from outside the house but the higher vantage point makes it even more breathtaking. It's also much quieter up here, with none of the sounds of cars or motorbikes. And there's less birdsong—only the odd tweet.

The sun's about to disappear behind the mountain and is spilling out rays of pumpkin, apricot and peach.

"I don't think I've ever been anywhere as beautiful," I tell Theo.

"I know. And it's so romantic." He takes hold of my hand. "It makes me realize how much I love you, Adam."

He moves in to kiss me on the lips.

"I love you too, Theo." I snuggle up and rest my head on his shoulder.

Even though we've only been going out for eighteen months, I've already decided I want to spend the rest of my life with him. He's all I've ever wanted.

But I've always worried that the turmoil around Theo's divorce—plus the hostility from his kids—might one day get in the way, that it might lead him to the conclusion that the relationship is more trouble than it's worth, that all the negativity weighing down on him might overwhelm the love he says he feels.

I tell myself that we could come here to get away from the stress and negativity. This could be our happy place.

There must be some way of keeping it. . . .

I sit up. "I just thought, I could apply for voluntary redundancy. I'm sure they'd give it to me: if I went they could hire someone younger and cheaper. And you know the job doesn't make me happy. I've been bored of it for years."

Theo blows out his cheeks. "I've always said you're wasted in it. You could do with a change."

"Well, now I've got one—or the chance of one." I feel excitement taking hold. "I've been in the job for more than ten years so I'm pretty sure I'd get a year's salary. If I threw in my savings I'd probably have enough to pay the inheritance tax *and* do some basic renovations. Although we might have to chip in and do some of the work ourselves."

Theo inches forward. "That's OK. But what would happen afterwards? How would you earn a living?"

"I'd put it on the market as a holiday let."

"Is there a demand for that?"

"I don't know but I imagine so—loads of people come here on holiday. And I think it's mainly posh people with money."

Theo tilts his head so it catches the sun's rays, taking on a tinge of apricot. "Would you manage it yourself?"

"I guess so." I run my hands along the rough stone. "But we wouldn't rent it out all the time: we'd keep a few weeks free so me and you could come here too."

Theo waggles his eyebrows. "I must admit, that does sound appealing."

My heart's thumping. "Why don't we come here in the summer and just get on with it? You've got the school holidays—we won't get that opportunity for another year."

He frowns. "Yeah, but I'd still have work to do."

"Well, I could get Wi-Fi installed and you could do it from here." I slap out a rhythm on his thigh. "What do you reckon?"

Theo chuckles. "It does sound superb. But what about the kids?"

I feel a clutch of fear. "Didn't you say Kate's taking them to the States?"

"Yeah, she's taking them to her sister Shona's. So I'll probably only have them for a week anyway."

I release a breath. "Well, you could always fly home for that week."

"Or I could bring them here. . . ."

Shit.

I suddenly realize my plan could backfire. What if Theo finds out how much his kids hate me? I wouldn't be able to cover it up if we were together all the time. And then he might get scared. He might realize how difficult the relationship's going to be, long-term. He might look to the future and decide the relationship's impossible.

"But do you think they'd like it?" I attempt, meekly.

"Ads, how could anyone not like this?" His forehead puckers. "Alright, they might moan a bit at first but I'm sure they'd fall in love with it in the end."

I pause and watch the sun disappear behind the mountain.

I smile back at him. "Go on, let's do it."

"Are you sure?"

"Yeah. It's only a week. What could possibly go wrong?"

Three months later

Chapter 1

"Six weeks?"

We're in my kitchen and Theo's on the phone, talking to his ex-wife. He has her on speaker as he irons his work shirt for tomorrow. At the start of the conversation I was happy to listen in, sitting at the island pretending to do my online Italian course. But then Kate told Theo she's had a change of plans for the summer: her sister in Atlanta has found her an interior design job and it runs over the entire school holidays, so she won't be able to take the children after all. She said they'll have to come to Italy for the whole six weeks. At which point Theo stopped ironing and I spilled my glass of wine—thankfully not on my laptop. I stand up and grab some paper towels to wipe it up.

"Kate, it's not as if I don't *want* to spend the summer with them," Theo says, resting the iron in the cradle. "You know I was gutted when you said I could only have them for one week. But all six? It changes our whole summer."

"Well, what do you want me to do about it?" snaps Kate. "I can hardly dump them on Shona."

I put the sodden paper towels in the bin as quietly as I can and tiptoe back to my seat.

"I'm not suggesting that," protests Theo, unplugging the iron. "But couldn't we split the time?"

Kate huffs. "Theo, I can't leave them with her for *three* weeks. She's got a job, remember?"

"Oh yeah."

He widens his eyes at me as if to say, "What can I do?"

I slosh more wine into my glass.

"And before you ask," Kate steams on, "I'm not saying no to this job. I put my career on hold for years to have *our* children, to bring up *our* family. And you threw it back in my face when you walked out on us. So now I need to claw something back and build it up again. And I won't let you stop me!"

Theo rubs the crease between his brows. "I understand, Kate. And I'm not trying to stop you. But this isn't just my summer—it's Adam's too."

Bad move, Theo!

Kate makes a sound as if she's being strangled. "Right, so you're not satisfied with making me put my career on hold for *you*—now you want me to do it for your *boyfriend*!"

I can just imagine the face she's pulling as she says that word. I've only met Kate once—and that was briefly when she came to Theo's flat to drop off the kids. He was on the phone and I had to answer the door. I have to admit, part of me was glad I had an excuse to see what she looked like in real life. And she was pretty, slim and stylish, with honey-blond hair cut in an asymmetrical bob. But she refused to say hello and looked at me as if a bird had just shat on my face.

"That's not what I'm saying, Kate," Theo insists.

"That's *exactly* what you're saying!" Kate fires back. "You know, you really are unbelievable. You want to dump your kids on *my sister* so you can go swanning off to some castle in Italy with your rich boyfriend!"

I want to point out I'm not rich. But if she finds out I'm listening, it'll only make things worse.

Thankfully, Theo does the job for me. "Kate, Adam's not rich."

She scoffs. "That's what all rich people say."

"He grew up in a two-up two-down."

"Well, he's not living in a two-up two-down anymore. From

what I hear, that place in Italy is enormous. And he can hardly be strapped for cash if he's giving up his job."

I feel a kick of anger but try not to let it take hold.

Theo lets out a sigh. "Kate, Adam's taking redundancy."

"I'm not interested, Theo! The point is, he doesn't need to work. And you're not going to be working over the summer, so what's the problem?"

Theo kneads his eyelids. "We're supposed to be renovating a house. And I'm just not sure the kids will enjoy it—at least not for six weeks. And, you know, they were excited about America. They were excited about the pool."

"Stop pretending you're thinking about the kids," Kate barks. "As usual, you're just thinking about yourself. You know, you didn't used to be so selfish. It's like you're a different person now you're gay."

"He's always been gay!" I want to yell at her.

But Theo looks as if he's been wounded: she's hit him in his weak spot.

I move over and give his back a rub.

"I suppose this is Adam's doing, is it?" Kate blasts on. "Is *he* putting you up to this?"

I take a step back.

"Bloody hell, Kate," says Theo, "how can it be Adam's doing? You've only just told me about it."

There's a beat. "Wait a minute, is he *listening*? Is that why you're on speakerphone?"

Theo picks up the phone and trudges out of the room.

I can't hold my anger back any longer. Theo stayed in the closet for years to protect his family. We've talked about this a lot, so I know that when he was younger, he was confused about his sexuality: he knew he was attracted to men but also thought he was attracted to women. When he slept with Kate, he felt good about himself. But he didn't realize this was because he desperately didn't want to be gay. By the time he'd worked that out, they were married with a baby—and he wanted to do the right thing. That's why he ended up sacrificing his own happiness and living a lie for years. Until he couldn't do it anymore. And I do understand that it must have been really difficult for Kate, but she's showed Theo no compassion—and still refuses to forgive him.

I fill my lungs and let out a long breath. I decide to empty the dryer and start pairing the socks and piling them on the worktop.

The kitchen's my favorite room in the house, a house I moved into five years ago, when I became a first-time buyer at the age of forty, just a few years after finally paying off my student debt. It's a small townhouse in Prestwich, just outside Manchester city center, and couldn't be more different to the property in Montemagno. First of all, it was a new build when I bought it, so has no period features. There are three bedrooms—the smallest of which I use as an office—and one lounge. The kitchen is the biggest room, with a separate dining area, so it's perfect for hosting dinner parties—which is my favorite way to socialize.

As the pile of socks builds, my anger fades. Some of Theo's clothes have sneaked into the wash, which doesn't surprise me, as he's spending three or four nights a week here. When he split with Kate, he couldn't afford to buy anywhere for himself—at least not anywhere big enough for the kids to stay—so he rents a place in Sale, not far from the family home in Altrincham. But it's characterless and not very comfortable, which is why he spends so much time here. Although I'm more than happy about that. After our trip to Italy, we've been closer than ever. And making the decision to spend the summer together has given us a shared short-term future. That is, as long as his ex-wife doesn't ruin it.

Theo comes back into the room, looking crestfallen. "Ads, I'm so sorry."

I leave the socks and go over to hug him. His hold is strong and I can feel the hairs on his forearms tickle the back of my neck.

"It's alright," I reassure him. "It's not your fault."

We break out of the hug and sit at the island.

"No, but I know how much this means to you," he says. "I know how much you're giving up."

I take a sip of my wine. "It wouldn't be so bad if she'd given us more notice: we leave in ten days. The flights are going to be expensive."

"Don't worry, I'll deal with that. And hire a bigger car."

I force out a smile. I don't like to remind him that he hasn't got much money—ever since he gave in to pretty much all Kate's financial demands.

Theo spreads his hands on the table. "But you know, maybe it's happening for a reason. I know it's going to be a challenge, but it could work out for the best."

I can tell how desperately Theo's trying to convince himself as well as me. But I'm not going to argue. And I'm not going to criticize his kids. I can't: I hardly know them. After all these months, I've still only managed to establish a bond with Archie. He's eight and is into Marvel superheroes, WWF wrestlers and the card game Top Trumps, building up a collection of several of the different sets. We're not an obvious match but I like playing with his action figures—it's surprisingly imaginative—and we've managed to find a set of Top Trumps called Great British Bakes that works for both of us. But the older two—Callum, who's fifteen, and Mabel, who's thirteen—just refuse to engage with me. Their barriers are up the whole time. Last weekend, we took them to an Italian restaurant to try to get them excited about the holiday—which at the time we thought was only for a week. That's when we told them about the house and castle, information they must have passed on to Kate. The irony is, when we showed them pictures, they didn't seem remotely interested. They said the house looked boring, that the castle was just a load of rubble, and moaned that there was no swimming pool. No, I can't see how this is going to work out for the best.

"I suppose I was just looking forward to us having some romantic time together," I venture, diplomatically.

Theo sips his wine and swirls it around the glass. "I'm sure we can still do that. Callum's older now and very responsible. He's been babysitting for the other two for a while."

Great, so we'll get the odd evening out.

But I can't say that. I force out another smile. "I'll look forward to it."

Theo inches his stool closer and gives me a serious expression. "Ads, I know it isn't ideal. I know Callum and Mabel are still struggling with all the changes. But they're great kids, I promise.

They just need to get to know you. And this could be the perfect opportunity."

I remember the state of the bathrooms, that the builders have told us the kitchen will be out of action for two weeks. I remember that the earliest I can get Wi-Fi installed is mid-August—which would have been fine when the kids were joining us at the end of the holidays but not when they'll be there from the last week of July. And I remember how hot it was the last time I was there, which was only June—and there's no air-conditioning.

I have a premonition that sends a chill down my spine: the kids turn their dad against me and he dumps me—just like all my exes have in the past. All those exes who told me I was insecure, oversensitive, *needy*. . . . Wait a minute, is that what's happening now? Am I getting in my head, worrying needlessly and am going to end up scaring him off?

Whatever's going on, it's not as if I have any choice; if I want to spend the summer with Theo, I'll just have to accept his kids. And if I don't make an effort, that'll be a surefire way to lose him.

"You're right," I manage, brightly. "Let's see this as an opportunity. Let's make the most out of it!"

Although my expression is cheerful, I'm feeling dragged down by dread. My dream summer is turning into a nightmare and it hasn't even started.

Chapter 2

It's the day after my work leaving do but I'm not remotely hungover. We just went to a few bars around the corner from the office in Spinningfields. And there were several people leaving, two of them because of ill health, so the evening fell a bit flat. I ended up slipping away after a few hours, which suited me fine. Although I've been in that job for more than ten years, as soon as I made the decision to leave, in my head I moved on. I started looking forward to the future—and the next chapter of my life in Montemagno. This time next week we'll be on the plane.

As I've listed my house on Airbnb and rented it out for pretty much the whole summer, I'm going from room to room packing up everything personal. My Auntie Julie's going to manage the lettings for me and has said I can leave a few boxes of belongings in her garage. So I'm taking down framed photos, clearing the bathroom of toiletries, and wrapping up breakable vases and ornaments. I don't really like the idea of strangers staying in my home but will have to get over it: if I'm paying two sets of bills for six weeks I'll need the extra income.

Since Easter I've been back to Italy twice, once with Theo during half-term, and once on my own in June. When my *codice fiscale* finally came through, I set up a bank account, with the help of

Signor Mancini. Then we had to attach a value to the estate, work out the duty and complete a tax return. Only once this was done could he arrange for the deeds to the castello to be transferred into my name. And I could start filling out—with the help of my translation app—several online forms to set up accounts for the utilities, plus the Italian equivalent of council tax.

Signor Mancini also introduced me to the Italian couple who live in the property closest to ours—Stefano and Luisa Fiore. They're the couple who found Wilfred dead in his bed, but I decided against bringing that up at our first meeting. Stefano's a farmer and Luisa a history teacher in the high school in the closest town of Camaiore—and, thankfully, she speaks excellent English. Not that we had much time to speak at all as they were on their way out when we called. Although we did have just enough time to learn that Stefano used to maintain the vineyard and olive grove for my uncle—keeping seventy-five percent of the harvest for himself and giving twenty-five percent to Wilfred—an arrangement I was happy to renew. And for Luisa to explain that she runs the local history society, following this up with a request to do a dig of the castle—something she's been trying to set up for years. I pointed out that the deeds to the property state the castle is protected by all kinds of regulations, but Luisa reassured me she'd be working with the staff from the local museum, who know all about this kind of thing. I gave my permission and they've set up a dig for the summer: as she's a teacher, our dates coincide perfectly.

Other than that, Theo and I bought three new beds from a branch of IKEA near Pisa Airport. We also met with several builders and gathered their suggestions and quotes for the renovations. In the end, we hired a man called Giuseppe. Giving him the edge was the fact he's married to a British woman and so he speaks good English. But I've told him we don't want him to start until we're actually staying in the house, just in case anything goes wrong.

In the meantime, I've doubled my efforts to learn Italian—although I keep getting distracted so haven't made much progress. But everyone tells me the easiest way to learn is through immersion in everyday life so I expect that'll become my plan.

I've also researched the lettings market in Tuscany and it's more lucrative than I expected. Even without a pool, if the property is rented out for the full season I should be able to stay off work. If not, I'll have to pick up some contracts as a freelancer or find a part-time job. But I want to give myself the best chance of avoiding that—and that's one of the reasons I'm putting the house in Manchester on Airbnb.

I take down a photo of me and my best gay friends—who I call my sisters—on a wild singles' holiday to Gran Canaria. There's a selfie I took of me and Theo on Canal Street a month after we met, on the night he asked me to be his boyfriend. Then there's my favorite photo of my mum.

It was taken the summer before she died, when she and Dad took me on holiday to Newquay. I remember we'd just eaten our tea in the caravan when Mum insisted we all go outside to watch the sunset. Dad said she looked beautiful in the soft light and went back in to find his camera. In the photo she's smiling, relaxed and tanned, holding a glass of gin and tonic, sitting at a table on which stands her usual jar of Nivea hand cream and packet of Silk Cut cigarettes, around her neck the silver S she wore for her name, Suzanne—an S she'd often run up and down the chain as she was talking. Mum's hair was naturally fair but she dyed it butter-blond and had just had it permed, which was the height of fashion in the late '80s.

She was beautiful. I'm sure everyone thinks their mum's beautiful but I know mine was because everyone said it—not just Dad but shop assistants, bus drivers and strangers who'd stop her on the street. She loved the attention but would giggle and pretend to be embarrassed, then catch my eye and give me a wink.

I wrap the photo in old newspaper and slot it into the box. I've got lots to do. There's no time to be sentimental.

That evening, I take the boxes to Auntie Julie's. As an only child, I don't have much family and after Mum died, Auntie Julie brought me up. All these years later, we're still close.

Although they got on well, Mum and her only sister were very different. If Mum was known as a beauty—with an enviably slim figure—Julie was often called "big-boned" or people would comment on her "lovely personality." Unlike Mum, Julie didn't dye her hair, which I always thought was the same shade of brown as the sugar we used in baking. And while Mum liked nothing more than getting dressed up to go out, Julie preferred to stay in wearing her slippers and an apron. She's always been happiest in the kitchen—and inspired my passion for cooking and baking.

When I arrive at the house, Julie's partner Jason is just leaving. He works nights as a security guard in the Trafford Centre, even though he's a talented carpenter and is always building things in the garage. But he also has a stutter and is shy around people he doesn't know—and this has held him back. As a tall, well-built Black man, he's always managed to find work in security, which I worry could be a sign of racial stereotyping but he insists doesn't bother him. And, as he often points out, working in the Trafford Centre introduced him to Julie. She works in the shopping mall's HR department—which is another area in which she's influenced me. On Jason's first day—just over twenty years ago—he had to report to her to fill in some forms, something that made him nervous. But Julie immediately put him at ease, so much so that shortly afterwards he asked her out for a drink. Possibly because of his stutter, Jason had never married or had children. I wonder if Julie never married because she had to look after me.

I give Jason a hug and together we load the boxes into the garage. Once he's left for work, Julie puts the kettle on and makes us both a mug of tea, which we take through to the lounge. It's a cozy room, with lots of scatter cushions—all in Julie's favorite pink—plus several well-tended houseplants and a vase of magenta roses. As this is the house where I moved to live just before my twelfth birthday, it still feels like home.

"So are you all set, chuck?" Julie asks, as she makes herself comfortable in her favorite armchair.

"Yeah, pretty much." I sit on the sofa opposite. "This thing with the kids has thrown a spanner in the works but I'm still excited about it."

"Good." She blows on her tea. "You know, I still can't get over it. It still doesn't feel real."

"You're telling me. A few months ago, I didn't even know where Wilfred lived and now I'm moving into his house."

Julie arches an eyebrow. "Wilf, I think they called him. I've just remembered. Or at least my mum and dad did. On the rare occasions they mentioned him."

"That's interesting." I stand up and walk over to the windowsill, where I pick up a photo of Julie's parents—my grandparents. I peer closer and examine the face of my grandma—Wilf's sister—to see if she looks like him. I think there may be a resemblance.

"So do you still have no idea why they fell out?" I ask, sitting down again and pulling some of the cushions out from behind me.

Julie lifts a hand to tidy her hair, which is shorter than it used to be and much lighter. "I'm afraid not. I was four years younger than your mum, remember. Nobody told me anything: they treated me like a kid who needed protecting. That is, until I started working things out for myself. . . ." A shadow scudders across her face.

"What are you talking about? Working out what for yourself?"

She has a sip of tea. "Nothing. I've told you, I don't know anything about Wilf. I always just assumed he got some Italian girl in the family way."

"But the lawyer in Italy said he had no kids."

Julie puts her head to one side. "Then maybe he just ran off with one. This was only a few years after the war, remember. And my granddad—his dad—wouldn't have liked him seeing anyone from Italy. He fought the Italians and for a long time was a prisoner of war."

"Oh yeah, I didn't make that connection." I have a gulp of tea. "The only thing is, the lawyer said Wilf wasn't married. So if he did run off with an Italian girl, it can't have lasted. In those days wouldn't they have got married?"

"Not if she was married in the first place."

I turn my mug between my hands. "I didn't think of that."

Julie sits back and puts her feet up on the pouffe. "I remember once, when we were kids, your mum mentioned Wilf to our granddad. He went berserk and clipped her round the ear. Afterwards, Grandma took us to one side and said he didn't want to talk about Wilf as he found it too upsetting."

I frown. "So whatever happened, it must have been bad."

"Especially as beforehand Wilf was a bit of a golden boy. He was the first in our family to go to university and was an English teacher." Julie takes a swig of tea and sets her mug on a pink coaster. "That must have been a big deal for someone from our background. We lived in a council house, remember. My grandma and granddad—Wilf's mum and dad—left school at fourteen and worked in the mill."

Now I'm even more intrigued. "So were you never tempted to look him up on social media?" I'm not sure why I'm asking that question—I've already looked him up several times and found nothing. I just told myself that he was eighty-nine when he died so it was hardly surprising.

Julie screws up her nose. "I'm sorry to say that by the time social media was a thing I hardly thought about him."

"It's just such a mystery."

"I know, chuck." Julie folds her arms under her ample bust. "But you've got a good chance of solving it. You've just inherited his house—and presumably all his stuff."

I remember the wardrobes and drawers in Wilf's bedroom stuffed full of old clothes, his study stuffed full of bills and bank statements, and the wine store stuffed full of everything but wine. "Honestly, there's loads of it," I say. "I wouldn't know where to start."

"Well, maybe you should forget about Wilf and just enjoy what you've got," says Julie. "Maybe it's better not to dwell on the past. What good can it do? Start afresh. A big old house like that is going to be full of ghosts. Sweep them out and make it your own."

Chapter 3

The night before we leave for Italy, I say goodbye to my three closest friends—my sisters. We meet for dinner in Manchester's Northern Quarter, in a restaurant that serves excellent seafood and has stylish décor, with oak furniture, ochre walls, dusky filament lighting, and succulent-lined shelves. The only thing is, it may be a little sedate for what looks like it's going to be a raucous night.

"Ladies, I need to tell you about my latest pull," announces Gloria. "He had a face like a tortoise's minge but I swear down, he banged me like a shed door in a hurricane."

We gasp and giggle.

Gloria is the loudest, most outrageous of my sisters. We met on a night out, when I spotted him dancing on a pole to Geri Halliwell's "Bag It Up" and decided we had to be friends. His name is actually Paul—a name chosen by his Ugandan parents to give him the best chance of fitting into their adopted country. But fitting in was never on the cards for a bald, six-feet, four-inch-tall Black man who's overweight, has a beard that's usually covered with glitter, and a penchant for wearing bright makeup, synthetic wigs and gold or silver lamé body stockings. At some point in the long-forgotten past, someone had decided the name Gloria would be much more suitable.

"So are you seeing him again?" I ask.

Gloria looks at me as if I've just suggested he lick a slug. "Girl, I don't even remember his name. All I know is it was Eastern European and sounded like some poison the Russians would use."

There's another burst of laughter. We've just finished eating and a waiter appears to clear our plates and unload a tray full of cocktails. I take a swig of mine: I've no idea what it is but it tastes like smoke.

"How about you, Dom?" asks Gloria, twirling the ends of his purple wig. "Have you had any action?"

I snicker. "When has Dom *not* had any action?"

Of the four of us, Dom is the one with the most crowd-pleasing looks. His white skin only needs marginal exposure to the sun to acquire a tan, and he has thick hair, an equally thick moustache and a smattering of chest fur that are the color of dark chocolate. He also has a deep voice, chunky wrists, and—as a former football player—calves like hams. Since birth, Dom has been deaf in one ear, but most men only seem to think that makes him more attractive, almost as if without this flash of vulnerability his looks would be too intimidating. He and I met on a hookup arranged on the website Gaydar, in the days before they were even known as hook-ups. I would have taken it further but Dom made it clear he wasn't in the market for a relationship. After I saw him out on Canal Street a few times, we eventually became friends—and then sisters.

"Alright, alright," says Dom, sitting at an angle so his good ear is directed at us. "I did actually hook up with someone last week. He was fit and I liked him. But I got the impression he's looking for a boyfriend."

"At which point you bolted," I chip in.

Dom gives a rakish smile. "You know me too well."

"Dom, every gay in Manchester knows you've got the sexual appetite of a baboon in the mating season," quips Gloria. He takes his vape out from under the table and turns his back to have a sneaky puff.

"Honestly, you girls make me feel like a dried-up old spinster," says Ian. "The closest I get to an orgasm these days is driving over a speed bump."

We laugh and Gloria slaps Ian on the arm.

At fifty, Ian's the oldest in our group. He's mixed-race, with silver glasses and equally silver hair, and tonight is wearing another of his collection of check or gingham shirts—this one in orange and green—with chinos and brown leather trainers. I met Ian at university, when I was an undergraduate and he was studying for an MA, in his spare time running the student union's GaySoc. Like my other sisters, Ian is single. Unlike them, this is because his long-term partner died five years ago, after one uncharacteristic and experimental line of cocaine aggravated an undiagnosed heart condition. For a long time, Ian was floored by grief. When he finally started to pick himself up again, he abandoned his career in marketing and became a life coach specializing in working with LGBTQ+ clients. But he's never shown any interest in returning to dating.

"My sister, we need to reawaken your inner ravishing, sensual woman," says Gloria, caressing his gold lamé-covered body.

Ian gives him a curled look. "Gloria, I don't think I've ever been *any* of those things."

Gloria gives him another slap. "Hush your mouth! You are fifty and *fuckable*!"

The straight couple sitting at the next table looks over disapprovingly.

"And how are things with our favorite twink?" Dom asks, turning the attention onto me. My sisters often wind me up about having a cute, clean-cut, boyish look—a typical twink. Although recently that's shifted to winding me up about being an *aging* twink.

"Here, I've got a joke for you," cuts in Gloria, after another puff on his vape. "What do you call a twink over forty?"

"T'was?" guesses Ian.

"Twinked?" says Dom.

"Twunk?" I pitch in.

Gloria shakes his head. "Nobody calls a twink over forty!"

We gurgle with laughter.

Ian takes his glasses off and cleans them on his shirt. "Ignore her, Adam. She's just jealous because you've bagged yourself a gorgeous man."

"Yeah, how's it going with Theo?" asks Dom. "More to the point, why's he not with us tonight?"

I smile. "It's brill, thanks. But the kids only finished school today so he took them shopping and now he's doing their packing."

Gloria whistles and fans himself with a menu. "Girl, he could pack my suitcase any day. That is one serious zaddy."

"And that whole headmaster thing is a massive turn-on," adds Dom, loosening his collar and blowing down it.

Gloria adopts the voice of a little girl and flutters his fake eyelashes. "Please, sir, can I have a detention? I've been *ever so naughty*!"

Our laughter is starting to sound like cackling. The woman at the next table looks over again, this time turning up her nose as if she's caught a whiff of an open sewer.

I decide the restaurant is definitely too sedate. I don't know why I hadn't noticed before but it's frequented almost exclusively by couples. Theo and I actually came here on our first date. After matching on a dating app, we'd migrated to WhatsApp and chatted for a few weeks, then decided to meet in real life. By that stage, I already knew he'd been married to a woman and had three children. What I didn't realize was that he'd only been out of the closet for six months—and not just that but was still uncomfortable expressing his sexuality in public. At one point I leaned across the table to touch his hand—but he pulled it away. Warning bells rang.

I excused myself and went to the toilet to message my sisters on our WhatsApp group. I'd missed warning bells in the past but did I need to listen this time? Ian replied first and confirmed that this kind of behavior was a red flag. "If he's only just started to accept himself, then he's probably not ready to love another gay man."

The others agreed.

I thanked them and returned to the table, determined to pull back. But I couldn't. Theo was so handsome, with his blue eyes, hairy forearms and chest, not to mention those cute tortoiseshell glasses he wore to read the menu. Plus he made me laugh and made me feel safe in a way none of my ex-boyfriends had. There was no way he'd cheat on me or disappear for the weekend on a drink- or drug-fueled bender. I couldn't even imagine him chipping away at my confidence or putting me down—wrapping insults in compliments if we were in company—as so many of my exes had. That I was attracted to him and not to yet another man who could only ever bring me misery and heartache felt like a major step forward. I'd just have to try and ignore the warning bells.

At the end of the night, we stood outside the restaurant and I risked giving him a goodbye kiss. I was relieved when he didn't flinch and the kiss developed into more than a quick goodbye. Alright, he may have had a few glasses of wine but he didn't seem awkward and didn't look around to check if anyone was watching. That's when I knew that, if he was still adjusting to life as a gay man, he was at least ready to push himself and grow. Plus, he was a fab kisser.

The next day, Theo got in touch to say he'd booked us places on an Italian cookery course I'd mentioned reading about, only to find it was fully booked for months. But Theo knew one of the instructors and had somehow secured us places for the following Saturday. This was particularly sweet as I discovered he's a terrible cook: he put one egg too many in the dough for his tagliatelle so it ended up soggy; he didn't seal his ravioli parcels properly, so they all burst; and I don't know *what* he did to his *cantuccini* biscuits but they came out so hard that when he bit on them he chipped a tooth. We did have fun, though—and we laughed *a lot*. It was then that I knew there was no way I could stop seeing Theo, even if he had only recently come out. If he was still on a journey, I was going to be there to help.

"Seriously," says Ian, "how do you feel about spending the summer with the kids?"

I drain half of my glass. "To be honest, I'm not looking forward to it."

"I'm not surprised." Gloria purses his purple, pink-lined lips. "It sounds as dreary as hanging out with a white girl who wants to discuss race."

"What's that saying?" offers Dom. "Kids are like farts—you can only stand your own."

Now we really do cackle.

Gloria sneaks another tug on his vape. "I'm sure you'll have a fab time, Addy. And if you don't, that's where the gin comes in."

Dom runs his hand over the muscles on his forearm. "The important thing is, Theo's really into you. You know what, I bet you'll be engaged by the end of the summer."

I scoff. "As if! His divorce only came through the other week."

Gloria sits up. "I just thought, could that be why the ex-wife's causing trouble?"

I wrinkle my nose. "I don't see why; he gave her everything she wanted."

Gloria wags his finger. "Addy, that bitch is on a revenge trip. I bet she's plotting how to ruin your summer."

"You'd better keep an eye on her," agrees Dom, smoothing his moustache. "This may not be the end of it."

I tip back the rest of my drink. "Fuck. That's all I need."

"Yeah, but look on the bright side," chirps Gloria. "Whatever happens, we've still got our sisterly weekend."

As soon as I told my friends that Theo and I were spending the summer in Italy, they started researching flights—and within a few hours had booked to come and visit for the first weekend in August. At the time, that was three weeks before the kids were arriving, so I thought it would work well. Now I'm not so sure.

Dom rubs his hands together. "I can't wait to get to that castle, dump my stuff and open Grindr."

Gloria lets out a whinny of excitement. "Same! I've always loved a nice, thick Italian salami."

"You'll be pleased to know I've already been researching the gay bars," says Ian. "There's one about twenty minutes away—on a gay beach!"

"Yes!" squeals Gloria.

"Get in!" booms Dom.

I smile but can feel my anxiety rising. What's it going to be like seeing my two worlds collide? What's going to happen when my sisters come face to face with a pair of sulky teenagers—and an eight-year-old boy who just wants to play Top Trumps?

When the waiter arrives to clear our plates, I excuse myself to go to the toilet. When I re-emerge, Ian is waiting for me in the corridor.

"Alright, my sister?"

"Yeah, what's up?"

He frowns. "I just picked up on a bit of anxiety behind your smiles."

I lean on the wall and let out a breath. "I am anxious, yeah. I'm anxious about the kids. I'm anxious it'll all be too much for Theo."

A woman with sharp cheekbones emerges from the Ladies and totters past us on treacherously high heels.

"I know it's going to be challenging," Ian answers. "But basically you've got to try and relax. Don't put too much pressure on yourself. And don't let your abandonment issues get in the way."

I turn to face him. "What's that supposed to mean?"

"Adam, every time you've been out with someone you've spent your whole time terrified they'll leave you."

"And they did! They all left me, every single one of them."

That's not to say that it hurt the same every time. I once dated a man called Jeff, who was addicted to steroids and building up muscle in the gym. As his personality was ninety-percent pectorals, I hardly batted an eyelid when he left me. But then there was Steve, the sweet estate agent I dated in my early thirties and became convinced was cheating on me with his best friend—not that I had a scrap of evidence. Until he announced he'd had enough of my paranoia and walked out on me just before our third anniversary. Even revisiting the memory all these years later, I still feel the flare of shame.

A man who's spilled a dollop of what looks like cheese sauce down his shirt walks towards the Gents, unzipping his fly in advance.

"But it was like you were *expecting* it," Ian continues, "almost goading them to leave you. And when they did it was like you were relieved, or felt vindicated, because you'd proved you were right. You had more evidence to back up that story you tell yourself, that everyone leaves you."

I feel exposed and wriggle my back against the wall. "God, Ian, I don't know what was in those cocktails but you're not holding back."

"Sorry, my sister, I just know how important this is to you. I know how high the stakes are."

From the other side of the restaurant comes the sound of a coffee machine hissing.

"Yeah, well, I wouldn't want to be with any of my exes now," I say. "So it all worked out for the best."

Ian nods. "Theo's a much better bloke than all of them."

I mime shock. "Excuse me, that's not what you said at the beginning!"

"I know but we were just looking out for you. We only knew Theo on paper. Once we got to know him, we all came round."

The man with food on his shirt re-emerges from the Gents, rearranging his crotch.

"You know, all I ever wanted was to find a man who loves me," I say, "a man who'll never stop loving me. And this is the best chance I've had. Probably the best chance I'll ever have."

Ian tugs a hand through his silver hair. "That's why I don't want you to be insecure and introduce any unnecessary tension. I just want you to get it right, Adam."

"Excuse me, *I* want to get it right. I don't want to feel vindicated, or whatever it was you said earlier."

"Good." Ian pulls out his stick of lip balm and runs it over his lips. "Just because something's been your story for a long time doesn't mean it has to be forever."

"Absolutely. I'm not that person anymore." But even as I say the words, I'm not sure they're true.

"Right, coaching session over." Ian pushes himself off the wall.

"Thank fuck for that!"

We wind our way back through the restaurant and over to the table, where we find Gloria chatting up a bemused-looking waiter. "In case you're wondering," he says, batting his eyelashes, "I identify as sensational."

The waiter offloads a tray of shots and dashes away.

"What are these?" I ask, sitting down.

"Sambuca," Gloria answers, lifting his vape from under the table and no longer bothering to hide it. "It's Italian, isn't it?"

Dom lifts a glass. "Whatever it is, it'll do me."

We each tip back a shot. The hot aniseed burns my throat.

"Now let's pay the bill and get out of here!" tweets Gloria.

"I need to get away from these loved-up couples before I catch something," says Dom. He turns to me, as if he's just remembered. "No offense, Adam."

Gloria opens the camera on his phone and reapplies his lipstick. "Luckily for you bitches, I've booked us into a drag show in the Village."

I roll my eyes in mock exasperation. "Gloria, you know I've got a flight at nine in the morning."

He bats away my objection, his bracelets jangling. "Yeah, yeah. It's not every day your sister moves to a castle in Italy. We've got to give you a good send-off!"

Chapter 4

The next morning, my hangover is brutal. As Gloria would say, I feel like I've been dug up and belted with a shovel.

It did indeed turn into a raucous night. Just as we arrived at the drag bar, the Sambuca shots kicked in. After downing another round, we were all wasted. Dom successfully fended off the attention of three former hook-ups and disappeared into a corner with a blond man whose biceps were thicker than my waist. Ian spent a long time giving impassioned life advice to a straight woman he'd just met who'd been dumped by her boyfriend, insisting she was an inspiration, a goddess and a warrior, while she sat there wailing, showing no evidence of being anything of the sort. And Gloria got up on stage to belt out a female empowerment anthem by Dua Lipa, alongside a pair of drag queens called Bonita Gooch and Perry Anal. I managed to sneak off at around 1:30 a.m., grabbing a chicken burger from McTucky's on the way. When my alarm went off at 5:30, the remains of it were scattered around me on the bed. I was fully clothed, with a piece of cucumber stuck to my cheek and a blob of mayonnaise in my ear.

I stand up and start stripping off my clothes but give a little stagger and realize I'm still drunk. How am I going to get through the day? I curse myself for getting the summer off to such a bad start. I'm supposed to be a responsible adult. I'm supposed to be the host!

I knock back a strong coffee, jump in the shower, knock back another, and when the minibus arrives, crash out on the back seat.

My phone pings with a text. I look at the home screen and see it's from Dad. That's all I need.

Alreet, lad, it reads. *Is it today ur off to Italy? Have a beltin time. Dad*

My stomach lurches. I put the phone away.

A few minutes later, I'm feeling worse and have to ask the driver if he'll pull over so I can get out and throw up. I lean on a wall at the side of the road and empty my guts into a drain, tears streaming from my eyes as passing cars sound their horns. I feel the sting of humiliation.

When I look up, I see a little old lady pulling along a canvas granny trolley, who's stopped to stare at me.

"Sorry, it was a heavy night," I mouth, feebly. Then I find myself adding, "We went to a drag bar."

The old lady gives me a wink. "Don't worry, love. We've all been there."

Fifteen minutes later, the minibus pulls up outside Theo's flat. By now I'm sitting up, wearing my sunglasses—despite the fact the sky is slate gray—and chewing gum.

"Morning!" I screech, then realize I sound borderline deranged.

Thankfully, Archie gets in first and sits next to me. "Want to play Top Trumps?" he bursts out, the kink at the front of his ginger hair looking more upright than usual. "I've got our favorites!"

Theo slides in next to him, takes one look at me and knows how I'm feeling. "I think Adam might need some quiet time, squirt. Maybe at the airport."

"Why does this minibus stink of booze?" says Callum, thumping himself down on the back seat and squeezing his long limbs into the leg space.

"Is it you, Adam?" asks Mabel, sitting next to Callum, wearing her usual baggy top and sweatpants. "Oh my god, are you an alcoholic?"

"Mabel, Adam's not an alcoholic," states Theo.

"Mum says alcohol's a drug," Mabel crows. "She says it's a poison."

"She's right," I groan.

"Well, I'm glad you think that," Theo says to Mabel. "I'll remind you of it when *you* want to go out drinking."

Mabel tugs on a strand of her long fair hair. "As if! I'm *never* going to touch alcohol!"

"How do you say *alcohol* in Italian?" gabbles Archie, his green plastic glasses slipping down his nose.

Theo pushes them up again. "I've no idea, squirt. We can look it up later."

Callum makes a gagging sound. "Seriously, that smell is minging." He opens his window so wide that the sound of the motorway overrides any attempt at conversation. That works for me.

Mabel puts her earphones in and starts listening to music I imagine is her usual Harry Styles or Taylor Swift, while I see from the screen of Callum's phone he's listening to Oasis. I close my eyes and imagine I'm sitting in Montemagno, enjoying the sunset. I look at my watch: I just have to get through the next five hours and I'll be there.

When we arrive at the airport, we discover our flight's been delayed until lunchtime. Deflated, we trudge through security, battle our way through the crowds, and manage to find four seats that have just become empty. Theo insists on standing and I clear away the remains of the previous occupants' breakfast—which makes me want to throw up again. Over his shoulder I notice a bar packed with early-morning drinkers and am suddenly desperate for the hair of the dog. But I couldn't bear to defend myself against more accusations of alcoholism. Besides, when we get to Italy I want to drive: that way I won't have to do too much talking.

To pass the time, Theo suspends his usual rule and allows Callum and Mabel unlimited screen time. Archie and I lose ourselves in a marathon game of Top Trumps—playing not just with our favorite set Great British Bakes, but also Wonders of the World and Creatures of the Deep. I focus on the detailed description of manatees and conger eels and, by the time we hear the call for boarding, think I've memorized every statistic for the Blue Blubber Jellyfish.

"Adam, can I sit next to you?" squeaks Archie. "I've got Skyscrapers and Dinosaurs in my bag!" He smiles, revealing a gap where his two front teeth recently fell out.

"Of course you can!"

Across the aisle from us, an argument erupts between Callum and Mabel over who gets the window seat, then—when Theo tries to settle it by taking the seat himself—they start elbowing each other for control of the armrest. Once we've taken off, Theo has to sit between them, setting his stopwatch to split their time in the window seat.

"How many people are on this plane?" Archie asks me.

I look around and give him a rough calculation.

"How high does it go in the sky?" he continues.

I find the answer to this in the airline's brochure.

"Why does it not fall out of the sky?"

This I have no idea how to answer but Archie's eyelids are drooping. Soon, he's nodded off—and I'm not far behind.

Miraculously, I manage to sleep for over an hour. By the time we're landing, I feel much less rank.

It takes us nearly an hour to clear customs and collect our luggage, but when we finally emerge from Pisa Airport, one of the first things we see is a cluster of those tall, slender cypress trees that I always associate with Tuscany. Above them, the sun's blazing in a sky that's almost exactly the same blue as Callum's Manchester City football shirt. And all around us, we hear the distinctive sound of crickets rubbing their wings together.

I feel a rush of excitement. "Get a load of that, kids! We're on *holiday*!"

"Yeah!" warbles Archie, wiggling his bum. "Woo-woo!"

An Italian couple who are passing give him a smile. "*Che carino!*" says the woman.

I've no idea what that means but guess it must be something about Archie being cute—and he is, with his freckled cheeks, carrot-colored hair and skinny little legs. I return her smile.

Mabel, on the other hand, scowls. "Archie, you're so cringe!"

In response to this, he begins circling her and wiggling his bum even more.

Theo steps in. "Gang, look at that sunshine. Isn't it superb?"

Callum runs a hand over his short fringe. "Mum's text—apparently the weather's sick in Atlanta."

"*Everything's* sick in Atlanta," adds Mabel.

Theo and I exchange a look of solidarity. We lead everyone to the car-rental terminal—dragging our suitcases behind us—but when we arrive at the desk there's a long line.

"Why do they always have to be so slow?" I ask Theo. "Everyone's filled in the forms online. Why can't they be ready to go?"

We pick apart the process, joking that we should be management consultants and could whip the industry into shape.

"Why do adults have such boring conversations?" interjects Callum.

Theo and I burst out laughing.

"I've got to admit, that *is* a bit boring!" says Theo.

Am I imagining this or is there a hint of a smile playing at the corner of Callum's mouth?

"How do you say *car* in Italian?" cuts in Archie.

I look it up on my translation app. "*La macchina.*"

"Try to remember that," says Theo, laying his hands on Archie's shoulders. "In fact, let's learn as many Italian words as we can."

"Dad, why do you have to make everything about *learning*?" moans Callum, all traces of his smile gone.

"We're supposed to be off school!" agrees Mabel, pulling her sleeves over her wrists.

I can't help thinking that she must be hot in her long-sleeved top and sweatpants but don't say anything. I know she's still growing into her adult body and is struggling to shed the puppy fat. That's why she prefers to cover up—and pulls her long, wavy hair in front of her face. She's also conscious of her big boobs and hunches over slightly in an attempt to make them less noticeable. Callum, on the other hand, has shot up to over six foot but still hasn't started filling out. I assume from the number of protein bars and muscle-building shakes he gets through that he must hate being skinny. At least he'll wear shorts and T-shirts, although he does stoop to make himself shorter. And he avoids smiling, to hide the train-track braces on his teeth. I suddenly remember how miserable it is being a teenager.

Theo ignores his older children as he and Archie look up the Italian words for *engine*, *gear stick* and *steering wheel*.

When we've finally reached the front of the line and picked up the keys, Mabel announces she's desperate for the loo. We follow the sign to the other side of the terminal but she refuses to use the Ladies, saying it's too dirty. "Dad, there's a turd in there!"

Theo chuckles. "It won't bite you—flush it away!"

Mabel looks horrified. "What if I catch salmonella?"

"What's sallomella?" asks Archie.

"Mabel, you won't catch salmonella," Theo reassures her.

He finds a disabled loo, goes inside to check it's clean, and Mabel slinks in after him. When she eventually emerges, Theo says, "That better, chicken?"

Her face falls. "Dad, I've told you not to call me that!"

"Alright, alright." Theo flashes her an impish grin. "Sorry, chicken."

Mabel growls and turns her back on us. I can't help but feel relieved.

As we lug our cases to the car park, Theo asks if I want him to drive.

"No," I insist, "I'll do it!"

We find the car but discover it's a much tighter fit than either of us expected. We purposefully ordered the smallest five-seater so it wouldn't be difficult to maneuver down the lane through the olive grove. But the boot isn't big enough for our luggage, and Theo and the kids have to sit with bags balanced on their laps and wedged in between their feet.

Once I've adjusted my seat and mirrors, I type the address into the satnav, then remember that we need to stop at the supermarket; otherwise, we'll have nothing to eat tonight. I delete my first search and type in the name of the supermarket nearest the house. We set off.

Within seconds, I narrowly miss colliding with a concrete bollard. I feel a judder of fear: I haven't had much practice driving on the other side of the road and I'm not a great driver at the best of times. To make matters worse, the kids are falling out before we've even left the car park.

"Dad, I'm squashed!"

"Dad, Mabel's breathing on me!"

"Callum's leg's digging into me!"

As an only child who didn't even grow up around cousins, I've no sense of how siblings interact, or what level of acrimony is normal. Theo doesn't seem concerned. Then again, he is buried under suitcases.

In an attempt to lift the mood, I point out a field of sunflowers. "Look at that, kids! Isn't it beautiful?"

"We grew sunflowers at school," snipes Mabel. "*Primary* school."

"How do you say *sunflowers* in Italian?" asks Archie.

"How do you say *annoying little brother* in Italian?" grumbles Callum.

"Come on, gang," says Theo, "let's try and make an effort."

I decide to zone out and concentrate on my driving. The view soon becomes dull, with nothing to see other than motorway, drab residential developments and nondescript farmland.

Wait a minute. . . .

"Theo," I say, under my breath, "I don't recognize this."

"Are we lost?" shrieks Mabel.

Shit!

At the first turning, I exit the motorway and pull over in a dusty layby. By now the kids aren't just yelling at one another but exchanging physical blows. While Theo excavates himself from under cases to intervene, I consult the satnav. I discover we've driven south rather than north.

Fuck!

I must have accidentally clicked on the wrong branch of the same supermarket. I prise myself out of the car and explain my mistake to Theo. He gives my shoulder a supportive bump. "It's OK, Ads. Don't worry."

He lowers his head into the back of the car. "Sorry, gang. We've made a mistake."

The three of them groan.

"Dad, can *you* drive?" asks Mabel.

"Adam doesn't know what he's doing," says Callum.

There it is again: that sting of humiliation.

"Cal, Adam *does* know what he's doing," Theo argues. "We just made a mistake. It happens to everyone."

Even in the face of fierce animosity, I appreciate Theo's *we*.

"Sorry, kids!" I say, brightly. "I'll correct it in no time."

Theo and I slide back into the car and I turn it around. But by the time we're passing the airport again, the sun's setting. I'm gutted as I was looking forward to watching the sunset from the house. Now we won't get there till it's dark. I wonder if the shops will still be open but decide not to bring this up and hope for the best.

At least the route soon looks familiar.

"Are we nearly there yet?" asks Archie.

"My leg's gone dead," moans Mabel.

"Not long now," Theo reassures them. He reaches over and gives my knee a squeeze.

I try to interest the kids in the mountains up ahead, the ancient trees running along the side of the road, the dried-up river that flashes in and out of view behind them. "It looks like it hasn't rained in ages," I comment.

But they're not interested—and soon the light's faded completely.

When we arrive at the supermarket, it's closed. Through a chorus of groans, I drive to another, but that's also closed.

"Dad, I'm going to faint," whimpers Mabel.

"If I don't eat soon I'll die," bleats Callum.

We discuss finding a restaurant but Theo doesn't want to leave the car with everything in it. I tell him I'm pretty sure I left a few packets of pasta and a jar of sauce in the house.

He taps a beat on the dashboard. "That'll do!"

We set off along the road that winds up the hill to Montemagno. As we drive through the village, it's so dark I decide not to even point it out.

"Nearly there!" says Theo.

I turn left and drop down into first gear in order to mount the steep hill. This road is single-lane and whenever I drive up it I dread seeing another car. Once we reach the Fiores' house, I know I'm in the clear. Relieved, I take a left turn, into our olive grove.

"This is it, gang!" Theo pipes. "You're entering the Castello Montemagno!"

Very slowly, I proceed down a gravel lane that's so narrow it's only a few centimeters wider than the car—with a steep drop on either side.

"This is just a load of trees," says Archie. "Where's the castle?"

Before anyone can answer, Mabel screams.

I slam on the brakes.

A few meters ahead of us—emerging from the olive trees—two wild boars come trotting across the lane. One of them is clearly the mother, the other much smaller. The mother stops and turns to face us, blinking in the headlights. Her body's black with long, white hair that looks bristly and coarse. Her piglet, on the other hand, is light brown, with even lighter stripes running down its body.

Theo whistles. "Well, you don't see that in Manchester!"

"What are they?" whispers Archie.

"Wild boar," Theo whispers back.

"Will they attack us?" asks Mabel.

"No," Theo replies. "They're much more frightened of us than we are of them."

For a moment, we sit in silence, the five of us united in awe. Then the mother boar turns and trots off into the bushes, her piglet toddling after her.

"What about that?" I say, swivelling round to look at the kids. "Wasn't that fab?"

But just like that, the special moment has passed.

Callum shrugs. "It was OK."

Mabel flicks her hair. "If you like that kind of thing."

I hit the accelerator.

"Who wants to know how to say *wild boar* in Italian?" asks Theo.

Archie is the only one who answers. "Me!"

"*Cinghiale,*" says Theo. "I know that because the first time we came to Italy, Adam and I ate wild boar pasta."

"And it was delicious," I add.

Mabel mimes the sound of retching. "You two are gross!"

Theo chuckles. "Oh, give it a rest, chicken!"

"Dad, I *told* you not to call me that!"

We park in front of the garage and tug our cases across the patio towards the house. I look to see the kids' reactions but they're so tired—and so bad-tempered—they barely even glance up at it. They don't even notice the sea. Theo does, though.

"Look at that, Ads," he says, nuzzling the side of my head. "We made it."

"Yeah, we made it." I want to kiss him but feel self-conscious in front of the kids. "Come on, let's get inside."

I unlock the front door and we step through it. I switch on the lights, revealing the kitchen. There's a beat of silence. The wooden units are even more dilapidated than I remember and the light bulbs so dim, the room looks dingy and unwelcoming.

"Is this it?" asks Mabel.

"What's that minging smell?" says Callum.

"Just the smell of old houses," I sing-song. "It probably needs some air." But even as I say that I can't help thinking that the kitchen's usual smell is laced with something else—something dirty.

"Why don't you guys put on some mosquito spray?" I suggest. I open a drawer and thrust a can at Theo.

While he takes them outside to supervise the operation, I fling open the cupboards and look for the pasta. But the packets I left have been bitten through by some kind of rodent—and the contents obliterated. All that's left are crumbs and droppings. So *that's* what the smell is. . . .

I slam the door shut.

I remember leaving a small box of cereal in another cupboard, one that's on the wall and raised from the ground. I open it and see that amazingly, I also had the foresight to leave a carton of UHT milk. There's not enough for all of us, but it should at least keep the kids quiet.

I explain the situation to Theo and he puts three bowls on the kitchen table and rations the food between them. I insist I'm not hungry, hoping he can't hear my stomach roaring.

Mabel pulls a face. "What's the matter with this milk? It tastes funny."

"Nothing," says Theo, "it's just long-life."

"Dad, it's knocking me sick." She pushes her bowl away.

Just as I'm thinking I'll have it, Callum swoops in and slides the bowl towards himself. "What's the Wi-Fi password?" he barks, spraying crumbs all over the table.

This is the moment I've been dreading most.

Thankfully, Theo handles it for me. "We'll deal with that tomorrow. As soon as you've eaten, we're going to bed. After the day we've had, we all need some sleep."

Unbelievably, no one argues.

I show the kids up to their rooms, promising them a full tour of the house tomorrow. We've decided Theo and I will sleep in the cottage: even though it's connected to the rest of the house by an interior door, it feels a little more private. Mabel and Archie will sleep in the rooms on the top floor—in the new beds we bought on our last trip—while Callum will go in Wilf's room on the middle floor.

When he sees it, he tugs at his fringe. "It looks like some old man lives here."

"Not anymore," I chirrup. "It's where my uncle used to sleep."

Callum recoils. "What, so some guy *died* in that bed? *Dad*!" he shouts through the door. "I can't sleep in here!"

Theo steps into the room, Archie's toothbrush in his hand. "Cal, we can pick up another mattress tomorrow. You'll just have to make do for one night."

"Actually, we can swap it with the one in our room," I suggest, cheerily. "That way we won't have to buy another."

Theo agrees and the two of us heave the mattress off our bed and haul it through the house, trying not to let it catch on the dusty floor.

"You're sure nobody died on this one?" Callum asks, as we toss it onto his bed.

"Positive!" Theo and I say in unison. We look at each other and smile.

At that moment, I hear a buzzing sound and remember the mosquitoes. Shit, we've only got two nets. I was going to pick up some more to hang over the kids' beds—before their arrival was brought forward.

I decide to give one to Mabel and the other to Callum, provided he'll let Archie share his bed, just for tonight.

"Yes!" cheers Archie, bouncing into the room in his pajamas. "Sleepover!"

Callum groans and pulls a pillow over his head. "This is proper shit!"

"Cal, don't swear!" booms Theo.

From outside comes the *twit-twoo* of an owl.

"Dad, is this house haunted?" shouts Mabel from upstairs.

"Why, do you want me to come and give you a cuddle?" Theo shouts back at her.

Mabel screams and slams her door.

By the time Theo and I finally collapse onto our bed, we're too tired to even kiss.

And I'm really annoyed at myself.

I've made a mess of our first day. The holiday didn't have to start so badly. I've let myself down. And I've let Theo down.

I'll have to make up for it tomorrow.

Chapter 5

I'm woken by the sound of a cockerel crowing. I've no idea where it's coming from. I turn over and squint at my watch. It's just before six a.m.

Well, I'm awake now so I might as well get on with it.

I sit up and take in my surroundings. Light's streaming through a little window we left open because it was so hot—and some of it falls on Theo's face. He's gorgeous when he's sleeping, but he looks very different when he's awake. Ordinarily, he's strong and authoritative, especially when he's around his kids. But there's a gentleness to him when he's asleep, a vulnerability, a fragility. It offers me a glimpse into the man who tried to protect a trans pupil from bullying only to end up having a mental health crisis of his own, a crisis that led to him coming out. I'm overcome by a need to care for him, to make sure he's never hurt again.

I feel an itch coming from my lower body. I look down and see a trail of mosquito bites on my left leg and a cluster around my right ankle. Shit! They must have got in through the open window.

I stand up as quietly as I can and close it. I'm pretty sure there's some antihistamine cream in a drawer in the kitchen. I put on a pair of sliders and a light dressing gown I found in Wilf's wardrobe and sneak downstairs.

As I pass through the house, I don't open any of the shutters as I don't want to wake anyone. Once I've found my cream, I pull open the big front doors as quietly as possible—which isn't very quietly at all as they catch on the floor. I pause and listen to see if there's any stirring from upstairs. When there isn't, I step outside and onto the patio. I slather my bites in cream, then sit down on a wooden bench, holding my dressing gown open so the cream can dry.

Even though the house and the grounds—*my* house and grounds—are starting to look familiar, I'm struck by their beauty all over again. There's much more greenery than when I first came here at Easter. The trees and bushes are in full leaf, various grasses and ferns have shot up and fanned out, and there's even the odd prickle-covered cactus. The vine twisting in and out of the pergola is bursting with heart-shaped leaves, and hanging from it are bunches of small, not-yet-ripe purple grapes.

The view of the valley and the rippling hills is also much greener. It's still specked with the gray of buildings and the blue of swimming pools but it no longer contains much brown. Although, curiously, the lawn and patches of grass around the house have turned brown, presumably burned by the sun. I realize they won't have been watered since Wilf died and make a mental note to do this regularly. Likewise, the plants at the edge of the lawn bear signs of neglect, although some of them—presumably the hardier ones—have come into flower: bursting out of the green are lilacs, pinks, oranges and a dash of blue. I wonder if the edge of the hill has eroded over the years. Where was it when Wilf arrived and has it crept back, closer to the house? I can't escape the sense that, not only are we surrounded by nature, but we're almost battling it, trying to hold it back or halt its advance.

A white butterfly flutters from flower to flower and a twittering comes from the birds swooping through the sky. I'm hopeless at identifying species but I can tell that these are swallows because I once dated a man called Mark who had a tattoo of a swallow on his right thigh. Until he got to know what I was like and dumped me for a nude life-model who had pierced nipples with bolts through them. Not that this was the first time he'd cheated on me;

from what I heard, when I wasn't around he'd behave like a sailor on leave. In fairness, he had told me on our first date that he was struggling with sex addiction—but I convinced myself I could help him beat it. Actually, had I? Or was Ian right when he said the whole relationship was some form of self-sabotage? Some way of proving to myself that I wasn't good enough?

Although my relationship with Mark is hardly a happy memory, I'm glad it's popped into my head. Because it reminds me of what I have with Theo—however challenging the kids may be. It reminds me of why I want to fight for it. And it makes me even more determined.

But before I do anything, I need a coffee.

I fasten my dressing gown, go back into the kitchen and twist open the gas canister that's under the stove. Then I make myself a coffee in Wilf's old aluminum moka. When I first took possession of the house, I had to Google how this worked, but now I can whiz through the process in seconds. Once the pot's smoking, I pour my coffee and go back to sit on the bench.

By now the population of the valley is stirring. I can hear the ringing of church bells, the low hum of light Sunday-morning traffic, plus a bus giving a hoot of its horn as it rounds a tight bend in the road that winds up the hill.

Oh, the kids are bound to come round. They *have* to like this place. And if they don't, there must be some way of *making* them like it.

I look up the opening hours of the supermarket and decide to slip on some clothes and drive down. But first, I'm going to clean out the kitchen cupboards and remove all trace of the rodents.

Yes, those kids are going to *love* this place!

Pushing my trolley through the aisles of the supermarket, I marvel at the size of the tomatoes, the fragrance of the bundles of fresh basil, and the plumpness of the cherries and artichokes. I pile everything in, along with an abundance of cheeses and hams. My mind is already buzzing with ideas for sauces and salads I can make. But right now I need to plan breakfast—a breakfast to win the kids round.

I pick up several bags of fresh oranges that I'm going to squeeze using Wilf's old lever-arm juicer, visit the bakery counter for a crusty *ciabatta* and a herb-topped *focaccia*, and grab a few boxes of eggs and a selection of yogurts and jams. I also buy the kids some of the treats I know they love: milk chocolate buttons for Archie, the same brand of white chocolate Theo gets in for Mabel, and a handful of protein bars for Callum. I feel the same excitement as when I'm shopping for a dinner party and am confident my menu is going to hit the target. At the same time, it's strange to be shopping for a family. It's something I never imagined I'd be doing.

When I reach the front of the line, I smile at the assistant, a middle-aged woman with a bored expression. "*Buongiorno!*"

"*Buongiorno,*" she echoes, with noticeably less enthusiasm.

As I pack my groceries, I wonder who she thinks I'm buying for. Does she assume my partner is a woman or is it obvious I'm gay? I wonder how she'd respond if my Italian was good enough to say, "I'm shopping for my boyfriend and his kids."

When she's finished scanning, I reach into my wallet for my new credit card—held jointly in the names Mr. T Armstrong and Mr. A Webb—and feel a thrill as I hand it over. Theo set it up, saying it would be the simplest way for us to buy food and essentials, saving us the hassle of working out who owes what with every bill. While I don't dispute this, it also felt like a sign we were taking our relationship to the next level.

But I remind myself Theo's a dad. He and his kids come as a package. So I can only really take our relationship to the next level if I can bring them along with us.

When I get back to the house, Theo has lifted the outdoor table and chairs out of the wine store and arranged them on the patio, where he's sitting drinking a coffee. At his feet, Archie is wearing a Captain America baseball cap and playing with his action figures, organizing a rescue operation for Black Panther, who's stuck in a plant pot.

Theo stands up and helps me with the shopping.

"Did you sleep well?" I ask, as we carry the bags into the kitchen.

"Yes, thanks. I feel like a new man."

I load the milk and butter into the fridge. "Brill! So you didn't get bitten by mosquitoes?"

"No. They didn't come near me." He lifts out two cantaloupe melons and puts them in the fruit bowl. "I seem to remember it's got something to do with blood groups."

"Or maybe they're just not that into you," I quip.

"Maybe." He chuckles. "How about you?"

"They're *really* into me!"

He grabs me around the waist and pretends to nibble my ear. "I'm not surprised—you're bloody gorgeous!"

I slap him away, giggling. "Theo! Archie's outside!"

"And?"

I grab the bottles of water and slot them into a cupboard. "Anyway, it's fine. I've got some cream and I'll pick up more spray and candles this afternoon. What time do you want breakfast?"

Theo tells me that Callum and Mabel still haven't got out of bed but he's going to give them till eleven o'clock, then wake them. As that's only forty-five minutes away, I start work.

"What can I do?" asks Theo.

I thrust some dishcloths and antibacterial spray at him. "Give the table a wipe and set it."

While Theo gets on with that, I clear myself a space on the only available worktop. Not only does the kitchen have hardly any counter space but most of the knives and peelers are blunt, I have to crack my eggs into a salad bowl to beat them, and all the pans are ancient, with no nonstick covering and their undersides black. Theo also tells me there's only just enough crockery for the five of us—and that's after taking down a decorative plate from the wall and giving it a wash.

"Didn't your uncle cook for anyone?" he asks, as he towels the plate dry. "Didn't he have any friends?"

"I don't know." I pause my chopping and shrug. "Maybe he didn't. Maybe he didn't like people. Or maybe they didn't like him."

"How could anyone not like someone related to you?"

I roll my eyes. "You're very slushy this morning."

"I can't help it," he chirps, "it's the Italian air. It makes me feel *molto romantico*!"

I laugh and go back to chopping my onion. Once I've fried it and added it to the mix for a spinach and ricotta *frittata*, I leave it to bake in the little oven and start squeezing my oranges. As I do, I feel a rush of happiness. Cooking for people is the thing I've always done best. I'm on safe ground.

By the time my *frittata* is ready, it's eleven o'clock. Theo goes upstairs to rouse Callum and Mabel. A few minutes later, the two teenagers come sloping downstairs, wearing baggy T-shirts and sulky expressions. As they enter the kitchen, the atmosphere changes. Straightaway they're moaning about being woken up, sleeping badly in the heat, and picking up the odd bite from mosquitoes.

"I don't know how that happened," I say. "We mustn't have closed your nets properly. We'll have to be extra careful tonight."

"You know, Archie and I haven't been bitten at all," comments Theo. "I think we have different blood groups. You two must take after your mum."

Callum shoots Theo a look of contempt. "Dad, that is proper out of order."

"Why do you always have to take it out on Mum?" hisses Mabel.

Theo winces.

I sweep between them and direct everyone to sit down. "We've got fresh orange juice and I've made a *frittata*!"

Theo smacks his lips. "Superb!"

Callum eyes the *frittata* warily, as if I've just placed a bomb in the center of the table.

"What's that?" asks Archie, his glasses on the end of his nose.

Theo pushes them up again.

"It's the Italian version of an omelet, but you bake it in the oven," I explain.

"What's in it?" Archie goes on.

"Eggs, onion, spinach," I say, "and an Italian cheese called ricotta."

"Amazing!" gushes Theo.

"I don't like spinach," Callum announces.

"Me neither," says Mabel.

"Can't you give it a try?" pipes Theo. "You might be surprised."

Mabel looks outraged at this suggestion. "Dad, I'll vom!"

Theo sighs. "How about you, squirt?" he asks Archie. "Will you try some?"

"Yeah!" says Archie, swinging his little legs excitedly. He pops a forkful in his mouth but grimaces. "Dad, I don't like it."

All my earlier happiness trickles away.

"That's alright!" bursts out Theo. "Well done for trying!" He hands Archie a piece of paper towel so he can spit it out, then tucks into his own *frittata,* closing his eyes as if in ecstasy. "Mmm, this is outstanding!"

But I can tell he's overcompensating to try and make me feel better.

Oh, why did I go and make a stupid *frittata*? Everyone knows kids like bland, unfussy food—not something with spinach and some strange cheese they've probably never heard of.

"Gang, I'd like you all to have a glass of orange juice," Theo orders.

Callum pours some into his glass and examines the contents. "I can't drink this." He looks as if he's spotted scum floating on the surface.

"Why not?" asks Theo.

"It's got bits in it!"

A frown crosses Theo's forehead. "You *can* drink it, Cal. You just open your mouth, pour it in and swallow. What you mean is you don't *want* to."

"Mum buys it smooth," points out Mabel. "She knows what we like."

Theo looks like they're testing his patience. "You know, you kids are so ungrateful," he says. "Adam's spent ages juicing those oranges."

I bat away his comment: the last thing I want is for the kids to turn on me. "It's alright! Now, who fancies some of this nice Italian bread?"

I hold up the basket, optimistically.

Callum looks at the *focaccia* and scowls. "What's that green stuff on it?"

"Herbs," I answer. "I expect it's rosemary."

"What's rosemary?" asks Archie.

"A herb," I say, trying to remain calm.

"What's a herb?"

"It looks minging!" Callum pronounces, talking over his brother. "I'll have some of that." He points at the *ciabatta*.

"Please," Theo reminds him sternly.

"Please." Callum almost spits the word out.

"Mabel?" asks Theo.

"I'll have the same," she says. "But I only like that kind of bread toasted."

"Me too," says Callum.

I detect a hint of a snigger passing between them. Are they taunting us?

If they are, I'm not taking the bait. I stand up and force my face into a smile. "OK, I'll toast some."

"No," insists Theo, pushing back his chair, "I'll do it."

"No, no," I argue, "it's alright—I need to do it under the old grill and it's a bit fiddly." While this is true, I also want an excuse to leave the table.

When the grill has finally warmed up and the bread's toasting, I poke my head around the door and see that Archie's eating some *focaccia* and Mabel a yogurt. Progress!

I butter the toast, pile it on a plate and bring it out.

Callum flinches at the sight of it. "There's too much butter on that!"

Theo doesn't even glance in his direction but continues eating. "You'll just have to scrape it off then. You can put your own on next time."

Reluctantly, Callum picks up a piece of toast and starts scraping at the butter. I imagine his hunger must be winning through.

But there's no disguising my breakfast is a disaster.

I tell myself not to worry: at least I still have the treats up my sleeve.

Somehow we make it to the end of the meal. At least everyone has eaten something, even if it is mainly bread and yogurts—the two things I didn't make.

I clap my hands. "Right, time for a little surprise!"

I nip inside and come back carrying a tray of treats.

Archie squeals at his milk chocolate buttons, cramming them into his mouth and smearing chocolate on his cheeks, even getting some on his glasses.

Callum grunts as he picks up a protein bar and nibbles on the end. "It's too hard," is his verdict. "It'll damage my brace."

Mabel sits in stony silence, staring at her white chocolate.

"What's the matter?" Theo asks.

"I don't like white chocolate," she states, flatly.

"Yes, you do," says Theo, "it's your favorite. Adam's got you the exact same brand I get at home."

She wrinkles her nose. "I used to like it but I've gone off it."

"Fine, don't eat it then." Theo stands up, briskly. "Cal and Mabel, get up: you can help us clear away."

They look at him as if he's just suggested they clean the floor with their tongues.

But Theo refuses to acknowledge their outrage. He thrusts the treats at them with the jug of leftover orange juice. "You can start by putting these away."

Mabel stomps into the kitchen and flings open the fridge door, fire flashing in her eyes. "There's no room in this fridge!" she snaps.

Theo and I position ourselves behind her and look inside the small fridge that must have been fine for Wilf but is now bulging with food.

"And where am I supposed to put my skincare?" she wails.

Theo shakes his head. "Mabel, what are you on about?"

She gasps. "Dad, if I don't keep my skincare products in the fridge they'll go off! At Mum's I have a mini fridge in my bedroom."

Theo rests his hands on his hips. "Well, how many skincare products have you got? I'm sure you can squeeze them in somewhere."

"Dad, this fridge is stuffed full of beer and wine." She eyes me, dubiously. "Adam, are you *sure* you're not an alcoholic?"

"Mabel, Adam is *not* an alcoholic."

"I don't know," I want to chip in, "it's not even midday and I could murder a beer."

But I keep quiet. And I bend down and slide a couple of beers out of the fridge. "Look, why don't I put these in the larder and make some space for your skincare?"

Mabel smiles, possibly genuinely placated, but I suspect more than likely she's savoring her little victory. I think she and Callum have been enjoying this.

I can't bring myself to smile back at her. Because a warm beer isn't the end of the world but once we've washed up, I know Theo and I are going to have to coordinate everyone's showers. And with the house's old plumbing, only one person can use the hot water at a time. Even before Theo's explained, I can hear the kids moaning.

I can't bear to imagine what they're going to be like tomorrow. Because at eight a.m. the builders are arriving—and the situation is going to get a whole lot worse.

Chapter 6

After everyone has showered—an operation that was as fraught and frenzied as I predicted—Theo and I show the kids around the house. Their responses are just as predictable: Archie skips around, spotting corners and crannies where he can play with his figures and asking questions neither Theo nor I can answer; Mabel finds fault with everything, pointing out potential perils and expressing fear for her safety; and Callum just grunts and groans, refusing to engage. Theo and I exchange a look of camaraderie and lead them outside.

"Who's ready for the next adventure?" Theo bellows.

"Me!" squeaks Archie, leaping in the air and giving a twist.

He's dressed in tracksuit bottoms and a long-sleeved baseball top, which Theo chose for him so he wouldn't get scratched by brambles. Mabel was happy to follow her dad's brief and is wearing jeans, a long-sleeved raglan top and her scruffiest trainers. Callum, however, insisted on wearing gleaming white trainers that'll be dirty in minutes, shorts, and his cherished Manchester City away shirt that has short sleeves. Theo was about to tell him to get changed, till I took him to one side and said Callum might be self-conscious about how much he sweats. So he let him off and saved himself for the battle over hats and suncream.

That turns out to be epic. Thankfully, Theo wins.

He and I put on our sunglasses and matching Panama hats.

"Right," says Theo, "we're all ready. Ads, show us round your estate!"

I stiffen slightly, remembering Kate's comment about me being rich. "It's funny you should say that," I chirp. "Where I grew up, *estate* had a whole different meaning."

Theo laughs but the kids don't even register my comment.

"Come on!"

I start the tour by showing them the vast space above the garage, which is accessed from the lawn by climbing a short wooden ladder. As I lift my sunglasses and push open the door, I ask, "So what do you think this is?"

"A dungeon!" squeaks Archie.

"That's a good guess," commends Theo. He points out the sections of walls that have been tiled diagonally, to create ventilation gaps.

"It was probs to dry out grain or something," says Mabel.

"That's an outstanding guess," says Theo.

Callum flashes her a look from underneath his bucket hat. She rearranges her features into an expression of boredom.

"The truth is we've no idea what it is," I cheep. "But if you look at this and the garage downstairs, I reckon it's as big as your dad's flat in Manchester."

"Then maybe he shouldn't have left our house," snarls Callum.

I look at Theo's wounded expression and feel a surge of anger: I can't believe Callum would seriously want his dad to sacrifice his own happiness to stay with them. Then I remember he's still a child. *Of course* that's what he wants. That's what I wanted from my dad.

I lower my sunglasses and jump down onto the grass. "Come on, let's go round the back of the house."

I guide everyone past ivy crawling up the trunks of dead trees and over dried grass and twigs that crunch and crack under our feet. Tacked onto the back and sides of the house are several stone sheds or outhouses, which are stuffed full of old wood, rusty barrels and farm machinery, and chipped plant pots. There's also a pizza oven, but its tiled roof has collapsed inwards.

"What happened to that?" asks Archie.

"I haven't a clue," I answer. "But the builders are going to fix it so we can make our own pizzas!"

"Yes!" he says, punching the air.

I turn to Callum and Mabel. "Do you two fancy making pizzas?"

Callum shrugs.

"Whatever," says Mabel, suddenly fascinated by the ends of her hair.

Unsurprisingly, the kids show little interest in the chapel.

"It's just a wall," mutters Callum.

"Actually, you can still make out Saint Bartholomew," protests Theo, pointing at the mural.

"Religion's proper boring," comments Callum, licking his finger and wiping a bit of dirt off his trainer.

I become aware of how hot it is and feel the sweat beading on my brow.

I lead everyone up to the olive grove and, just a few meters along the gravel driveway, we spot a pile of empty gun cartridges. Archie is fascinated.

"Whose are they?" asks Callum, nudging them with his toe.

"I don't know," I say, "maybe the neighbors'. I'll ask Stefano. Maybe people are allowed to hunt wild boar."

Mabel looks panicked. "Wait a minute, are we going to get shot?"

"No, Mabel, we're not going to get shot," Theo assures her. "But if you're worried you could always moan a bit louder; then the hunters know we're coming."

She shoots him a vinegary smile. "Very funny, Dad. But what if the pigs attack us?"

"They won't, Mabel." Theo breaks into a playful grin. "The hunters will shoot them first."

I can't help chuckling, but Mabel stomps off, up the path.

When we reach the olive grove, I pause to take in the view. The trees are spaced out pretty evenly over the lumps and bumps of the hillside, their trunks knotted and knobbly, their leaves somewhere between green and gray.

"Adam," Archie says, squinting as he looks up at me, "how many trees are there?"

"Don't tell us," interrupts Callum, his tone mocking, "you don't know."

Theo folds his arms. "Give it a rest, Cal. Hey, squirt, why don't you help us by counting them?"

While Archie's doing that, I step under the shade of a tree. The sun feels hotter here and more brutal. The trees look parched and the grass between them is burnt the color of golden sand. I pull a branch towards me and examine one of the black olives. The harvest must be some way off as it's still only very small.

"Olives are gross," pronounces Mabel.

"Proper minging," agrees Callum.

"Fifty-three!" Archie shouts out. "There are fifty-three trees!"

"Superb work!" says Theo, pulling down the peak of Archie's cap.

Thinking we've probably exhausted all interest in the olive grove, I decide to take them to the castle. I've deliberately saved the best till last. But, as we're walking down the driveway, the kids start moaning about the heat.

"Just a minute," I say, "I'm pretty sure it's hotter than this in Atlanta."

"Yeah, but Auntie Shona has a pool!" Mabel fires back.

"Why don't *you* have a pool?" asks Archie.

I frown. "I don't think my Uncle Wilf had any money."

"*You* could put one in," suggests Mabel, as if the solution's obvious.

I lift my hat to wipe my brow. "But I can't afford it."

She snorts. "As if! You've got loads of money!"

"I don't know what gave you that impression."

"Mum—"

Callum elbows her and she stops herself. My mosquito bites are really itching.

We reach the bottom of the driveway and come to a stop.

"Now, when you were all looking down at those empty shells, you missed the best thing about this place." I turn and gesture up the hill. "The castle!"

Everyone looks.

Archie's eyes bulge. "Whoa! Is it real?"

"It is, squirt, yeah." Theo points out some gaps in the walls, through which soldiers would have fired their arrows.

Archie can hardly stand still. "Can we go and look?"

"Yeah!"

I steer everyone round to the bottom of the path. It's decided I'll lead, with Mabel following, Callum in the middle, then Archie, with Theo following him in case he trips or slips. The scramble is even more difficult than when Theo and I first did it, because of the extra overgrowth. There's a tense moment when Mabel gets a bramble caught in her hair. I take a few steps back to help her but she stiffens. Then, realizing there's no one else close enough, she relents and lets me untangle it.

"Thanks," she hisses, clearly furious—although whether that's at me or herself, I don't know.

Once we've reached the top, we dust our hands and inspect the damage to our clothes. Callum's legs and arms are dotted with blood, his white trainers coated in dirt, and his football shirt plucked several times.

"This top is proper ruined!" he yowls. "And look at my creps!"

I want to shout, "Your dad did warn you not to wear your nice trainers!" But he seems genuinely upset—and there's something about his expression that reminds me of Theo: Theo when he's hurting.

"I did try to explain, Cal," Theo says, gently. "Maybe next time try and listen to your boring old dad."

How he manages to be so patient is beyond me.

Speaking of patience, Archie has none whatsoever. He's already slid through the overgrowth and is in the clearing, bouncing up and down the various levels.

"I'm the king of the castle!" he sings. "You're the dirty rascal!" He points at Mabel and wiggles his bum.

"Yeah, very mature, Archie."

"Isn't this amazing?" says Theo, opening his arms. "Can you believe it's a thousand years old?"

As I look at the stone walls, a tingle runs up my spine. This place is every bit as magical as the first time I saw it.

"And look how high up we are," Theo goes on, admiring the

view from a gap between two trees. "It's like we're on top of the world!"

Archie looks up and starts spinning around. But he spins a little too close to the edge and Theo swoops in and lifts him up. "OK, squirt, let's not do that here."

Callum and Mabel walk around the clearing, poking at the earth for holes, pressing on walls, and lifting up stones—while doing their best to look disinterested.

"What do you think, gang?" Theo rests Archie on his hip: he's only small and still—just about—light enough to carry.

"There's not much left," Mabel mumbles.

"Yeah, it's just a load of rubble," says Callum.

"Who lived here?" gabbles Archie. "Was it a king or a knight?"

Rather than revealing this is something else I don't know, I say, "Hopefully we'll find out soon. Some people are coming tomorrow to start digging for clues. And who knows what they'll find?"

"Skellingtons!" bursts out Archie, his face blazing with excitement.

"You mean *skeletons*!" Theo corrects him. He helps Archie repeat the word till he gets it right.

"Until then you're going to have to use your imaginations," I say.

I lower myself onto the wall and imagine all the stories that have unfolded in the castle. I imagine people running around it hundreds of years ago, engrossed in their own dramas, their own passions, their own love stories—people just like us, fighting for their own dreams and ambitions.

Mabel scoffs. "Or we could just Google it."

I feel a clang of doom. Theo's been dodging the subject of Wi-Fi all day, keeping the kids busy, their minds on other things.

I make one last attempt. "I've tried that—no joy, I'm afraid."

But Callum isn't distracted. "You still haven't given us the Wi-Fi password."

Theo lowers Archie to the ground and draws in a breath. Suddenly, my mosquito bites itch more than ever.

"Cal, there is no Wi-Fi," Theo says. "Not yet, anyway."

Callum splutters, "W-what do you mean?"

I jump in. "We are getting it installed but the earliest they can come is mid-August."

Callum lets out a moan that sounds like it's coming from a wild animal caught in a trap.

Mabel rushes to his side. "What, so we're cut off for *three weeks*?"

Theo rubs the back of his neck. "We're not cut off. We've got mobile reception: you can always use my phone."

"And mine," I trill. "I've got loads of free minutes!"

Mabel sneers. "As if. Nobody speaks on the phone anymore. I need Wi-Fi for my Snapchat."

"And what about my gaming?" growls Callum. "I've brought my Switch so I can play FIFA."

Theo gives them a sympathetic expression. "I'm sorry, but you'll just have to wait."

Mabel shakes her head. "I am devo!"

Callum throws his hands in the air. "This is proper shit!"

"Callum," Theo booms, "don't swear in front of Archie!"

Mabel bursts into tears. "Dad, you ruin our lives and all you can think about is swearing?"

"You lied to us!" Callum shouts at Theo.

"Just like you *always* lie to us!" wails Mabel.

Theo rears back, as if he's been shot.

I wish they hadn't said that.

An injured, tense silence sets in.

I feel a wave of tiredness and remember how little sleep I've had. I can't resist any longer: I crouch down and start scratching my bites.

I need to go back to the house and put some cream on. Besides, there's no point staying here. The magic has been shattered.

"Come on," I say. "Let's go back down."

Chapter 7

At eight o'clock the next morning, our neighbor Luisa comes striding down the path. She's in her forties, with an athletic figure and brunette hair that's swept back in a pixie cut.

"*Buongiorno!*" she calls out, giving me a brisk wave.

"*Buongiorno!*" I repeat, immediately regretting not finding the time to do any more of my Italian course.

Trailing Luisa is a group of seven or eight volunteers who'll be working on the dig. Once she's given me a kiss on each cheek, she introduces them—but there are too many names for me to remember. Except Vito: that's the name of a man who's a foot taller than anyone else and the head curator at the museum, although he only looks to be in his thirties. Most of the others are past retirement age, although one woman is much younger and, I'm told, a student. More importantly, it becomes obvious they're all Italian. I'm bombarded with a jumble of expressions but I assume they're all friendly, as everyone's smiling. I feel another stab of guilt for not being able to communicate. Then I remember the word for *welcome*.

"*Benvenuto!*" I burst out in my best Italian accent.

"*Benvenut*-i!" Luisa corrects me, kindly. "It's plural as you are welcoming lots of us."

Shit, I can't even get that right. "*Benvenuti!*" I repeat, grinning hysterically.

Everyone is dressed for work, wearing mainly multi-pocket cargo shorts, utilitarian tops with long sleeves, and sturdy, steel-capped walking boots, their heads covered with sunhats or bandanas. I realize why they'll only be digging between eight and one: after that it'll be much too hot. They're also clutching hiking sticks, lugging heavy rucksacks, and pulling along trolleys of boxes packed with trowels, tape, notepads, water and snacks. Just as I'm about to ask how they're going to get everything up the hill, a severely dented, dusty van comes chugging round the corner. It has an open back and sitting around the sides are six young men, all of whom are dressed in faded shorts and T-shirts, their exposed skin browned by the sun. Strapped in the center is a portable toilet and behind the wheel is our head builder, Giuseppe.

"Will you excuse me for a minute?" I ask Luisa.

"Don't worry about us," she insists. "We can look after ourselves."

"Are you sure?"

"Yes! We'll speak later." She chuckles. "We'll be here all summer: soon you'll be sick of us!"

I laugh and insist otherwise but I can't help wondering if she may be right. Is it going to be too much having the dig take place at the same time as all the building work?

Well, it's too late to do anything about it now.

I stride over to greet Giuseppe, who gives my hand a firm shake. He's in his thirties, with a muscular physique, jet-black hair in a buzz cut, and a short beard.

"Good morning," I say, not bothering to attempt any Italian.

"Good morning!" he replies in English.

He introduces me to his builders, listing their names and nationalities. They're mainly from Eastern Europe, although there's also a Tunisian and an Egyptian. But their names are unfamiliar and I only catch one of them—Arjan, who's from Albania.

"What an international team," I observe. "But how do you communicate if you all speak different languages?"

"In English!" says Giuseppe. "The international language!"

Thank fuck for that! is what I think. What I say is, "Brill!"

Then I ask, "So are you all set? What's the plan?"

Giuseppe takes out a stack of notes and spreads them out on the bonnet of his truck.

"Today we split into three teams," he explains. "One team starts making the road wider." He points to the gravel driveway snaking around the bottom of the hill and up into the olive grove. "This is the most important job: after that, the trucks can come with our materials."

I nod, briskly. "Fab."

"The second team works on the roof," he goes on. "As you do not have money to replace this, they see which tiles are broken and which tiles are missing. They fix everything."

"Thank you," I say.

"The third team works inside the house," Giuseppe continues. "There is a lot to do here so we need to start. Today they destroy the first bathroom!"

"Fine by me," I chirrup. "Destroy away!"

"And remember we switch off the water in half an hour," Giuseppe says, one eyebrow raised. "That is still OK?"

"Yes, absolutely."

Wait a minute, is it?

As the men start unloading their tools, I glance back at the house. I wonder how Theo's getting on rousing the kids and making sure they've all had a shower. I hope they slept well and won't be as cranky as yesterday.

At least they each had a bed to themselves. After the bust-up at the castle, I went to a hardware store to buy more mosquito nets, plus plug-in repellents and some citronella candles and spirals the assistant recommended. I also picked up three fans that look like they belong in an office but should help with the heat. And Theo insisted that all the kids went to bed early. Theo and I also had an early night as our alarm was set for seven—although the cockerel woke me up again at six. But I feel much better, at least physically. And I haven't got any new mosquito bites, which is a major result.

I wish the builders well and leave them to set up the portable toilet in the garage, where it'll also be accessible for the diggers. Then I go back to the house to start preparing breakfast.

I'm being much less ambitious today, just laying out a buffet of cereals, toast and hard-boiled eggs. It goes against my instincts as someone who prides himself on being a good host but I have to remember this isn't a normal holiday and it's fine to serve a functional, no-frills breakfast.

Archie comes down the stairs first, clutching an action figure in each hand, his ginger hair sticking up not just at the kink but all over.

"*Ciao!*" he cheeps, grinning and revealing the cute gap between his front teeth. "Dad says that means *hi*!"

"It does," I reply. "*Ciao*!"

Theo's next, looking beleaguered, followed by a stony-faced Callum and Mabel. But the interesting thing is, once the kids step outside and catch sight of the builders in the driveway, their scowls disappear. A memory from my childhood flickers to life but I can't quite grasp it.

Once we've all sat down and are eating, I outline the renovation project. I explain that over the next six weeks, the builders will be changing the electrics in the house, damp-proofing the ground floor, replacing all the windows, and stripping out and refitting the kitchen and bathrooms. Once that's done, they'll replaster the walls—except for those that have been left with exposed stone—and give everything a fresh coat of paint. There are other things I'd like to do but this is already pushing the limits of my budget.

"Before the builders can get going," I tell everyone, "we need to clear out the house. And that's where you come in."

"What do you mean?" asks Callum, pulling at a piece of cereal that's stuck in his brace.

"You're going to help us," says Theo.

Callum flicks the cereal onto the lawn.

"We're throwing away most of my great-uncle's stuff," I explain. "And anything that's broken or seen better days."

"Which basically means the entire house," murmurs Mabel.

"Not quite the entire house," I chirp. "I want it to keep the look and feel of an old Tuscan farmhouse. But we will be throwing away lots. And what we can't recycle or donate we'll burn on a bonfire."

"I love bonfires!" says Archie, biting into an egg.

"Me too." I lean on the table. "So what do you say? Will you help us?"

"Yeah!" Archie whoops.

"Superb," says Theo, smoothing down Archie's hair. He turns to Callum and Mabel. "But we're going to need you all to chip in and do your bit."

"Dad, that's slave labor!" Callum burbles.

Mabel pouts. "You can't make us!"

But I notice that their protests are much quieter than usual and they glance over to check the builders can't hear them.

"This is a working holiday," Theo says, firmly. "We were always clear about that."

Callum pushes his bowl away. "Well, *I'm* not working."

Theo spreads jam on his toast. "Fine. You can do some schoolwork. As you're going into GCSE year it's probably a good idea to get a head start."

"Dad, that's not fair!"

But the builders are approaching and Callum and Mabel contort their faces into smiles.

"Hello!" the men chorus as they lumber past, tools slung over their shoulders and tucked under their arms.

"We are sorry we invade your house," says one of them, a man with a tattoo of a scorpion on his neck.

"That's OK," I insist. "As soon as we've eaten this, we'll start clearing everything out."

"My children were just saying how much they're looking forward to helping," adds Theo. "Isn't that right, gang?"

Archie warbles a loud yes. Callum and Mabel's is much quieter—but it's a yes all the same.

"Very good," says the builder with the tattoo. "Very good children."

And just like that, the matter's settled.

If only the builders could come seven days a week.

An hour later, the house is full of the sound of banging and crashing. The builders who went inside are on the top floor, ripping out the first bathroom.

One floor down, Theo and the kids join me to sort through

Wilf's stuff. We start in the smaller lounge, where I point out an almost threadbare rug, some rickety white chairs with worn-down cushions, and what seems to be a full-sized but purely decorative spinning wheel, which we pile up and haul outside, dumping it all behind the wall of the chapel.

I pause when I come to some framed watercolor paintings that are hanging on the walls. They're landscapes, with several of mountains and seashores.

Callum recognizes one: "Isn't that the view from in front of the house?"

"Oh yeah," says Theo, stepping over a rolled-up tapestry to get a closer look. "Well spotted, Cal."

"And this is the castle," says Mabel, "looking up from the bottom of the hill."

"So it is." I peer into the corner and read the name W. TREADWELL. "It looks like my Uncle Wilf was a painter!"

We examine the remaining pictures and decide they must all be scenes from the local area. From upstairs comes the sound of something ceramic smashing on the floor.

"Was he famous?" asks Archie, his glasses already covered in dust.

"I don't think so," I answer.

"But his work's good," says Theo, lifting off Archie's glasses and cleaning them on his shirt. "He's got a confident stroke."

I feel a grin spreading across my face: this is my first glimpse into Wilf's character, his energy, his spirit.

"So what do we do with them?" asks Callum.

There can only be one answer. "We're keeping them! Let's stack them up against the wall and cover them with a blanket."

Once we've finished clearing out the smaller lounge, we move on to the study. I start by examining Wilf's shelves—and his rows and rows of books.

"He was also a big reader," I announce.

I run my fingers over leather-bound classics by Dickens and Austen, plus yellowed paperbacks by the likes of E. M. Forster, Henry James and James Baldwin. And there are several titles I don't recognize, such as *The Heart in Exile*—billed as a "noir thriller"—by Rodney Garland. I decide not to throw any of his books away, telling myself it'll be good to have a well-stocked library when we rent out the house.

"Theo, please could you bring up some of those crates from the wine store and box these up?" I say. "We'll keep them in the garage till the builders have decorated."

Theo sets off downstairs, with Archie skipping behind him.

At the end of the shelves stand two framed photos. They're both of Wilf with the same man from the picture in the bedroom but from different periods. One looks like it was taken in the mid-1980s, as Wilf's caramel hair is in a mullet and he's wearing a pastel blue linen suit, a mint green T-shirt and white espadrilles, although the other man's look hasn't changed: he's still dressed traditionally, in smart trousers and shoes, with a pale blue shirt and a navy jumper tied around his shoulders. In the second photo, the other man still hasn't changed his style, although he looks significantly older, drawn and his clothes are hanging off him. Wilf, on the other hand, still has an eye on fashion, even though by this stage he must be around sixty and his hair graying: he has a very '90s look, wearing baggy jeans, a white T-shirt and a check flannel overshirt.

"Is this your uncle?" asks Callum, nodding at the second photo.

"Yeah, that's Wilf," I answer.

"Nice drip," says Callum.

"What does that mean?"

"His clothes are cool," offers Mabel. "Who's this other guy?"

"I don't know," I answer. "He must be a friend."

Callum frowns. "But why do they look so serious? It's like they don't like each other."

"They're probs just embarrassed," suggests Mabel. "Maybe they hate having their picture taken, like me."

Callum runs his hand over his fringe. "But why are there only photos with this one guy?"

"Were they boyfriends?" asks Mabel.

"That does seem like the obvious thing," I say. "But I assume not. It would have been very difficult to live as a gay couple in those days." And surely someone from my family would have told me?

Theo comes back in holding several crates, and he and Archie start loading up the books. As the study's only small, I take Callum and Mabel through to Wilf's bedroom. Callum's suitcase is lying open on a chair, his clothes hanging on the back of the door.

"Right, let's make some room for your stuff," I tell him. "There's no point keeping any of Wilf's clothes. Let's bag them up and take them to the charity bins near the supermarket."

I fetch a roll of black bin liners and fill them with Wilf's old trousers, jeans, shoes, shirts and shorts—but I keep a belt for myself and a pair of light canvas espadrilles for Theo. Although it's only mid-morning, it's already getting hot and I have to switch on one of the fans. When the bags are full, I hand them over to Callum and Mabel and ask them to take them out and put them next to the car.

While they're doing that, I bend down and look under the bed. There's nothing there, except for a few clumps of dust and a daddy longlegs that disappears into a crack in the wall. Although under the wardrobe I do spot a couple of shoeboxes. I pull out the first, take the lid off and see that it contains a handful of letters—and next to it is another that's stuffed full of them. I feel a rush of excitement. These are sure to provide an insight into Wilf's story. They might even explain how he got here.

Hang on a minute, I can't read them—it wouldn't be fair to pry into someone else's secrets. And I absolutely can't let the kids read them. What if there are things in there Wilf wouldn't want us to know?

I slide the boxes back and wedge them against the wall, so they aren't visible at all.

Chapter 8

Once the builders have gone for the day, we walk through the olive grove and leave what I don't think I'll ever get used to calling my estate. We pass the Fiores' house and wind down the hill, through more olive groves belonging to other people, until we get to the main road. It's time to explore the village of Montemagno.

The first thing we see—directly opposite—is a women's clothes shop, with some old mannequins in the window wearing comically cheap wigs and clothes that could best be described as frumpy.

"Nice drip," I say to Callum and Mabel.

They both laugh and I want to jump up and punch the air.

I gesture to the right and lead everyone down the main road as it runs through the center of the village, in between houses that have been painted shades of butterscotch, Parmesan and honey. There's a brick-fronted church and a war memorial standing on what seems to be a cross between a square and a car park, which—as far as I can decipher from the plaque—is named after a hero of the Italian Resistance. Continuing up the road—keeping to the side to avoid the occasional car and hordes of cyclists—we come to a cluster of cafés, each with its own terrace. These seem to be set up less for locals and more for cyclists: one of them has a repair shop tacked onto the side and they all sell gear and gadgets that make me realize just how big the sport is around here. At the village's farthest limit, there's a platform looking out over the valley, but it offers pretty much the same view as we have from the house. Even so, Archie insists on perusing the valley through the coin-operated binoculars.

Once his time is up, we meander back up the road to check out the two restaurants and Theo and I are delighted to discover that neither of them is expensive. That decides it: we're eating out this evening. Theo has already said that if the kids can pick their own meals, there's less potential for arguments. As one of the restaurants is closed on Mondays, the choice is made for us.

When we walk inside, we discover we're the sole customers. But it's only seven o'clock, which I imagine is early for Italians to eat their evening meal. One of the waitresses leads us through the terracotta-tiled reception, past a pizza oven and into the main dining room. This is dominated by several thick marble pillars, dotted with glass pendant lights with frilled edges, and the tables are surrounded by wicker-backed chairs, covered with plain white cloths, and decorated with matching napkins fanning out from the wineglasses. It's homely and feels authentic and I catch the smell of something delicious coming from the kitchen.

The waitress seats us at a table in front of a mural of a Tuscan landscape. "*Allora*, what you like to drink?" she asks.

I decide not to order any alcohol, fearful of attracting the kids' disapproval, and opt for a fizzy water.

Once the waitress has gone, we pick up our menus.

"This is our first restaurant of the summer!" says Theo, putting on his tortoiseshell reading glasses. "Let's enjoy it, gang!"

Archie whoops in excitement but Callum and Mabel don't react.

"Now who knows what an *insalata tricolore* is?" Theo asks, peering over the top of his glasses.

Callum rolls his eyes. "It says here, Dad: it's a salad with tomato, avocado and mozzarella."

"Yeah but who knows *why* it's called a *tricolore*?" says Theo.

Mabel huffs. "Here we go again—it's like being at school."

"Because it's green, white and red," Theo explains, undeterred. "The colors of the Italian flag, which is called the *tricolore*."

I quirk an eyebrow at him. "How can I have got to the age of forty-five without knowing that? I love an *insalata tricolore*!"

Callum mimes a yawn. "Dad, that's proper boring."

Theo ignores him and changes tack. "Hey Ads, I wonder if your uncle ever ate in here."

I put my menu down. "I didn't think of that."

Callum snaps his menu shut. "Adam, how come you don't know anything about your own uncle?"

"He was my great-uncle, actually." I lean back against the wall. "There was some argument in the family, but it was way before I was born. I think my mum was around but she was very little."

"So why don't you ask her?" caws Mabel.

"I can't. She died when I was eleven."

There's a bump of silence.

Archie pulls Hulk and Iron Man out of his pockets and stands them up on his plate.

"How did she die?" Mabel asks, a little more gently.

Theo takes off his glasses and puts them away. "You know, you don't have to talk about this, Ads. Not if you don't want to."

"No, no, it's fine. It was a long time ago now." I turn back to the kids. "She was hit by a car."

"Did she walk across the road without looking?" asks Archie, glancing up from the fight between his figures.

I give a stiff smile. "Something like that, yeah."

"Dad says I should always look before I cross the road," Archie comments. And with that, he lifts up Hulk and makes him punch Iron Man so hard he falls back onto the tablecloth.

"He's right," I comment.

"What about your dad?" asks Callum. "Is he dead too?"

"No, he's alive. I just don't speak to him very much. We're not close." That's an understatement. I haven't even replied to the text he sent when I was on my way to the airport. Just reading it made me feel worked up and triggered.

"Does he not like you being gay?" Callum says, bluntly.

For a moment I'm not sure how to answer that. As a child, I *did* think my dad didn't like me being gay—or coming across as gay would be a better way of putting it, seeing as I was so young. And that hurt and tormented me, a hurt and torment I still haven't been able to shake off. That's probably because, as an adult, we haven't really discussed it. Although I came out to Auntie Julie at eighteen—and she was fine, having fully expected it, her reassurances long-rehearsed—I never properly came out to Dad: I think I was too scared. Instead, I just fudged it. When I was writing him an email, I casually mentioned going on a night out in the Gay Village. In my next email, I dropped the name of some man I was dating, but in a way that was so vague he could have been a friend. But Dad fudged it, too, by declining to respond to either comment. He did meet one or two of my exes, at a party for his sixtieth birthday and the wedding of one of my stepbrothers. But their status in my life was never openly acknowledged: I just introduced them by name and no questions were asked. So it wouldn't be strictly accurate to say that's why he and I aren't close—or his text made me feel triggered. Or at least it's not the whole story. It's more complicated than that.

Luckily, the waitress reappears and Callum loses interest in his own question. Once she's offloaded our drinks and taken our food order, he asks her for the Wi-Fi password. Then he and Mabel promptly switch off from their surroundings and disappear into their phones.

For once, Theo doesn't mention his rule of no phones at the table—presumably overriding it because they've gone without Wi-Fi for so long. I don't say anything as it's good to be able to chat to him. But, when the food arrives, Theo does tell the kids to put their phones away.

Seconds later, his own phone rings. He angles the screen towards me so I can see it's Kate. "Perfect timing," he mutters under his breath.

"Gang," he says to the kids, "your mum's on the phone."

Theo greets her, then hands the phone to Archie.

"I've got a pizza!" Archie says, through a mouthful. "Cheese and tomato . . . yeah. . . . I like it here. . . . It's a big house. . . . Yeah. . . . We went to the castle. . . . Yeah. . . ." He looks at Theo. "Dad, what was that animal called? The one we saw on the first night?"

Theo stabs into a roast potato. "A wild boar."

"A wild boar," Archie repeats to his mum. "It was a mummy with a baby. But it didn't attack us. It was nice."

He rests Theo's phone on the table and crams more pizza into his mouth.

Callum snatches up the handset and thrusts it back at him. "Archie, say goodbye to Mum. I want to speak to her."

"Bye, Mum!" Archie shouts, his words barely audible through a wall of pizza.

Callum lifts the phone to his ear. "Mum, I've got to be quick. I'm starving and my pizza's just arrived."

But that's all I catch, because he stands up and walks away from the table.

"How's your pizza, Mabel?" Theo asks.

"Yeah, it's alright." But she's only nibbling at the edges.

When Callum comes back, Mabel takes the phone, bounces out of her seat and disappears behind a marble pillar.

"Everything alright, Cal?" Theo asks.

Callum grunts and plugs his mouth with pizza.

Once I've finished eating, I excuse myself and go to the loo. The restaurant's filling up and I have to weave my way through customers who've pushed their chairs back into the aisles. Just before I go downstairs, I spot Mabel, leaning against the pillar and chatting into the phone. Wait a minute, is she crying?

I move closer, hiding on the other side of the pillar.

"But Mum, I miss you," she's saying, in between sniffles. "Why did you have to leave us?"

All of a sudden, I'm twelve years old again, missing my dad and wondering why he's left me. Poor Mabel.

I don't want her to spot me listening so I jog downstairs to the loo.

By the time I return to the table, Mabel's sitting back down, her eyes dried, her face hidden behind her hair. She's prodding at her pizza but hardly eating it.

"Was it nice to speak to your mum?" I ask, cheerfully.

She shrugs.

"Come on, Mabel, eat your pizza," Theo says.

She pushes it away. "It's cold."

"I like cold pizza," Theo chirps.

"I don't," Mabel snarls.

His tone becomes firmer. "Well, you need to eat something."

I smile at Mabel as compassionately as I can. "Come on, listen to your dad."

She shoots me an icy glare. "You don't even speak to yours!"

"Yeah, you can hardly lecture us!" snaps Callum.

I wish I hadn't told them that.

I look at my watch: it's eight o'clock. We'll be able to wind the meal up soon. But it's looking like it's going to be a long summer.

Chapter 9

On Tuesday morning, Theo walks down to the village, to one of the cafés that he noticed advertises Wi-Fi. He has to do a few hours' work but sets off early so he can be back as soon as possible.

"I'm sorry to leave you with the kids," he says, as he hugs me goodbye.

"That's alright," I reply, squeezing him tightly. "There's no other way around it."

With any luck, Callum and Mabel won't get out of bed till he's back.

When the builders arrive, I chat to Giuseppe about their plans for the day. He tells me the men who are widening the road will be cutting away some of the earth from the hill around the castle and transporting it via wheelbarrows to dump in a disused part of the estate. Meanwhile, work will continue on the house, on the roof and top-floor bathroom.

As the builders inside are working next door to Archie's bedroom, the noise wakes him up first. At least I don't have to worry about showering him, as Theo did that last night. I get him dressed, give him some cereal and orange juice, then he comes upstairs to help me clear out Wilf's desk.

This is rammed full of bank statements and utility bills dating back to the late 1990s. With no shredder, Archie and I have to rip them up by hand. But he seems to enjoy this and we have a competition to see how many pages we can rip at once, a competition I let Archie win, after which he flexes his biceps and roars like a lion.

We haul the bags of shredded paper up through the olive grove and all the way to the car, which we've had to park outside the grounds as the driveway is out of action. On the way back, we stop to observe the builders at work, which Archie finds thrilling—especially when one of them lets him hold one of the handles on his wheelbarrow as he pushes it up the driveway and tips the contents over a hill. The joy on Archie's face and his desire for me to watch him makes me feel a fluttering in my stomach.

All morning, Archie is such a delight—skipping along at my side, at one point taking hold of my hand—that I forget all about Callum and Mabel. By the time they're stirring, Archie and I are in the larder, crouching in front of the sideboard and sorting through the contents.

"Morning!" I sing-song. "You've done well to sleep through the noise!"

"Why didn't you wake us up?" snaps Callum.

I put down the bowls I'm holding and stand up. "I wanted to let you have a lie-in."

"But Dad's gone to the café without us," Callum protests.

"I am devo!" says Mabel. "I told you I needed to use the Wi-Fi!"

I'm not sure how to deal with this. Discipline seems to come easily to Theo: he just adopts a firm tone of voice and they know not to argue with him.

I try to do the same. "Well, I'm sure it can wait."

Mabel explodes. "Adam, you don't understand! I'm the only one of my friends who can't snap! Sharita's going to forget about me!"

I've heard her mention Sharita before and know the two of them are close. "I'm sure she won't. Not if she's a good friend."

This only seems to wind Mabel up more. "She *is* a good friend! But Aurora's taking her off me: I know it!"

Callum chips in, "And what am I supposed to do about Charlotte?"

"Who's Charlotte?"

He gasps in outrage. "My *girlfriend*! We've been going out for two months!"

"Oh, yeah, sorry." I feel flustered: teenage relationships and friendships are unfamiliar territory for me. "Didn't you message her last night?"

Callum's face hardens. "Yeah, but she didn't reply. And she's a bit of me. If she dumps me I'll never get anyone like her again."

I decide against telling him this may seem like a major drama now but he's bound to find someone else in the future.

"Adam, this is all your fault!" cuts in Mabel, her nostrils flaring. "It's your fault for dragging us to this dump!"

I feel shaken by the intensity of their upset. "Look, why don't I make you both some nice scrambled eggs?" I suggest, my voice cracking. "Once you've had something to eat, things might not seem so bad."

They stomp off into the kitchen, huffing and blowing.

But they do actually eat. In Mabel's case, it isn't much, but at least she eats something.

It's after breakfast that things take a turn for the worse. First, Callum and Mabel refuse to wash up. Then they refuse to help me and Archie clear out the larder.

"Come on, guys," I mewl. "Please."

Callum shoots me a look of defiance. "Or what? What are you going to do about it?"

What am I supposed to say to that? What *can* I do about it?

Just as I'm wondering if I can find an excuse to call the builders down so they'll witness the kids' behavior, Mabel screams.

"There's a lizard!" She points to the hook on which I've hung my Panama hat. "Over there!"

I try to sound blasé. "Oh, yeah. Haven't you seen it before? I think it lives behind that unit."

She squirms as if her skin's crawling. "But it's massive, Adam. It's like a crocodile!"

Callum, on the other hand, is transfixed and takes his phone out to film it. "That is sick!"

Archie moves forward to get a better view but his jerking movement scares the lizard and it slithers off up the wall. "Is it a boy or a girl?" he asks.

"I don't know," I say. "What do you think?"

"I think it's a boy."

Mabel screams again. "There's another one! Next to the radiator!"

"Oh yeah!"

Callum pans across to video the second lizard, which is slightly smaller than the first.

"That one's a girl," pronounces Archie. "I can tell."

Callum picks up the broomstick and tries nudging the lizard with the handle.

"Callum, please don't hurt it," I say. "It's not doing us any harm."

"But what if it bites?" Mabel says, her voice straying into a higher pitch.

I'm just about to reassure her that lizards don't bite when I realize I don't actually know whether or not that's true.

"Are they boyfriend and girlfriend or brother and sister?" gabbles Archie.

"Archie, will you shut up!" hisses Mabel.

I've no idea what to do. In desperation, I shuffle everyone out of the room and slam the door shut. "Right, let's just leave the lizards till your dad's back."

Callum and Mabel stomp upstairs and disappear into their bedrooms.

"Come on, Archie," I say. "Let's go back upstairs."

We go into the larger living room and start sorting through Wilf's furniture. I decide to keep his sofas but get rid of the faded, frayed, flattened cushions. I like an antique wooden chest it looks as if he used as a footstool but decide against keeping a collection of ceramic vases that are attached to the walls. There's another stack of books—illustrated coffee-table books about art and famous painters. These look like they've been read much less so I don't mind throwing some of them away. Archie and I sort through them and pull out the ones we don't like.

As we carry the rejected books downstairs, the builders are making so much noise that Mabel doesn't hear us entering the kitchen. She's standing in front of the fridge with the door open, eating the white chocolate she refused to touch on our first day.

I can't resist saying, "So you like white chocolate now?"

She spins around, her face ablaze. "Are you *spying* on me?"

"No, I'm not spying on you." I gesture to the books. "We're taking these out."

She slams the fridge door shut. "Well, for your information I *don't* like this chocolate. It's minging. I'm only eating it because I'm starving. Those scrambled eggs you made were gross!"

She swallows what's in her mouth and tosses the rest of the chocolate in the bin.

"God, I hate this place!" she rails, pushing past us and flying up the stairs. "I've no privacy!"

"I think Mabel's angry," Archie comments, screwing up his little, freckle-covered nose.

I can't resist ruffling his hair. "You can say that again. Come on."

As we add the books to the crates behind the chapel, I feel a stab of annoyance at Mabel, but I'm also annoyed at myself. Why did I have to go and do that? I shouldn't have made her feel like she's being watched: that's only going to make things worse.

Archie totters off to watch the builders as they continue cutting away the hillside. I lean back against the chapel wall and let out a sigh.

I feel like a failure. Aren't gay men supposed to be great with kids? Isn't that the stereotype? Why can't Theo's kids just like me? What am I doing wrong?

A tapping sound comes from the roof of the cottage and I turn to see a builder replacing some tiles. Farther down the house, two more builders are erecting scaffolding along the back wall. Signs of their activity are everywhere and at the bottom of the driveway someone has put up a sign saying LAVORI IN CORSO, which I assume from the image means "Building work in progress." At least the builders are making progress—which is more than can be said for me with the kids.

Theo steps into the big lounge. He's wearing khaki cargo shorts, a burgundy T-shirt and sandals, and takes off his Panama hat. "Where is everyone?"

I look up from a stack of opera records I've found: I would never have thought anyone from my family would be a fan of opera, but evidently, I was wrong. "Archie's playing in the other lounge," I say. "Callum and Mabel are in their rooms."

"Have they behaved?"

He looks careworn and I don't want to add to it. "I've had a fab morning!"

Theo sits next to me on the sofa. "Yeah, but did they help?"

"Archie's been brill. And so adorable."

He narrows his eyes. "And Cal and Mabel?"

I frown. "They didn't exactly help, no."

He looks away and I can see how much this upsets him.

"But it was fine!" I add quickly. "Honestly, we got loads done. Although you might have to talk to Mabel about the lizards."

"I was wondering when she'd spot them."

"Well, it's happened. I suppose it was always going to."

Theo nods, gravely.

I stand up and slide the vinyl that's in good condition down the side of the record player, leaving the scratched records by the door. "How about you? Did you get everything done?"

"Well, I sent those emails I needed to. But I also spoke to my parents." He dashes his hand over his eyes.

So *that's* why he looks troubled.

Theo's parents live in Hertfordshire, which is where he was born and brought up, before moving to Manchester for university then settling in the city. They go out of their way to stress that they don't disapprove of him being gay: they just don't understand why he couldn't have waited a few more years till he came out. Their reasoning is that this would have been less distressing for the kids, but they don't seem to have any awareness of how distressing it was for Theo to stay in the closet. It doesn't help that Kate got to them first, turning up on their doorstep and breaking down in tears as she related how hard the breakup had been for her.

I swallow but can feel my throat going dry. "And what did they say?"

He lets out a weary sigh. "Just the usual. I mentioned the problems we've been having with the kids and they basically told me the same old story about it being my fault. Apparently my sister feels the same."

I go back to sit on the sofa. "Theo, you can't listen to them."

"No, I know." But he doesn't sound convinced.

In an instant, I feel vulnerable and exposed. Because if he believes his parents—even if a tiny part of him believes them—where does that leave me? After all, if he hadn't come out we wouldn't have met.

But I manage to keep my anxiety inside. What I actually say is, "Theo, you did the right thing. You've got to hold onto that."

He massages his stubble. "Ads, I just want my kids to be happy. And they're not. At least not Callum and Mabel."

Out of nowhere, I feel a flash of irritation. "And what about you, Theo? Don't you deserve to be happy?"

I didn't intend to raise my voice and immediately regret it.

"But that's just it, Ads," he says, sounding tetchy. "I'm a parent. I *can't* be happy unless they are."

"And what about *my* happiness?" I want to say. "Or does that not come into it?"

But I can't: that would only put him under more pressure. And it would pit me against his kids, forcing him to choose between us. I know how that would end.

In a flash, I remember how I behaved when my dad introduced me to the woman who'd become my stepmum. Did I ever think about his happiness—or hers? Did I consider either of them for one second?

I mop a hand through my hair. "We can't give up yet, Theo. We've only been here three days."

Theo blinks and furrows his brow. "Ads, who's thinking about giving up?"

"Nobody!" I bounce onto my feet and force out a smile. "We'll get there, I know we will!"

But I'm not sure I do know that.

I grab the car keys.

"Where are you going?"

"I need to take some recycling into the village. A load of paper me and Archie ripped up."

What I don't tell him is I also need to be alone with my fears. To do everything I can to stop them from overwhelming me.

"OK," Theo says. But his beautiful eyes have a look of sadness.

As I walk to the door, I want to kiss him.

But I hold back, afraid he might pull away.

Chapter 10

"I am very sorry," says Giuseppe. "My men make a mistake."

I'm standing behind the chapel, inspecting a stone wall that's started to sag and looks like it's about to fall down. The scaffolding the builders set up on the side of the cottage somehow put too much pressure on the wall's foundations and undermined them.

"It is a modern wall," explains Giuseppe, running a hand along his black beard. "Maybe thirty, forty years old. It is supposed to contain the land behind the chapel but it is not very strong. Maybe your uncle does not have enough money to build a good retaining wall."

I've noticed that Giuseppe speaks great English but only in the present tense. Not that I have any right to criticize: I've basically given up on my Italian course.

"Well, if that's the case, I'm sure it would have fallen down anyway," I reassure him. "Don't worry about it."

But I can't help thinking this is another job to be added to the list—and it'll cost more money, which I don't have. I wonder if there's anything in the house I can sell. Anything I can be sure wouldn't have been of sentimental value to Wilf.

Giuseppe explains that his men will clear away the stones and make it safe by pinning back the land until they can build a new wall.

"Brill," I pipe. "Sounds like a plan!"

His builders start lifting the stones and piling them up, out of the way. As they're all shirtless—their muscles flexing and glistening with a light film of sweat—it feels indecent to watch. I turn away and spot a stone that has landed near my feet and has some scratches on it. I pick it up and read an inscription: WILF + ARNALDO.

The sight of it knocks the breath from my chest.

Is Arnaldo that man in the photos? Does this mean he and Wilf *were* boyfriends?

I'm not sure what to do with the stone. But I don't want anyone to know about it until I've worked out what it means.

I slip away and stash it in my bedroom.

Luisa and Stefano stand by the stones from the dismantled wall. Luisa picks one up and turns it around in her hands.

"These stones were taken from the castle," she declares.

"Really?" I say.

"Yes. This used to happen a lot when castles were destroyed: the stones were taken to reuse elsewhere." She balances her stone carefully on top of the pile.

"So what do we do?" I say.

"We should take them back up to the castle. We can use them to rebuild what remains of the front wall."

"Are you sure?"

"Yes. When you rebuild this wall you can use new stones. We have lots at our house. You're welcome to take them. You won't be able to tell the difference."

I nod in agreement. "Thank you. I'll speak to Giuseppe tomorrow."

We walk round to the patio and join Theo and the kids. They're sitting around the outdoor table, which I had to clean thoroughly after the builders had finished for the day, even though they hadn't been working anywhere near it. They have an incredible ability to get dust everywhere—even through the plastic sheets we've thrown over furniture, even through the cotton sheets we've gaffer-taped around doorframes. And we didn't have enough outdoor chairs, so I had to bring out a rickety wooden one from the kitchen, which I've insisted on sitting on myself. It doesn't feel too safe but it'll have to do till I can buy some more.

Although the sun won't set for another hour or so, it's low in the sky, giving off a soft, golden light that makes the view over the valley look particularly stunning, the sea sharp and clear. The air is heavy with the smell of citronella, which is rising from the candles and spirals we've dotted around the patio to ward off mosquitoes.

We've invited Luisa and Stefano for dinner, as I wanted to get to know them. But this is our first time entertaining at the house and I'm on edge. I want it to go well.

"Who fancies a Prosecco?" I ask, once everyone's seated.

I pour three glasses but Theo doesn't like fizz so serves himself a beer.

"Cheers!" I say, holding up my glass.

"*Salute!*" chime Luisa and Stefano.

We bring our glasses together with a clink.

"Can I do it?" asks Archie, holding up his no-added-sugar fruit juice.

"*Salute!*" says Luisa, giving his glass a clink.

"*Salute!*" replies Archie, beaming.

Although it's only an informal dinner, Theo and I wanted to change out of our scruffy work clothes so are wearing chinos, linen shirts and leather loafers. Archie, too, looks smart in chinos and a little short-sleeved shirt with a pineapple print, and as a treat we've put some of my textured gum in his hair, so it's sticking up all over rather than just at the kink. Callum, on the other hand, refused to dress up and is wearing an England football shirt—which I hope doesn't offend Stefano—and Mabel is dressed in one of her usual baggy tracksuits, hunched over and cowering behind her hair. I'm hoping she and Callum will be shamed into toning down their hostility in the presence of our guests.

"So how's the dig coming along?" I ask Luisa.

"It's always slow at the beginning as it's rare to find anything interesting near the surface," she explains. "But I'm very happy that we've started. This is the very first time the castle has been excavated."

"What's *excavated*?" asks Archie, tucking his hands under his thighs.

"Dug up, squirt," says Theo.

"You know, I love your red hair," Luisa says to Archie, her eyes sparkling. "That's something we don't see very much in Italy."

Archie doesn't know how to react to the compliment. "Does the castle have a dungeon?" he asks.

"We don't know yet," answers Luisa, "but it may do."

"Is it true it's a thousand years old?" Theo asks, rolling up his sleeves. Even though it's 7.30, it's still very warm.

"The truth is, we don't know, exactly," says Luisa. "But it's mentioned in local archives for the first time in 1099."

Theo's eyes widen. "Did you hear that, gang? So it could be *more* than a thousand years old."

Callum and Mabel shrug.

I pick up a plate. "Would anyone like a bruschetta?"

Not only is this our first time entertaining at the house but it's also the first outing for my new crockery set—which is plain white and the cheapest I could find. In just over half an hour I'll be using it to serve lasagna with a big salad. I was slightly nervous to make lasagna for real Italians—especially as the kitchen here is so basic—but I learned it on the cookery course Theo and I did in Manchester and whenever I've made it for my sisters, they've loved it. The choice of menu also means I can do all my preparation in advance, put the lasagna in the oven, then relax and nibble on bruschetta, plates of fat, juicy olives, cubes of Parmesan and slices of prosciutto.

Theo turns to Stefano and the hairs on his forearms catch the golden light. "Adam tells me you're a farmer," he says.

"Yes. I have a vineyard that is small but more big than this one. I also grow tomatoes. But mostly olives." Stefano isn't confident with his English and it comes out falteringly. He's a short, stocky man, with black hair and weather-beaten skin.

"When is the olive harvest?" I ask.

"The end of October," says Stefano. His expression hardens. "But this year will not be so good."

"Oh no. Why?"

Stefano gives Luisa a long explanation in Italian. She turns to us and translates: "There's a type of fly that punctures the olive and lays an egg inside. When the egg hatches, it eats the olive from within."

I pull a face. "That sounds a bit grim."

"We have a plague of these flies," Luisa continues. "There's a spray to kill them but we only used to have to spray twice a year—now we must spray four times a year. So it's expensive. Also, it only works up to thirty degrees and climate change is making our summer much hotter. And olives need rain and it hasn't rained much this year."

"OK, so we won't expect many olives," I joke.

"Yes, but you'll discover that Stefano is always pessimistic," Luisa quips. "A typical farmer!"

We laugh and I offer around the Parmesan. "Have you two always lived in Montemagno?"

"No," Luisa answers. "We're from other villages in Versilia."

"What's Versilia?" asks Archie. I notice that his glasses are smudged with fingerprints and take them off to clean them on my shirt.

"This area of Tuscany," says Stefano, his chunky arm leaning on the table. He has earth under his fingernails and scratches on his hands. "It is very special because it has both the sea and mountains."

"We moved to Montemagno fifteen years ago when I got a job—a promotion—at the high school in Camaiore," expands Luisa.

I position Archie's glasses carefully back on his nose.

"How did that work for Stefano?" asks Theo. "I would have thought it's difficult for farmers to move."

"He wasn't always a farmer," says Luisa. "He used to work in logistics, for a marble distribution company." She pops a cube of Parmesan in her mouth.

"Marble is very typical of this region," explains Stefano. "Carrara marble is famous but there are lots of mountains in Versilia that are made of marble."

Luisa swallows her Parmesan. "You'll see it as you drive around. Some of the mountains have white tops, with chunks of marble sliced out of them like a cake."

"Superb!" Theo looks at the kids. "Gang, are you taking this in?"

Callum kicks at the patio but says nothing.

"I'm not into marble," comments Mabel, with the faintest suggestion of an eye roll.

"What's marble?" burbles Archie.

Theo explains. "So why did you give it up?" he asks Stefano.

Stefano pauses. An emotion zips across his face but it's too fast for me to read it. He looks to Luisa.

"He was not happy," she answers. "He had a little depression. So we decided to make some changes to his life. And he'd always enjoyed working on the land."

"My father was a farmer," Stefano adds, rolling up a slice of prosciutto and driving it into his mouth.

"So we bought several hectares of land off Wilf," Luisa goes on. "He needed the money and was selling some of his estate. That was twelve years ago."

"And are you happier now?" I ask.

"Yes, very much," answers Stefano. "And we like living in Montemagno. It is not too busy."

"What's the population?" Theo asks, stretching out his legs.

"Four hundred people and twenty-one swimming pools!" pipes Stefano.

We laugh.

"Shame there aren't twenty-two," mutters Callum.

Luisa doesn't hear him—or at least pretends not to. "Do you like it here?" she asks the kids.

"Yeah!" bursts out Archie. "We've got two lizards! They live in the larder."

"It's alright," mumbles Mabel. "But I miss my friends."

"Yeah," concedes Callum. "But it's really hot and there's dust everywhere. It's ruined my creps."

"That means trainers," I tell Luisa. I decide to deflect the attention away from the kids. "By the way, how come you speak such fab English?"

A smile lifts her fine features. "Thank you. I've been to England several times, to London and Brighton, Hastings and Cambridge."

Callum looks up. "What about Manchester?"

"No," says Luisa. "I've never been to Manchester."

"But Manchester is very famous," chips in Stefano. "Everyone knows Manchester United!"

"I support City," Callum states. "I'm missing the first match of the season."

Theo shoots him a glare. "You can't have everything, Cal."

Luisa gestures with her arms to the scene around her. "And how lucky you are to live in this beautiful house for the summer. With your two dads!"

"Adam's not our dad!" Mabel barks at her, clearly horrified by the suggestion.

Luisa's face falls. "Sorry, *step*-dad."

"He's not my stepdad!" Mabel fires back. "He's our dad's *boyfriend*."

A flush of humiliation works its way up my body.

I tell myself not to be so sensitive. I'm pretty sure I said worse about my stepmum. And she actually *was* my stepmum.

I fix my features into something approaching a smile. "I think what Mabel means is Theo and I haven't been together that long."

"Their mother and I separated a while ago but only recently got divorced," clarifies Theo. "It'll take some time to adjust."

"Now, who wants a top-up?" I ask, perkily.

Stefano and Luisa hold out their glasses and I fill them with Prosecco, some of it frothing over and onto the patio. Theo goes inside to get himself another beer.

"You know, you look like your uncle," Luisa says, examining

my face. "Of course, by the time we knew him, his hair was gray, not brown. But he had the same dimples."

"How well did you know him?" Theo asks, sitting back down.

I've asked them this on our previous meetings so already know the answer.

"Not very well," says Luisa, pausing to sip her drink. "He kept himself to himself."

"I just don't understand how a working-class bloke from Manchester ended up here, in the hills of Tuscany," Theo presses on. "Do you have any idea?"

"I'm sorry, we don't," says Luisa. "Wilf was a very private man. He always refused my requests to do a dig at the castle, saying he didn't want strangers coming and going. And he didn't like it if we asked personal questions. So eventually, we stopped."

"There are a few photos around the house," I say cautiously, "and they've all got another man in them. I don't suppose you know who he is?"

I spot Callum and Mabel looking up from their plates.

Luisa puts her glass down. "I think in the past Wilf lived here with a friend—a special friend."

I raise an eyebrow. "Do you mean a boyfriend?"

"Yes, I think so."

So he *was* gay!

"You don't happen to know this man's name?" I ask, my heart rate soaring.

"I'm afraid not. When we arrived here, he'd already died and Wilf was on his own. But people in the village mentioned him. I know he was Italian."

Arnaldo! That's him!

Suddenly, I'm desperate to know more.

I remember the letters hidden in Wilf's old bedroom. There's no way I'm going to be able to stop myself reading them now.

But what if they contain something shocking? Or something I wouldn't want to know? I'll just have to wait for the right moment, when no one else is around.

Inside the house, the timer on the oven gives a ping.

I get up to take out my lasagna.

Chapter 11

"Surprise!" Theo bellows.

I'm not sure how to respond. I know how I'd like to respond but I'm not sure I should. How did I end up here?

The kids have been awful all day, almost as if having to behave themselves for Luisa and Stefano used up their stock of goodness—and they only had badness left. Callum and Mabel have done nothing but snap and snarl at me and all three of them have fought like rats in a sack. Theo suggested they needed a run-around to expend some energy and I was so tense and overwrought I thought I'd benefit from the same. But he wouldn't tell us where we were going—he insisted on keeping it a surprise. And he's just parked up outside a football pitch.

"What do you think, gang?"

I hate football: that's what I think. It reminds me of how I didn't fit in at school, of how the other boys mocked me, of how I disappointed my dad. And it makes me feel like a failure. But I've never dared tell Theo as he loves football. Whenever he's asked, I've just said it isn't my thing. I don't want to disappoint him, too.

Now isn't the time to spell out my feelings: the boys are that excited they've already bounded out of the car and are flinging open the gate and running onto the pitch.

"Woo-woo!" squeals Archie.

"This slaps!" gushes Callum. I don't understand what that means but can tell it's positive.

Mabel, however, looks less positive. "Dad, it's a football pitch," she states, flatly.

"Yeah, I thought we could all have a game," Theo says, turning off the engine.

Shit, how do I get out of this?

Mabel angles her head as she thinks it over.

"You *like* playing football," Theo coaxes. "Or at least that's what you always say. You love it when we watch the Lionesses."

Mabel pulls out a hair tie and puts her long hair up in a ponytail. "OK."

I don't want to bring down the mood so don't comment. "How did you find this place?" I ask.

As Theo gets out of the car and opens the boot to grab a sports bag, he tells us that while he was in the café, he did some research online, saw there was a pitch on the outskirts of Camaiore, and reserved it for an hour.

"Brill," I force out. But I'm feeling anything but. The prospect of spending a whole sixty minutes playing football is grim.

I slope after Theo, onto the pitch. It's not full size—I expect it's meant for five-a-side—and is surrounded by a tall wire fence, beyond that a bland, modern housing estate. It's covered in Astroturf so feels divorced from nature. There aren't even any trees around, just a ring of mountains in the distance that from here look like cardboard cutouts. Theo opens his sports bag and produces a ball he tosses to the boys. They start kicking it around and soon Mabel joins in.

I hang back.

"What's the matter, Ads?" asks Theo, holding onto the fence to stretch out his glutes. "Is everything alright?"

My face thickens. "You know I'm not into football."

He shrugs. "Yeah, but I thought it'd be different with the kids. Come on, it'll be fun."

Can I do this?

"Dad, are we sorting teams?" breaks in Callum.

Theo switches to stretching his calves. "I thought it could be you and Adam versus me, Mabel and Archie."

Callum looks as if Theo's just suggested he eat a plateful of spinach topped with herbs. "I don't want Adam on my side. I bet he's crap."

In a flash, I'm back at school at the start of a PE lesson. Whenever we played football, none of the other boys wanted me on their side.

"Adam's gay," they'd moan to the teacher. "He can't play."

They'd do impressions of me kicking like a girl, squealing with fear when the ball came towards me, or running around with a limp wrist. They'd sometimes lift me into the bin that was used to store the balls and the teacher would join in their laughter. If he did call them out for bullying, they'd insist they weren't bullying—they were just "clearing up litter." Eventually, the teacher would help me out of the bin, but I'd sense his relief when I offered to sit at the side.

"Cal, don't be like that," Theo says, sternly.

"It's OK," I say, sitting on the Astroturf and leaning back on the fence. "I *am* crap. I'm happy to just sit here and watch."

"Please play," says Archie, tugging at my hand and trying to lift me up. "You can be on my team!"

I let go. "No, thanks. I really don't fancy it."

Theo massages his elbow, then gives a firm nod. "OK, so it's me and Archie versus Cal and Mabel."

He splits the pitch in half and creates a second net from some towels he produces from his bag.

"Right," he says, throwing the ball in the air, "game on!"

As I watch the four of them running up and down the pitch, kicking and chasing the ball, I feel shut out and excluded, just like I did at school. But I can tell they're having fun: their faces are flushed, there's hollering and cheering, and Callum and Mabel even let out the odd giggle. Now and then Theo provides a commentary in the style of a passionate TV pundit. And when I look at him, I see my dad.

My whole body deflates.

When I was a boy, Dad was always trying to get me into football. It was obvious he wanted a son who shared his love of the game. But after countless hours attempting to teach me the basic skills, after enrolling me in a junior club for a course of training, and after several trips to Old Trafford to watch Manchester United—with no sign of the slightest stirring of love, or even anything that came close to like—he abandoned it.

Then he married Debbie and they took me on holiday with her sons, Trevor and Keith. We stayed on a campsite somewhere in northern France and Dad was keen that I get on with my new stepbrothers. As they were both obsessed with football, on the first day he organized a game on the beach. It was him and Keith versus me and Trevor, and the three of them got all fired up about it. For me, though, it was a miserable, demoralizing experience. Trevor and Keith made fun of my ineptitude and did impressions, just like the boys at school. Dad ended up getting angry with them and we had to abandon the game. But I couldn't help wondering if he was angry with me, too. And I hated myself for it.

All these years later, I tug in an unsteady breath and let it out slowly.

Dad knew I didn't like football. Why did he make me play?

When the game pauses so Callum can fasten his shoelaces, Theo trots over. "Ads, are you sure you don't want to play?"

"Yes, I'm sure!" I bark. "Will you leave me alone!"

He holds up his hands and backs off.

Shit, why did I go and do that? Now he really is going to get angry with me.

I take out my phone and see I've got 5G. I decide to WhatsApp my sisters.

"Ladies," I type, "I'm at a football match."

"What the fuck?" replies Ian. "You hate football more than me."

I explain I'm watching Theo play with the kids.

"Girl," pipes Gloria, "I can just see you sitting there looking like a bulldog passing a kidney stone."

I send a few laughing emojis.

"Let's not joke about it," chips in Ian. "Me and Adam have a painful history with football. And we're not the only ones."

"I keep telling you it's not like that anymore," points out Dom.

"All the current England squad are pro-gay. They wear rainbow armbands and shoelaces. And look at all the queer teams and supporters' groups."

"Yeah and footballers are gorge," offers Gloria. "All those thick, muscly legs. Do you remember that one I got off with in Mykonos? I swear down, he had a dick like a water bottle."

I add another laughing emoji but feel dirty joking about this kind of thing in front of the kids. Even though they're several meters away, I shield my phone.

"Never mind that," Ian types. "Respect your feelings, Adam. And if you find it triggering, go off and do something else. Don't put yourself through it."

"Did I tell you I'm going to the summer social for Dom's old team?" continues Gloria. "Apparently, it'll be packed with quality cock."

"Touch wood," writes Dom.

"That's what I'm hoping," quips Gloria.

I add another string of laughing emojis but feel dirty again.

The ball crashes into the fence a few feet away and I give a start.

"Sorry!" calls out Theo.

My insides compress. Don't tell me I have to kick it back?

Thankfully, Archie bounces over to retrieve it. But just then, Gloria sends a dick pic and it pops up on my screen. I've no idea who it belongs to but quickly shut down my phone.

I catch my breath.

Ian's right: if I'm not enjoying this, I should go off and do something else.

I shout to Theo that I've remembered a few things we need to pick up from the supermarket. And I get up and leave.

Chapter 12

At the end of our first working week, we treat ourselves to an early finish. Not only have I managed to sort through the entire house—clearing out Wilf's belongings and all the furniture that won't work in a holiday let—but I've also accompanied Giuseppe to hardware stores, builders' merchants and bathroom and kitchen studios. I've pored over brochures, websites and artists' impressions, and made all the important decisions on everything from units to surfaces, shower curtains to storage racks. I deserve a break.

Theo suggests driving into Lucca to show the kids the Italian tradition of *la passeggiata*, or early-evening, sociable stroll. But they interpret this as an attempt to smuggle through a bog-standard walk and revolt—Archie included. So Theo pivots to a bike ride, remembering that when he and I stayed in Lucca, many Italians didn't just stroll along the path over the city walls, but they also cycled it.

"What do you reckon, gang?" he booms. "Shall we do it?"

Archie is the only one who answers but Theo interprets this as a "yes" from all of them.

We remember seeing a bike hire shop just inside the city walls, by the Porta Santa Maria, so look up the address, enter it into the satnav and set off.

It's a twenty-five-minute journey and I insist on driving, largely to avoid engaging with Callum and Mabel, who won't stop moaning about being dragged away from the house, even though they moaned about being *in* the house. But it's a difficult drive, with heavy traffic and two junctions that don't make any sense, plus countless cyclists riding double and sometimes triple file. When we eventually arrive, there's little parking, forcing me to try and parallel park at the side of a street—which I can't manage at the best of times, never mind before an audience of sniggering teenagers. Eventually, I accept defeat and let Theo do it.

When we arrive at the bike shop, Theo goes inside to make our booking, while I wait with the kids, perusing the long lines of bikes to choose which we want.

In the children's section, Archie spots one that's bright green. "Can I have that one, Dad?"

I wince at his mistake.

"As if Adam's our dad!" Mabel hisses.

"Of course you can," I cut in. "It'll match your glasses."

"Green's my favorite color," Archie announces, proudly.

He snuggles into me and I put my arm round him. Then I worry that Mabel will think I'm encouraging him, that I *want* him to think of me as a second dad. All of a sudden, I feel hopeless.

It's a relief when Theo comes back, stuffing his wallet into his denim shorts. "All set, gang?"

We each take the bike we've chosen, adjust the seat and familiarize ourselves with the gears. Then we push them over the pedestrian crossing, mount the seats and cycle up onto the tree-lined path that runs along the Renaissance fortifications.

"This way round!" shouts Theo, taking the lead.

Callum follows, then Mabel, with Archie cycling at the side of me. There are several other people riding bikes but most are on foot, strolling and chatting, pushing babies in prams and toddlers in buggies, or being pulled along by dogs, usually pugs or dachshunds. There's a relaxed, friendly atmosphere and the early evening sun glints at us through the trees.

On our left is an expanse of grass on which teenagers are sunbathing and smoking, young men are exercising in an outdoor gym, and older women are doing yoga or tai chi. On our right is the city itself—the roofs of its tightly packed mustard, rhubarb and vanilla houses tiled with terracotta, the odd church steeple or factory chimney rising amongst them—the deep green Apuan Alps forming a protective ring around it.

"*Mamma mia!*" a cyclist shouts as she almost crashes into her friend. Theo turns back and we exchange a smile: although this is a regular occurrence, we still enjoy hearing Italians saying it.

I gaze out over the city and remember our first visit to Lucca—our trip to see the trees at the top of the Torre Guinigi, our browse around narrow streets packed with old and new shops, and our look around the rather austere cathedral, balking at the sight of the mummified body of some dead saint on the altar. We made a hasty exit and found a bar in the square opposite, where we enjoyed an *aperitivo,* and—as this was the night after Signor Mancini showed us the house—our conversation fizzed with excitement.

"Look, no hands!" Archie shouts, raising his arms up in the air. "Look, Dadam!"

Mabel flips. "Archie, what's *wrong* with you? You're such a thicko!"

Theo swings his bike to a stop in front of Mabel. "Don't say that. He's only eight. There's no need to be cruel."

Instantly, tears spring to her eyes. "Stop having a go at me, Dad! You're always having a go at me! I can't take it anymore!"

She turns and cycles off in the direction we came, wailing loudly, attracting the attention of Italians on their *passeggiata.*

"Mabel, come back!" shouts Theo.

But she ignores him.

He sets off in pursuit, calling to us, "Just give me a minute."

But it's obvious that this is going to take longer than a minute.

"Come on," I say to the boys, "let's follow them. We don't want to get split up."

"Is she running away?" Archie asks.

"I don't know *what* she's doing," I answer, trying not to sound weary.

The three of us ride back, keeping our eyes on Mabel. But she turns off the wall and flies down the path leading to the road. When she reaches the bottom, she misjudges her speed and has to slam on her brakes. But it's too late: she comes to a stop with her front wheel on the tarmac, directly in the path of a silver Fiat. It swerves out of her way and bumps into an iron bollard.

Fuck!

"Get off your bikes!" I instruct the boys, quickly. "We're not cycling down there."

Callum's face has drained of color. For once, he doesn't argue.

By the time the three of us reach the site of the accident, a small crowd has gathered. But no one's been hurt and Theo looks like he's managed to placate the driver—who happens to be Scottish—and is handing over his insurance details.

"I'm so sorry," he repeats.

"It's alright," the man replies. "It's only a hire car. I'm sure the wee girl has learned a lesson."

Mabel is standing by her bike, sniveling. But she doesn't look remorseful in the slightest. She whips out her phone and starts typing. I hope she isn't messaging her mum.

I've no idea how Theo's going to handle her, because we've barely had time to push our bikes back to the shop when his phone rings.

"Hi, Kate," he says, flashing me a rictus smile. "Gang, your mum's on the phone!"

I suggest we grab a table outside the café next door and order us all a soft drink while, one by one, the kids step away to speak to their mum.

Theo and I sit in silence.

When Archie comes back, he looks troubled and confused. Callum is sullen and unreachable. Mabel's blazing with defiance.

She thrusts the phone at Theo. "Mum wants a word."

It's difficult for me to follow the conversation with only Theo's responses, but—as far as I can make out—Kate's using the accident as an excuse to challenge his competence as a parent. "Kate, I understand that but they're perfectly safe. . . . Yes, I know she's upset and I know this is hard for her. . . . You know, I am capable of keeping an eye on my own children. . . . You're very welcome to speak to your lawyer. . . . Bloody hell, I was not distracted by Adam. . . . Kate, he's a perfectly good driver!"

He turns away so I can't hear any more. But I've heard enough.

I can't delude myself any longer. My sisters were right and Kate's trying to sabotage our summer. She's out to destroy me—or at least my relationship with Theo. And not just that, but it looks like she's manipulating Mabel—and maybe Callum, too—to achieve her ends.

Once again, I feel upturned by an awful feeling of despair. What can I do? I can't fight back. I'd never win against their mum.

And I wouldn't want to: I wouldn't want to turn any children against their mother. I still miss mine and would give anything to have her back.

I'll have to discuss it with Theo later.

When we get back to the house, Theo puts Archie to bed, while I go up to the castle to watch the sunset.

The climb is getting more difficult as the earth continues to erode. I've already asked the builders to construct a proper path—which they've said they'll do, using logs to create steps and iron staves to hold up a rope handrail—but I'm going to have to persuade them to move this up their list of priorities. God knows how Luisa and the other diggers have been managing to get here every morning.

When I enter the clearing, I discover that the diggers have divided the land into some kind of grid system that's mapped out with red string. There are sticks with measurements on them and little numbered markers poking up at the corners. It only looks like a thin layer of soil has been removed from a handful of the squares. But I don't want to touch anything, not even the squares in which the digging hasn't started. So I skirt around the edges, dodging boxes of equipment and stacks of what look like sieves with wooden frames.

I find the spot on the stone wall where Theo and I sat the first time we came to the house. As then, the sun's about to dip behind the mountain and is spilling out sensuous rays of pumpkin, apricot and peach.

I smile.

I find myself thinking about my mum. Although I loved watching the sunset with her, she'd always imagine what other people were doing around the world, other people with different dreams and passions, other people in more glamorous, exotic places, but living under the same sun. She never seemed to talk about our life or what we were doing in Manchester. After a while I worried that she wasn't happy and wanted to be somewhere else. That she didn't want to be with me. That I wasn't good enough for her. And I tried to be good enough, convincing myself that if I could just make myself better, Mum would be happy.

In the weeks leading up to her death I worried even more. She started to behave suspiciously, having hushed phone conversations and quickly hiding things whenever I walked into the room. Once, she told me she was going to the local tanning shop to use the sunbed but I saw her sitting on a bus going into town. I sensed she was covering something up but didn't want to tell Dad in case he got angry at her and she became even more unhappy—or in case she got angry at me. Then came that awful morning when I found out she was dead. Dad told me she'd been hit by a car on a night out with Auntie Julie—but I could tell that he was hiding something, too. I decided Mum must have killed herself. And I couldn't escape the feeling that it was my fault.

I've never brought up the subject with Dad—or Auntie Julie. I couldn't bear to hear them confirm my worst fears. What would it say about me if I wasn't even good enough for my own mum to want to stay alive?

I hear the buzzing of a mosquito and bolt up onto my feet. I need to go down to the house and put on some spray.

I turn my back on the setting sun.

As we get ourselves ready for bed, I ask Theo how he dealt with Mabel.

"We had a long talk." He cups the back of his neck with his hand. "She said she's sorry."

"Yeah, right," I want to say.

"I believe her," Theo adds.

I force out a "Brill."

I strip down to my underwear and stuff my clothes into the already full laundry bag. I must remember to buy some kind of basket—and a couple more for the kids' rooms.

"We've agreed she's going to email the driver of the car and apologize properly," Theo continues. "And as a punishment, she's going to give our car a bloody good clean. I mean, it'll be covered in dust again the next day but it's the principle."

"Absolutely," I state, without much conviction.

We're in our bedroom, on the upper floor of the cottage. I can only assume Wilf didn't come in here, as it's the shabbiest part of the property. The white walls are browning in places, yellowing in others, with clumps of plaster flaking off. The radiators are rusty, the window frames are rotten, and there's a wardrobe that's made of some kind of fake, reconstituted wood, looks about forty years old and sways like a drunk whenever you open the doors. But the thick chestnut beams running along the ceiling give the room character. Once the builders have given it a good going-over—and I've replaced the furniture—I'm sure it'll look fab.

I move into the bathroom, which has a floor covered in tiles with an ugly brown swirl pattern and a suite that, when I sent a picture to my sisters, Gloria called gonorrhea green. I cleanse my face—using cold water that splutters out of the taps so aggressively I have to step back—then apply my moisturizer. I pause to look in the mirror. With all the suncream I've been slathering onto my skin, my face is becoming a bit greasy. I probably need to change my products but don't have the time to do any research. At least my hair is looking good: it's already been lightened by the sun and is now the color of golden syrup.

I floss my teeth as I walk back into the bedroom. Theo has taken off his clothes and is in his briefs. I admire his toned body, which has bulges in all the right places. He's been going for a run in the early evening—while we let the kids have some quiet time and I make the meal—coming back to do press-ups, squats and sit-ups. I, on the other hand, haven't done any exercise at all—and bulge in all the wrong places. Conscious of my expanding gut, I step back into the bathroom. I really don't feel attractive.

"And what about Kate?" I ask through the open door.

"What about her?" says Theo.

"Well, it was obvious she was winding Mabel up."

Theo steps into the bathroom and I pull in my stomach.

"I don't want to think about that," he says.

I feel a prickle of irritation. I understand Theo feels guilty about breaking up the family—and I understand it will have been hard for Kate—but I'm sick of letting her walk all over us.

I drop my floss into the bin. "Yeah, well, you might have to soon."

"What do you mean?"

I squeeze toothpaste onto my brush. "Theo, she's not going to stop at this."

"She'll calm down." He gives my shoulders a little massage. "Come on, let's brush our teeth and go to bed."

Once we're lying on our pillows—on top of the sheets because of the heat—Theo moves in to kiss me.

I open my mouth and respond, but I feel stiff. I tell myself to relax but it's no use.

Theo pulls back and gives me a wolfish grin. "You know, I bought some lube when I was in the supermarket the other day."

I sit up. "You don't seriously want to have sex, do you?"

"Yeah, we haven't all week." He shrugs. "Why not? Is there a problem?"

I grimace. "Well, for a start, I'm fat."

"You're not fat. You're gorgeous, every little bit of you." Theo kisses me on the shoulder and starts stroking my nipple.

I pull away. "It's not just that. I don't want to mess up the mosquito nets. I stink of spray and I've been sweating all day."

"So what?" he says. "I've been sweating, too."

"This old mattress squeaks," I go on. "And the kids are in the other room."

He smirks. "Ads, they're on the other side of the house."

"Yeah, well, the doors are thin. And I'm sorry but it doesn't feel right."

Theo sits up. "Why? I used to do it with Kate."

"I don't want to think of you shagging your ex-wife, thanks very much."

"Alright, point taken. But what I want to say is, straight couples have sex while their kids are in the other room—sometimes the same room when they're in a hotel."

"I know," I say, even though I don't. "I'm just not feeling it, that's all."

I give him a peck on the lips, slip in the mouth guard that stops me grinding my teeth, and turn over.

Theo sighs. Then he lets his sigh hang in the air. The silence thickens.

He sits up and switches out the light.

The first time we came to Italy, Theo and I couldn't keep our hands off each other. I couldn't get enough of him.

I feel a surge of anger at myself. What if he goes off me?

And I can't escape another thought: if he does, it'll be my fault. I'll have driven him away, just like I've always done. Just like I've done with everyone I care about.

Chapter 13

I'm on the top floor of the house, cleaning the third—entirely redundant—lounge. Following Theo's comment about families sharing rooms when they're on holiday, I've had the idea of converting this into another bedroom—meaning the top floor will have one big bedroom, a double and a single leading off it, plus a shared bathroom—and we can advertise it as a family suite. If it isn't taken by a family, it could always be used by a group of friends: I'd be happy to stay somewhere like this with my sisters.

The space has the potential to be stunning, with walls of exposed stone and sturdy wooden beams holding up a vaulted, textured ceiling. Plus, it's the only room in the house to have a big window along the back wall, offering a view up into the mountains, rather than down over the valley. Best of all, repurposing it won't cost any more money than I already have in my budget—I'll just switch from buying a sofa and armchairs to a bed and a wardrobe. The only thing is, with most of Wilf's old furniture stripped out, patches of thick grime have been exposed on the tiled floor. So I'm on my hands and knees, scrubbing it with hot, soapy water.

As it's a Saturday and the builders aren't working—and Theo has driven the kids into the village so they can use the Wi-Fi—I've taken off my T-shirt and put on my swimming trunks, sliders and a pair of banana-yellow washing-up gloves. I've already got a pile of laundry and don't want to add to it: this way I can jump in the shower when I've finished. And I won't need to wash my hair, as I'm wearing a shower cap to protect it. I'm aware I must look ridiculous.

I'm listening to one of Wilf's opera albums, which is blasting up from the old record player on the floor below. It's Puccini's *La Traviata*—not my usual thing but I'm surprised to find it works well in this setting.

Wait a minute, never mind cleaning—while everyone's out I can read Wilf's letters. . . .

I drop the scourer into the bucket of water and snap off my washing-up gloves. I march downstairs to Callum's bedroom and yank the boxes of letters out from under the wardrobe. I sit on the bed and open the first shoebox.

My heart rate quickens as I pull out just three letters. They're all addressed to Arnaldo Silvestri at Azienda Silvestri, in a town called Prato. So Arnaldo must have worked for some kind of family business.

All three envelopes are postmarked with the year 1958. I look to see which has the earliest date.

As I pick it up and slide the letter out, my heart takes flight.

I tug in a breath and start reading.

Carissimo Arnaldo,

How was your journey home? I hope it wasn't too gruelling. I hope it was lifted by memories of our time together.

Even now, a week later, I can hardly believe we met. Everything that happened over those ten days was like a dream. So much of it took place in that one hotel room that it felt separated from life. It didn't feel real.

However, it was real. When the memories come back to me, I thank the stars I had such good fortune. Thank goodness I met you on your first night in Manchester and not at the end of your stay. Thank goodness for the Union. Thank goodness there's a hotel that accepts folk like us. I'm not quite sure what to call us. 'Homosexual' sounds like something the doctor would say. 'Queer' is a wretched word. I can't for the life of me think of any nice words. What do they call us in Italian?

I didn't tell you this in Manchester but the first time I went in the Union, just to the pub downstairs, was on my birthday last year. I'd had tea with my mam and dad and my sister called round with our Suzanne and baby Julie. I blinking love those kiddies and Suzanne sat on my knee and helped me blow out the candles on a Victoria sponge Mam had made. That's a cake, in case you haven't guessed. Any road, it was a lovely evening but, strangely enough, I felt lonely. I felt like the odd one out and started to fret that the older I got, the more this would be obvious. The more folk would start to ask questions. I suppose I was feeling sorry for myself. Happen that's why, rather than going home, I ended up walking into town.

I'd known about the Union for a while. I'd read about it in the Evening News, when the landlord was sent to prison for running a 'disorderly house'. Obviously, I was terrified by that but happen I was intrigued too because I held onto the information. For some reason, the night of my birthday it popped back into my head and took hold of me. I was powerless to resist.

When I arrived outside, I was shaking like a leaf. I had to pace up and down Canal Street, trying to pluck up the courage to go in. Even though the windows were painted black, I was frightened someone would see me walking through the door. Every time I approached it, a passer-by seemed to appear on Princess Street and gawp at me. Actually, do you understand that word? It means 'stare'. I should say your English is marvellous, by the way. I have a lot to thank that Irish nanny for!

Any road, when I finally made it inside, I found all sorts of folk. There were doctors and builders and shop workers and solicitors, folk of all classes, colours and creeds. The one thing they had in common was they were all men and they were all like us. It was a real boon! Some of them were broken wristed but some were very masculine and you wouldn't be able to tell they were that way at all. I thought it was splendid. I didn't feel lonely any more. I realised I belonged to this wonderful freemasonry of homosexuals, this delightful coterie of queers.

After that first foray, I started going to the Union every Saturday. If they asked, I told my mam and dad I was going for a pint with some of my school pals. I did, now and again, but only early doors, just in case they bumped into any and asked questions. Whenever I did, I'd have to stop myself looking at my watch. I couldn't wait to get to the Union.

The only thing that spoiled it was that the atmosphere was always tinged with fear. Whenever the door opened, everyone's eyes would look up to see if it was the police. A few of the fellas had been in the pub when it was raided. The police arrested everyone they could get their hands on and went through their personal belongings. One of the men they caught kept a diary and the police read it and found out the names of all the other fellas he'd been with and went after them. Wretched things happened to those who were arrested. If they weren't put in prison, they were given electric shocks or injections of some chemical to stop them wanting to be with men (although apparently neither of those strategies works). All the men were disowned by their families and lost their jobs. Some of them carried on going to the Union, as they'd lost everything already. Most of those who hadn't started to use false names.

It's blinking terrifying when you think about what can happen to men like us. As a schoolteacher, there's no question that if I were caught I'd be sacked. Folk often say queers can't be trusted around children, or that we want to corrupt them. I know my mam and dad would never speak to me again. I can't help myself, though. It's like I have no choice.

I did think about how much of this I should put down in a letter and I've probably been freer than I intended. I'm going to take this to the Post Office as soon as I've finished. When it reaches you, it'll be in a foreign language, although you'll have to hide it from your family if they also speak English.

Any road, I'm not sure why I've written so much about the Union. I suppose it's because I didn't want to bring it up when we were together. I didn't want you to think I'd been going out looking for trade because I'm not like that. I've certainly never gone looking for it in public toilets, like lots of the fellas I know. Or cottages, as they call them. Each to their own but I wasn't interested in nookie. Sorry, sex. You already know that with you it was my first time. That's because I was looking for someone to love. I know lots of folk think it's daft or even disgusting for one man to say that about another, but I don't care. When I told you I loved you and you said you loved me back, it was the happiest moment of my life. Just thinking about it makes me want to cry.

That brings me on to why I'm writing. You said we should both take some time to think about what we want, and consider the consequences. I have thought about it. I've thought about it a lot. I haven't thought about anything else, truth be told. I imagine this won't come as a surprise but I've decided I do want us to be together. I'm ready, Arnaldo. I'll give up everything and go anywhere in the world to be with you.

Just writing that and looking down at the words on the page gives me goose pimples. Do you know what they are? It's when your skin goes bumpy and the little hairs stand on end. Although it's terrifying, I also think it's romantic. Yes, I can see you rolling your eyes and teasing me, just like you did when you were here. I'm a romantic, Arnaldo!

Now that I think about it, it isn't just romantic but it's a blinking miracle you and I found one another. We're from different countries and speak different languages. You're from a posh family and I'm from a poor one. You're so much older than me, almost a whole generation. It isn't long since we were on opposite sides in the war. These things would be serious obstacles for most folk, but I think the only thing that matters is love.

What do you think, Arnaldo? Do you still feel the same? Are you ready to give up everything to be with me?

Please know you are my one true love and always will be. I hope you still think of me as your tesoro.

I'm signing off with another Italian expression you taught me: con tutto il mio cuore,

Wilf xx

I look up from the letter, stunned. I sit in silence, the record having ended while I was reading.

It's like Wilf's come bursting into life, like I'm seeing him—and experiencing his story—in 3D, high definition, laser-sharp focus. Even his handwriting—with its neat lines and curls but a hint of contained flamboyance—adds to the picture, as does the thick, ivory paper, black ink and old-fashioned fountain pen he used, the tools of a regular writer and someone who respected the act of writing.

I try to swallow but it's difficult. Tears have welled in my eyes. I sniff them back and clear my throat.

It isn't just Wilf's story the letter has opened up: it's like I've been offered entry into a whole other world, a forbidden world, a world I knew existed but would never have been able to imagine. I wonder how many men lived like this. I wonder how many of them didn't dare to keep letters or diaries. I wonder how many of their stories have been lost forever.

At one point Wilf even mentioned my mum. Until now I couldn't really see any connection between them. I couldn't get my head around how Wilf fit into my family. But now I can see it very clearly.

It's a lot to take in.

I carefully fold the letter up again, slide it back into its envelope and pick up the second.

Carissimo Arnaldo,

Thanks very much for your letter. I'm so happy—

I'm interrupted by the sound of voices.

Shit. It's Theo and the kids.

I stuff the letter back in the envelope. I don't want anyone to know about them—not yet, anyway. And I certainly don't want the kids to see me dressed like this.

I pick up both boxes and dash through to the cottage, where I slide them under the bed, next to the stone inscribed with the names WILF + ARNALDO.

I quickly take off my shower cap and put on some clothes.

Chapter 14

On Sunday, I know the five of us are going to be together all day. As I'm not going to get the chance to read the letters, I try not to think about them. We've decided to go on a day trip to the nearby seaside resort of Viareggio. But things don't go according to plan.

Theo had wanted to leave the house after an early breakfast so we could find a parking space close to the front and a spot on the public beach. But Callum refused to get out of bed till nearly eleven, which he insisted was early for a Sunday. And then Mabel announced that she's on her period and couldn't possibly do beachwear. Theo looked almost as embarrassed as I was by this—and only marginally less out of his depth. It struck me that it must be hard for Mabel being the only girl, something I hadn't considered before. We agreed to abandon the beach.

The drive to Viareggio takes ages. As it's a Sunday, the roads are full of cyclists, many of them in such large groups I struggle to overtake. Callum and Mabel sit with their earphones in, but still manage to scoff and snigger at my driving. By the time we arrive, the only parking space we can find is a fifteen-minute walk from the front. The kids complain all the way to the promenade.

We decide to stroll down the concrete pier, its walkway covered in crazy paving. On our left is a marina full of yachts and speedboats, bobbing and clinking in the water; behind that, a much bigger and more industrial-looking shipyard. Theo tries testing Callum and Mabel on the flags flying from some of the boats but they're not interested.

On our right is a long stretch of beach packed with people. The coarse sand isn't quite golden: it's slightly darker, like a burnished gold. But the Mediterranean laps the shore and the sky is an uninterrupted slab of clear, sharp blue.

Theo gestures at the view. "Look at that, gang! Isn't it superb?"

"Woo-woo!" says Archie. He climbs onto the wall separating the pier from the beach. I walk alongside him in case he needs to grab onto something.

"I hate the beach," whines Mabel, pulling her wide-brim straw hat down at each side.

"I hate the sand," Callum agrees.

"Are there any sharks?" asks Archie.

Callum scoffs. "Not in the Med, Archie. There might be jellyfish though."

Mabel looks up. "What about sea urchins?"

"I'm not even engaging in this conversation," Theo says, pausing to shake a stone out of his slider. "We're not going on the beach so let's all just stop moaning about it."

We continue walking, past the end of the sand and the start of a strip of enormous rocks that have been arranged along the side of the pier, presumably to break the waves. Theo has to restrain Archie from jumping off the wall and scrambling over them, especially when he spots a few fishermen. Perched on a little outcrop is a bronze statue of what looks like a family. We read the plaque and discover it's called *L'attesa*—which translates as "the wait"—and is meant to signify hope. I could do with a bit of that.

When we reach the end of the wall, Theo lifts Archie down and we stand on the square platform, looking out to sea. The other arm of the marina stretches around us, its main wall decorated with graffiti. I turn to take in the view back to the beach, the town behind it and the now familiar mountains behind that. But this is the first time I see that one of them has a white peak, with chunks of marble sliced out of it, just like Luisa and Stefano said. I point it out to Theo, whose face lights up. When he shows Callum and Mabel, their faces darken.

"Boring," dismisses Callum.

I want to take some pictures of us all but Callum and Mabel refuse. So I take a selfie with Theo, his arm around me, the two of us tipping back our Panama hats so our faces aren't in shadow. As we stroll back down the pier, I post it on my Instagram with the caption *Mi amore*. The kids might be doing their best to spoil the summer but that's not going to stop me showing off my gorgeous man. Then Archie holds my hand, which could brighten up the most miserable day.

At the bottom of the pier, we come to the start of the promenade. Unusually, this doesn't run directly along the beach but is separated from it by a row of elegant shops, cafés and restaurants, as well as private beach clubs, which all seem to have pools. On the opposite side of the promenade is a row of palm trees, beyond that the road, beyond that a long stretch of hotels and villas. The architecture is all in the same style, with lots of arches, curving lines and ornamentation, often patterned with flowers and leaves. Theo and I think it might be Art Deco but he checks online and discovers it's Art Nouveau.

"What do you think of the architecture?" Theo asks Mabel.

"Dad, I've got period pains," she grumbles. "I couldn't care less about the architecture."

Theo frowns. "Sorry. Is there anything I can do to make it better?"

She glowers at him. "I *knew* you wouldn't understand! I wish Mum was here!"

"I'm starving!" chimes Callum.

I let out a weary sigh. "Look, shall we just go and get some lunch?"

Theo agrees.

But after much trudging around, the only place we can find with a table for five is a very basic pizzeria that's three blocks away from the seafront. And it isn't till we sit down that we realize the menus are only in Italian.

"That's a good sign!" insists Theo. "It means this place is for locals."

I have to hand it to him: he's doing everything he can to flip the mood.

"It's also cheaper," I chip in. "So you'll get no complaints from me." I try not to think of all that extra money I have to find for the retaining wall. At least Giuseppe said I can settle any fees outside the original budget at the end of summer.

We manage to place our order—in very inept Italian—but when the food arrives, Mabel gives a yelp. "Dad, this isn't meant to have olives! It's a *capricciosa*—when I get them at home they never have olives."

Theo's unfolding his napkin on his lap. "Can't you just pick them off?"

"Dad, they've touched the rest of it. I'm *allergic* to olives!"

Theo exhales. "You're not allergic, Mabel; you just don't like them."

She gives him a withering look. "It's the same thing."

"We've been through this: it's not the same thing."

Mabel folds her arms. "Well, I need another pizza. I'm starving and it's my period and I've got a heavy flow."

Theo blushes. He calls over the waiter and orders her a Margherita.

The rest of us sit in silence, eating our pizzas. Callum drives slices into his mouth with one hand, while tapping furiously on his phone with the other. Theo must be too exhausted to argue with him. Mabel, meanwhile, devours a packet of breadsticks—then mine and Theo's, too.

When her second pizza arrives, she declares she isn't hungry.

Callum finally looks up from his phone. "I'll have it!"

Without saying a word, Theo lifts the plate from in front of Mabel and plonks it down in front of Callum.

By the time we've paid the bill and are walking out the door, it's a relief.

Archie's attention is caught by a shop across the road. "Dad, can I have an ice cream?"

"Of course you can, squirt," says Theo. "You ate all your pizza."

"Can *I* have an ice cream?" asks Mabel, tartly.

I can't contain myself any longer. "I thought you weren't hungry."

She gasps. "Adam, it's good for period pains!"

I can't argue with that.

We buy five ice creams. Theo tries to encourage the kids to try some Italian flavors—like his favorite *bacio*, which he tells them is chocolate and hazelnut—but they insist on ordering what they usually have at home. I choose a scoop of *pistacchio* and another of *stracciatella*, which reminds me of the Wall's Viennetta my mum used to love. Both are delicious. Even better, we manage to commandeer one of the few tables outside.

As he licks his chocolate, Callum continues tapping away on his phone. But he struggles to do both at once and spills ice cream down his football shirt. As he grabs a napkin to wipe it up, Theo catches sight of what's on his screen.

"Cal, what's that?"

Callum shields his phone. "Nothing."

"It doesn't look like nothing."

Callum tugs at his fringe. "It's just something my mates sent me."

"I'd like to see it, please." Theo stabs his plastic spoon into his ice cream.

Callum pretends he hasn't heard and continues licking his.

"I said, I'd like to see your phone," Theo repeats in a tone that's much firmer. This time, Callum knows not to argue.

Theo takes hold of the phone, looks at the screen, and flicks through several images. His face sets hard. "These images are inappropriate for a fifteen-year-old."

Callum huffs. "Dad, I didn't *ask* to see them!"

I hold out my hand and Theo passes me the phone. On the screen is an explicit GIF of two men having sex. As I scroll down, I discover it's the latest of several images of gay porn Callum's been sent over the last hour. Each is accompanied by jokes about "fags," "faggots" and what they—*we*—do in the bedroom.

All of a sudden, I'm back on the school bus, being pushed up and down the aisle, listening to words like *poof* and *queer*, listening to boys tell me what happens to men who have gay sex, that when I grow up I'll have to use tampons because I'll be incontinent and will end up dying of AIDS. I feel nauseous and push away my ice cream.

"Can I see?" asks Archie, banana-flavored ice cream smeared around his mouth.

"Can I?" says Mabel, who's barely touched her strawberry.

I thrust the phone back at Theo, as if it's about to blow up.

"No," answers Theo. "No one's seeing it. Cal, I want you to delete these videos immediately."

He gives the phone back to Callum.

"My pleasure," says Callum. "They're gross!"

As he goes through his phone deleting the GIFs, Theo questions him and it turns out that several of his friends have been tormenting him about having a gay dad, saying that it runs in the family so he must be gay, too.

"But I'm not," he stresses. "I'm not gay."

I'm taken aback by how keen he is to make this point.

"Yes," says Theo. "Don't worry."

"But it would be fine if you were," I want to add. I tell myself now's not the moment.

Thankfully, Theo says, "But I'd love you whatever your sexuality. And I know your mum would, too."

Callum twists his face in disgust. "As if I could ever do that kind of thing. It's proper minging."

"You're a shit-stabber," I hear a boy on the school bus shout at me. "A fudge-packer. A Marmite miner."

Even though we're sitting in the shade, I swear it's getting hotter. I feel sweat collecting under my arms and on my forehead. I take my hat off and use it to fan myself.

"Cal, we'll talk about this later," Theo says, gesturing to Archie.

He cracks a smile. "How's your ice cream, squirt?"

"The best ever!"

"Superb!" Theo turns back to Callum. "And when we get home I'm going to speak to the boys concerned. And their parents, too, for that matter."

"But Dad," Callum protests, tugging at his fringe wildly, "it's only bants."

"Really, Cal? It didn't look like you were enjoying it to me."

"Can't you take a joke?" I remember one of the boys at school saying, after he'd spread a rumor that I'd been caught masturbating with a cucumber. I feel a trickle of sweat run down my back.

"Dad!" Callum howls. "It's bad enough having you at my school without you laying into my mates!"

Mabel pipes up, "You've no idea how cringe it is to have a gay dad!"

Out of nowhere, I feel a surge of sympathy for the kids. But I can also tell how much Theo's hurting: from the look on his face, he's crushed.

It was bad enough for me, thinking my dad was ashamed of me. I can only imagine how awful it must be for Theo to hear his kids actually telling him they're ashamed of him. I inch closer to him and rest my hand on his knee.

"Dad, if you have a go at them it'll only make things worse," Callum argues. "I can handle it, honestly."

Theo runs a hand across his eyes. "Well, if it happens again—if it happens in term time—I'm going to intervene."

Callum screws his empty tub into a ball and tosses it in the bin.

"What I don't understand is," I say, throwing my ice cream after it, "why's this suddenly happened now?"

Callum sneers. "They saw your Insta post, Adam. That pic you posted of you and Dad."

Shit.

I'm about to apologize but stop myself. We're no longer in the '80s and I won't allow myself to be shamed like I did when I was at school.

Before I can think of how to reply, Theo steps in and says, "Adam, you know I'm not supposed to be on social media."

"What do you mean?" But I know exactly what he means: his school has a strict social media policy, forbidding all teachers from posting personal content, a policy he repeats to me now.

"Sorry," I bleat. "I must have forgotten. It's just that school seems a million miles away."

"Oh my god," Mabel says, dramatically, "Dad's going to get sacked!"

Theo lets out a weary sigh. "It's fine," he says. "I'm not going to get sacked. I can't be absent from social media completely: I just can't post anything personal myself."

Mabel looks disappointed.

I apologize again and open my Instagram to remove the post.

Theo puts his hand on my arm. "Leave it," he says. "It's not as if you've tagged me in. I'm not even on Instagram."

"You know, you could always make your account private," Callum suggests, looking me in the eye.

"That's a good idea," I say. Then I stop myself again. Actually, I'm not sure it *is* a good idea. Wouldn't that be accepting that my sexuality should be hidden away like a dirty secret? Shouldn't we have moved on from that kind of thing?

Theo intervenes. "No, don't do that, Ads. We've nothing to be ashamed of."

I smile and put my phone down. It's a relief to hear him saying that.

The only problem is, from the look on his face I'm not entirely sure he believes it.

"They're homophobic," I say. "They're actually homophobic."

I've come up to the castle to speak to Ian on the phone.

"And I know it's only because the kids at school have said awful things," I add. "It's perfectly normal for them to be affected by it."

"But that doesn't mean it isn't going to be triggering for you," Ian observes.

I tap the back of my heels against the stone wall. "I have to say, today was pretty grim."

I can hear Ian sitting up and rearranging his cushions. I picture him in his living room, on his olive-green sofa, under relaxing low lighting and surrounded by calming candles.

"But what you've got to remember is, phobia means fear," he goes on. "It doesn't necessarily mean hatred. The kids are probably just scared of what they've heard, just like you were at that age."

"But I thought things were better now," I protest.

"They are," Ian says, "they're much better. Come on, remember how awful it used to be."

For some reason, I don't think about my experience but Wilf's.

I think of him and his friends in the Union, living in terror that the pub would be raided, that they'd be arrested and their families would disown them. I want to tell Ian about the letters, but not until I've finished reading them.

"No, you're right," I admit. "They are much better. I suppose the kids' situation is very unusual."

"And no one can blame them for reacting like that, not at their age. I'm sure once they're older, they'll come round."

I look at the sun falling in the sky. Tonight it doesn't give off pink rays but is glowing a deep orange. "Yeah, but it's not just that, my sister. Callum and Mabel have been a nightmare the whole time. They literally hate me. And I'm not very good at being hated."

"OK, so which of those two sentences do I start with first?"

I chuckle. "Take your pick."

I hear the familiar sound of Ian taking out his stick of lip balm, running it along his lips, then clicking it shut. "Right, so you say they hate you. But I'm sure you told me you used to hate your stepmum."

"I did. Funnily enough, I've been thinking about that."

"And?"

"This is different. My mum had died, remember. My dad had dumped me."

Ian pauses, then says, "Had he? I thought he wanted you to live with him and Debbie?"

"Yeah, but that was *after* he'd dumped me on Auntie Julie for a year."

Just saying the words, the pain rushes back, cutting through me. The pain of being abandoned, of Dad not wanting to see me. Just after Mum hadn't wanted to see me.

"OK, so it's not exactly the same," Ian concedes, "but imagine Theo's kids enjoying their nice, happy life. Imagine Mabel being a daddy's girl and thinking she and Theo have their own special bond. Imagine Callum going through puberty and worrying about being a man and wanting to talk to his dad about it. And then as far as they see it Theo basically upends their lives and their happiness is shattered. And not just that but for something the other kids make fun of. Of course Mabel's going to feel betrayed and Callum's going to feel like less of a man."

I bump my fist against the wall. "Yeah, yeah. I get it. Why do you think I'm still here?"

"Well, try not to lose sight of that. Try and hold onto how you felt in similar circumstances."

I pick up a twig and start turning it around in my hand. "I have tried but that wasn't exactly the happiest time of my life. I don't really like going back there."

"No, but it could be the key. Maybe you need to dig a little deeper."

I'm not sure I do need to dig deeper. I'm not sure my feelings are buried very deep at all. I can remember very clearly being insanely jealous of my stepmum: I thought my dad loved her more than he loved me. I was jealous of my stepbrothers, too. They were younger than me but I was convinced Dad preferred them, that he saw them as a chance to have another stab at molding boys into men and this time get it right.

"When you say your dad dumped you," Ian continues, "would it be fair to say part of you thought this was because you were gay?"

I stop flipping the twig and wrap my fist around it. "I did think that, yeah."

Just like I thought that was the reason my mum didn't love me enough to bother staying alive.

"Which brings me onto your second sentence," says Ian. "I've talked to you before about low self-esteem, about your need to make people like you, to prove to everyone that you're good enough."

I wriggle, awkwardly. "I'm not sure I like where this is going, but yeah . . ."

"And we've talked lots about Theo having to get over his gay shame."

"Yeah . . ."

"Well, are you sure you're not still hanging onto some?"

My insides give a lurch. But I remember how instantly the childhood taunts came back to me when I saw the insults on Callum's phone. I remember how quickly the game of football transported me back to PE lessons at school.

Then another thought occurs to me: could this be the reason I don't want to have sex with Theo?

But it's too much.

I snap the twig in half and toss it over the side of the hill. "I don't know," I say, "I think I'm probably just finding it difficult because I haven't really been around teenagers—not since I was one myself. And it's so hot here I haven't been sleeping well. *And* I keep getting bitten by mosquitoes."

Ian sounds like he's repositioning himself and sitting up. "OK, so you need to focus on self-care. Make sure you go to bed early and stay fit and healthy."

"I actually saw a cheap exercise bike in a sports shop the other day."

"What about a normal bike?"

"You haven't seen the hills around here. And you haven't seen the Italian drivers." I remember how bad my own driving has been. "Not to mention the tourists."

"Alright, point taken. An exercise bike sounds like a great idea."

"I'll pick it up tomorrow." I rise to my feet and dust the back of my shorts. "Anyway, enough about me. What's going on at home?"

"Well, that's a handbrake turn!" he jokes. But I hear a meow: one of his cats must be joining him on the sofa. Ian has two, girls he named Celie and Nettie after the characters in his favorite film, *The Color Purple*. Thanks to them, it looks like I've got away with it.

As I stand, savoring the sunset, Ian tells me he's about to start his first course of group coaching, which he's organizing through the Proud Trust, one of Manchester's LGBTQ+ charities.

"That's brill news. And what about Gloria and Dom?"

"We went out last night. Gloria got off with some bloke with blue hair. Apparently his dick was like a Coke can. He said it was short and stubby but that thick he couldn't get his hand around it."

I let out a honk of a laugh. "And Dom?"

"Oh, same old Dom. He shagged some artist with thousands of followers on Instagram. He's doing some photography project on all the men he's slept with and asked Dom to pose."

"After that Dom'll dump him."

"Already happened. Honestly, I've had cups of tea that have lasted longer than his relationships."

I grin. "I miss you girls."

"We miss you, too. But don't worry, we'll be with you soon."

My stomach flips. I was already worried about bringing my two worlds together—and that was before Callum added homophobia to the mix. What's he going to be like around my sisters?

I can't think about it right now.

"Yeah, but brace yourselves," I joke. "You've no idea what you're letting yourselves in for!"

Chapter 15

At the start of our second week, I carry one of the bins up through the olive grove—we have five altogether and I had to ask Luisa to translate what each is for. Today's the day for *RUR*, which I couldn't work out until she told me it's for general rubbish, anything that can't be recycled. Once I've done that, I decide to tackle the massive pile of laundry.

Theo has always insisted he'll do this but it's my house so that goes against all my instincts as a host. That aside, I'm surprised by just how much laundry there is. Archie seems to have a special talent for spilling every drink, meal and snack down himself. Callum thinks every item of clothing needs washing every single time he wears it, even if it's a pair of jeans or denim shorts he's only had on for a few hours. Mabel, on the other hand, dumps all her clothes on the bedroom floor, so—even if they don't need washing—they do after that. Without wanting to provoke an argument, I scoop it all up off her floor—being careful to leave the underwear—and stuff it into the washing machine.

Once the first load is done I hang the clothes up on the washing line I found behind the chapel. Then I go and find Theo and the kids, who are cutting back the ivy that's growing up the fig trees. I offer to drive them down to the café in the village for a fix of Wi-Fi, on my way to the sports shop. I'm going to buy that exercise bike, pleased to be following some of Ian's advice and focusing on self-care.

As I wind the car down the hill, around bend after bend, I can feel the tension in my shoulders. The road's so narrow, every time I use it, I dread a car coming in the other direction. Then—for the first time—one does.

Shit.

To make matters worse, it's on a stretch of road that runs along the brow of an olive grove, with no barrier to protect us from a sheer drop. I try to reverse but am disconcerted by the bend and—after a few attempts—the kids start screaming that we're going to fall over the edge.

"Alright, alright!" I yank on the handbrake.

"Dad, I don't think Adam should be driving," bursts out Callum.

"I don't think Mum would be happy," jumps in Mabel. "We could die!"

I draw in a deep breath. "Theo, would you mind taking over?"

I step out of the car but don't get back in the passenger seat. I decide to wait while Theo maneuvers into the nearest passing place. But the driver of the other car is waving. She beckons me over.

Oh no; is she going to criticize my driving?

I trot along, smiling desperately. When she winds down her window, I see she's a blond woman in her seventies, wearing fire-engine red lipstick and lots of expensive-looking jewelry.

"*Buongiorno!*" I say, contorting my face into a smile.

"You can speak to me in English," the woman trills. "I'm German. My name's Angelika. I live further up the hill."

She holds out a hand that's much more wrinkled than her face. Does that mean she's had a facelift?

"Good to meet you," I say, giving her hand a shake. "I'm—"

"—Adam," she interrupts me. "I've been looking forward to meeting you. You look just like your Uncle Wilf."

I blink, several times. "What? Sorry?"

Angelika tilts her head. "When I met Wilf he was already older than you—in his late fifties—but he still had a boyish face. I always said he looked much younger than he was."

I give my head a little shake. "What, so you and Wilf were friends?"

"Darling, he used to call me his sister."

The shock wipes me blank.

Angelika nods at my car. "But I didn't think you had children."

"They're not mine," I manage to say. "They're my boyfriend's. From a previous relationship." I decide not to add "with a woman" as it'll only complicate the matter.

I turn around and see the kids are getting fractious. Mabel is elbowing Archie and Theo's turning around to remonstrate with them.

"In that case, I offer you my solidarity," Angelika drawls in her light German accent. "I know how hard it is to bring up someone else's children."

Before I can respond, Mabel winds down the window and shouts, "Adam, hurry up! I'm suffocating!"

"And dealing with their hostility," Angelika adds, with a wry smile. "Go on, you'd better get back in."

"But . . . sorry. . . ." I stutter. "I want to talk to you."

"Oh, darling, you will!" Her eyes twinkle at me.

Amazed, I jog back to the car and slip into the passenger seat.

"Finally!" groans Callum.

"Can we go now?" moans Mabel.

"What was that about?" asks Theo.

"You're not going to believe this," I gush. "That woman was a friend of Wilf's!"

Before he can reply, Angelika pulls up alongside us in her sleek, black Audi convertible. She signals for me to wind my window down.

"Now you're settled," she says, one hand hanging out of the window, her red nails glinting in the sun, "would you like to come and visit?"

Theo leans forward. "Hello!"

Angelika gives him a broad smile. "You too. All five of you."

"Dad, do we have to?" Mabel mutters, in a tone of voice I can only assume she thinks is too low to hear.

But Angelika hears. "Suit yourselves. But my house is very different to yours: I don't have any farmland, I have a big garden *and* a pool. I swim in it first thing every morning; then it's empty all day. You'd be welcome to use it."

I turn around and see Mabel's face. Suddenly, she looks like a sweet, innocent, excited girl. Next to her, Callum's nodding furiously, his expression both pleading and apologetic. Once again, a flash of Theo passes across his face.

I turn back to Angelika. "That's very kind of you. Yes, please. We'd love to."

"*Klasse!*" Angelika gives me a conspiratorial wink. "I'll message you on social media."

It's only as she's driving away that I wonder how she'll do that. Does she even know my surname?

When we arrive back at the house—my exercise bike in the boot—the builders have left. That isn't surprising as it's after five o'clock, but outside the garage—next to a skip that's overflowing with the contents of the top-floor bathroom—there are piles of stones, tiles, bags of sand, plaster and cement, plus three new bathroom suites. Now the driveway has been widened, they must have taken several deliveries. Most of these are covered with dust sheets, some of them are left open to the elements, and a few are blocking the path to the house. The five of us dodge around them, Theo carrying my exercise bike through to the larder, where we've agreed it'll be stored when I'm not using it.

Theo's planning to go for a run and I'm looking forward to slipping up to our bedroom and reading more of Wilf's letters. But I only make it as far as the chapel, when a trail of dust catches my eye. I follow it around the back, where the builders have left out a workbench, on which they must have been cutting tiles or stone. There's dust all over the windows of the cottage, the trees, bushes and plants, and—worst of all—the washing on the line. Shit, I'm going to have to do it again.

Mabel appears from behind me, dashes over to her favorite lilac top and gives it a shake. "Adam, I didn't ask you to wash this! You've ruined it!"

"I haven't ruined it, Mabel," I attempt, feebly. "It just needs another wash."

She fires bullets at me with her eyes. "But it'll fade if it's washed too much!"

"It won't fade," I try to reassure her, "not if I do it on thirty."

She gives a little scream. "I *hate* you!"

She stomps off towards the house, shouting, "Dad! I need to use your phone!"

Resigned to another argument—probably involving Kate—I slowly take the washing down and drop it in the basket. Rather than getting annoyed at the builders, I decide it was my fault for not asking what they were doing. In the future, I'll only peg out when I know they're inside.

I trudge round to the house and find Theo sitting on one of the new chairs on the patio, talking into his phone. The boys must have gone inside but Mabel's on the chair next to him, her face animated.

"Clothing's very intimate," Kate is crowing over the speaker. "And what about her underwear? Did he go through that, too?"

Theo massages his temples. "Kate, he didn't touch her underwear."

"Well, it's extremely inappropriate. And as a mother, I'm outraged. It's a violation of my daughter's privacy."

Theo's forehead ruts. "Kate, how did you think Mabel's clothes were going to get washed? Did you think she'd do it? Or did you think we could all bring enough for six weeks?"

"No, but I thought you'd at least speak to her before letting your *boyfriend* go rummaging through her room!" Once again, when Kate pronounces that word, I can imagine the look of distaste on her face.

Theo looks at me and rolls his eyes. I rest the washing basket on the table.

"Adam's here, Mum!" Mabel chirps. "He's listening to our conversation!"

Kate gives a low growl. "Well, I can't be expected to speak to him. Theo, you're going to have to explain that from now on, we need some boundaries. Mabel deserves to feel comfortable. And Adam needs to respect her privacy."

Theo gives a long, disenchanted sigh. "Alright, Kate, leave it with me."

Something breaks inside me. "Leave it with me?" As if I'm some naughty child who needs reprimanding. Why can't he just tell her to fuck off?

Mabel shouts, "Thanks, Mum. I knew you'd be on my side!" She flashes me a triumphant smile.

Determined not to explode, I pick up the basket of laundry and take it inside.

I wish I'd left her clothes on the floor now.

Later that night, Theo and I sit on the bed going over the argument with Kate. My anger has been building all evening and adrenaline's coursing through me. I won't be fobbed off with any more empty assurances that Kate's going to calm down.

"She's a bitch, Theo," I say, shocked at how harsh the word sounds coming out of my mouth. "There it is, I've said it."

Theo pinches at the bridge of his nose. "Ads, I know she's being antagonistic but I wouldn't go that far."

Why does he always have to be so measured and diplomatic? "Well, I would," I assert. "And she's managed to convince the kids she's some kind of saint and I'm the devil!"

He tries to put an arm around me but I shake him off.

He retreats to his side of the bed. "They don't think that. They're just caught in the middle. Kate wants them to think by being hostile to you they're being loyal to her."

"Yeah, and you let her get away with it!" I want to scream.

But the last thing Theo needs is animosity coming from me as well as Kate, Callum and Mabel. So what I actually say is, "And what do you suggest we do about it? I can't just sit here and take it, without anyone to defend me."

Was that too critical?

Theo scrapes his fingernails through his hair. "Ads, it's bloody frustrating . . ."

"You can say that again."

". . . but if we rise to the bait, Kate will only get what she wants. She knows she's got the kids on her side and she's trying to create a war between us and them. I suspect she wants you and I to fall out, too."

I breathe in and out a few times. He's right. I know he's right.

I just need to control my anger.

"Yeah, well, she won't succeed," I say. But I can't bring myself to smile.

"That's the spirit," says Theo, his relief visible. "Look, from now on, I'll do the laundry. It should have been me doing it in the first place."

Brill. Now he's going to get sick of the whole setup. So much for our romantic, magical summer. "I don't know," I object. "Are you sure?"

"Yeah. Who do you think does it at home?"

But, even though Theo doesn't seem bothered by the prospect, even though he gives me another of his gorgeous smiles, I can't help worrying that this could be the beginning of the end. It's exactly as I thought when I heard the kids were coming with us: he's going to realize the whole thing is too much stress and too much trouble. And he's going to want out.

Then another voice inside me says, *He was always going to dump you sooner or later. You might as well get it over with now.*

I hear a loud crash coming from outside. "What was that?"

It's followed by the pitter-patter of rain on the windowpanes.

"Was it thunder?" I ask.

"Bloody hell," says Theo, "it's a storm."

"Fuck!"

We jump up and close the windows.

This is all we need.

Chapter 16

On the first day of August, we wake up to find the storm has ended—but has left some serious damage. A tree has blown down and is blocking the driveway, the bags of plaster, sand and cement that weren't covered are spoiled, and the rain has washed away tiles from the roof and patio, plus some of the land behind the chapel, where the retaining wall has yet to be built. The water has also crept under the turquoise doors and flooded the kitchen, which needs mopping up. As if all that isn't enough, our electricity has been cut off.

"How are things up at the castle?" I ask Luisa.

"Actually, fine," she says, stabbing a hiking stick into the driveway. "Stefano warned me there was going to be a storm so we covered everything with thick black plastic and secured it down."

Giuseppe tips back the remains of his coffee. "Adam, I am very sorry. Luisa tells me about the storm but I do not believe her."

It takes me a second to work out he should be speaking in the past tense.

"Yes, but it's very unusual weather for this time of year," Luisa counters. "I'm not surprised you didn't believe me."

"Look, there's no point worrying about it now," I chip in. "Let's just concentrate on fixing everything. Assuming we *can* fix everything?"

Giuseppe gives the uprooted tree a pat. "Yes, we move this. And I order more materials."

Dread curdles in my guts. "And how much is it all going to cost?"

"I pay for the materials," Giuseppe says. "It is not very much and it is my fault they are damaged."

"No, I can't have you being out of pocket," I insist. "I'll pay. But what about the extra jobs?"

He tilts his head as he does a rough calculation—and then lets me know. I feel all the heat leave my body.

He gives me a kindly smile. "But remember you pay me for extra work at the end of the job."

"Yeah, thanks." But even then I still have no idea how I'm going to get the money.

"Do not worry about the patio," Giuseppe offers. "We plan to lay new tiles anyway, but we plan to do this at the end of the job so we do not damage them. Next we must push back the land behind the chapel and build the retaining wall."

I just about manage a weak smile. "OK. And what about the electricity? How do I fix that?"

Giuseppe runs his hand over his freshly shaved scalp. "I take care of this. It is the least I can do. First we need to find out what is the problem, then I call the company."

He dismisses himself and steps back to issue instructions to his men.

"This evening, you must come and eat at our house," says Luisa.

I raise an eyebrow. "What, all of us?"

"Yes, you, Theo and the kids."

I wipe my palms on my shorts. "That's nice of you, but I'm not sure about the kids. They're not behaving too well at the moment and I wouldn't want them spoiling things."

Luisa gives me a warm smile. "Don't you worry, I have just the thing to . . . how do you say in English? 'Soften them up'?"

"Yeah, that's right."

"But whatever it is," I want to add, "I doubt it'll work."

* * *

We're coming to the end of an incredible meal, the best I've had so far in Italy.

We started with a pasta dish—as is the custom, explained Luisa and Stefano—of *pappardelle* with porcini mushrooms. The mushrooms were picked by Stefano on his own land, and bursting with even more flavor than those Theo and I had on our first night in Lucca. This was followed by a main course of roast lamb with garlic and rosemary, which was heavenly. I was relieved when Luisa served the kids meat from the ends of the joint so it wasn't too bloody and Callum didn't complain about the rosemary but discreetly scraped it off onto the side of his plate. Midway through our main course, I received a text from Giuseppe—who was working late to fix the electricity, re-erecting a pole that had come down and liaising with an engineer to reset the circuit—letting me know that we were reconnected. At which point Theo and I relaxed and enjoyed the meal even more.

"Very often in Italy we eat fruit for dessert," Luisa explains, as she passes around a big bowl of delightfully chubby cherries and perfectly round peaches.

"I've noticed that," says Theo, cutting up Archie's peach and taking out the stone.

"I like it," I comment, doing the same with his cherries. "It's unfussy and refreshing."

The tension between Theo and me has eased, possibly because we've been dealing with storm damage all day. The force of nature somehow made everything else seem less important.

We're sitting under an awning on the Fiores' patio, which is at the back of their house. This has been concreted—rather than paved—and is more functional than ours, with several items of farm machinery lying around, plus a bright pink mop and bucket. Then again, it's decorated with pots and hanging baskets containing well-tended shrubs and pretty flowers. Opposite the driveway—and across the little road that leads to my olive grove—is a small, corrugated iron garage, which is packed with tractors, other items of farm machinery, implements and tools. To the right of that, and across the road that leads up the hill, is the first of Stefano's fields, the slope of which is lined with vines, the flat section at the bottom tomato plants. Bordering this is a shack housing several hens and one cockerel—probably the one that wakes me up in the morning—surrounded by a wire fence to keep out foxes.

Stefano tops up our glasses with red wine made from the grapes from my vineyard. I've cooked with the oil from my olive grove before—he gave us a vat, which I've decanted into several bottles—but this is the first time I've tasted the wine. It's sweet, not very strong and possibly not the most sophisticated wine, but that's more than made up for by the knowledge that it came from my land.

Theo asks Luisa for more information on the castle, which she's happy to give. "It may seem small by today's standards but we know that the nobility of Montemagno lived in a luxurious palace at the top. The castle also housed the military quarters and, for the residents of the village, it was a refuge in times of siege."

Archie's face lights up, his mouth and fingertips stained red by the cherries. "So did they have battles?"

"No question," says Luisa, slicing into her peach. "Lots of battles!"

"Who were the baddies?" asks Archie. He has a smudge of cherry on his glasses and I lift them off his nose to clean them.

"I don't know if you children realize," she says, "but it's only in the last two hundred years that Italy became one country. Before that it was made up of lots of separate city-states. They often fought against each other."

"Was Montemagno part of Lucca?" I ask, batting a fly off my polo shirt. I notice that Callum has finished his fruit and is sitting up, listening.

"It was. But it often came under attack from Pisa. Both states wanted to control the castle because it overlooked the Via Francigena."

Mabel spits a cherry stone into her hand. "What's that?"

Theo and I flash each other a smile.

"It was an ancient route for trade and pilgrims," answers Luisa. "It ran all the way from Canterbury in England down to Rome."

"That's actually sick," acknowledges Callum.

I'm about to translate but realize Luisa must understand because she's smiling. "We know there was a major battle in 1242," she continues, handing round more fruit, "because that's when the castle was destroyed."

"Oh, no, so we lost?" says Archie. Now that his mouth is empty, I notice that his adult teeth have started to come through in the gap at the front.

"We lost, I'm afraid," confirms Luisa. "But that's pretty much all we know—which is why we have to keep digging!"

Once we've finished dessert, the kids go back to playing with the kittens. This was Luisa's plan to soften them up: her cat Camilla has three kittens that have just turned five weeks old. There are two girls and a boy and they're gray and white, unbelievably fluffy, and make a cute little squeaking sound. And she was right: they do have a soothing effect on the kids. Mabel coos and giggles in a way I've never heard before. Archie shows previously hidden capabilities of being soft and gentle. Even Callum has a tickle and a cuddle, until Stefano offers to connect him to their Wi-Fi and he switches to flicking through his phone.

"Do you have any pets in Manchester?" Luisa asks.

Theo shakes his head. "The kids always wanted a cat or a dog. . . ." He stops.

"Our mum's allergic to pet hair," fills in Mabel, stroking a kitten with each hand.

"Dad, can we keep one?" asks Archie, scratching a kitten's stomach. "Can we take it home?"

Theo slips off a loafer and starts massaging his foot. "I only have a little flat, squirt. And the kittens have all this lovely countryside here."

"*I* know!" says Archie. "How about we keep one here, in Adam's house?"

Theo frowns and slides his shoe back on. "We're only here for the summer. And I don't think these kittens are ready to be taken away from their mum."

We all look at Camilla, who's stretched out on the concrete, licking her paws, glancing up every now and then to check on her young.

"Where's their dad?" asks Mabel. I notice that she's pushed her hair behind her ears so the kittens can't claw at it, but she doesn't seem self-conscious.

Luisa shrugs. "In the animal world, dads don't always raise their young. Once they've mated with the mother, they tend to leave."

I wince, in expectation of a criticism of Theo. It doesn't come.

"Where are *your* kids?" Archie asks Luisa.

There's an uncomfortable silence.

"I'm sorry," says Theo. "He can be a bit blunt sometimes."

"It's OK," insists Luisa.

"We do not have any children," answers Stefano, standing up to slosh more wine in our glasses.

"Why not?" persists Archie.

Luisa gives a sigh. "I suppose when Mother Nature was creating me, she made a little mistake."

And just like that, I'm ten years old again, watching a TV debate in which a Tory MP said gay men were mistakes, evidence of nature misfiring.

"Not necessarily," pipes Mabel. "The planet's overpopulated so people who can't have children could be part of nature's plan."

I'm impressed by her thinking, but also the way she stepped in to relieve Luisa's discomfort. In my stomach I feel a little flutter.

"That is a very interesting idea," agrees Stefano.

"It is," I add. I wonder if any scientists have argued that human beings are gay for the same reason. I remember reading an article about gay animals but can't remember if it said anything about population control.

"We were very sad at first," Luisa reflects. "It's why Stefano gave up his job and we changed our lives. But now we've adjusted and are happy. Did *you* want kids, Adam?"

I'm thrown by her question and take a swig of wine. "When I was growing up, the thought didn't cross my mind. You just didn't see queer parents in those days." But if it weren't for that, would I have wanted kids?

"The best thing you can do for the planet is *not* to have children," declares Mabel.

"Do *you* want children?" Luisa asks her.

She lifts up a kitten and gives it a nuzzle. "I haven't decided yet."

"Well, it's very rewarding," Theo says. "But it can also be hard work." He sneaks her a wink.

I notice a half-smile playing around Mabel's lips. And I feel another fluttering in my stomach.

It dawns on me that I've been presented with the chance of inheriting some kind of family—and creating some kind of role within it—however challenging that may be. And it's a chance people like Wilf didn't have, so I should take it seriously.

"Well, you're doing a very good job with those kittens," Luisa observes. "Maybe you could help us look after them."

"*I* will!" bursts out Archie, making the kitten in his hands mewl.

"How about you start by helping us pick some names?" Luisa suggests.

Mabel's smile spreads across her face. "Really?"

"Yes. But they'll have to be in Italian. Stefano must be able to pronounce them."

"Bella!" erupts Mabel. "For one of the girls. I heard somebody say it the other day."

"Donnarumma!" booms Callum. He looks at me. "He's Italy's goalie—and a mint player!"

"Spaghetti!" yells Archie.

Everyone laughs.

After much discussion, we settle on Sophia—after Sophia Loren, Luisa's favorite actress—Roberto—after Roberto Baggio, apparently another footballer but one who used to play for Stefano's team, Fiorentina—and we stick with Spaghetti, which pleases Archie no end.

Then Theo announces that it's gone nine o'clock and past Archie's bedtime.

I finish my wine and rise to my feet. "Well, thanks for a brill evening."

Luisa and Stefano stand up and push in their chairs.

"It was our pleasure," says Stefano.

Luisa turns to the kids. "Come back and see the kittens soon."

All three of the kids smile. And that's when I realize the fluttering in my stomach was what I've been looking for—hope.

Chapter 17

I lift up my exercise bike and lug it back into the larder. Getting up early to have a workout was grim but after ten minutes of pedaling—looking out over the valley from the lawn—I was glad I did. Now that I've finished, I feel energized and excited about the day.

The builders have just arrived and drag the new windows across the patio and stack them up against the front of the house. One of the most important parts of the refurbishment is replacing the old single-glazed windows—many of which have rotten frames and cracked panes—with more durable, double-glazed models.

As I drink my orange juice and munch on a bowl of cornflakes, I watch the builders at work. Every now and then, they do something that reminds me of my dad, who was a window fitter before he retired. When I was little, I'd sometimes accompany him on a Saturday, when he was doing a "foreigner"—an off-the-books job for friends or family. As Mum worked in a shop selling women's fashions, she wasn't around on Saturdays. At the time, I looked up to Dad and idolized him. I thought he was so skillful and talented. But then he tried to teach me the basics of window fitting and I just couldn't grasp it. Nor could I grasp joinery or tiling, or any of the DIY activities he tried teaching me. I started to ask if I could go to Auntie Julie's when he had a job on Saturdays. It was bad enough registering his disappointment, but when I'd come home with cupcakes or a trifle we'd made, he'd look baffled, like he didn't know what to make of me, like I was some kind of alien. In Dad's eyes, the kitchen was a female domain—despite the fact Mum couldn't even make beans on toast and used to joke that she could burn water. He couldn't understand why his son would choose to spend a day cooking or baking over going out with him. It made me feel miserable and rotten. And why should I forgive him for that? Aren't parents supposed to love their children unconditionally?

Now that I think of it, this could be another reason I didn't consider becoming a dad—because my relationship with mine wasn't great. But if circumstances had been different, would I have wanted kids?

I finish my cereal and take my crockery indoors.

I don't understand why all these years later, revisiting this in my head should make me feel just as miserable and rotten.

Maybe Ian's right and I am still holding onto some gay shame.

I'm going to make a pot of coffee and take one up to Theo.

At five o'clock, we drive the kids into Pietrasanta. It's another medieval town but in the opposite direction from Montemagno to Lucca. It's also smaller, more upmarket, its streets and squares dotted with public art, much of this made out of local marble. Luisa has told us that the town's many shops and galleries are renowned for art, interior design, ornaments and soft furnishings.

After browsing a couple, I see she's right. "This place is fab! I'm picking up loads of ideas!"

But Mabel scoffs at my efforts, comparing me unfavorably to her mum and her talent in this area.

"Alright, alright," I say, putting back some bookends in the shape of chess pieces. "I'm not a professional, only an amateur!"

I hold up a Venetian blown-glass vase that's streaked with the colors of the rainbow and suggest it might make a nice nod to the Pride flag.

But Callum screws up his face. "Adam, it's proper tacky."

One step forward, two steps back!

I tell myself not to be downhearted: I couldn't afford it anyway.

After buying a couple much cheaper plant pots, a marble bowl that will be good for our house keys, and a bigger moka to make coffee for the builders—who seem to drink it all day—we stop in the main square. This is dominated by a marble cathedral and a red-brick bell tower, and is currently acting as an exhibition space for various big bronze sculptures of open and closed hands by the artist showing in the municipal gallery. The plan is to sit at a table outside one of the bars so the kids can connect to the Wi-Fi and check in with their friends, while Theo and I enjoy an *aperitivo* and observe the *passeggiata,* which seems to be in full swing even though it's only a Wednesday. Once we're sitting down, he orders his usual beer, while I ask for an Aperol Spritz.

"Can I have one of those?" cuts in Callum.

Theo tilts his head as he considers this. "Alright, just the one." He looks at me and shrugs. "It isn't very strong."

But I notice that when we're leaving the bar, Callum spots the remains of someone else's Aperol Spritz on another table and tips it back while his dad isn't looking.

"Is everything alright, Callum?" I ask.

"Yeah!" he snarls. "What's your point?"

I decide not to push it.

When we get back to the house, Callum announces he doesn't want dinner and slinks off to his room. But as soon as Theo and I have a moment alone—which is when Mabel and Archie are washing up—I tell him what I witnessed. He goes up to check on Callum and discovers that he's smuggled a bottle of Aperol out of the larder and has already drunk half of it, neat. I only find this out when I'm drawn upstairs by the sound of raised voices.

"Cal, what are you playing at?" Theo is demanding, standing in the doorway.

But Callum pushes both of us out of the way and lurches over to the bathroom, where he throws up into the toilet.

I go back downstairs and bring him a bottle of water. When I enter the bathroom, Callum's telling Theo that while we were in Pietrasanta, he heard Charlotte has dumped him for another boy. She didn't even tell him herself—he had to hear it from a friend.

"I hate being here!" he wails. "This is the worst summer ever!"

Make that three or four steps back.

Theo helps him to the bedroom and sits on the bed next to him. I decide to leave them to it: Callum's probably feeling humiliated as well as angry. He won't appreciate me hanging around.

When I'm walking through to the big lounge, I find Mabel, hiding in the study, listening to what's happening.

My heart drops in my chest. What's Kate going to say when she hears about it?

Later that evening, when Mabel and Archie have gone to bed and Theo and Callum are having a chat on the patio, I finally spot the opportunity to go back to reading Wilf's letters. I sit on our bed, under the mosquito net, propped up against my pillows, and pull out the next one.

Carissimo Arnaldo,

Thanks very much for your letter. I'm so happy you feel the same as I do. Well, I knew you felt the same because you told me several times, but I'm happy you haven't had a change of heart. The day after your letter arrived, one of the teachers at school said I was grinning like a Cheshire cat. I had to pretend it was because I'd spent the evening with my nieces.

As for your idea of finding a house in the hills, a long way away from anyone else, I'd say it's blinking marvellous. I didn't know in Italy it isn't against the law to be homosexual, or omosessuale *as you say. At least it means we won't be outlaws and won't have to live in fear of being arrested and going to prison. However, I hear what you say about the way folk think and the way they treat men like us. That sounds more or less the same as it is here, although it does sound like the Catholic Church can aggravate matters.*

That story you told me about your pal is terrible, by the way. I've been thinking about it a lot. I'm sure he only went cottaging because he was lonely and desperate to meet men like him. To be dragged down the street and given a beating, with folk standing around, cheering! And a priest, too!

Just writing about this is getting me all het up. Actually, do you know what that means? It means fired up or angry. I don't care what anyone says: it isn't fair that men like us have to hide away or pretend to be normal. It isn't our fault we're like this. Not that I'd want to change, even if there were an injection or electric shock that could do that to us. Not now I've found you, carissimo.

Any road, I understand why you had to tell your family. In this regard, your situation is quite different to mine. You can hardly move a few miles away and not offer them any explanation. Their response, however, is shocking. Some of the things your mother said are unforgiveable. I don't know how she can live with herself.

Happen you are better off staying in a hotel and, if they do cut you out of the business, you should set up your own concern. You've worked in textiles all your life, so are bound to make a success of it. You're a marvellous man and I have every confidence in you, Arnaldo. I can't help thinking, though, that it's odd it was the rag trade that brought us together. I've always hated the mills around Manchester, with their smoke and smells. Many a time I've dreamed of escaping somewhere more beautiful, somewhere more romantic. I'd never have thought it would be the rag trade that would give me the opportunity. I'd certainly never have thought it would lead me to a man who loves opera. I still don't know how I'll get on with that, by the way. Growing up here, I've never really come across it, although I do remember my music teacher at school once playing us some Caruso on an old gramophone. Who knows, though? If it's important to you, happen I'll grow to love it.

Any road, after hearing what happened with your family I've decided I'm not going to tell mine, at least not until after I've left. I know what they'll say, Father in particular. I hear exactly what he thinks about 'queers' every time there's a story in the newspapers, such as when Lord Montagu or John Gielgud were arrested. I've also heard his stories about some queer soldier he knew in the war, a man he called a 'brown-hatter' and he and the other soldiers tormented, even though they were supposed to be fighting on the same side. My brother-in-law isn't much better, truth be told. He often talks about some fella at work he thinks is a 'pansy'. It's as much as I can do to sit there and say nothing once the two of them get on the subject, especially if they've had a few pints.

Once I've arrived in Italy, I'll write to my family explaining why I've gone. I much prefer putting my thoughts on paper and find it easier to order them. Whenever anyone in my family needs to write a letter, they ask me to do it. Now they'll be getting one from me. Just thinking of their faces when they read it sends a shiver down my spine, but I won't let that stop me.

I've already started preparing for the trip. I've been to the library to borrow some novels set in Italy so I can familiarise myself with the culture. I think I told you I'm an avid reader, but what else would you expect from an English teacher? I've taken out A Room with a View by E. M. Forster and The Wings of the Dove by Henry James. They're both about posh folk, nobody like us. Or nobody like me, I should say. Oddly enough, I've heard rumours that both of the authors are homosexual, although I don't know how I could determine that for sure.

By the way, I've just finished reading a book called The Heart in Exile by an author called Rodney Garland. One of my pals in the Union told me about it and passed his copy onto me. Oh, Arnaldo, it's a wonderful book! The lead character is actually homosexual, which shocked me at first as I've never seen that before, not in the pages of a book. My heart was racing as I read it. Of course, he's another posh fella and he does have odd ideas about working-class folk, although it's nothing I haven't heard before. The main thing is he isn't a villain, although he does suffer and has to live in exile, or should I say exiled from the emotions in his own heart. I think that's what the title means, or at least that's what the English teacher in me thinks. I believe the book has been popular, which gives me hope. I need as much of that as I can get before you and I go into our own exile.

Although I'm committed to your plan, I don't mind admitting that I'm also blinking terrified. It's an enormous undertaking for us both and we each stand to lose everything. You'll lose your home, your inheritance, your friends and your position in the family firm. It sounds like you've already lost your family. I'll lose my home country, my position, and also my family and friends. We won't have any money but I'm not too fussed about that. I grew up with very little and it's only recently I've started to earn a decent wage. I also lived through the war and rationing, so I know I'll cope. We'll just have to be everything to one another.

I'm enclosing some photographs that I hope will tide you over until I arrive. I know it's reckless to be sending them in the post, but I trust you'll forgive me. I hope they bring back happy memories of the two of us sneaking into that booth in Central Station in the dead of night. When I look back, I can hardly believe we did that, although I suppose it was much safer than taking a film to be developed in a shop. A fella from the Union was arrested when he did that and you don't want to know what happened to him. Any road, thank goodness we did, as these may be the only photographs we ever have of the two of us together, that is unless we go into a booth again. You may have forgotten about them because I kept the whole roll for myself and didn't mention them again. Sorry, but I just couldn't bear to part with them. I was frightened you'd arrive back in Italy and change your mind about wanting to be with me, and I'd have nothing to remember you by.

Better late than never, I'm enclosing your half of the strip. I hope it eases the pain of us being apart. Very soon we'll be together once more.

You are my carissimo and I am so happy to be your tesoro,

Wilf xx

I put the letter down and find the top half of a strip of black-and-white photos in the bottom of the envelope.

Both photos show Wilf and Arnaldo embracing and in the second shot, Wilf's kissing Arnaldo on the cheek. He looks so young, far too young to have lived through some of the experiences he writes about. Arnaldo is smiling in the first shot, laughing in the second, his face a picture of joy. The photos are so different to the stiff, awkwardly posed ones we found in Wilf's bedroom and the study. There's so much affection—so much love—between the two men. And there's another emotion in there, something like an extreme release.

I have to find the bottom half of the strip.

I slip out of the mosquito nets and go down to the study. When I was clearing out the room, I came across a box of photos similar to the ones in frames. Although they didn't seem particularly interesting, I couldn't bring myself to throw them away. I pull out the box and begin thumbing through them. There aren't many photos, considering Wilf and Arnaldo were together for decades, and they're all similar to the ones in frames: both men are holding back, suppressing their emotions, concealing their love for each other.

Underneath the pile is a faded brown envelope. I open it and pull out another heap of loose photos. But these are all in strips. They were all taken in photo booths.

Sitting on the top is the second half of the black-and-white photos taken in Manchester. I hold it up and see the sequence continues with a shot of Wilf and Arnaldo kissing on the lips. Then—in the final shot—they each turn to the camera and grin, their faces aglow.

Tears spring to my eyes. But this time I can't hold them back. Soon they're streaming down my cheeks and falling onto my bare chest, as I look through decade after decade of photos, the fashions changing, Arnaldo's hairline receding, Wilf's forehead wrinkling, color eventually replacing black and white. But one thing never changes—the joy on the men's faces.

A handful of the photos are dated and I realize they were all taken on the same day—22 April. So this must have become Wilf and Arnaldo's annual tradition. But the last of the photos is dated 22 April 1997, after which I can only assume Arnaldo died. Surely by that stage they could have lived a little more freely? Or did they get so used to hiding that they lost the ability to express their feelings in the open, in anything other than the strictest of secrecy, in anywhere other than a photo booth?

I wipe my tears on my bare arm, careful that they don't fall onto the photos. I try to sniff them back but can't stop the flow. I'm ripped through with grief, grief for the life Wilf and Arnaldo never had, for the love they had to keep buried.

I give myself over to full, body-racking sobs.

I'm going to have to put the photos away. And I'm going to need a break before reading the final letter.

Chapter 18

On Thursday, we find the beginning of a footpath that leads from my grounds—from in front of the garage—down to the village. Stefano told us about it but it hasn't been used for so long it's almost completely overgrown. The plan is to clear it to create a shortcut to our favorite café.

Theo walks at the head of our group, slashing at the brambles with a sickle we found in one of the outhouses. A few steps behind him, I prune what he missed with a pair of secateurs. Behind me comes Archie, then Mabel, with Callum bringing up the rear.

We pass the ruins of a laborers' cottage—with its own stable block—which I've seen on the deeds but is almost completely overgrown with brambles and bamboo. I try not to think about how long it'll take for the path we're clearing to be reclaimed by nature.

It's early afternoon and the hottest time of the day. I wipe the sweat from my forehead and notice that Theo is developing a damp patch on his back. As he swings his blade from side to side, he lets out a little grunt.

"It's like watching Indiana Jones," I joke.

"Hardly," quips Theo. "And didn't Indiana Jones have a whip, not a sickle?"

"I've no idea but you look very manly."

"Urgh, will you two stop flirting?" complains Callum from behind us.

"It's gross!" agrees Mabel.

Defiance cuts through me. I think about Wilf and Arnaldo, having to hide their love away. "Guys, you shouldn't say things like that. Your dad and I have every right to express our feelings for each other."

Callum scoffs. "I didn't know we were coming on a Gay Pride march."

My defiance surges. "Actually, Gay Pride marches are important. For years, couples like us were made to feel ashamed of who we were. Remember it was a gay couple who owned this house before us. And if you think the boys at school can be savage, imagine what kind of things people said in those days."

Before he can reply, into our path lands a snake. It just appears from the bushes and slides to a stop before us.

Instinctively, Theo and I jump back.

"Bloody hell!" he bursts out.

I howl in terror.

The kids lean forward, peering around us.

"What is it?" asks Callum.

The snake's coiled up but must be more than a meter long. It's dark green, with black markings. We're so close I can see its scales.

When Mabel registers what it is, she screams, louder than I've ever heard her scream.

"It's OK," says Theo, reverting to his usual calm. "Stay still and nobody panic."

We do as he says and the snake slithers off, into the bushes on the other side.

"It was only a grass snake," Theo's quick to reassure us. "I know it was a shock but it couldn't have done us any harm."

Mabel, however, has gone into some kind of panic, breathing in and out shallowly and frenetically. "Oh my god, we nearly died. Oh my god, we nearly died. Oh my god, we nearly died."

Archie ignores her. "Can we go into the bushes and find it?" he asks, tugging on his dad's hand.

"No, squirt," says Theo. "I think it wants to be on its own."

Theo tries to calm Mabel down but she won't listen to him. She just continues repeating the same line. "Oh my god, we nearly died."

Soon, Callum is irritated. "Mabel, will you stop being such a drama queen?"

"Right, let's all just stop and have a minute," Theo commands.

After a short discussion, we decide that I'll walk back with Mabel and Archie. I'll take them to the village via the usual route, through the olive grove and down the winding road. Theo and Callum, meanwhile, will continue clearing the footpath and meet us in our usual café.

For the entire walk—which lasts about half an hour—Mabel refuses to say a word.

Archie, however, takes hold of my hand and merrily skips along, telling me everything he knows about snakes—most of which he learned from a pack of Top Trumps.

"That's brill, Archie!" I gush, keen to encourage him. "You're so clever!"

When we reach the village and arrive at the café, Mabel connects to the Wi-Fi and gets straight on the phone to her mum. I order everyone a soft drink and find a table on the terrace. As soon as Theo and Callum arrive—looking triumphant but sweaty and covered in leaves, thorns and pollen—Mabel thrusts the phone at Theo.

He sighs and slumps onto one of the plastic chairs. "Alright, Kate?"

"Theo, what's going on?" Kate blasts over the speaker. "Apparently you've just been attacked by a snake. And last night Callum got drunk—no doubt on one of Adam's bottles of booze."

Something snaps inside me.

"Kate . . ." Theo begins. But he stops. And he throws his hands in the air, as if in surrender.

"Come on," Kate pushes, "I want to hear what you've got to say."

"What *can* I say?" Theo replies. "What difference would it make?"

"Look, I'm worried about my children," Kate steams on. "As a mother, I'm perfectly entitled to be concerned about their welfare. And I've got to be honest, I think Adam's a negative influence."

At that point, I stop listening.

All that matters is that Theo is just sitting there, stabbing at the ice in his drink. He doesn't defend me at all.

"Why didn't you stand up to her?" I bark, when Theo and I are alone in our room. "You didn't stand up to her at all!"

Theo flops back on the bed. "Oh, Ads, I just felt so defeated."

He lets out a shaky sigh and I can tell how much he's suffering. But I'm so gripped by anger—an anger that's been building ever since the phone call—that I can't stop myself.

"Defeated or guilty?" I fire back, pacing around next to the bed. I'm only wearing my underpants but it doesn't occur to me to hold in my stomach.

Theo turns to face me. "What does that mean?"

I stop and look him in the eye. "Theo, it's obvious you feel guilty about leaving Kate. Go on, deny it!"

He sits up and smooths down his shirt. "I do feel guilty about lying to her. Although if I hadn't, we wouldn't have the kids so I don't know what to make of that. I don't think I feel guilty about leaving her. Maybe just some of the details. Maybe the timing."

I shake my head. "Brill! So your parents have got through to you."

"No, it's not that. It's just . . . I don't know, it's complicated."

I gasp dramatically. "'It's complicated'. Where have I heard that before?" Pretty much every single time a bloke has dumped me, I say to myself.

Theo shuffles towards me on the bed. "Ads, what do you mean?"

I tuck my hands under my armpits. "Look, Theo, this isn't complicated at all. It's perfectly simple: if you hadn't left Kate when you did, you wouldn't have met me. So do you *regret* meeting me? Is that what you're saying?"

He stands up. "Bloody hell, Ads, that's not what I'm saying. That's not what I'm saying at all."

But I'm so angry I hardly take it in. "Bullshit, Theo! You're ashamed of me. You're just not brave enough to say it!"

Theo walks down the little staircase to shut the door so the kids won't hear. "Ads, I'm sorry about earlier," he says, calmly. "You're right, I should have stood up to Kate."

But I don't register his apology. And now I've pulled the cork on my feelings, I can't stop them splurging out. "Oh, this is all such a nightmare. This whole trip's a disaster. Callum and Mabel hate me."

Theo starts tugging off his clothes. "They don't hate you, Adam. It's just hard for them. I expect it is for all kids who have a parent that gets a new partner."

I roll my eyes dramatically. "It's not like we had an affair! It's not like I *stole* you off Kate! And it could never have worked between you two, anyway!"

Theo stuffs his clothes in the laundry bag. He's wearing only his briefs, but I don't even notice his body.

"I know, but they're still getting used to having a gay dad." A note of testiness enters his voice. "It doesn't help that their friends have been teasing them about it. Their world's been turned upside down."

I lean into him. "I understand that, Theo! But when are you going to understand that you couldn't have carried on sacrificing your own happiness?"

Now it's Theo's turn to snap. "Couldn't I? Isn't that what a parent's supposed to do? Make sacrifices? Put their kids first?"

Red mist clouds my vision. "Aha! Now we're getting down to it! So you *do* feel guilty! You *are* ashamed of me!"

He hurls the laundry bag back into the corner. "I'm not, Adam! Bloody hell, I'm not ashamed of you!"

I go back to pacing the room. "You know, it's no wonder the kids hate me. They can probably sense it. They can probably sense that you resent me ever coming into your life!"

"Adam, that's not true!" Theo lowers himself onto the bed. He looks like a broken man—and I hate myself for attacking him.

I know I'm driving him away. But for some reason, I'm compelled to keep going.

"Why don't you just leave, Theo? It's obvious you want to dump me. Why don't you just put both of us out of our misery?" I can hardly believe those words are coming out of my mouth. As a shocked silence sets in, they almost crackle in the air between us.

But I realize I'm slipping into an old pattern and part of me *wants* Theo to leave me. Because at least then I could relax. It'd be like unclenching a fist, a fist I've been clenching ever since he and I got together. And I could go back to normal, to being dumped and on my own, just like I always am.

But another part of me is desperate to avoid that. Another part of me knows that's not what I want at all. It's the *last* thing I want.

No, I won't let it happen. I need to end this argument before I do any more damage.

"Sorry, Theo. I didn't mean that. Just ignore me. I only said it because I'm upset."

He kneads his face with the heel of his hand. "That's OK. I think we're both are."

I sigh heavily. "Let's call it a day."

He nods, somberly.

"Let's go to bed before we say anything else we might regret."

Theo looks at me, his face etched with sadness. "Alright, deal."

I lie down with my back to him and close my eyes.

I try not to think that Wilf's letters to Arnaldo—relating their struggle to be together—are hidden under the bed.

Chapter 19

In the morning, Theo and I don't have the chance to talk. But that's a situation of my own making. After lying in bed rigid for most of the night—tormented by what I said to him—I get up early and grab the first excuse to get out of the way. I go to the supermarket to stock up before my sisters arrive.

But as I walk around the aisles, I'm still tormented by our argument. Have I blown it? Have I fucked it all up?

The same thought darts around my mind when I get back to the house and unpack the shopping. It's on my mind when I clean and set up the first bathroom finished by the builders, which now has a dove-gray suite and sage-green tiles and I would think is gorgeous if I were able to concentrate. It's on my mind when I clear out the bathroom on the middle floor so that the builders can start stripping it on Monday. And it's on my mind as I make everyone lunch, insisting I'm not hungry as I ate a massive bag of crisps in the car—which is true, although that's something else I did on purpose.

Throughout the meal, Theo is much quieter and more introverted than usual. I daren't imagine the thoughts going through his head.

In the afternoon, Giuseppe gives me his usual end-of-the-week progress report. I can just about concentrate as he shows me the finished work on the retaining wall behind the chapel and the new, user-friendly path up to the castle—both of which are very impressive. But my concentration slips as he outlines next week's schedule. And it goes completely when he starts talking about damp proofing and rewiring. All I can think is, I can't believe I told Theo to leave me. What is *wrong* with me?

Anxiety rages in my head. It doesn't help that I've hardly slept. When Giuseppe finishes his report, I go to make myself—yet another—strong coffee.

I need to pull myself together before my sisters arrive.

And my two—very distinct—worlds, collide.

At four o'clock I receive a message from the girls letting me know they've arrived in Montemagno. Our original plan had been for them to stay in the house, but that was before the kids were coming for the whole summer. I felt so guilty asking them to stay elsewhere that I found them an Airbnb just off the main road in the village and insisted on paying for it myself—although I regret that now Giuseppe's bills are mounting up. Worried that Gloria's luggage wouldn't fit in my little car, I also booked them an extra-large taxi from Pisa Airport. At least the work on the kitchen isn't starting till Monday so I can cook them a welcome meal. Although the thought of my sisters, the kids and Theo sitting round the same table sends my anxiety soaring.

I drive down to the village but don't make it to the Airbnb before I spot my sisters in the square outside the church. Ian is wearing a short-sleeved check shirt, cargo shorts and Birkenstocks, and studying the plaque by the war memorial. Dom is dressed in tiny drawstring sports shorts and an equally tiny vest—his muscles and chest hair spilling out of it—doing triceps dips on a bench. And Gloria is in half drag—or "hag" as he calls it—wearing a pink, bobbed wig and heart-shaped dangly earrings, with a strappy silver top and fitted trousers, both of which show off his ample curves. He's currently shimmying down a potted olive tree, when he reaches the bottom twerking furiously. I feel an ache in my gut as I realize just how much I've missed them.

"Ladies, it's fab to see you!" I gush, flinging open the car door and rushing towards them.

"You too, *mia sorella*!" trills Gloria, in a flurry of kisses and hugs.

"In case you're wondering, that's 'my sister' in Italian," translates Ian. "We looked it up in the airport."

"While we were drinking the bar dry," booms Dom in his deep voice, his moustache tickling me as he plants several kisses on my cheeks.

"Bitch, this place is as dead as Kerry Katona's career," Gloria declares. "Take us to your castle!"

I frown. "Just so you know, it's not very glamorous."

Gloria raises a nail-varnish-tipped hand in dismissal. "Don't worry, girl, we *are* the glamour!"

I chuckle. "Yeah, it's also a building site."

"In that case, it'll be full of hot builders." Gloria jumps in the car and gives a few taps on the ceiling. "Addy, hit that accelerator!"

When we arrive at the house, the girls jump out of the car and start looking around.

"It's as hot as a swamp up here," drawls Gloria. "It's a good job I brought my fan." He produces an elaborate lace fan, which he throws open with a loud click, and begins wafting himself.

Theo trots over to greet us, trailed by the kids.

"How's my favorite zaddy?" Dom bellows, giving him a hug and pat on the back.

"You've only been here two weeks and look how blond you are!" observes Ian.

"Even the hairs on your arms have gone blond!" says Gloria. He gives a little growl. "If you weren't dating my sister . . ."

Theo gives a bashful smile, but I can tell he isn't uncomfortable. Which is more than can be said for the kids. They seem taken aback by just how loud—just how forceful a presence—my sisters are. As do a couple of builders, who are dragging out an old bath and chucking it into the skip, doing everything they can to avoid establishing eye contact.

Theo introduces the kids to Ian, Gloria and Dom. While everyone is polite, each side is clearly wary of the other. That can't be helped by the fact that I've kept my sisters updated on some of the kids' more challenging behavior. Not that I regret that: without their support, I wouldn't have made it through the last two weeks.

Archie seems fascinated by Gloria, all six feet, four inches of him—and that's before adding on his pink, patent leather stack heels.

"Are you on stilts?" he asks.

Gloria gives a broad grin. "No, my angel. Just heels."

Archie points at Gloria's pink wig. "Is that real?"

"Nothing about me is real!" says Gloria, theatrically. "I'm a work of art, my own special creation!"

The reference to "I Am What I Am" is lost on Archie, but it doesn't matter because my sisters' attention has already shifted onto the builders. Gloria and Dom are mesmerized, especially as the men are—as usual—working shirtless. Giuseppe in particular is a big hit and my sisters insist on going over to introduce themselves.

"*Buongiorno!*" says Dom, eyeing him up, approvingly.

Gloria flutters his false eyelashes. "I think I'm suffering from subsidence. Can you spread some cement on my foundations?"

Ian tries to contain his laughter. "I'm not getting my translation app out for that."

"There's no need," I say, torn between embarrassment and amusement. "Giuseppe speaks English. He's married to a British woman."

"Sorry, you lost me at 'married'," quips Gloria, with a click of his fan.

To my relief, Giuseppe seems to be reveling in the attention. I try not to notice that the other builders are scurrying off with their heads down. Arjan, in particular, looks terrified.

Wait a minute, what would they be like if a few straight women had arrived and were flirting with them?

"Come on, let me show you girls round," I suggest, brightly.

I start with the castle, which I know will be empty since the diggers left at lunchtime—not to mention away from the builders. Even though the newly constructed path and steps make the climb much easier, Gloria struggles in heels—and it doesn't help that he's vaping.

"I feel like those queens at the end of *Priscilla, Queen of the Desert*," he groans. "When they're climbing Ayers Rock, or whatever it's called now."

"Uluru," provides Ian.

"Try saying that with a mouthful of cock," Gloria chirps.

Everyone cackles. I glance behind us to check the kids aren't in earshot but they've gone inside.

When Gloria reaches the top of the hill, he tugs on his vape, and lets out a long, pink plume. "Ladies, gentlemen, friends, family, fans . . . I hereby declare the queens have arrived at the castle!"

Despite the fanfare, we're not able to explore much of it as the majority is marked out for the dig. But we step around the markings and I am at least able to show the girls the view.

"You know, this would make an amazing meditation space," comments Ian.

"Do you think if I went to sleep, a handsome prince would wake me up with a kiss?" says Gloria, adopting a breathy, distressed, female voice.

"As if you'd settle for a kiss," pipes Dom.

"Yeah, I'd at least want a blowie!"

The cackling accompanies us down to the olive grove, where Gloria skips around in a flight of fantasy. "You know, I've always wanted to be ravaged in an olive grove by a rough Italian farmhand."

I give him a wry smile. "You might want to be careful. We saw a snake around here the other day."

Gloria narrows his eyes. "Now you're talking!"

When we make it back to the house, the builders are just leaving and I feel the relief wash over me. We enter through the cottage and I give our visitors a tour. All three of them love it and they each have ideas on how they'd transform it if they were in charge of the refurb. Dom would turn the big lounge into a home gym, for example, while Ian would turn it into a coaching studio and Gloria would turn it into a disco room—complete with dance floor, stage and bar.

"Speaking of bars, is anyone going to crack open some fizz?" warbles Gloria. "My mouth's drier than a nun's snatch."

From outside, I hear the kids squabbling and feel a rush of fear: soon we'll all be out there together.

We go down to the kitchen and I serve everyone drinks, including an extra-large one for myself. I also take a chicken cacciatore I've prepared out of the fridge and slide it into the oven. Then I bite the bullet and invite everyone to sit at the table, gabbling nervously about the new chairs I bought. I busy myself spreading out nibbles, as the kids huddle around Theo—as if for safety—at one end.

"I can't get over how beautiful this place is," says Ian, marveling at the surroundings. "It's like being on a film set."

Gloria looks around and nods. "I could get used to it. Lounging around in my kaftan, nipping to the opera on my Vespa . . . what else do Italians do?"

"Going to church on a Sunday," says Dom, joining his hands in prayer. "Bless me, Father, for I have sinned."

"Girl, I'd be in there all day!"

The three of them laugh.

I feel buoyed up by my sisters' positive energy and lack of inhibition, their pride in who they are. But Archie seems quieter than usual and a little overwhelmed, plus Callum and Mabel just sit there, stony-faced. I've no idea how Theo's feeling.

Gloria takes a drag on his vape and lets out another pink plume. "Now then, how well do you kids know our Addy?"

A cold slick of dread passes through me.

"They've been getting to know each other," offers Theo.

Gloria puts down his vape. "Who wants to hear the story of how he got his name?"

"Me!" squeaks Archie.

I know this story well, so am able to relax a little. I open a second bottle of Prosecco and fetch Theo and Dom another beer.

"When his mum was pregnant," Gloria begins, "she got sick of being stuck in the house so his dad took her out for a pub lunch. The baby wasn't supposed to arrive for a couple of weeks so she was nice and relaxed, enjoying her Yorkshire pudding, when her waters broke. They called an ambulance but it all happened so quickly, Addy was born in the car park."

"And who can guess the name of the pub?" tosses in Dom.

Theo and the kids look blank.

"The Adam and Eve," I reveal.

The adults laugh. There's even the hint of a smile on Mabel's face.

"Ads, how do I not know that story?" asks Theo.

I think he may be smiling but I daren't look at him.

"It sounds like you need to spend more time with his sisters," says Ian.

"We could tell you a few other things he's done in a pub car park," quips Dom.

Gloria laughs so hard his earrings rattle. Callum looks appalled, while Mabel and Archie don't seem to have understood the joke. Theo did and is chuckling. So why do I feel embarrassed? Would I feel the same if I were straight and being teased by my friends?

I look at Dom and widen my eyes. "Yeah, thanks, my sister."

"Can I ask a question?" Mabel crows. "Why do you call each other sisters?"

"Because we are sisters, my angel," says Gloria, rubbing his beard. "A sister isn't just someone with the same parents. It can be anyone you've shared an important experience with. What matters is the bond."

"Basically, queer people used to be rejected by their families," explains Ian, taking off his glasses to clean them. "So we have a history of what's known as 'found family', of creating our own families."

"But you're not even girls," snipes Callum.

"No, but we also have a bond with women, because we too have been oppressed by the patriarchy," Ian answers, pushing his glasses back up his nose.

"What does that mean?" asks Archie, screwing up his face.

"Before I was bullied for being gay," Gloria explains, "I used to get called a girl and laughed at for not being masculine enough. But that's just another expression of misogyny."

"What's mis. . . . ?" asks Archie, struggling to pronounce the word.

"Misogyny," supplies Theo. "It means hating women."

"By calling each other girls, we're reclaiming the insult," Ian goes on. "And refusing to see being feminine as something negative. We're also refusing to fit into any fixed understanding of gender, because that's limiting."

I can tell that, begrudgingly, Mabel at least is impressed. Callum is out of his depth. And Archie just looks bewildered.

"Speaking of feminine, your hydrangeas are gorge, my sister," says Gloria, gesturing to a bush at the edge of the lawn.

"Thanks," I reply. "I've been watering them every day since we arrived."

"Gloria's a florist," Theo tells the kids.

Ian takes out his lip balm and runs it over his lips. "And what do you three want to be when you grow up?"

"I'm going to be a lawyer," Mabel declares, determinedly.

"Sensational," cheeps Gloria, tipping back his Prosecco. "You can help us fight the patriarchy!"

Callum says he doesn't know—and I can't help noticing him squirm slightly. He looks for his dad's reaction.

"We haven't worked it out yet," Theo says, reaching out and giving Callum's shoulder a rub. "Cal's very practically minded: academic work isn't really his thing. He loves sport."

"Me too," says Dom, chugging his beer. "I used to hate school."

Callum raises an eyebrow but doesn't pursue the subject.

"And Archie wants to be a wrestler," Theo goes on. "Don't you, squirt?"

Archie shakes his head. "Not anymore. I'm going to be a builder now."

Theo nods. "Archie loves watching our builders."

"He's not the only one," says Gloria, picking up his fan and giving it a click. "That Giuseppe is smoking hot. He could renovate my downstairs any day."

Ian and Dom burst out laughing and I can't help joining in, as does Theo.

But Callum and Mabel exchange looks of horror. I feel a spike of resentment towards them. My mum and her friends from the shop always used to talk about who they fancied. Every time they'd had a few glasses of wine they'd fantasize about what they'd do with Michael Douglas or Harrison Ford. How's this any different?

I suddenly realize that all the time I've been in Italy, I've been holding some of myself back, frightened of behaving inappropriately around the kids. But in the process have I been compromising who I am?

Maybe I was stupid to try and make this work. Maybe I should just tell Theo it's a mistake and let him take the kids and leave.

Then I can go back to Manchester with my sisters.

Chapter 20

When Theo wakes up, he says he's going to take the kids out for the day, starting with a trip to see the kittens. "We'll give you guys some space."

I'm about to ask if what he really means is he wants to get out of my way, just like I did with him yesterday. We still need to untangle our argument—but I can't go there now my sisters have arrived.

"Brill," I manage, weakly. "Thanks."

The girls and I decide to go to La Lecciona, the gay beach in between Viareggio and the next resort along the coast, Torre del Lago. It's another gorgeous day and we arrive to find a stretch of sand that's much softer and closer to golden than the beach in Viareggio. The sea is a perfect turquoise, the reflection of the sun on its waves so bright I can hardly look at it, even with sunglasses. And framed by the much deeper blue of the sky is a Pride flag, curling and snapping in the gentle breeze.

As we spread out our towels, I feel uneasy about taking off my clothes. Regular sessions on the exercise bike may have stopped my weight gain but I still haven't lost any of the weight I originally put on. I scan the beach, however, and can make out bodies of all types: there are old men and young men, fat men and thin men, handsome men and not-so-handsome men. And I spot biceps, pecs, glutes and delts, but also guts, moobs, chicken legs, and loose flaps of skin hanging from arms. But nobody seems self-conscious. Some men are even nude—and this isn't, to my surprise, the ones with the best bodies. I clearly have nothing to worry about.

Of our group, Dom is the first to strip off, flaunting his spectacular, gym-sculpted physique in a pair of tiny black Speedos. Ian's next, his slim frame covered only with tufts of silver hair on the chest and gray, shell-patterned swimming shorts. And a wigless, bald Gloria flings off his clothes to reveal a woman's jade-green bandeau swimsuit that accentuates every inch of his head-turning figure. If he's rounded off the look with a coral sarong, I know this isn't to cover himself up but to give him something to swish around.

The four of us lie in the sun and spend most of the day chatting. I tell my sisters about Wilf and what I've discovered of his story so far and they're gripped, insisting I keep them updated—although I feel a pang of guilt as I still haven't told Theo. We discuss Gloria and Dom's most recent sexual encounters and they open Grindr to make contact with men and line up some options for later.

After lunch in a nearby beach club, Ian settles down to read his book; Dom plays volleyball with a group of similarly jacked, Speedo-sporting men; and Gloria slinks off into the dunes with the guy who was walking up and down the beach, selling drinks and fresh fruit.

"I need a closer look at his watermelons," he jokes.

I slip off for a swim. The water is the perfect temperature: not cold but cool enough to provide some respite from the heat. As I plunge beneath the surface and reemerge to find my stroke, I feel a sudden rush of freedom. I realize how good it is to have a break from all the tension and hostility at the house, and a taste of my old, much simpler, life. I wonder again if I should let my new one fall apart and then I can just go back to it.

I stop swimming, let myself float and close my eyes, breathing in and out, deeply. Maybe I was never meant to take on a family. Maybe I'm not cut out for this kind of complicated relationship or emotional baggage. Maybe it's time to have a rethink and start again.

One thing's for sure: I love being surrounded by people who like me, people who enjoy my company and actually want to spend time with me.

Being disliked is horrendous. And so exhausting.

I swim back to the shore, stand up and stride out of the sea. I throw myself down on my towel, ready to dry out in the sun.

Several hours later, we've showered and changed and arrive at the local gay club, which is a few hundred meters behind the beach, back in Torre del Lago. The four of us step through the doors arm-in-arm, and being out with my sisters makes me feel a power surge.

The club has a large indoor space but an even bigger courtyard that doubles as a dance floor. This is lined with painted rainbows, crowns and palm trees—some of them bordered with flashing lights—and packed with people. The crowd is mainly made up of men, several of these signaling their gayness with colorful wigs, fans and dog masks. A minority are women, some of them doing the same with their lesbianism, others looking more likely to be friends and allies. Those who aren't dancing are kissing or fondling someone—or more than one person—while others are downing shots in lurid colors or watching a drag queen in a blond Afro and a zebra-print catsuit strutting up and down the stage belting out a song by Christina Aguilera.

As I wait at the bar to buy our first round of drinks, I feel a rush of excitement to be back amongst my community. There's only one problem: most of the people here are younger than us—significantly younger.

"Are you sure we're not too old for this place?" I ask the girls, as I hand out their drinks.

Gloria shakes his head, defiantly. "We'll never be as young as we are now!"

Age doesn't seem to dent Dom's appeal. He's wearing purple Speedos and a matching sequined harness, and within minutes is surrounded by a huddle of much younger admirers.

"Sometimes I think that girl must glow with a permanently applied Instagram filter," offers Gloria.

We laugh. But I worry about Dom's hearing as he struggles in loud venues. I spot him repositioning himself so his good ear is facing a tall man with his hair in curtains, who's marveling at him, his eyes gleaming.

Wait a minute, I know that man. . . .

"That's Vito!" I tell the others. "He works in the museum and is helping with our dig."

Ian raises an eyebrow. "So he's clever with a proper job. Slightly off-brand for Dom but an interesting pivot."

We keep an eye on the two of them. By the time we're hitting our third drink, they're kissing. By the time we're on our fourth, they've disappeared.

Gloria lets out a gasp and grabs onto my arm. "Girl, look at that go-go dancer!" He points at the raised stage, at a muscled man wearing a studded leather thong, black wraparound sunglasses, and nothing else—except a bolt through his left nipple and what looks like an entire bottle of baby oil slathered over his body. "I'd rinse out his jockstrap."

Without any further discussion, Gloria plunges into the throng, weaving his way towards the stage. A few minutes later, Ian and I spot him in his silver lamé leotard, writhing around the dancer, hair-whipping his electric blue wig, and sending clouds of glitter flying out from his beard into the crowd.

"Come on," says Ian. "Let's get another drink."

"Do you want to see if there's anyone you fancy?" I suggest.

Ian pushes his glasses up his nose. "No, thanks, I'm perfectly happy as I am. Why do I need a man when I've got my sisters?"

I smile and take his hand.

When we reach the bar, there's a scrum of people pushing and shoving to get served. Ian insists it's his round and thrusts himself in, while I wait at the back, leaning against a wall.

"*Ciao!*" comes a voice from behind me.

I turn around to see a tall man with smooth, wrinkle-free skin and thick black hair in a quiff, wearing smart jeans and a heavy blazer.

"Are you not hot?" I find myself asking him.

"No," he replies, "but you are."

I'm just about to insist otherwise, pointing to my thin T-shirt, when I realize he's flirting with me. I giggle, flattered.

"My name is Salvatore," the man says. "In Italian that means I am here to save you."

He smiles and it feels like the sun's breaking through the clouds. "From what?" I ask, hoping he can't tell I'm drunk.

"You tell me." Salvatore grins and his eyes glisten.

I suddenly remember Theo and my gut twists. What am I *doing*?

I dismiss my objection. Why shouldn't I flirt with this bloke? Theo's going off me anyway. It's only a matter of time till he dumps me.

I tell Salvatore that I recently inherited a house between Lucca and Camaiore.

"Really?" He moves closer and I can smell his woody aftershave and some sugary cocktail on his breath.

"I'm here for the summer," I add.

Salvatore's so confident, his presence so commanding, that I can't take my eyes off him. But could I actually get off with him? Would I be capable of that?

"And do you like my country?" he asks.

Before I can reply, a drink's thrust into my hand.

"Here you go," says Ian.

I smile as I take hold of it. I register a look of surprise on Ian's face. He'd never judge me but suddenly I can see how tacky and cheap I must look.

"*Ciao,*" Salvatore says, unenthusiastically. He turns back to me. "Is this your boyfriend?"

"No, he's my sister." I pause as I consider what to say next. "My boyfriend's back at the house."

The muscles in Salvatore's face tense, ever so slightly.

"With his kids," I elaborate. "He used to be married to a woman."

Salvatore runs his hand through his quiff. "And do you have an open relationship?"

I purse my lips. "No. Sorry if I gave you the wrong impression."

Ian leans into my ear. "Shall we get away, Adam?"

"Yeah." I say goodbye to Salvatore but he's already turned his back.

"What was all that about?" Ian asks when we're walking upstairs.

I let out a groan. "I don't know, he just came over and chatted me up. I wasn't expecting it, to be honest. And I know it's awful but for a minute I actually considered getting off with him."

We reach the balcony and take up a spot by the balustrade, looking out to the beach. I watch the moonlight dance over the waves of the sea and breathe in the salty air.

"It's not awful," Ian says. "He was hot. And you've had a tough few weeks."

I rub my jaw. "It's just really hard with Theo. Well, not Theo: the whole situation."

"I know. But remember what it is you want: you've always said you want to fall in love with a man who'll never stop loving you."

I tip back my drink. "But that's just it, Ian. At the moment I can't see Theo sticking it out."

Ian stirs his drink with the straw. "Yeah, but that might be your abandonment issues talking."

"Maybe. Or it could be that I was only attracted to him in the first place because I sensed he wasn't ready for a gay relationship and wanted to punish myself."

"Adam, where's all this coming from?"

"I don't know." I grip the balustrade. "Oh, Ian, what if I'm just not meant to be with him? What if the whole family situation isn't right for me? What if I'm meant to move out here with you guys and set up some sort of queer commune?"

Ian smirks. "I must admit, that does sound appealing."

"You always say you don't need anyone because you've got us . . ."

"Yeah, but I've had my great love," Ian goes on. "And it may not have lasted as long as it should but I consider myself lucky that me and Greg had the time we did."

I stab at my ice cubes, remembering Greg.

"You haven't had yours," Ian continues, "or you may have found it but you haven't seen it through yet. And not everyone wants a great love but you've got to be honest with yourself and work out if you still do."

I gaze out to beach and sigh. "You know, Theo and I came here on our second trip to Italy. We were just going for a walk on the beach, before we even knew it was gay. Then we saw the flag and it felt like a sign. We were so excited, so hopeful. I miss that."

"Do you want to get it back? *Do* you want to see this through?"

I take another swig of my drink. "But what do I do about the kids?"

Ian leans on the balustrade and steeples his fingers under his chin. "Could you ever see yourself being happy to have them in your life? I mean, actively happy. Or would you only ever be putting up with them to please Theo?"

I think of Callum when I catch a flash of Theo in his features. Or when I sense he's worried about sweating too much, or being too skinny, or disappointing his dad. I think of Mabel when she's playing with the kittens—and knowing there's a sweet, uncomplicated girl hiding in there. And I think of Archie when he holds my hand. Or when he asks me to peel his fruit. Or when I take off his glasses to clean them, and he accepts it without a word.

"I like the person I am when I'm with the kids," I answer. "I just don't see how that's compatible with the other side of me. With me being proud of who I am as a gay man."

Ian finishes his drink and rests the glass on the floor. "Why shouldn't it be? Being a parent or step-parent or whatever doesn't have to involve hiding away your sexuality. Not unless it's something you think is bad and could corrupt them. Not unless you think being gay is just about having sex."

Shit, is that really what I think?

"All you're doing is presenting a slightly different version of yourself when you're around the kids," Ian continues. "And yes, it would be inappropriate to talk about sex in front of them but that's true of a lot of people."

I tap my foot against the balustrade. "I suppose it's like when I'm with Auntie Julie or my old boss. I wouldn't talk to them about sex. But that doesn't mean I'm pretending not to be gay."

"Exactly. And why shouldn't you be able to express all those different sides of yourself at different times? Why should you have to limit yourself to any one side of your personality? They're all part of you."

I finish my drink and put it down next to Ian's. "You know, this is brill, being here, being with my people—but I wouldn't want it all the time."

I turn around as a man struts past in Speedos and a bow tie in a Keith Haring print, followed by a drag queen wearing a crimped blond wig and a pink kimono.

"Can you imagine?" I say. "It'd be too much!"

We laugh.

"And do you think you'd have wanted kids?" Ian asks. "If things had been different?"

It's the question that's been on my mind ever since we had dinner with Luisa and Stefano. Although it gets right to the heart of the issue, I still haven't been able to answer it.

"Yes, I think I probably would," I admit for the first time. It almost sounds as if someone else is speaking. At the same time, I'm not surprised by my answer. I'm not surprised at all.

Ian nods, thoughtfully. "Care to elaborate?"

"I think the problem is I've never really known a happy family. I've certainly never known a happy queer family. So I've never been able to picture myself as part of one."

Ian reaches for a fix of his lip balm. "Well, if you have no template to follow then you just have to create something new. But maybe that's a good thing, an opportunity. We're all unique so our relationships should also be unique. But the starting point has to be what's in here." He puts his hand over my heart. "And you've got to stay true to what *you* want."

I smile at him. "Thanks, my sister."

Ian puts his arms around me and gives me a hug.

"Oh, and I do want Theo," I add, as I break away. "Of course I want him. I've only ever wanted him."

"I'm glad we've cleared that up." Ian grins.

"Kids and all," I toss in.

Ian's grin grows. "Good to hear it."

"Now come on, let's find the girls."

Chapter 21

The next morning, Gloria and Dom are hungover, but I'm relieved to see all three of my sisters packed up and ready to go when I drive down to the village. They have to leave their Airbnb by ten o'clock but they have less luggage than I expected—Dom's tiny outfits making up for Gloria's multiple wigs—so I cancel their taxi to the airport and say I'll drive them. Before that, though, I'm taking them up to the house for brunch.

In the car, Gloria and Dom relive last night's adventures.

"I can't believe that go-go dancer binned me off," Gloria moans, "for some skinny white boy with a face like a chewed caramel."

"That's outrageous!" we chorus.

"At least one of us got some action," Gloria says. "Come on, Dom, spill the T."

"The T is we went for a walk on the beach," Dom says. "And Vito's great. He's really interesting."

"'Interesting'?" teases Gloria. "Since when have you given a fuck about 'interesting'? Come on, did you show him your Leaning Tower?"

Dom grins. "I may have done."

"How about your Trevi Fountain?" jokes Ian.

We all screech with laughter but, intriguingly, Dom doesn't answer.

Once I've parked the car, my sisters greet Theo and the kids. Everyone seems more relaxed than at our first meeting. And I observe each of my sisters slip into a slightly different persona—just as I do. But Theo and I still haven't chatted since our argument. When I got back last night it was late and, just as I was waking up this morning, Mabel burst in wailing that she'd found a patch of skin cancer—only for Theo to examine it and tell her it was a large freckle.

It's a beautiful morning and the usual sound of crickets and birdsong is accompanied by the distant ringing of church bells, these setting off the barking of dogs. I serve a buffet of local cheeses, cooked meats and breads I picked up from the bakery in Camaiore. There's also smoked salmon with dill and capers, a tomato and basil salad, and a huge pan of creamy scrambled eggs. Everyone helps themselves and chats in little groups, which is what I was hoping, as it must be less intimidating for the kids than speaking to a table full of intent faces.

Archie is soon full and starts studying a pack of Top Trumps cards. "Adam, did you know 'the Gigantosaurus could run for long distances at great speeds due to its shock-absorbing muscles'?"

"No, I didn't but that's fascinating." I lean in and rest my forehead against his temple. "You know, Ian loves Top Trumps."

He pulls back. "Really?"

"Yeah, he told me that when he was a kid it was his favorite game." Ian did actually reveal this after spotting a pack of the cards while I was showing him round the house. "Why don't you ask if he wants to play?"

Archie jumps up and toddles over. When Ian smiles in agreement, he starts dealing the cards.

Dom, meanwhile, is mixing himself a protein shake. As he glugs it back, I notice Callum watching. He looks like he wants to ask a question but is lacking the confidence.

"You know, Dom's a personal trainer," I tell him.

Callum gives his head a jerk of acknowledgment.

"I used to be the skinny, weedy kid," says Dom, wiping some shake off his moustache. "When you're already deaf in one ear, that's not great. So when I was around your age, I started packing on muscle."

"How did you do it?" asks Callum. "How did you get that rig?"

As Dom shares information about exercise and nutrition, I treat myself to some mortadella.

Mabel, on the other hand, isn't mixing at all but skulking behind her hair, sticking to the side of her dad. I scour my brain for interests she may share with my sisters. Again, I think how tough it must be for her as the only girl.

When Gloria's finished eating, he takes out a compact and tops up his lip gloss. I remember Mabel's interest in skincare and decide to take a chance.

"You know, Gloria's fab with makeup. If there's anything you want to ask . . ."

Gloria snaps his compact shut. "Girl, you've got a sensational bone structure."

Mabel pulls more strands of hair over her face. "As if."

"Hush your mouth! I would *love* to practice on you!"

She writhes in her seat. "Would you?"

"Hell, yeah!"

Mabel considers this. The crease of tension on her face suggests she's going through some sort of internal struggle. Then a smile lifts the corners of her mouth. "OK."

I don't want her to feel like she's being watched, so I quickly turn away and cram my mouth full of *pecorino*. When I catch Theo's eye, he gives me a smile. It's the first we've shared in days. I'm relieved to feel my heart leap.

"Now who wants the last of this orange juice?" I ask.

"I'll have it." Dom reaches over for the jug, then spots Callum watching. "Sorry, mate, do you want it?"

"No, thanks," replies Callum. "It's got bits in it."

Dom raises an eyebrow. "Dude, when you meet a really hot girl and go round to her house for the first time, what are you going to say if she gives you orange juice with bits in it?"

A smirk traces itself on Callum's face. He holds out his glass.

I daren't look directly, but out of the corner of my eye I'm stunned to see him drinking it.

As I survey the scene, I'm even more stunned that everyone's chatting and smiling—my outrageous gay sisters and my boyfriend's kids. I wonder what Wilf would make of it. When no one's looking, I slip upstairs, open the window, and put on one of his opera records.

When I come back—to the sound of *Tosca*—I see that Gloria's been to the car for his beauty bag and is doing a full face of makeup on Mabel.

"I do this with my nieces," he's saying, as he contours her cheekbones, "although obviously they've got a different coloring to you."

"What's your heritage?" asks Mabel.

"My family's from Uganda," Gloria answers. "Which at the moment is one of the worst places in the world to be gay."

"Really?"

Gloria steps back to examine his work, then gives a few more swipes of his brush. "Yeah, but my parents are cool with me. Well, they are now. Let's just say we've been on a journey. You've got to work on these things, my angel."

"You can say that again," I want to throw in. But I keep my distance and start clearing away the plates and leftover food.

Theo stands up to help me. "Everything alright, Ads?"

He smiles at me again and again I smile back.

"Yeah, thanks."

His smile grows into a grin. "I'll wash, you dry."

"You're on!"

"That's good to see," Theo says as he rinses the first plate and slides it into the water. "Everyone getting on."

"Yeah," I say, taking it from him to wipe. "It is, isn't it?"

I kiss his shoulder and we continue working in a contented silence.

Once we've finished, Theo and I go back outside to find Gloria teaching a fully made-up Mabel how to throw a fan, and Dom training Callum and Archie in various football skills.

I pick up the juicer and the big bowl of squeezed oranges and turn to take them indoors.

"Wait a minute!" calls out Dom. "You're not throwing those away, are you?"

When I answer yes, he yanks them off me and lines up the boys on the side of the hill. He takes half an orange, draws back his arm, and throws it up into the sky. It arches over the trees, skims some of the branches, and lands in the overgrowth with a little rustle.

"See if you can beat that!" he booms.

Callum and Archie start lobbing oranges over the hill, winding each other up about whose reaches the farthest, and laughing riotously. Mabel jumps up to join in and the laughter only increases. Soon, they're throwing two oranges at a time, then one with their backs turned. Next, Theo stands up to take a turn—and trounces them all.

I can't stay sitting any longer—even if I know I'm going to be rubbish. "Can I have a go?" I ask Dom.

He holds out the bowl. "Of course."

I pull back my arm and throw my orange in the air, as high as I can. And I don't do too badly.

Everyone cheers.

When I get back from taking my sisters to the airport, Theo's sitting on the patio with a bottle of wine and two empty glasses.

"How was it?" he asks.

"Fine, thanks. I was sad to see them go, but Gloria says visitors are like fish: three days and they go off."

Theo laughs.

There's a pause.

He runs a hand over his stubble. "Callum and Mabel are putting Archie to bed."

"Oh, brill," I reply. "But where did that come from?"

He shrugs. "I asked them and they said yes."

There's another pause.

"I thought you and I could use some time on our own," he says. "I thought we could go up to the castle and watch the sunset."

I smile. "I'd like that."

Once we've climbed up and are sitting on the wall, Theo fills our glasses with wine. We look out at the sunset, its palette of pinks and oranges giving our skin a golden tinge.

"I just want to reiterate that I'm sorry about the other day," Theo says. "I should have defended you to Kate. Putting up with her interfering can't have been easy for you."

"No, but I'm sorry for laying into you," I say, resting my wine on the wall. "I know it hasn't been easy for you either. And I do know you're not ashamed of me. I've no idea why I said that. I think I was just frightened."

Theo rests his wine next to mine. "Of what?"

"I don't know . . ." But I do: I just don't want to say it.

Theo must sense that I'm holding back—he must sense I'm still frightened—because he reaches out and hugs me. I nestle into his embrace and squeeze him tightly.

"Don't leave me," I let slip. "Please don't leave me."

Theo kisses my head gently. "Is that what this is about? Is that what you're frightened of?"

"I think so," I confess. "It's just that everybody leaves me."

Theo kisses my head again. "Well, that may have been true in the past. But I promise I've no intention of leaving you."

I remember Ian's line: "Just because something's been your story for a long time doesn't mean it has to be forever."

For once, I can imagine myself believing it.

I pull Theo tighter. "I love you, Theo."

"I love you too, Ads. Please don't ever doubt it again."

My mind jumps back to the first time Theo told me he loved me. He didn't do it with any fanfare or grand gesture; he just told me one perfectly ordinary morning, while we were in bed. But I knew what a significant moment it must be for him and that it must be the first time he'd said it—or at least to a man. Just like it had been for Wilf, it was the happiest moment of my life and a tear had slipped from my eye and onto the pillow. But, unlike Wilf—or at least unlike anything he'd said in the letter—part of me hadn't let myself fully believe it. Part of me had doubted it from the start.

I let out a sigh. "I won't. I won't doubt it—not anymore."

"If you do," Theo says, "I'll just have to remind you."

I relax and rest my head on his shoulder. "I'm pretty sure that'll work."

Chapter 22

On Monday, my priority is to find some time to read Wilf's final letter to Arnaldo. But it's a big day for the builders: as they start demolishing the kitchen, the house fills with the sound of banging, thudding and crashing.

We set up a temporary kitchen in the big lounge on the first floor, where there was already a dining table. Giuseppe plugs in the fridge and the little electric oven, next to a single-ring portable gas stove he lends us—all within easy reach of the bathroom in the cottage, which we designate as our washing-up station. The plan is for us to eat breakfast at the dining table and prepare simple lunches we can eat outside, accessing the patio via the exterior door and a short flight of steps. I've no idea what we'll do in the evenings: we certainly can't afford to eat out every night.

At least our first breakfast in the new setup goes well. All three children drink some orange juice and afterwards, we go outside to throw the oranges over the hill. Then Theo has to nip down to the village to send an important email, taking the kids with him and walking down the new footpath. I think this could be my chance to read Wilf's letter but am accosted by Giuseppe, who wants clarification on several details of the kitchen design. Before I know it, Theo and the kids are back—but they scatter around the top two floors of the house, each doing their own thing. Theo's reading some documents, Archie's playing with his action figures, and Callum's doing the workout Dom devised for him, which is made up of strength-building exercises using the bench on the patio, big bottles of water for weights, and a portable pull-up bar that Dom set up in his bedroom doorframe. I've no idea what Mabel's doing. But I spot my chance to read the letter.

Just as I'm walking to the cottage through the temporary kitchen, I notice that the washing-up still hasn't been done. As I don't want to disturb the quiet, I decide to do it quickly myself. But when I load up the washing-up bowl and lug it through to the cottage bathroom, I find Mabel. And I find out what she's doing: she's running my toothbrush around the rim of the toilet bowl.

I'm so shocked I almost drop the bowl of crockery. Then—weirdly—I find myself laughing.

Mabel looks up. "What are you doing here?"

"What does it look like?" I reply, gesturing to the washing-up bowl. "Didn't you hear me?"

She looks down, unable to meet my eye. "No. There's so much banging I can't hear anything."

I put down the washing-up and sigh. "Mabel, what's the matter?"

As she struggles for words, I'm hit by a memory: I'm around her age, wiping a piece of toast I made for my stepmum on the kitchen floor. Except on that occasion, I wasn't caught. But I felt so guilty, I quickly threw it away and made her another. Seeing the shame on Mabel's face takes me back to exactly how I felt on that day. And I'm not sure how to respond. I can't muster up any anger, but amusement—or even admiration—would be inappropriate.

"Actually, don't answer that," I interject. "Just go. Let me get on with this."

She gingerly places the toothbrush on the windowsill and scurries out.

As I fill the sink with hot, soapy water, I can't help but feel sorry for her. Because I'm pretty sure I know what the matter is. Theo told me while they were in the village, she received several messages from her mum. Apparently Kate saw the pics Mabel posted on Instagram of the makeup job Gloria had done on her—and said she was finding it difficult being away from her while she's having such fun. Mabel must have felt guilty: that would explain why she's pulling back and expressing her loyalty to her mum.

Once the sink's full, I start washing the pots, rinsing off the suds in the bath, where I carefully stack them to dry. Theo also told me that Mabel exchanged messages with her friend Sharita, who she's sensed has been pulling away from her all summer. Sharita said she's been invited on holiday with Aurora and her family in the last week of August, news that must have hurt Mabel. Possibly even more so after seeing me with my friends. Now she's lashing out.

"What's going on?" Theo's standing in the doorway, thick lines on his forehead. "Mabel says she's done something bad but won't tell me what."

As I scrub the cereal bowls, I fill him in.

Theo looks appalled. He wants to go and confront Mabel but I beg him not to. "She'll only resent me. Just let her sit with it for a while and maybe chat to her later."

Theo puffs out his cheeks. "Well, she owes you one bloody big apology."

"I'm not going to argue with that."

"She can also buy you a new toothbrush." He clenches and unclenches his jaw. "I'm going to take her out for one now."

While Theo takes Mabel to the shops—and Callum and Archie tag along—I close the door to the cottage and sit on the bed. Now, finally, is my chance to read Wilf's third letter.

Carissimo Arnaldo,

I'm writing this in haste so forgive me, but I need to tell you what's happened.

Last night, I went round to our Kathleen's for baby Julie's first birthday. As it was Saturday, after tea everyone disappeared to the pub, but I stayed to help Kathleen clear up. We were drinking stout and laughing and joking, and I don't know why but I told her I'm queer and have fallen in love with you. Happen the booze had loosened my tongue. Happen I thought I was safe with my own sister, especially as we've always rubbed along so well. I was wrong. She refused to talk about it and went ever so quiet for the rest of the night. Not thoughtful quiet but angry quiet. I went home feeling sick with dread.

This morning, my brother-in-law Gerald turned up at the house and exploded. He says I can't go round to their place any more, that I can't be trusted around kiddies. It was terrible as I love those girls and would never do anything to harm them. Gerald then went and told my mam and dad and they came to the house and went berserk. Sorry, that means 'mad' where I'm from. Father was bawling and shouting, calling me a pervert and a freak of nature. He said if that's the way I want to live, then I'm no son of his. He also said if being queer wasn't bad enough, I've been carrying on with an Italian, after everything he went through in the war. I wasn't sure what to say, even though I've been thinking about this a lot and had already started composing the letter I was going to send. I was just so shocked and felt so foul, all I could do was sit at the table skriking. Sorry, there I go again. Skriking means 'crying'. Any road, Father didn't take pity on me, not one bit. Nor did Mam. She just stood there watching, her arms folded and her face like thunder. To think she gave birth to me and nursed me. How could she forget that? I feel abandoned and utterly wretched.

I won't let my feelings get the better of me, though. I need to pack a case and make arrangements to leave Manchester. After work tomorrow, Father and Gerald have arranged to meet to decide what to do about me. Apparently, they're too angry to decide now and need time to calm down. I've no idea whether they'll go to the police, but if Gerald thinks I'm a danger to children I'm quite sure he'll tell the school. Either way, I'll end up in prison. There's a slight possibility Father will be too ashamed to let the secret out of the family, but I can't take a chance. I've got one day to escape.

First thing tomorrow, I'll go to the telephone box and tell school I'm poorly. I'll have to write a proper letter of resignation to the headmaster from Italy (and try not to feel guilty about giving him no notice). After that, I'll go to a travel agency to book my trains to Italy and my passage on the overnight ferry to France. I'll call into the Post Office to send this letter and I'll also go to the bank to draw out my savings, although I've never been abroad so goodness knows where I go to change it into French and Italian currency. Happen a clerk at the bank will tell me. As for my little house, I've paid the rent until the end of the month so I'll just do a flit. Do you know what that means? It's when you move out without telling anyone, usually if folk are coming after you for money. If folk come after me, it won't be for money. Any road, I won't let them find me. I'm going to London to stay in a hotel until I can catch my train to the continent.

As for what happens when I arrive in Italy, I like the sound of that house you've found in the hills, the one with the old castle. It sounds like it's surrounded by nature, which is marvellous. It doesn't bother me that it isn't very modern and parts of it are dilapidated, although it does sound like it's in a remote setting, so I hope you can hold on to your car. Nor does it bother me that we won't have any money to fix it up properly. Once you've set up your own concern and I've found work as an English teacher, it'll be different. Please go ahead and buy it as soon as you can. The last thing we want is for the owner to find out he's selling to two queers and pull out.

You said the house isn't far from Lucca, so I'll go there, find a hotel, and write to you. If my letter doesn't arrive, or if someone in your family intercepts it, I have a back-up plan. I found an old guidebook in the library and it mentioned a square called Piazza dell'Anfiteatro. The square was a hundred years old when the book was written so I can only assume it's still there, and still will be when I arrive. Apparently, it's used as a food market during the day so I'll avoid that as it'll be busy, but I'll wait there every evening from 7 o'clock until you come and find me. I know you won't let me down, carissimo.

In case you're wondering, I don't regret anything. I may be upset and blinking petrified, but I'm also sick of hiding and pretending, always trying to act like a proper man so nobody will spot the way I am. It's no way to live. At least what we're doing is more honest, even if our families do hate us for it. We don't need them, any road. We'll create a new family ourselves, just the two of us.

Oh, Arnaldo, I'm shaking like a leaf and goodness knows how I'm going to sleep, but I'm also excited that very soon we'll be together once again.

Come Hell or high water, I'll see you in Lucca!
Con tutto il mio cuore,
Wilf xx

As I put down the letter, this time I don't feel upset. My heart is thumping against my ribcage and I'm burning with rage. How could Wilf's parents—my great-grandparents—have treated him like that? How could Mum's parents—*my own grandparents*—have been so cruel?

My granddad died a few years before I was born so I have no memories of him, but I do remember my grandma. She died when I was eight or nine and before that, we spent a lot of time together. Did she ever express disapproval if I behaved in a way that made her suspect I was gay? Were there ever any judgmental looks or raised eyebrows? I can't recall.

I fold the letter up again. I want to know what happened next but this is Wilf's final letter. Obviously, he made it to Italy and the two of them made it to this house, so if Arnaldo didn't receive the letter about where Wilf was staying, I can only assume they met on Piazza dell'Anfiteatro.

As I slide the letter back into the envelope, I feel a pulse of shame that I ever doubted Theo's love for me. Wilf and Arnaldo had a much tougher time than we have but Wilf never doubted Arnaldo's feelings—all he ever asked for was confirmation of his commitment. That was all it took for him to risk everything.

I open the second shoebox—the one that's stuffed full of letters—but the envelopes of the first few are addressed to Arnaldo and the senders' names and addresses are all Italian. Even if I could read what's in them, it wouldn't be fair: they contain other people's stories, possibly even their secrets.

I'm interrupted by a knock on the door.

"Who is it?"

"It's me," comes a mumble, "Mabel."

"Just a minute!" I quickly stuff the letters in their boxes and push them back under the bed. "Come in!"

Mabel enters, her head down so I can't see her face, clutching a new toothbrush. "I just want to say I'm sorry. What I did was awful. I've thought about it and I'm devo."

I let out a breath. "In that case, apology accepted."

I'm not sure what else to say as I'm still immersed in Wilf's story—and my heart is hammering. But I can tell Mabel's sorry. When she raises her head, she looks thoroughly miserable.

"You know what, it was an old toothbrush," I say, with forced jollity. "I needed a new one anyway."

She shuffles up the stairs and hands it over.

"Thanks," I say. And I give her a smile. I hope this isn't going to set us back, just when I thought we were making progress.

I smooth out the bed sheets. "We all make mistakes, Mabel. Let's just forget this ever happened. Tomorrow morning, let's wake up and start again. How does that sound?"

She nods, meekly. "OK."

I stand up, trying to put Wilf and his story out of my mind. "Come on, let's go and see what the others are up to. It's nearly five o'clock, so we should finally get a rest from all that banging."

Chapter 23

Theo has decided to buy a barbecue. He says he feels bad that I do all the cooking, and he may be lousy in the kitchen but at least he can make up for it by doing his bit on an outdoor grill. Now that our kitchen is out of action, this is an obvious solution to the problem of what to do for our evening meals. So we round up the kids and drive to the retail park, where we buy the cheapest model available, then go on to the supermarket to stock up on meat. As it's a sweltering day and the kids behave well, we call into Camaiore on the way back to treat ourselves to an ice cream.

It's five o'clock but there aren't many people around. We stroll down the main street that runs through the old town, skirting churches, cafés and shops, many with their original—now antique—fittings, many with window displays of sun-bleached stock that doesn't look far off antique status itself. We pass a woman pushing her disabled son in his wheelchair, two priests chatting on a stone bench, and an elderly woman gliding along on a mobility scooter. A farm laborer passes us, at the wheel of a Vespa scooter that has been adapted into a little three-wheeler van, a vehicle I remember Stefano telling us is called an *ape,* or "bee" in Italian. But that's about it. It's clear Camaiore is a sleepy rural town, far away from the urban bustle of Lucca, the seaside cheer of Viareggio, or the genteel sophistication of Pietrasanta. It's also clear that it doesn't attract any tourists—other than us.

I imagine we must stand out like a cluster of peacocks in a flock of pigeons. Theo, Callum and Mabel have hair that's now almost Prosecco blond, and Archie's red flame draws attention like a lightning rod. To make matters worse, Callum's wearing an England football shirt. I start to feel self-conscious. And I'm not the only one.

Mabel pulls down the sides of her straw hat, while Callum does the same with his bucket hat. Archie transfers Thor into his left hand and grabs onto mine with his right.

We spot a fridge full of ice cream in the window of a scruffy old café. We join the line at the serving hatch, overlooked by a trio of aging Italian men huddled around a table. They're drinking beer and smoking cigarettes, empty packets and glasses strewn between them. One of them has ruddy, vein-threaded cheeks, another a burgundy, bulbous nose, the third a belly that looks like a balloon resting between legs he's spreading widely. As this man scratches his crotch and sneers at us, my heart slams into my throat.

The other day, the kids came to Camaiore just with Theo. Whenever I've come—usually to pick up bread from the bakery—I've been on my own. This time, however, Theo and I are wearing our matching Panama hats, almost advertising our status as a gay couple—a gay couple with some kind of family. And it's not one it looks like these men accept.

"Right, what does everyone fancy?" I chirp, when we reach the front of the line.

To my surprise, each of the kids asks for an Italian flavor. Callum goes for *stracciatella*, Mabel *frutti di bosco* and Archie *panna cotta*.

"Superb choices, gang!" says Theo.

One of the old men mutters something to his friends. Suddenly, I wish I could speak Italian. His friends respond with disdainful laughter, one of them veering into a hacking, smoker's cough. Actually, I'm glad I don't speak Italian.

Archie gets his ice cream first and goes to sit down at the only other available table, directly next to the men. A nervous-looking Callum and Mabel follow.

Theo and I pay the bill and take our ice creams. While I have my usual *pistacchio*, this time partnered with *nocciola*—or hazelnut—Theo has his usual *bacio*, with a second scoop of *fior di latte*. We sit down and tuck in. Theo asks if he can have a taste of mine and, with one eye on the old Italian men—and a determination not to hide—I scoop some up and feed it to him. He misses the spoon and it hits the side of his mouth. We both giggle and I give him a slap on the shoulder.

"*Maniaci!*" snarls the man with red cheeks.

"*Degenerati!*" hisses the one with the purple nose.

"*Depravati!*" growls the one with the belly.

I don't need to consult my translation app to know they're insulting us for being queer. It's like I've been slapped across the face. Theo looks equally startled and tries to break out of it by coughing into his fist.

Thankfully, Archie is too absorbed in his ice cream to have heard anything. Callum and Mabel, on the other hand, did.

"Dad," asks Mabel, "did they just say something homophobic?"

Callum's forehead is rutted. "You're not going to let them get away with it, are you?"

Theo sighs and leans towards them. "What can I say? We don't even speak Italian."

I let out a short breath. "Look, let's just not rise to it."

"Exactly," says Theo. "It's not as if we care what they think."

"Let's just sit here, hold our heads up high, and enjoy our ice creams."

We try, but it's difficult to avoid the men's staring. And none of us is enjoying our ice cream, except Archie.

A tear rolls down Mabel's face. "Please can we go," she says, wiping it away with the back of her hand.

"Yeah, I've had enough," says Callum, pushing his ice cream into the center of the table.

"This *nocciola*'s rank," I say, trying to inject some humor.

"Come on," says Theo, pushing back his chair. "Let's go back and set up that barbecue."

While Theo assembles the barbecue, I sit on the patio, looking out over the valley. Above my head, the vines that twist in and out of the pergola are hanging with bunches of increasingly plump grapes. And breaking through the usual sounds of crickets and birds is the familiar *twit-twoo* of the owl that we still haven't seen.

But this evening I don't give it a second thought. Because in my head I'm replaying the old men's insults. And I'm blazing with rage. How dare they? How dare they think we're bad people, just because our love is different to theirs?

A lizard slithers over the rocks bordering the lawn and comes to a stop by my feet. I'm amazed at how perfectly still it holds itself. As I'm wondering if it's one of those that lives in the larder, another insult crashes into my head—it's Wilf's dad calling him a freak of nature.

I shift in my seat and the lizard slithers off across the patio and up the wall of the house.

The atmosphere is sullen. Mabel is sitting at the opposite end of the table, her earphones in, listening to Harry Styles. Archie is inside, in the smaller first-floor lounge, playing with his wrestlers.

Callum appears in the doorframe. "Need any help, Dad?"

I'm about to raise an eyebrow but stop myself.

"Thanks, Cal, but I've just finished," says Theo. "Although I'm glad you're joining us. I think we could do with a group chat."

Callum tugs on his fringe and takes a seat between Mabel and me. Theo signals for Mabel to take out her earphones. She doesn't object.

"Now, I don't want you two to be upset by what happened earlier," Theo begins, sitting down opposite them.

"Dad, it was awful," whimpers Mabel.

"Yeah, but you need to know the world's a much better place than it used to be for people like Adam and me—or at least it is in Europe. You do still come up against these attitudes and you do still find pockets of intolerance. But we need to make sure they don't upset us."

Callum curls his hands into fists. "But Dad, how can you just accept it?"

I'm interested to see that he looks genuinely outraged.

Theo leans forward. "I don't accept it, Cal. But sometimes the best way to fight these attitudes is to show the bigots we're better than them."

"Also, those men were pretty old," I offer. "I expect their attitudes are dying out."

An orange, black and white butterfly lands on a trunk of vine and basks in the glow of the evening sun.

Mabel turns towards me. "What do you think it was like for your uncle, when he went into town with his boyfriend?"

Again, I'm about to raise an eyebrow: until now the kids haven't shown much interest in Wilf's story. But I stop myself. Part of me would like to show them Wilf's letters and photos—or at least the stone—but that doesn't feel right. Besides, I still haven't shown Theo.

"I don't know, but I imagine it was very hard for him," I answer. "We're seeing his friend Angelika tomorrow, so we'll be able to ask her."

The butterfly flutters away.

"But even when Adam and I were growing up it was hard," points out Theo. "Have you heard about something called Section Twenty-Eight?"

Callum and Mabel look at each other and shake their heads.

"It was a law brought in by Margaret Thatcher's government in the 1980s," Theo explains. "It made it illegal for anyone employed by local councils—including teachers—to say anything positive about gay people."

"Why?" asks Callum.

"Because they thought this would corrupt children and 'turn them' gay. Basically, the government thought being gay was so awful that people had to be protected from it. But Section Twenty-Eight meant there was nobody to defend children who *were* actually gay and being bullied for it. And it made life very difficult for gay teachers. If they were open about who they were, they could lose their jobs."

Callum picks at his brace. "Is that why *you* didn't tell anyone?"

A little frown appears between Theo's eyebrows. "It's one of the reasons, yeah. When I first became aware of my feelings, I tried to bury them. Because everyone would think I was a terrible person, but also because I wouldn't be allowed to have the career I wanted."

I've never heard Theo talk about this before but it makes perfect sense.

Mabel cocks her head. "That's so wrong."

"It's fucked up," Callum agrees.

Theo nods. I notice he doesn't tell Callum off for swearing.

"But the point I want to make is," he goes on, "that law doesn't exist anymore. There are still laws like it in places like Russia, but not in our country. And not in Italy, either."

"But there are still horrible old men," comments Mabel.

"Yeah, but they're in the minority," insists Theo, weaving his fingers together. "Look at all the other people we've met in Italy. All the other people we've seen when we've been out and about. They haven't said a word."

"No," concedes Mabel. "But what happens the next time we go into Camaiore?"

"We make sure we're feeling strong," I answer. "We don't hold back from being ourselves and we don't let horrible old men stop us from doing what we want."

"And we stick together," Theo chips in. He opens his mouth again—possibly to add "as a family"—but stops himself. "What do you say?"

"Alright," responds Mabel.

Callum extends his arm and sweeps a leaf off the table. "OK."

"Superb," says Theo. "Now, I'm going to fire up that barbie. Who fancies a burger?"

Theo and I climb up to the castle and sit on the stone wall to watch the sunset.

After dinner, Callum and Mabel offered to clear up and put Archie to bed, an offer I immediately accepted. After the day I'd had, I really wanted a quiet moment with Theo. I really wanted to bring him up here.

Theo takes hold of my hand. "Ads, I know what happened today was bloody unpleasant. But at least it's made the kids think. And it does seem to have softened them a little."

I nod. "Let's hope it's a sign of things to come."

I inch closer, so our arms are touching and we're leaning onto each other, as we delight in the sun's colors.

"Just think about all the people who used to live in this castle," I say. "Do you think any of them were like us? Do you think any of them were men who fell in love with men?"

"There must have been some." Theo gives my hand a squeeze. "Although I can't imagine what it was like for them—living in terror of being found out."

"I wonder what would have happened if they were caught," I say. "According to Luisa, they used to burn gay men at the stake in Italy. But I don't know when that started or stopped."

Theo tugs in a breath. "Me neither. I know they were executed in England but I think that was by hanging."

I shake my head. "How could anyone possibly fall in love knowing that's what would happen to them? How could anyone be proud of who they were?"

"I expect they weren't," reflects Theo. "And I expect lots of them fought their feelings. But we'll never know, as it had to be so secret. And now all those secrets are buried. All those secrets from all those men stretching back all through time." He pats the wall.

I rest my free hand on the stone. "Well, they're not all buried."

"What do you mean?"

I swivel to face him. "Theo, there's something I need to tell you."

He turns to look at me. "I'm glad you've said that, because there's something I need to tell you, too."

Chapter 24

Theo and I are sitting on our bed. Spreading out around us are the photos of Wilf and Arnaldo, Wilf's three letters, and the stone inscribed with their names. I wanted to go first with my revelation as I wanted to get it off my chest.

As he sifts through the photos, Theo's mouth hangs open. "Ads, these are amazing." He grabs his reading glasses and opens one of the letters.

"They're about how they met in Manchester," I comment. "How everyone turned on them and they had to fight to be together. It's really upsetting but quite inspiring, too."

"It's like the missing piece of the jigsaw," Theo observes. "Now everything makes sense." He looks up from the letter. "I want to read these properly. It sounds like there's a lot to take in."

I scratch the side of my nose. "Yeah, sorry, that's kind of why I didn't tell you about it sooner. I just needed a bit of time to get my head round it."

"You don't need to explain." Theo removes his glasses and his face darkens. "I've put off telling you something, too. And when you hear it, I'm worried you'll be mad at me."

Fear pricks at my insides. "Why? What is it?"

Theo rubs at the little marks left by his glasses. "Ads, I cheated on Kate."

His words bust the breath out of me. "W-what? When?"

"When Mabel was a toddler," he answers, grimly. "It was only a one-off and I'm not proud of it. I'm actually really bloody ashamed."

I snatch a breath. "I can't believe it. You're going to have to tell me exactly what happened."

He puts the letter back in the envelope. "It was when I was in London for a work conference. On the last night, a few of us went out in Soho for some drinks. It was early summer so we were standing outside a pub and I kept seeing all these gay men walking past, in couples and groups of friends. I wanted to follow them, I wanted to join them, and as soon as the idea entered my head I just couldn't resist. So I told everyone I was tired and going back to the hotel, but I walked down the street and slipped into a gay bar. And it was weird: I was only in there for five minutes and all these men started chatting me up and flirting."

"That doesn't surprise me. You're hot." I give him a smile but immediately regret making light of his story.

"Anyway, I got talking to this American guy who seemed nice and was staying in a hotel nearby." Theo pauses and pain skitters across his face. "You know what, let's skip the details and just say I went back to his hotel and woke up there the next morning."

"OK," I say, gently. "I don't need to know more."

Theo starts wringing his hands. "And I felt terrible about it. Absolutely bloody terrible. So as soon as I got home I told Kate. Except I didn't tell her it was a man—I just couldn't. So I changed the pronouns and told her it was a woman."

So that's what he meant when he said it was complicated.

"And what did she say?" I ask. "How did she react?"

He exhales shakily. "She was devastated, completely broken. Then she got angry and threatened to tell the kids—and my parents."

My eyes widen. "And did she?"

He goes back to wringing his hands. "No, she calmed down and eventually forgave me. We agreed to work on the marriage and give it another go."

I inch closer to him. "But Theo, that was your chance. You

could have saved yourself so much torment if you'd taken it and broken free."

He frowns. "But I wasn't ready. And the circumstances wouldn't have been right: I hated myself for what I'd done."

"And let me guess—Kate made you feel grateful to her for forgiving you." I realize my lip's curling. I wipe the bitterness from my face.

"She didn't *make me* feel grateful," Theo corrects me. "I *was*. Not everyone would have done that, Ads."

I tip my head to one side. "Fair point. I'll give her that."

Theo lays his hands flat on the sheets. "Anyway, Kate had always wanted a third baby so we agreed to start trying. She thought it would bring us closer together."

"I bet she did," I'm tempted to add, but stop myself.

"And when Archie arrived," Theo goes on, "in a funny way it did."

It dawns on me that this really is complicated. I let out a long breath. "I guess it's like you said the other day: you can't regret your actions if they're the reason you have kids."

"Exactly. And I was so happy to have Archie in my life, I just pushed my feelings down again. But sooner or later they came bubbling back up to the surface." He breaks off and smooths out a crease in the sheets. "And, well, you know the rest."

My eyes settle on the new laundry basket that's overflowing. I'd do the washing myself but promised to leave it to Theo.

I turn back to face him. "But Theo, there's one thing I don't understand."

He looks up. "What's that?"

"Why are you telling me now? Why didn't you tell me sooner?"

Theo mistakes my curiosity for disapproval. "I'm sorry, Ads. I didn't mean to lie to you."

I shake my head. "You didn't lie to me, Theo. What you said was the truth: you just simplified it and missed out some detail."

"But I did lie to Kate."

"Yeah, but that was only to spare her feelings. And what you did wasn't the cause of the problem: it was only a symptom of it. The problem in your marriage was you were gay."

He rubs his jaw. "Yeah, well, I'm not going to argue with that."

I inch even closer, so our knees are touching. "You know, if Kate thinks you cheated on her with a woman, it might have made things harder for her. It might have made her think your relationship stood a chance."

Theo drags a hand through his hair.

"Maybe you need to tell her the truth," I add.

I spot a wince in his eyes. "Yeah, but I can hardly do that at the moment. Not when she's on the warpath and lashing out at every opportunity. *That's* why I'm telling you now—so you know all the background."

"No, but maybe if she knew the truth she'd be less angry. And less inclined to lash out."

He nods, slowly. And I can see just how much he's hurting, just how much he's blaming himself.

I take hold of his hand. "You know, you've got to be easier on yourself, Theo. You're a good man."

He squeezes my hand. "Am I? Am I really?"

"Yes. And I love you for it. Come here." I open my arms and he leans into them.

As I kiss his hot, clammy forehead, I realize that knowing his story has given me a much clearer picture of his feelings. I understand now why he wouldn't stand up to Kate. And I don't resent him for it at all.

More than anything, I want to alleviate his guilt. But I know the only way this would happen is if he told Kate the truth. And, reluctantly, I have to accept that right now, that just isn't possible.

Chapter 25

The next morning, Theo goes down to the village to work and the kids and I get on with clearing all the debris out of the pizza oven. At the start of the job, they're more enthusiastic than usual. But then Callum tugs out a piece of wood that gives him a splinter in his index finger. I pull it out with a pair of tweezers and apply some antiseptic, but after this his enthusiasm drops—and so does Mabel's. They start handling wood with the tips of their fingers, as if it's radioactive. As we've nearly finished the job, I persuade them to keep going with the promise that after lunch we can visit Angelika—and her pool.

When we arrive at the address Angelika sent on Facebook, I discover that her house is surrounded by tall railings and accessed through intercom-operated security gates. Once they're buzzed open, we pass through to find Angelika waiting for us in a cheetah-print kaftan, her platinum-blond hair pulled back in a ponytail, her lips and nails painted fire-engine red. Over her head, she's holding a dainty lace parasol, and her eyes are hidden behind gold-framed sunglasses.

"Darlings, welcome!" she trills. "Leave your bags at the door and I'll show you round!"

Angelika lives in a handsome stone house that's roughly the same size as ours. It used to be a traditional Tuscan farmhouse but has been converted into a luxurious, ultra-modern, open-plan living space, with a kitchen that looks like something out of a spaceship and clean, white walls hanging with colorful, abstract paintings—as well as several of Wilf's watercolors running up the stairs.

As we leave behind the air-conditioning of the house, the heat hits us again. I fan myself with my Panama hat and gaze out over vast landscaped gardens that are bursting with flowers—the dominant color being red—and populated by several modern, outlandish sculptures. At the bottom of a sloped lawn is the—surprisingly large—pool.

Without any prompting, Archie runs towards it, flinging off his T-shirt and kicking his sliders in the air. I run after him and grab him by the back of the shorts. "Not so fast!"

I take off his glasses, quickly apply his suncream, and instruct him to wait for it to dry while I see to Callum and Mabel. They each apply their own but Callum begrudgingly lets me do his back. As I run my hands over a light coating of hair, I feel him tensing. He probably doesn't realize how many men remove their unwanted back and shoulder hair, his dad included. I'm about to crack a joke about smearing Veet on Theo's back being a test of how much I love him but stop myself: it would probably be better if Theo had a quiet chat with him about it. Mabel, meanwhile, is wearing a swimming costume that covers up—but can't disguise—her big boobs. Even after I've rubbed suncream into her back, she keeps it turned. The second I tell her the suncream's dried, she straps on her goggles and plunges into the water.

Angelika and I take seats at a table under a giant parasol on the paved poolside.

"I can't get over how glamorous this place is," I gush. "How long have you lived here?"

She takes off her sunglasses. "Since 1992. Edgar and I had been together a few years, but at first we had to keep our relationship secret. You see, he was married. And I was the mistress, or the 'side chick' as they say now."

From the way her eyes sparkle, I sense she's enjoying the revelation.

"Tell me more," I say, smiling so she knows there's no judgment.

"We were both living in Frankfurt but when Edgar left his wife, she turned the children against me. Not that I blamed her: I did steal her husband." There it is again: that sparkle in her eyes. "We thought we'd move here to create some distance."

"Was it tough?"

Angelika takes a packet of cigarettes out of her handbag and screws one into a gold holder. "It was. Edgar's oldest son was twenty at the time and thought I was trying to get my hands on his dad's money. In fairness, Edgar did have a lot of money. He was a banker."

"And what did you do for a living?"

She lights her cigarette with a gold-plated Zippo and blows out a curl of smoke. "I was an air hostess, darling. That's how we met. I was working in the first-class cabin on a flight to Hong Kong and served Edgar a glass of champagne. Although to listen to his ex-wife, you'd think I'd blown him in the aisle."

I laugh so loudly the kids look over.

"Are you coming in, Adam?" shouts Archie.

"Not just yet!" I call back.

Angelika waits for them to start playing again. "How are you getting on with the kids?"

"Better, thanks. Or at least I think so. But it's been hard work." I lower my voice. "The other day I caught Mabel running my toothbrush around the toilet bowl."

Now it's Angelika's turn to howl with laughter. "My younger stepson once pissed in a bottle and said he'd made me apple juice."

I howl some more. "That's rank! Did you at least catch him before you drank it?"

"Yes. And I remind him of it all the time. Believe it or not, we get on very well now."

I grab hold of my chair and pull it closer. "So how did you turn things around?"

Angelika sucks in a drag and blows out more smoke. "Funnily enough, the distance helped. Although I appreciate that's not much use to you. I guess I just didn't push it. I let them set the pace. And I tried to see things from their perspective."

As she flicks her ash into a gold-plated tray, I become aware of an argument erupting in the pool. I stand up and walk over. "What's going on?"

"Archie's splashing me!" wails Mabel.

"I'm trying to swim but he keeps getting in the way!" moans Callum.

"Please come in with us," begs Archie. "Please come and play!"

I frown. I am wearing my swimming shorts and have packed a towel, but I'm fascinated by the conversation with Angelika—and still haven't asked her about Wilf. "I'd love to, Archie, but I'm talking. Why don't you guys play a game?"

"Of what?"

Scrabbling around for ideas, I find myself revisiting the one holiday I went on with my dad, Debbie, Trevor and Keith. With two football-obsessed stepbrothers, I was always the odd one out, as they'd delight in reminding me—in between calling me *queer* and *poofter*. The only time I felt comfortable was when we played games in the pool. Dad would tell us to turn our backs, he'd throw his keys in the water and we'd compete to find them. As Trevor and Keith weren't very good swimmers, I'd sometimes win—and for a short time I no longer felt inferior to them. I outline the game to the kids and, when they express enthusiasm, go to my bag to find the house key.

"Will *you* throw it in?" asks Archie.

I screw up my face. "I'm sorry, you'll have to take it in turns."

I hand the key to Callum first.

"Make sure somebody keeps score!"

When I sit back down, Angelika has stubbed out her cigarette and served two glasses of Prosecco from a bottle that's been standing in a bucket of ice—but she's mixed it with raspberry liqueur to "give it a twist."

"*Prost!*" she says, holding up her glass.

"Cheers!" I reply, clinking mine against it.

We each take a sip.

"So tell me about you and Wilf," I begin. "You said you were close."

Angelika smiles. "Oh, yes. I organized his funeral. Although he didn't want any fuss so it was very quiet, just a basic cremation."

"So I heard. Apparently, even Stefano and Luisa didn't go."

Angelika tilts her head. "Isn't that the couple who looked after his house?"

"Yeah. Do you not know them?"

"I wave to them on the road but not really. I only live up the hill but we might as well be in different worlds."

I nod. "So how did you meet Wilf?"

She twists her gold watch around her wrist. "It was shortly after Edgar and I moved in. I spotted him one day, painting at the side of the road. As you've seen, I'm very interested in art, so I went over and introduced myself and we chatted. Of course, Willie pretended he was living with his 'friend' but I saw through that straight away. Being an air hostess, I was used to being around gay men. My gaydar was as sharp as a stiletto."

I chuckle. "From what I can make out, he and Arnaldo were very private."

She takes another swig of her drink. "They were, darling. And Willie was suspicious of me at first. I could tell he was holding back. But I told him stories about going out on the gay scene in San Francisco and Sydney. I remember telling him about trying to find the toilet in a bar and ending up in the dark room—but I didn't leave till I'd flicked on my lighter so I could check out what was on offer."

I roar with laughter. I look over to check the kids aren't listening but they're engrossed in their game.

"Willie loved that story," Angelika says. Then her smile falls. "Edgar was used to gay men, too, as he had a gay brother. But he died of AIDS. When I first met Willie that was all very recent. It was terrible, such an awful way to go."

I run my fingers up and down the stem of my glass. "I've heard it was really grim."

She nods and lights another cigarette. "I lost a lot of friends, but Edgar was extremely close to his brother. The first time I persuaded Willie and Arnaldo to come here for drinks, he burst into tears. But it was probably a bonding moment for us. I think Willie and Arnaldo could see we understood something of the challenges they'd faced."

Mabel walks past us and drops the key down the back of the steps to the pool. "On your marks, get set, go!"

There's a huge splash as the boys jump in.

"So did they go through a lot?" I ask. "Wilf and Arnaldo?"

Angelika drags on her cigarette. "They had a terrible time."

As Callum and Archie try to find the key, Mabel hovers by our table, her arms crossed, shielding her boobs.

"Was this when Wilf first came to Italy?" I press.

She nods. "And for a long time afterwards. That's why they used to tell people they were friends. They even set up a decoy bedroom, in case anyone came to the house."

I take another sip of my drink. "Which one was that?"

"The one in the cottage on the side."

"That's where we're sleeping!"

She gives a wicked grin. "How appropriate. That is, assuming sleep isn't all you do in there."

I don't like to tell her we haven't had sex this summer.

Angelika tips back the rest of her drink. "Anyway, despite their efforts, the news got out and there was a hideous scandal—down in the village but also in Camaiore. People spat at them in the street and shopkeepers refused to serve them."

"God, that's hideous," I say. I turn to Mabel. "Did you hear that? Angelika just answered your question."

She smiles, but Callum has found the key, so she jumps back in the water.

"At the time, Wilf was trying to find a job as an English teacher," Angelika continues, blowing smoke over her shoulder. "But there was no way any school would employ him. And people refused to do business with Arnaldo. He'd set up his own company but it fell apart within a few years."

"So what did they do for money?" I ask.

Angelika takes one last drag on her cigarette and stubs it out. "Willie found part-time work teaching English to adults at a night school in Lucca, and he gave a few private lessons. People were more accepting in the city. He was still working when I met him, although he stopped a few years later, once he qualified for his pension. They kept their heads above water but they never had much."

"Were they happy, though?"

Angelika serves us another drink. "Very much so. Especially when it was just the two of them at home."

"But the house is so different to what Wilf must have been used to. How did he cope being up here in the wild?"

She sits back, cradling her glass. "He loved being surrounded by nature. He used to say he embraced it, all of it—the good *and* the bad. He didn't try to fight it or hold it back."

I become aware that another argument has erupted in the pool. I excuse myself and walk over, only to find the kids are disagreeing about the score. Unsure how to settle the argument, I declare the game a draw.

"Come on," I say, "it's time to play something else."

"Will you come in?" repeats Archie.

I grimace. "I'd love to but not yet. Maybe later."

I return to my seat and take another swig of my drink. "One thing that's been puzzling me," I say to Angelika, "is how did Wilf find me?"

She smiles. "Oh, that's easy, darling: I helped him. We did it on my laptop, right here at this table."

I sit forward. "But I don't understand how he even knew I existed. How did he know my name?"

Angelika fiddles with her rings. "I thought your mother told him."

My insides flip. "My *mum*? But she died in 1989. And they weren't in contact. . . . As far as I know, he wasn't in touch with anyone from the family."

She lifts a plucked eyebrow. "Well, I have a vague memory that Willie did have some contact with your mother."

The shock of it stops my breath.

"I could be wrong," she adds. "Remember this would have been before I knew him."

I'm so shocked I can't speak.

"Anyway, when Willie was writing his will and wondering what to do with the property," Angelika continues, "he came to me and we looked you up on social media. He'd had the idea of leaving it to you but first he wanted to make sure you were gay."

"'Make sure'? What do you mean?"

"He already knew, darling."

I feel like I've been punched. "But how?"

"I'm afraid I can't remember. I've no idea at all. But I do know he was delighted to see pictures of you with your gay friends. There was one of you all at a foam party in Sitges and the caption said something about you being sisters. He loved that. I think I told you he used to call me his sister."

I try to shake the shock out of my head but all I can think is that Wilf was in contact with Mum. And he knew I was gay.

"That's when he decided he would leave you the house," Angelika goes on. "It was the one place he and Arnaldo could celebrate their love, so he thought it would be fitting to leave it to his gay nephew."

She explains that she accessed Edgar's old account on LinkedIn and looked for an Adam Webb who worked in Manchester. Once they'd found me, they scoured the company's website to discover my work email address. But I can't concentrate on any of it.

Callum, Mabel and Archie bound over to the table.

"I'm hungry!"

"I'm thirsty!"

"Have you got my towel?"

I snap out of my trance and hand over their towels.

"Let me get you some drinks and snacks," says Angelika. "I've stocked up for my granddaughters."

I blink. "Oh, so you've got kids, too?"

"No, they're Edgar's actually, but I've known them all their lives, so we don't bother with any of that step nonsense."

"Right, yeah."

She stands up and opens her lace parasol. "They were supposed to be coming this weekend but their trip's been postponed. I don't suppose any of you are fans of Harry Styles?"

"Yes!" blurts out Mabel. "I am!"

I smile. "She *loves* Harry Styles."

"Well, I was going to surprise my granddaughters with tickets to his concert in Lucca," says Angelika. "I'm too old to go myself but I was going to drive them there and pick them up afterwards. I don't want any money but the tickets are yours if you want them."

Mabel's face lights up. "Oh my god, I'd love to go. Thank you!"

"Just a minute, who will you go with?" I say. "You should probably ask your dad before you say yes."

Mabel screws up her face. "As if. Dad doesn't get Harry Styles. He says he's not a serious musician." There's a pause. "Adam, will you come?"

To my surprise, I find myself saying, "I'd love to."

"*Wunderbar!*" warbles Angelika. She turns to walk back to the house and sneaks me a wink. "Now, go on, darling, take off that hat and T-shirt and get in the pool!"

Chapter 26

After yesterday's visit to Angelika, I came back to the house thinking about Mum. I was desperate to speak to Auntie Julie and messaged to ask if she was free, but she and Jason are on holiday in Spain till Saturday. I've no idea how she'll respond to Angelika's suggestion that Mum and Wilf had been in contact—or if she's been hiding something from me—but don't want to push it while she's away. We've arranged to speak on Saturday.

In the meantime, I've decided to focus on Wilf and his story. After last night's barbecue, I updated Theo on what Angelika had told me. Again, he was moved and riveted and asked a lot of new questions I'm going to put to Angelika the next time I see her. But I didn't tell Theo what Angelika said about Mum—not until I've ascertained if it's true. To take my mind off her, I organized a game of cards, but it descended into squabbles when Archie got overexcited and couldn't stop looking at Callum and Mabel's cards—only for them to accuse him of cheating. In the end, we had to abandon the game. I went to bed to start reading *The Heart in Exile*, willing Mum out of my head.

Despite my efforts, when I woke up this morning, she was the first thing I thought about. I quickly forced myself to switch my focus back onto Wilf—and Arnaldo. I've decided to frame all forty strips of passport photos, splitting them into two lots so they're not too big. As I pedal away on the exercise bike—listening to *La bohème*—I consider where to hang them. The best option is probably on the gable wall in the big lounge, the most communal room apart from the kitchen. When I've finished my workout, I run the idea past Theo and he approves.

After breakfast—and all five of us have thrown the oranges over the hill—I drive into Pietrasanta to drop the photos off at a place I found online. I'm told my order will be ready at the end of the day.

By the time I get back to the house, once again I'm thinking about Mum. Thankfully, Luisa is on her way down from the castle. She's wearing rubber gloves and holding a square of fabric, on which sits what looks like a piece of shattered pottery.

"We've just made our first discovery!" she announces, her eyes wide.

"Fab!" I jog over to her. "What is it?"

She gently takes hold of it and lifts it up. "It's a fragment of what was probably a ceramic basin. Look at the glazing." She points out some black-and-blue stripes. "I'm pretty sure the black is manganese and the blue is cobalt. Which means it's probably from North Africa."

My eyebrows shoot up to my hairline. "North Africa?"

She wraps up the pottery in the cloth. "I can't be sure. I need to take it to the museum so Vito can have a look. He's the expert."

"Well, whatever he says, it's very exciting. And congratulations."

She smiles. "Thanks. I'm excited, too!"

I wish her luck and turn to walk over to the house but immediately collide with a cement mixer.

"*Fuck!*"

As I rub my shin, I become aware of piles of sawdust, planks of wood, and stray stones strewn everywhere—as well as the usual covering of dust. This place is a tip. There's a bag of plaster that has a hole in it and is spilling out over the patio and, worst of all, a battery-powered drill has been left standing on a wall. If Archie picked that up . . .

And he would pick it up . . .

I quickly grab hold of it, making a mental note not to get angry at the builders. It can't help that all the furniture, rugs, cushions and coffee-table books that we stripped out of the house are still piled up behind the chapel—together with that awful spinning wheel. If I'm going to tell Giuseppe he and his men need to be tidier and store their tools away, first I need to create some space.

"Theo, kids!" I shout. "It's time to light that bonfire!"

That should keep my mind off Mum.

When I get back from Pietrasanta, I peel the bubble wrap off the frames and the photos look wonderful. Each frame has two lines of ten strips, one above the other, starting with the original black-and-white photos that have been pieced back together. Viewed side by side, they form a document of Wilf and Arnaldo's relationship. From year to year, cuddle to cuddle, kiss to kiss.

Theo and I prop them up against the sofa and sit on the fireplace to admire them.

I feel a lump in my throat. "Oh, Theo, isn't it sad?"

"Is it?" he says. "I think it's quite joyful. The two of us are sitting in what used to be their home, basking in their love for each other."

I let out a breath. "I didn't think of it like that. But maybe Angelika was right: maybe that was the point."

Theo rises to his feet. "Come on, let's get them up on the wall."

He goes downstairs to fetch tools and a tape measure and, when he comes back, we set about hanging them. I'm glad Theo's good at DIY as I've always been clueless—much to my dad's disappointment. As an adult, whenever I've put up pictures, I've made so many mistakes and miscalculations that when I've taken them down, I've exposed walls that look like someone's blasted them with a machine gun. I wonder if Wilf or Arnaldo was good at DIY, if they both were, or if they worked best by combining their skills. I suddenly feel privileged to have been given this window into their lives.

Tears are building in my eyes. "Oh Theo, it's all a bit overwhelming. To have this link to the past—and everything they went through to be together."

"I know," says Theo, "I know." He puts his arms around me and gives me a hug. He smells of smoke from the bonfire but I don't mind. As I hug him tighter, my tears fall onto his shoulders. Soon, I'm sobbing.

"Are you OK?" comes a voice from behind us.

We turn around to see Mabel, flanked by her brothers, standing in the doorway.

"What's the matter?" asks Callum.

"Nothing," I say, stepping back from Theo and wiping away my tears. "We're just looking at these photos of Wilf and Arnaldo. What do you think?"

The kids step forward to take a closer look.

"They're alright," says Callum. But I suspect he likes them more than he's letting on.

"They're the only photos they had of them as a couple," I comment.

"Why?" asks Archie.

"Well, in those days you couldn't take photos on phones," Theo explains. "You had to have a camera and a roll of film that you'd take into a special shop to get developed. And if anyone saw photos of two men kissing, they could report you to the police and get you into trouble."

The kids look surprised.

"That's why Wilf and Arnaldo didn't really stand near each other in the photos you've seen around the house," I add. "But we found these, which they took in photo booths, where nobody could see them."

Callum nods, taking it in. "In that case, they're not just alright—I'd say they're pretty sick."

Theo cuffs him on the shoulder and I feel the lump in my throat melting.

"Isn't this lovely?" Theo says. "To have them here with us, like this?"

Mabel agrees. "Yeah, it is."

And the five of us stand in silence, admiring the photos.

Later that evening—after Theo's cooked us yet another barbecue—we play a game of cards, and this time the kids manage not to fall out. In between rounds, Mabel picks up her phone. "You know, we've not taken many photos on this holiday," she points out.

"You're right," I say, not wanting to remind her that it's only because she and Callum moaned every time I suggested it.

"Why don't I take one of you and Dad?" she offers.

Theo puts down the cards he was shuffling and stands up. "That's a superb idea."

"Go on," says Mabel, "stand in front of the house."

I pick up a napkin and blot my face—cursing my greasy skin—and Theo and I take up our positions in front of the big turquoise doors. He wraps an arm around my shoulders.

Mabel takes several pictures. "I think you'll like them," she pronounces.

"Let's have a look," says Callum, taking the phone and swiping through. "Yeah, they're not bad."

"High praise indeed," teases Theo. "Now, what would you say about taking one of the five of us? Can we do a selfie?"

There's a pause. I can't work out if Callum and Mabel are resisting. But eventually they skulk towards us, pretending to be taking part under duress. Archie, on the other hand, doesn't pretend at all. He springs out of his seat, skips over to take up position, and immediately starts striking poses.

Theo whips out his phone but can't work out how to take the picture without casting a shadow over our faces.

"Dad, you're so crap!" says Callum, miming exasperation.

He lifts out his own phone and directs us to shuffle around so there are no shadows. "That's better."

But he and Mabel aren't smiling.

"Everybody say *formaggio*!" chirps Theo.

"Dad!" Callum and Mabel elbow and slap him.

"Everybody say *parmigiano*!" I can't resist adding.

"*Adam!*" groan Callum and Mabel.

But I smile—we all do.

And Callum takes our photo.

Just as I'm about to ask if I can have a look at them, he shuts down his phone and slots it into his pocket. "Right," he says, briskly, "shall we play another round?"

Chapter 27

It's Friday night and Mabel and I are on our way to see Harry Styles. The gig's taking place in an open-air arena that's been set up on one of the huge lawns next to Lucca's historic walls.

We're in the car listening to Harry's latest album and compiling our top five of his songs. I don't like to say I don't know many of them. I'm nervous about tonight, especially after Theo designated it the perfect opportunity for Mabel and me to bond. I don't want to blow it. So I rearrange Mabel's songs in a different order, switching out "Watermelon Sugar" for "Music for a Sushi Restaurant," which I do at least know. That seems to do the trick.

We pass through a nondescript village and see a sign that tells us Lucca is just a few kilometers away. Mabel lets out a whinny of excitement, which I'm pleased she isn't trying to hide. She's also put on some makeup, including shimmery lip gloss and the false eyelashes Gloria gave her. And I may be imagining this, but she isn't cowering behind her hair as much as usual.

"Have you seen Harry before?" I ask, brightly.

In a quick-fire babble, Mabel tells me that she and Sharita tried to get tickets to see the tour when it came to Manchester, but her mum missed the deadline and it sold out. "I'm going to post loads of pics on my Insta. Sharita will be devo when she sees them! And Aurora's going to *die*!"

I hope they don't provoke jealousy in Kate.

I spit out a feather that's stuck to my lips. Mabel and I are wearing thick boas: hers is the tasteful green of a Tuscan artichoke, while mine is much less stylish, the same color as the oranges we throw off the hill. She'd seen on TikTok that Harry's hardcore fans wear feather boas when they go to his concerts. Apparently, this is inspired by some appearance he made at the Grammys. I hope she's right and we're not the only ones, as I'm starting to get a sweaty neck.

We pass the two dodgy junctions, but I don't have trouble negotiating them as there's so much traffic heading into the city, I just follow the flow. Besides, I'm starting to feel much more confident driving. When we arrive on the outskirts of Lucca, it takes us a long time to find somewhere to park and I have to settle for a spot that's a good distance from the city center. It's also tight and will test my parallel parking skills, so I brace myself for sniggering. It doesn't come—and I manage to maneuver the car into the spot in just two attempts.

When we leave the car, Mabel and I discover that, although we're a long way from the venue, there's a stream of girls heading in that direction, most of them chaperoned by older women, presumably their mums, mums' friends, and maybe the odd auntie. To my relief, many are wearing feather boas, some of which have already started to shed their feathers on the pavement. I pity whoever has to clear them up tomorrow.

"Good shout on the feather boas," I say.

Mabel gives a little skip.

Before long, the stream of fans has expanded into a river. And there's so much excitement in the air, I can't help but be affected.

"Nearly there now!" I tweet.

"He's probs getting ready backstage!" Mabel squeaks.

Suddenly, I'm fifteen years old again, on my way to the Manchester Apollo to see the Take That and Party tour with Auntie Julie; the two of us are linking arms and the excitement is vibrating through me.

I've no idea why I was nervous about tonight.

I hold out my arm for Mabel to link it. She threads hers through.

"That was unbelievable!" I gush. "He's literally a god!"

"Unreal!" chimes Mabel. "What was your fave bit?"

"'Sign of the Times'," I yap. "And I found 'Matilda' really moving. I should have put that in my top five, by the way."

"Oh my god, we'll have to do them again," declares Mabel.

We're in the car on the way back, our faces flushed, our voices hoarse from screaming, our legs aching from dancing. Although our feather boas are thinning and mine's plastered to my neck, neither of us wants to take them off.

"My fave bit was probs 'As It Was'," Mabel rabbits on. "I loved it when everyone sang along."

"Me too," I say. What I don't mention is that I particularly enjoyed singing along with her. "Oh, and I liked that One Direction song. When all the mums and aunties joined in."

"Yeah, that was fun."

It's dark, except when we pass through the odd street-lit village. When this happens, I notice Mabel has no hair in front of her face.

"I loved it when he wore those dungarees with hearts on them," she babbles. "They were so cute!"

"And when he held up the Pride flag and helped that girl come out!" I add, tapping on the steering wheel.

"Oh my god, that was incred! Although I think my fave bit of the whole show was when they told him he was the most popular singer they'd ever had in Lucca—and he started crying."

I smile and allow a pause to fall. "You know, not everyone gets to see that."

Mabel twists to face me. "Do you not think so?"

"No, you can't fake that kind of emotion." Although I'm not sure this is necessarily true, I think it's important for her to hear it.

"He did seem really emotional. He can't get like that at every concert." Mabel pulls down the sun visor so she can look at herself in the mirror and rearrange her boa. Even though I can't see her, I sense a huge grin on her face.

"Oh, and he's so hot!" I slip out. "I can't believe we haven't discussed that!"

Mabel remains silent.

Shit. I hope I haven't messed up. After all, I am in a relationship with her dad, and Harry Styles is probably twenty years younger than me. Will she think I'm gross?

But she lets out a giggle. "I know! I love his hair. And his smile!"

As relief rushes in, my grip on the steering wheel loosens. "And those tattoos!"

"I keep thinking if I could just meet him," she goes on, "he'd realize we're perfect for each other and he'd fall madly in love with me."

I don't like to tell her that every girl in the arena was probably thinking that. Instead I say, "I used to think that about Howard Donald."

"Who's Howard Donald?"

"He was in Take That. Well, he still is, but he was when I was obsessed with them. I used to fancy him so much, and he wasn't even gay."

"That doesn't matter," declares Mabel. "Harry Styles is a lot older than me, but I don't care. I love him. And I know he'd love me."

"You hold onto that feeling," I tell her. "Never forget it."

We come to the section of the road that's lined with cypress trees on either side: we're approaching Montemagno.

Mabel slides her hands under her thighs. "You know, you're much better at this than Dad."

"Well, your dad didn't really get his head around being gay till he was older," I explain. "I knew from a young age. But I couldn't express it, so I couldn't talk about this kind of thing. I couldn't tell anyone I fancied Howard Donald."

"Why not?"

"Because the other boys would have battered me!"

Her eyes bulge. "Oh my god, did that actually happen?"

"Yeah, all the time. So I learned to keep things in. Ian thinks that's why a lot of gay men act like teenage girls. Because all those things we're supposed to do as teenagers we didn't get to do."

We pass the walled cemetery that's just outside the village.

"At least that stops you from being a boring grown-up," observes Mabel.

I chuckle. "I'll take that as a compliment. I love being connected to my inner teenage girl. Although maybe that explains why I've got such bad skin."

Mabel shakes her head. "No, that'll be all the suncream you put on. What products are you using?"

I tell her and her face falls.

"You need to make some adjustments," she states, emphatically. "I can help you if you like. I know loads about skincare. I've watched everything on TikTok and Insta *and* YouTube."

I smile. "OK, that'd be brill."

We come to the old-fashioned women's clothes shop and turn off the main road.

"You know, I can't wait to tell your dad about tonight," I say.

Mabel doesn't respond, but I can tell that she does, too.

Chapter 28

The next day is—finally—Saturday, and I've arranged to call Auntie Julie at four o'clock. Although how I'm going to contain myself till then, I don't know. I'll just have to keep busy.

I'm thrown a lifeline while we're eating breakfast in the temporary kitchen. All of sudden, Mabel sits up and screams. "Oh my god, there's a mouse!"

I swivel around but can't see it. "Where? Where did it go?"

She lifts her feet up onto the chair and points to the far wall, on the other side of the lounge area. "Oh my god, what if we catch rabies?"

"What's rabies?" asks Archie, jumping up and running over to the wall.

"Mabel, we're not going to catch rabies," Theo reassures her. "Just try and calm down and tell us exactly what you saw."

"It was a mouse," she splutters. "It ran along the wall and disappeared into a hole in that corner."

I feel a tug in my gut. Since the day we arrived at the house and mice had eaten through the kitchen, I've spotted their droppings a few times—but I just kept sweeping them away and hoping no one would notice. I couldn't face setting traps to kill them and told myself that all the noise the builders were making would probably scare them off. Clearly this hasn't been the case. Just as I'm worrying that all the progress I've made with Mabel is going to be lost—or that she may tell her mum—Theo seizes control of the situation and turns it into a game. He and the boys get down on all fours and scour the room for holes. As well as the one through which the mouse disappeared, they spot two others and block up all three with pieces of cardboard. I'll ask Giuseppe to seal them properly on Monday.

"Remember he hasn't started on this room yet," I point out. "So there's bound to be the odd hole. But by the time he's finished, the entire house will be mouse-proof."

Callum looks disappointed. "Can't we set traps?"

"Yeah, can we not kill them?" asks Archie, excitement flaring in his eyes.

Over Mabel's shoulder, I catch sight of the photos of Wilf and Arnaldo hanging on the gable wall. I remember what Angelika said about Wilf deciding not to fight nature. "I'm afraid there's no point trying to get rid of them completely. The best we can do is just to stop them coming in."

To my surprise, Mabel declares, "I agree." She lowers her feet back onto the floor. "Besides, killing them would be cruel."

Theo stands up and returns to the table. "Come on, let's finish eating, then clear everything away. And the best way to stop attracting mice is to make sure we don't leave a single crumb."

As we do as he suggests, I console myself that the situation could have turned out much worse. And in fairness to Mabel, seeing a live mouse probably did come as a shock.

"You know what, it was only small," she concedes as she finishes her cereal. "It was probs just a baby. Now that I think about it, it was actually quite cute."

Under the table, Theo presses on my foot and I give him a smile.

As soon as we've finished clearing up, I remember my phone call this afternoon.

I look at my watch. Five hours to go. . . .

I decide it'll be the perfect distraction to get a haircut. After three weeks in Italy, Mabel's long hair is fine, but mine, Theo's and the boys' is starting to look unkempt. And Theo and I joke that our eyebrows and ear hair seem to be growing much quicker than usual, wondering if it's the sun or just a symptom of aging. Whatever's going on, we're in dire need of a trim and tidy.

Stefano has told us the best barber in the area is in Camaiore. While I'm not looking forward to going back to the town so soon after we were insulted, I think it's probably a good idea: we can hardly avoid it forever.

"Now, who's feeling strong?" asks Theo, when we're all in the car.

"Me!" Archie and I chorus.

"Who's ready to stick together?" continues Theo.

"Me!" Archie and I trill.

"And who's afraid of horrible old men?"

"Not me!" Callum and Mabel join us to shout, much louder.

We set off, through the olive grove.

But when we arrive in Camaiore—parking the car on a bizarre hybrid of a roundabout and a car park—I sense we're all a bit nervous. Theo and I put our hats in the boot, making the excuse that we're having our hair cut so don't want to take them off and forget them in the barber's. But we both know that isn't the real reason.

I remember the photos of Wilf and Arnaldo and feel a rush of defiance. "Actually, I am going to wear mine," I announce.

"Yeah," says Theo, straightening his spine. "Me too."

We lift them back out of the boot and place them on our heads.

As we walk down the main street, it's busier than it was on Tuesday and there are plenty of shoppers. But nobody really looks in our direction.

When we come to the barber's, I stop outside.

"Here we are," I say.

Loud rock music is blaring out, video screens are showing sports games, and a twentysomething with a bolt through his nose is hovering outside, tugging on a cigarette. The shop's name is scratched like graffiti over a painting of an angry bull, brandishing a pair of clippers like a weapon.

"What do you think, gang?" asks Theo.

Just as I'm about to say I'm not sure this is the right place for us, a voice shouts, "Adam!"

I turn around to see Vito bounding towards us—all six feet, five inches of him. He's dressed in navy chinos, a pale blue linen shirt, and moccasins, very different to the clothes we see him wearing on the dig, and very different to the crop top and shorts he was wearing in the gay bar at Torre del Lago. Although he does have a lapel badge of the Pride flag pinned to his shirt.

"Hi, Vito," I say. "*Ciao!*"

"*Ciao!*" chirrups Archie.

Vito greets us all in his excellent English. As he does, I notice how handsome he is, how thick his dark brown hair, how positive his energy. I hope Dom's let him down gently. To be on the safe side, I avoid the subject.

"What are you up to?" I ask. "Do you live around here?"

He smiles. "Yes, I do. I am on my way to the museum. But I am not officially working: I have come to examine the ceramic Luisa found at the castle."

I grin back at him. "Yeah, that's really exciting. I can't wait to hear what you think."

"You will." Vito gestures to the barber's. "Are you here for a haircut?"

"Yeah!" cheeps Archie. "I'm having wax in mine!"

Vito smiles. "Wonderful! I'm sure you will look very handsome."

"Actually, I was just thinking, I don't know if this place is quite right," I say, scrunching up my nose. "It seems a bit . . . I don't know . . . laddy."

Vito looks confused. "*Laddy?*"

I shake my head. "Sorry—very macho, very male." I lower my voice. "Very heterosexual."

Vito's eyes swell. "Ah, I understand. But Marco is very nice. He is my friend. And his mother is a lesbian!"

Theo and I quirk an eyebrow. We look around to check no one's listening, but everyone seems to be getting on with their own business.

Vito shouts Marco's name and a striking young man in a black string vest puts down his clippers and jogs over. When he's standing before us, I notice that his short black hair has bolts of lightning shaved into the sides. Vito speaks to him in Italian but I recognize the words *famiglia*, *castello* and *zio*—which Luisa taught us means *uncle*—and Marco nods in acknowledgment. He shakes all of our hands and tells us in decent English that we're very welcome.

"Dad!" interrupts Archie, and I can guess what's coming: "Can I have my hair like his?"

"We'll see, squirt," says Theo. Then he nudges me in the ribs and says under his breath, "We can hardly back out now, can we?"

But, as we step inside, I realize I wouldn't want to. And I regret ever thinking that just because a handful of old men were homophobic, the whole town must be.

"What do you think about that?"

I'm in the olive grove, where I've come for a bit of privacy as the kids help Theo assemble the furniture we've bought for the master bedroom in the new family suite. It's finally time for my phone call with Auntie Julie and I've just told her what I've learned about Wilf—that he didn't come here to be with an Italian woman at all, but an Italian man. And his family cut him off when they found out.

"Well, you could knock me down with a feather," Julie answers. It sounds like she's propping herself up with cushions, no doubt in her favorite armchair. "But now that I think about it, it does make sense. My dad was homophobic. And I remember my granddad making comments, too."

"Well, both of them made plenty of comments to Wilf—it's all in the letters. And when he got here, he had to put up with a load more." I relay some of the detail Angelika gave me.

"That's awful," says Julie. "They must have felt like it was the two of them against the world."

"I expect they probably did."

I'm leaning against a tree, but a knobble on the trunk is digging into my back. I wriggle around to make myself comfortable. I notice that the olives hanging from the branches have grown but are still some way off the size they need to be before they're harvested. And just a few weeks ago, the grass was the color of golden sand but now it's almost white, bleached by the sun.

"There's something else," I venture, warily.

"What's that?"

I pull up a few strands of grass and toss them down the slope. "This friend of Wilf's told me he'd been in touch with Mum."

There's a silence I can't read.

After a few seconds, Julie speaks. "Yeah, I think she did write to him."

I feel the choke of betrayal. "But why didn't you say?"

"To be honest, I didn't know at the time. I only found out after she died."

"What difference does that make? That was thirty-four years ago."

I sense she's hiding something from me and I don't like it. It feels like it's getting hotter and I blow down the neck of my T-shirt.

I hear Julie standing up and giving a little groan. "I'm going to put the kettle on. I'm desperate for a brew."

"Come on," I insist, "stop trying to dodge the subject. How did you find out Mum had been writing to Wilf?"

"I can't remember, chuck! There was loads going on, and in case you've forgotten, I was grieving for my sister."

"Oh, yeah, sorry." I can hardly argue with that.

Julie turns on the tap and fills the kettle. "But I wouldn't read too much into it. You know what your mum was like. She was probably just angling for a free holiday. I always said she had champagne tastes and a lemonade budget."

An electric current shoots through me. I wonder if whatever letter—or letters—Mum sent are still here. I wonder if they're in that second shoebox.

All of a sudden, I'm overwhelmed by the urge to look.

I shift gears and ask Julie about her holiday, which she seems to appreciate. Then I update her on mine and check in on how things are going with the Airbnb lettings in Manchester. When the kettle starts shrieking, I spot my opportunity and say I'll leave her to her unpacking.

"Bye!" I sing-song. "I'll speak to you soon."

"Yeah, see you, chuck."

Once I've ended the call, I sit still for a moment. I sit in silence, listening to the sound of the crickets and the birdsong.

While I am desperate to look for Mum's letters, I'm also frightened. What if I find out something I don't want to know?

There's a rustle in the undergrowth. I've no idea what it is but decide to head back.

I can't shake off the feeling that there's something Julie isn't telling me. But what if she's trying to protect me?

Yeah, I need to think about this.

Chapter 29

It's Sunday but, for once, Callum doesn't have to be dragged out of bed. He gets himself up early to do his workout. Through the open window of his bedroom, I hear him grunting and panting, as I sit on the patio, sipping my morning coffee, reading *The Heart in Exile*.

The book's lead character is a middle-class psychiatrist struggling against his nature—a nature that, like Wilf, he finds it difficult to name, although he sometimes uses the medical term *invert*. When his ex-lover dies in unexplained circumstances, the psychiatrist delves back into the underworld he gave up—because he found it "sordid"—to try and track down some answers. While the plot's gripping, I'm fascinated by the details of the subculture he describes—although the character's self-loathing and hatred of effeminate gay men can be wearing. And Wilf seemed to accept his class snobbery and treatment of working-class men as sex objects, but I find it difficult to stomach. Once I've finished the book, I'm going to scour Wilf's library to see if I can find any other novels about gay life at other stages of history.

I'm torn away from my reading when the others stir. After going up to the temporary kitchen to make a breakfast of orange juice and fried eggs on *ciabatta*—and after we've thrown the oranges over the hill—the kids do the washing up in the cottage bathroom. Then we look around the wine store collecting as many baskets as we can find and set about stripping the fig trees of their fruit. Stefano examined these the last time he came to the house and told us they were ready. Judging by the taste, he's right. I've never eaten fresh figs before but they're deliciously rich and sweet, somewhere between strawberries and currants, with a dash of dates. All of us eat as we work, making appreciative noises, Callum and Mabel breaking off to take the occasional photo. My favorite is of Archie holding up a fig in each hand, bolts of lightning shaved into the sides of his head, just like Marco the barber.

In the afternoon, we go shopping for hammocks, which we've decided we'll set up between the trees at the side of the house, the opposite end to the chapel. Everything I've read about holiday rentals says you need to create "Instagrammable moments." I'm sure the castle and its views are going to rank number one on our list but I want to create some more, inspiring our guests to post several times. We find two hammocks that aren't expensive and are in pretty much the same turquoise as the front doors. As Wilf and Arnaldo must have chosen this, I decide it's going to be our signature color.

"Is that the color you're doing the website?" asks Callum.

I suddenly realize that, other than registering the domain name for the Castello Montemagno—and setting up an Instagram account in the same name—I haven't done anything. In fact, I'd forgotten about it completely. "I haven't had chance to think about that yet," I say.

"Adam, you need to get on it," Callum argues. "It'll take ages to do the design and get everything set up."

"I know, I will!"

On the way back, we call at the supermarket to pick up everything we need to make pizzas. On Friday, the builders finished rebuilding the roof over the pizza oven and told us to leave it a few days; then we could use it. As we're still in the temporary kitchen, we're reduced to using ready-made bases, but the kids enjoy picking their own toppings and coming up with names for their combinations.

Next stop is the beauty aisle, where Mabel finds everything she's prescribed for my new skincare regime.

"I'm looking forward to this," I tell her. We exchange a smile.

Theo takes a detour down the sweet aisle, where he tells the kids they can each pick a treat for the car. Archie goes for his usual chocolate buttons and Mabel asks for a bar of white chocolate. I'm about to remind her she doesn't like that anymore when she volunteers, "I know I said I'd gone off it but I like it again now."

Theo and I try not to smirk.

"And I know I said these were too hard for my brace but I was basically talking crap," says Callum, picking up a protein bar.

Am I imagining this or do Callum and Mabel turn away so we can't see them smiling?

Once we're back at the house, we hang the hammocks, which are instantly claimed by Callum and Mabel. Archie feels left out but, as he's only interested in the hammocks for swinging, Theo has the idea of building him a rope swing. He remembers seeing a thick length of rope in the wine store and retrieves it, along with as many tools as he can find. The five of us spend the next two hours creating and erecting a swing from the thick branch of a tree that hangs over a slope. We saw, sand, drill, measure and tie, with Theo acting as foreman. Once the swing's ready, Theo and I insist on testing it out before any of the kids go on it, then we sit one on top of the other to really test its ability to carry weight. Mabel takes more photos and we all laugh loudly. I'd never imagined DIY could be so much fun. If only Dad could see me now.

Then another voice in my head says, Dad *could* see you now—if you'd let him.

I clap my hands together. "Right, who fancies a pizza?"

Theo fires up the pizza oven while the kids and I sprinkle our ready-made bases with our chosen toppings, then slide them in.

As we sit on the patio eating, congratulating ourselves on our taste combinations, Archie spots two lizards sitting on the doorstep. We recognize them as the ones that live in the larder. But this time Mabel doesn't scream and Callum doesn't attack them. We just sit eating, watching them. And they sit watching us.

Theo finishes his pizza and gently dusts the flour from his hands.

"Gang, I think we should come up with some names for these guys."

"Len," suggests Callum.

"Liz," says Mabel. "Liz the Lizard!"

"Lionel!" quips Archie, his mouth smeared in so much tomato he looks like a clown. "After Lionel Messi!"

"All outstanding ideas," judges Theo. Like a punch to the gut, I suddenly feel the force of his good looks—enhanced by his sharp, neat haircut. Something stirs inside me.

"Actually, not Liz," Mabel corrects herself. "I don't think they're boyfriend and girlfriend."

"Brother and sister!" yelps Archie, cramming the remains of his pizza into his mouth.

Mabel shakes her head, firmly. "I think they're two boys."

"Best friends!" says Archie, spraying tomato all over the table.

Mabel puts her pizza down. "I think they're boyfriends."

"Like Dad and Dadam!" chirps Archie.

I wince.

But this time Mabel doesn't correct him.

In the evening, Mabel gives me my skincare tutorial, while Archie is in bed and Theo is speaking to Callum about his back and shoulder hair—laying out options he may or may not want to follow.

I have to admit, Mabel's skincare advice is incredibly useful, although I do feel sheepish to be learning some of the basic principles from a thirteen-year-old, a week before I reach the age of forty-six. She ends with the instruction to store all my products in the fridge and I hope there'll be space in our new model when we're back in the kitchen.

Once Mabel's gone to bed, I have a shower. As I'm drying myself off, I become aware of Theo standing in the doorframe. He moves over to me and I sense an edge to his energy. He takes his shirt off, throwing it on the floor, and kicks away his sliders. He clasps his hands around my neck and pulls me closer.

He kisses me full on the mouth, his breath hot and quick. He tastes salty, like the sea. I run my nose up his cheek and breathe in his musk, the smoke of the pizza oven, the scent of the country.

"*Mio tesoro,*" he whispers in my ear.

I smile. "*Mio carissimo,*" I say into his mouth.

I let my towel fall to the floor so I'm naked. He lifts me up with his powerful arms and I feel them tensing at my sides. I wrap my legs around him, feeling the tickle of the hairs on his stomach. He kisses me hungrily, feverishly, and carries me through to the bedroom, as if I hardly weigh anything.

He lowers me onto the bed and tugs off his shorts, throwing them onto the floor. He's hard, huge. I move my mouth down to pleasure him, guiding him in and out, savoring his taste, his size, his readiness. He lets out a moan and buries his fingers in my hair. Then he pulls back and lets himself out of my mouth.

"Sorry," he says, "I need to be inside you."

"You *were* inside me," I say, with a giggle.

"Ads," he growls, "I need to fuck you."

He grabs the lubricant, gives a few pumps and slicks himself. Then he waits for me to do the same, his breathing growing faster and heavier. He kneels before me and pulls my thighs up ever so slightly. And with one push, he's inside me.

"Yes."

"Yes."

He waits, knowing I need to get used to his size. I pant, forcing myself to relax, knowing the pain will be over soon.

"Ready?" he whispers.

I give him an eager kiss.

He begins driving himself in and out of me, so forcefully that I gasp. He silences me with a hot, open kiss. I grab onto him, pulling him deeper and deeper inside me.

Suddenly, I've no idea why I've avoided doing this the whole time we've been in Italy. And I don't feel the slightest flicker of shame that the kids are under the same roof.

"I love you, Theo," I burst out.

"I love you, Ads," he rasps.

"I just love you so much."

"And I love fucking you. I want to fuck you forever."

I groan. "Yes, please!"

I run my hand down my body to start pleasuring myself. Theo gently tugs at my nipple with his right hand, his left holding up my flank. I feel him gaining momentum, his speed building. I want to scream but instead cling onto his muscular shoulders with my fingers. I dig into him as he bores into me, closer to my essence, the boundary between us blurring.

"I'm nearly there," he tells me. "I'm going to come."

"Me too," I say.

"Fuck," he cries. "I love you."

"I love you, too."

With a feral growl, Theo empties himself into me. At the same time, I climax, a wild, breathy grunt escaping me.

We fall back on the bed, catching our breaths. Then we both start laughing, loudly and uncontrollably.

I feel my entire body unclenching.

I remember just a few weeks ago thinking that if Theo dumped me, it'd be like unclenching a fist. But I realize now just how wrong I was. Because this is the ultimate unclenching, the ultimate release. I don't think I've ever felt so myself.

Theo moves in for another kiss. "I'll never leave you," he says.

I feel like I'm smiling with my whole body.

Chapter 30

"Mister Webb!"

I'm woken up at 7:30 a.m. by the sound of someone shouting my name in an accent that isn't Italian. I'm lying in Theo's arms, where I've slept against his chest.

"Mister Webb!" calls the voice again. There's a banging on the door.

I sit up. Shit, it's the Wi-Fi engineer!

Realizing I've overslept, I jump out of bed, throw on my dressing gown and bolt downstairs. I apologize profusely, not getting too close to the man in case I have morning breath. More to the point, I hope I don't smell of sex. But he smiles brightly, clearly used to greeting customers before they've woken up properly or made themselves presentable.

The engineer is a young, dark-haired, olive-skinned man, who tells me his name is Cristian and he's from Romania. But, as he doesn't speak much English and I don't speak Romanian—or Italian, come to think of it—we struggle to communicate. I make us a pot of coffee while Cristian unloads his van.

When Giuseppe arrives, he steps in to translate. As far as I can make out, the two men decide that the best plan is to lay Cristian's cables along the same route as the old phone line, which is erected on poles about five or six meters above ground and runs along the lower boundary of the olive grove. But I zone out. I stand there, holding my coffee and grinning, thinking of last night, thinking of Theo.

Once Cristian has started work, I go back into the bedroom and open the shutters. "Morning!"

Theo rolls over and smiles. "Morning."

He's naked on top of the sheets, the curve of his bum and thigh backlit by the sunshine streaming in through the window. My bones cry out for him but I tell myself to get a grip: the kids will be awake soon and the house is crawling with workmen.

Once Theo has got out of bed and the two of us have dressed and showered, we round up the kids and take them through our usual morning routine. Then we troop down to the wine store and fling open the doors. This is the only part of the house we haven't touched, mainly because I can't afford to do anything with it, so it hasn't been a priority. But even if we want to continue using it as a dumping ground—which Theo and I joke every house needs—first we need to strip it of Wilf and Arnaldo's dumped items, which almost fill it, in some parts up to the ceiling. We lift out tins of dried-up paint, broken heaters and fans, and dust-covered lampshades and stands. There's a gold cigarette case inscribed with the initials A.S. that I assume belonged to Arnaldo—but I have no idea why it's been tossed in here. I tuck it into my pocket so it doesn't get thrown away. We continue tugging out shabby old shelving units, a wooden chair that's missing so many slats it would be impossible to sit on it, and a rusty old barbecue. I pause to picture Wilf and Arnaldo enjoying barbecues on the lawn, just like we do. Then I plunge back in, instructing everyone to keep the old kegs and barrels, as they'll add to the atmosphere.

"Of what?" asks Theo, smirking. "A dumping ground?"

I roll my eyes in mock annoyance. "No, *mio carissimo*. Whatever we decide to do in Phase Two." I've no idea where that idea came from: until now I hadn't even thought of a second phase to the renovations. I also realize I just used the word *we*.

But Theo doesn't bat an eyelid. "Good thinking, *mio tesoro*."

He grins and I feel another pulse of love for him.

As the builders' skip was recently emptied, Giuseppe says we can throw everything we don't want in there. By lunchtime, it's full and the wine store is as empty as we're going to get it.

"That's it, gang!" declares Theo. "Job done!"

Towards mid-afternoon, the Wi-Fi is up and running, so we give the kids the code and connect Archie's devices. As Theo begins connecting his home office in the study, the kids retreat to their bedrooms. I feel a stab of worry that they might also retreat into themselves, that they might start distancing themselves from us again—or moving closer to Kate. But I check on them after an hour or so and they all seem relaxed and happy. They don't stay in their rooms much longer. Archie leaves his devices to play on his rope swing, while Callum and Mabel take pics and videos of the house and grounds, then lie in their hammocks, sending them to friends. A few video calls also take place, but I don't pay attention to who's on the other end. The important thing is, the kids seem to be enjoying showing off the house and telling people about their summer.

I decide to check my social media and catch up on the latest antics of my sisters. Ian's posted a coaching video about the dangers of catastrophizing, Dom's posted a few shirtless training pics—which, as far as I can tell, are identical to the last—and Gloria's posted a video of him in full drag, lip-syncing to some long-forgotten solo single by a minor member of Girls Aloud. I notice that on Callum's Instagram he's posted the pic he took of the five of us standing in front of the turquoise door. There's no caption but I guess it speaks for itself.

"I love your Instagram post," I casually mention when I find him in the temporary kitchen mixing a protein shake.

"Thanks," he says, screwing the top on his plastic bottle.

I open the fridge and pour myself a glass of fizzy water. "I meant to ask, what happened with those friends who sent you the gay GIFs?"

Callum shakes his bottle. "Oh, I dealt with that ages ago. I told them they were homophobic and out of order. They moaned for a bit but then they apologized." He flips the lid on his bottle and tips back the shake.

"Good on you," I say. "That's great to hear."

He trots upstairs to play FIFA.

After relaying Callum's news to Theo—and sneaking a kiss—I start preparing *arancini* rice balls for Stefano and Luisa, who are joining us for dinner. Just as I'm stirring the risotto for the stuffing, Mabel shuffles in. "Adam, I can't find this place on TikTok."

"That'll be because I haven't registered it," I confess. "Sorry, I know TikTok's really important but I'm literally clueless about it."

She pulls at a stray thread on her top. "You know, I could always have a look at some of the other accounts on there. It's not my usual thing but I could see what other people with places like this are posting. And let you know if there's anything that does well."

I rest my wooden spoon on the side of the pan. "Really?"

She shrugs. "If you like."

"That'd be fab."

Mabel bounces out of the room.

I sneak a quick glance at the photos of Wilf and Arnaldo and give them a smile. I go back to stirring my risotto.

The kids and I are sitting with Stefano and Luisa at the table on the patio. Theo is standing on the lawn, poking at the coals of the barbecue. A recording of *Carmen* is playing through the window, the smell of citronella surrounds us, and the view over the valley seems more beautiful than ever.

I tell everyone to tuck into the starters, which I've placed in the center of the table. On offer are the *arancini* balls with a marinara sauce, an *insalata tricolore* Archie and I made, and a selection of hams I picked up from the delicatessen in Camaiore. Plus, there's a choice of breads I bought from the bakery, knowing Callum is eating more than ever now he's training every day.

Stefano makes a lip-smacking noise. "Your *arancini* are very good, Adam. If I do not know you, I say you are Italian!"

"Thank you," I reply. "*Grazie.*"

I take Theo over a plate of food so he can eat while tending the barbecue.

"Superb," he says. "Just like you."

He gives a little growl and a giggle escapes me.

Once I'm sitting down again, Luisa updates us on the kittens' progress. The kids ask plenty of questions and arrange to visit them tomorrow. The conversation turns to the dig and Luisa tells us the team has recently found a jug handle, an iron nail, and a little bone she thinks was probably worn as a pendant.

"Is it from a dead body?" asks Archie, saucer-eyed.

"We don't know," answers Luisa. "It may be human; it may be from an animal. We need to examine it."

Archie forces a whole *arancini* ball into his mouth.

"And what about that piece of pottery?" I say, helping myself to some mozzarella from the *tricolore*. "Did Vito find out what it is?"

"It *is* a fragment of basin," Luisa replies. "And it dates back to the second half of the twelfth century."

"Amazing," says Theo.

"And it *is* from Tunisia," adds Luisa, holding a forkful of ham in the air.

"What's Tunisia?" asks Archie.

"One of our builders is from there," says Callum, wiping some breadcrumbs from his vintage Stone Roses T-shirt. "It's a country in North Africa."

"Very good, Cal," says Theo.

Callum smiles and loads his plate with ham.

Mabel is sitting upright, her hair pulled back in a ponytail, wearing an attention-grabbing raspberry-colored T-shirt I've never seen before. "But our builder will have caught a plane," comments Mabel. "How would a basin have got from there to here in those days?"

Luisa reminds us of the trade route. "The Via Francigena mainly connected Anglo-Saxon Europe with Latin Europe, but it was also accessed by countries much farther away. So it was important for the exchange of linen from Flanders and silks and spices from the East."

"That's fascinating." Theo starts lifting lamb skewers onto the barbecue. Over his shoulder he says to the kids, "Remember in those days people didn't travel as much, so they wouldn't have known about different countries. Imagine what it must have been like discovering them for the first time."

"I wonder what kind of person brought that basin here," I say. "I wonder what they thought of this place."

Theo turns to face us, a pair of tongs in his hand. "What do you think, gang?"

"I think it was a soldier who came to fight in a battle," squeaks Archie. "And he killed loads of people and that bone's from one of the dead bodies."

"I think it was a rich businessman who sold things in Italy and took all the money back to Tunisia," Callum suggests. "I think he lived in this mint palace in the desert and had, like, a hundred wives."

Theo and I exchange a smirk at the last detail.

"I think it was a warrior queen who was kicked out of her country because all the men were scared of her," pipes Mabel. "And she came here and became best friends with the queen who lived in the castle. They made a pact to look after each other and help each other out."

"Those are all outstanding guesses," says Theo.

"What about you, Adam?" asks Luisa. "What do you think?"

I pass around what's left of the *arancini* balls. "I think it was a handsome trader who came here to sell pottery but fell in love with a gorgeous knight who lived in the castle. And the knight's family accepted him, so he stayed and they lived happily ever after."

"I'll go with Adam's option," says Theo, flashing me another smile.

"Oh my god, will you guys stop making eyes at each other and just kiss?" jokes Mabel.

"OK!" says Theo, and he trots over to plant a kiss on my lips.

"Kissy, kissy!" teases Archie.

"And how about my beautiful daughter?" says Theo. "Do I get a kiss from her?"

Mabel covers her head with her hands but Theo bombards her with kisses. As she giggles and shrieks, we all laugh.

A familiar *twit-twoo* interrupts us from the sky. We all look up to see a tawny bird hovering, its wingspan huge. I whisper to Stefano, who confirms it's our resident owl—or *gufo*. Finally, it's made an appearance.

After less than a minute, the owl spots something and swoops down, out of sight.

"Now who's ready for their main course?" asks Theo.

Chapter 31

For a second day, I've been walking around grinning. Last night, once Stefano and Luisa had left and the kids were in bed, Theo and I ran upstairs to the cottage—tripping over some of the steps—and made love. Once again, I felt complete. I felt safe.

But today I'm feeling something else—something else that surprises me: I'm feeling brave enough to have a look and see if my mum did write to Wilf.

When Theo takes the kids to visit the kittens, I pretend I need to stay behind to do jobs. I creep through the house and close the door to the cottage, to shut out the banging that's coming from the builders. I reach under the bed, pull out the second box of letters and start sifting through it.

After a few minutes, I recognize Mum's handwriting.

Fuck!

I flip over the letter and read the name Suzanne Webb. My pulse tripping, I see the address she's given isn't that of our old house but the shop where she used to work. Why would she do that?

I tug in an unsteady breath.

I'm about to open the letter when I remember there may be others—and I want to make sure I read them in the right order.

I continue sifting through the pile and, sure enough, there is another letter. Again, Mum's given her work address. So she mustn't have wanted Dad to know she was writing to Wilf.

I continue looking but there isn't a third.

I lay the two letters on the bed next to each other. I read the postmarks and one is dated March 1989, the other a month later. Mum died on 5 May.

My heartbeat's in my ears.

Am I brave enough to do this?

But even as I ask myself the question, I know I have no choice.

Dear Uncle Wilf,

This is your niece, Suzanne. I know this must be coming out of the blue but I found a letter you wrote to your mum and dad explaining where you were if they wanted to find you and that's how I got your address. I came across it a few years back when I ~~were~~ was clearing out the house after my mum died. Actually, do you know she died—your sister Kathleen? Did anyone tell you? I'm sorry if that's a shock. Come to think of it, all the family's dead now, except me and our Julie. But you must know about your mum and dad?

Flamin eck, I'm making a right mess of this already. I'm sorry I'm a crap writer. I might as well get that out of the way now. I should probably have worked harder at school rather than messing about with the lads. Although I'm not sure I should be admitting that to a teacher. You are still a teacher, aren't you?

Anyway, I only found one letter so I'm assuming no one wrote back to you. I'm sorry, Uncle Wilf. Now that I think about it, my granddad ~~were~~ was a bit of a dick. Let's be honest, so was my dad. And he ~~were~~ was a shit husband. My mum was scared of him because he was always getting pissed up in the pub and would come home and knock her about. Not that I'm trying to make excuses for her not sticking up for you. I don't think there's any excuse for disowning your family and I'm sorry they all gave you such a shit time. In your letter you said you'd never change and you were happy with the love of your life and I think that's mega. And I know you must have been really hurt by what happened and having to move a long way away but I also think it's dead romantic you got your happy ending.

Anyway, I'm glad I found out what happened because nobody told me ~~owt~~ anything at the time and they all just acted like you didn't exist. I remember once I asked my granddad where you'd gone and he belted me so I never mentioned it again. I know I ~~were~~ was only young when you left but I really loved you and I used to love sitting on your knee when you read me stories and I loved it when you brought me sweets and took me to the pictures. You took me to see my first film, South Pacific, when I was only little. Do you remember? Anyway, for a while I thought you'd just dumped me and forgotten all about me and I must have done ~~summat~~ something wrong. But you know what kids are like, they only think about themselves.

By the way, I hope you don't think I'm being selfish by writing to you because you said in your letter you didn't want me and our Julie to know. I should say I haven't told her. We're very close but very different. Our Julie's sensible and has a posh job in an office, she ~~were~~ was never one to have her head turned by the lads, not like me. Anyway, if you want ~~nowt~~ nothing to do with me I'll understand. I just want you to know that the way you are doesn't bother me. I don't think anyone should be told they're a bad person because of who they love. Mind you, I would say that because that's kind of the reason I'm writing to you.

This isn't easy to admit, Uncle Wilf, but I'm having an affair. I've been seeing this bloke called Gary for about a year now and it's all built up and become this big thing and I don't know what to do about it. Sorry, I should probably tell you about my husband first. Flamin eck, I really am making a mess of this.

My husband's name is Martin but everyone calls him

Mart and I met him when I ~~were~~ was 18 and he's a mechanic which isn't very exciting but he was dead fit and everyone said he was Manchester's answer to Warren Beatty. All the girls fancied him and I wanted him for myself so they'd all be jealous. I sometimes wonder if part of the problem was I didn't really know what to do with myself after school. I was always the pretty one and I was rose queen and everything and people used to say I should be a model and I did once get chatted up by this bloke who said he was an agent in London and he gave me a card with his number on it but my dad went berserk when he found out and ripped the card up and threw it away. I told you he was a dick. I work in a women's clothes shop now and it's alright because the clothes are nice and me and the girls have a laugh, especially when we go out for drinks. But when I first left school I was working in this crap shop selling old lady clothes with this boss who was a right bitch and I hated it. I think that may be one of the reasons why I got married when I ~~were~~ was 20, I just wanted something else in my life, something more exciting and Mart was nice and I did think I loved him. The problem was, it all got dead boring dead quickly. I suddenly had all this housework and cooking to do and I can't cook, honestly I could burn water. I'm crap at ironing too. And then I got up the duff and our Adam ~~were~~ was born and he's going to be 12 this August and he's gorgeous and dead clever and does really well at school and I love him to bits. And right from the start I loved having a baby and he was so cute but Mart never wanted to do anything exciting anymore, he just wanted to stay in. And he never kissed me or told me I looked nice except when he'd had a few pints and he wasn't romantic or passionate and I just felt like I was invisible.

Then last year I was on this works do in town and I met this mega fit bloke called Gary. All the girls thought he looked like Michael Douglas and I've always fancied Michael Douglas, especially in that film Fatal Attraction. And he chatted me up and told me I looked nice and started buying me drinks and I felt like a film star. The funny thing was, I'd been chatted up by blokes before when I ~~were~~ was out with the girls but I'd never done anything about it because I wasn't looking for it—I'm not a slag or anything. But for some reason it was different with Gary. We sneaked off and before I knew it he ~~were~~ was kissing me and I liked it and then he came into the shop a few days later and pretended to be buying ~~summat~~ something for his sister and asked if he could take me out. He took me to this Italian restaurant and it was dead posh and I felt like a film star again and thought he must really like me. A few hours later, he booked us a room in this hotel and we ended up in bed together and it was mega and afterwards I just couldn't control myself. I knew I was in love with him and he always says he loves me and I know some people think it's wrong what we're doing but I don't think it makes me a bad person because how can it if it feels right?

I think our Julie can tell ~~summat's~~ something's going on, it's probably a woman thing, although I've denied everything. And I do feel guilty about cheating on Mart but I can't help it if I don't love him anymore and anyway he hasn't told me he loves me for years so maybe he doesn't and that makes the two of us. And I feel dead guilty about lying to Adam, although I keep telling myself I'm only lying to protect him and this doesn't change how I feel about him which it doesn't because nothing would ever change that. But at the end of the day this thing with Gary makes me happy and I just want to be happy.

I don't know why I'm telling you all this but I think maybe all the creeping around and keeping it secret is starting to be too much and I just need to get it out of my system. I suppose I also know you won't think I'm a bad person because people said you were a bad person but you knew you weren't and you were doing the right thing and look how it turned out for you. Maybe that's why I think you'll be able to help and will know what I should do. What do you think, Uncle Wilf? Should I leave Mart so I can be with Gary? All hell would break loose but I think it would be worth it. Am I right, do you reckon?

I hope you're still happy with your Arnaldo and he still loves you and makes you feel special like my Gary does. And I know this letter's rubbish and I am crap at writing but I want you to know that not everyone in our family hates you. And like I said, I wanted to say sorry for them. Even if you are annoyed at me for writing (but I hope you're not).

With lots of love and kisses from,
Your niece, Suzanne x

I sit on the bed, blinking.

I feel like I've been hit by a truck, that I'm suffering from a concussion or am regaining consciousness and haven't quite come round.

At the same time, Mum has burst back into my head exactly as I remember her and I can see her facial expressions and hear her voice much more vividly than I have for years. She's written on thin, lined paper that's been pulled out of a spiral-bound notepad, with what looks like a cheap blue biro, the pressure she exerted making her imprint come through to the other side. Her handwriting is more rounded and frilly than Wilf's, with circles over the *i*'s, but it's also sloppy—even sloppier towards the end of the letter. But it all fits the mum I remember: it's all unmistakably her.

My head's spinning with adrenaline and I struggle to fill my lungs.

I hold the letter to my nose and try to breathe it in, but it doesn't smell of Mum. It doesn't smell of Silk Cut cigarettes or Nivea hand cream.

Come on, Adam, get a grip.

Although I am shocked to hear about the affair, in some ways it doesn't surprise me at all. I remember suspecting something was going on, something I couldn't quite understand, but sensing very clearly that Mum was pulling away. Now it occurs to me, I probably started to feel abandoned even before she died. When she did, the knife just twisted in farther.

Suddenly, all the happiness and security I've felt over the last few days has been snatched away from me. All my anxieties and insecurities have come crashing back and my head's flooding with questions. What does this mean about Mum's death? Surely it can't be a coincidence that she wrote to Wilf just two months before she died?

From outside, I hear the sound of Archie's little feet clattering up the stone steps. "Adam!"

The sound of his voice hits me like a second truck from the opposite direction.

He bangs on the exterior door to the big lounge.

I ram the letter back in the envelope, replace both envelopes on top of the pile, and close the shoebox.

"Coming!" I call out.

I quickly tidy the box under the bed, telling myself it's a good thing to be forced to take a break before reading the next letter.

This is a lot to process. A *lot* to process.

"I thought it would be nice for us to watch the sunset together," says Theo, as the five of us sit down on the castle wall. "For us to say goodbye to the day."

I don't think Theo realizes the expression he's using—an expression I've used on him—comes from my mum. He doesn't realize I've been thinking about her all evening. He doesn't realize I've been tormenting myself, going over and over what she revealed in the letter, wondering how it affects what I've always thought, what I've always suspected.

Even so, he sensed something was wrong. A couple of times he took me to one side and asked if I was OK but I just fobbed him off. There's no way I can tell him—not yet.

Probably because he knows how much I love watching the sunset, after dinner Theo suggested we all come up here. Now we're halfway through August, the sun is setting earlier and there's no conflict with Archie's bedtime. But I'm worried this is only going to make me feel worse. Because watching the sunset always makes me think about Mum.

I look out at the orange sun arching closer to the mountain, a few thin stripes of cloud streaking around it. At the mountain's foot shimmers the unusually clear sea, its surface smudged by what I can only assume is a boat. Behind the mountain that embraces the sea, the sky burns a much deeper orange, like the embers of our barbecue.

I have a clear memory of Mum and I watching the sunset a month or so before she died—around the time she wrote Wilf the letter I've just read. I remember her saying that if she ever had to go away it wouldn't mean she didn't love me, that she'd never stop loving me. That's why I'd always thought she must have taken her own life: I thought she must have been trying to prepare me. She knew I was gay and was so repulsed by it, she couldn't bear to be near me, she couldn't bear to go on living. As everyone at school called me a dirty queer and everyone acted as if being gay was the worst thing ever, that seemed to me to make perfect sense.

At my side, Theo lets out a relaxed, contented sigh. "Right, let's think of all the things we did well today and all the things we want to do better tomorrow."

"I liked playing with Spaghetti!" cheeps Archie, sitting on my other side. "And on my swing!"

Theo grins. "Superb, squirt. But people don't have to tell us if they prefer to keep it to themselves."

We all fall silent and gaze out at the sunset. But I become fixated on what I realize is its imperfection. If I could just shift the sun over to the right, it'd be hovering directly above the sea—in the center of the V made by the mountains—its reflection on the waves forming a perfect straight line, until it disappears behind the horizon.

"Now, aren't we lucky to be doing this together?" says Theo, softly. "Not everyone gets to say goodbye to the day with the people they care most about."

Like a body blow, I realize just how much I miss my mum. All of a sudden, I start crying.

"Sorry, Adam," says Callum.

I knuckle the tears out of my eyes but they keep falling. "'Sorry'? What for?"

"For being so hard on you," he says. "When we first got here."

"Oh." I'm taken by surprise.

"I'm sorry, too," says Mabel. "I wasn't very nice, either."

"That's OK," I manage. "Although apologies accepted. Thank you."

Archie shuffles closer to me and takes hold of my hand.

"We want to make up for it," Callum announces. "Me and Mabel wondered how you'd feel about us doing your digital marketing."

"For this place," clarifies Mabel. "Callum could do the website and I could do the social media."

"We'll do a mint job, I promise," says Callum.

The two of them look at me, eagerly.

I sniff back my tears. "I'm sure you would."

"So what do you say?" chips in Theo. "Is that a yes?"

I force out a smile. "Yes, brill. And thank you. That's really exciting."

Archie squeezes my hand. "If you like, we can play Top Trumps tomorrow. Dad's got me a new pack in Italian. 'Awesome *Animali*'!"

I no longer have to force myself to smile. "You're on." I let out a breath. "Guys, I'm sorry I got emotional."

"Don't apologize," insists Theo.

"I was just having a moment," I go on. "But it's lovely to be here. And you're right: we are lucky to be doing this together."

I squeeze Archie's little hand and realize this hasn't made me feel worse at all. It's made me feel much better. Even if the sunset is imperfect.

I notice Archie's glasses are dirty. I let go of his hand, lift them off his nose, and clean them on my T-shirt. And I hold them up to inspect the lenses in the light of the setting sun.

Chapter 32

The next day, Theo is out of action to prepare for his school's A level results, which won't be released to students till tomorrow but the teachers find out today. He'd originally intended to fly back to Manchester, before our plans changed and the kids joined us. He feels bad about not being there but hasn't missed a results day in nearly ten years; plus, he has a supportive deputy head who's already been away so has offered to step in. But he still needs to be online and on the phone, which means I'm on child-care duty and won't be able to sneak off and read Mum's second letter. Part of me is relieved.

I take the kids to see Angelika, who's invited us to spend another day by her pool—and to meet her granddaughters, who've arrived for their delayed summer holiday. As we troop through the gates, she's standing waiting for us, wearing a tiger-print kaftan and gold jewelry that glints in the sun. On either side of her is a fine-featured, pretty, slim, blond girl. Angelika introduces one as Lina, who's sixteen, and the other as Freya, who's fourteen. Thankfully, they both speak excellent English.

"Our mum's British," Lina explains. "She's from Hertfordshire."

"Really?" says Callum. "So's our dad."

I notice him blushing slightly—and Lina does too.

Mabel gives Angelika a basket of figs to say thank you for the Harry Styles tickets.

"*Klasse!*" Angelika gushes. "I love Willie's figs!"

She drops the basket off in the kitchen, then leads us down to the pool, shielding her face from the sun with her lace parasol. She asks if we enjoyed the concert and Mabel and I tell her all about it as the kids strip down to their swimwear and I apply Archie's suncream. This time, Callum and Mabel come to me to offer up their backs. Mabel's bikini—a purple sporty number—is making its debut appearance and she doesn't appear to be self-conscious wearing it. Callum, too, is holding himself more confidently: while he's still skinny, his chest stands proud. I also notice Lina checking him out when she thinks nobody's looking.

"It seems to me that Callum's making quite an impression on my granddaughter," Angelika comments under her breath.

"I think Lina's making just as big an impression on him," I mutter back.

We share a smile and sit down at the table. A bottle of Prosecco is standing in an ice bucket, next to a crystal sphere of raspberry liqueur and two empty champagne flutes, which Angelika fills without any discussion. We slip off our sunglasses and bring our glasses together.

Angelika asks how the house renovations are going and I run her through our plans. "The kitchen and second bathroom will be finished by the end of this week, which means the only room left is the bathroom in the cottage. The builders are already getting on with the damp proofing and changing the electrics, or should I say there are holes and trenches in the walls and wires hanging everywhere. I don't quite understand what's going on and I'm not sure I want to."

Angelika releases a bracelet that's caught on the side of her kaftan. "Quite right, darling. You and I are far too fabulous for that kind of thing. When we renovated this place, I left it all to Edgar until they were done with the plastering. Now, tell me your plans for the décor."

I take a swig of my drink. "We're going to stay authentic so we'll probably paint the walls in warm, earthy tones. I need to start thinking about that, although I've already bought a few bits. And I put up some photos the other day."

I tell her about the passport photos we found of Wilf and Arnaldo—and the difference between these and the stiff, posed shots that stood on the shelves.

"I'll look forward to seeing them," says Angelika. "You know, Willie and Arnaldo didn't like to show affection in public—even when I knew them, when they could go down to the village and people were friendly. I think they just got used to holding it in and it became second nature."

I look at Callum and Lina, who aren't engaging with the others but sitting on the side of the pool, swinging their legs, chatting. Their faces are animated and their eyes sparkling. It wouldn't occur to them to worry about their attraction towards each other being seen—apart from maybe not wanting their siblings to wind them up.

"That's sad, isn't it?" I say to Angelika.

She lets out a sigh. "It is, darling. You know, the only time I ever saw Willie and Arnaldo expressing affection was when I turned up unannounced at the house once and caught them kissing on the lawn. Willie wasn't embarrassed in the slightest, but Arnaldo was."

We're distracted by a loud, theatrical giggle coming from Lina. Callum is smoothing his fringe and chuckling. At the other side of the pool, Mabel and Freya seem to be getting on well, trying out different dives. But Archie is left out, sitting on the steps, playing with Captain America. I excuse myself and go over to ask if he wants me to throw the house key into the water so he can find it. His face lights up and he tosses Captain America away. I direct him to turn his back and—knowing he's a good swimmer—throw the key into the deep end.

"What was he like, Arnaldo?" I ask Angelika, once Archie's searching the pool. "We hardly spoke about him the other day—it was all about Wilf."

Angelika screws a cigarette into her holder and lights it with her gold-plated Zippo. "He was quite restrained and buttoned-up, as you Brits say—much more subdued than Willie. I think his family was very religious. I remember once telling him about working on an airbus—where they used to have a private room for the crew—and walking in on two of my gay friends having what the British crews used to call a flying fuck."

I cackle loudly.

"Working for an airline was wild in those days." She takes an extravagant drag on her cigarette and blows the smoke over her shoulder. "Arnaldo didn't disapprove but I could tell he was uncomfortable with anything explicit. Willie, on the other hand, loved my stories."

I grin at her. "In that case, I know where I get it from."

I excuse myself again and go over to check on Archie. He's spotted the key at the opposite end of the pool and is swimming over. Lina, meanwhile, has got in the pool and is throwing a ball high in the air so Callum can catch it as he jumps in.

"So they were very different, then?" I ask Angelika. "Wilf and Arnaldo?"

"In some ways, yes. And their relationship wasn't perfect. Arnaldo could be very proud."

"What do you mean?"

She takes a swig of her drink. "Well, if they had a row, he wouldn't say sorry—he'd just brood. My Edgar was like that, so I sympathized. Arnaldo saw himself as a traditional man, the head of the household, so Willie did all the housework and the cooking. I wasn't sure it was a fair division of labor but it seemed to work for them. And they were very much in love. Willie was devastated when he died."

I watch as Archie dives down for the key and reemerges with it in his hand.

"That's brill, Archie!" I shout. "Well done!"

When he's given me the key back, I tuck it into a little recess that leads into some kind of filter just under the rim of the pool—hoping this will give me more time to talk. Once Archie's searching, I sit back down. "And how did Arnaldo die? Actually, *when* did he die? I don't even know that."

Angelika narrows her eyes as she works it out. "It would have been twenty-five years ago, because I remember Willie saying we were coming up to the anniversary. He was a heavy smoker and had lung cancer." She takes one last drag on her cigarette, blows out her smoke and stubs it out. "Willie hated smoking. He always said if Arnaldo hadn't smoked they may have had another five or ten years together."

I suddenly have an idea. But I put it to the back of my mind as Archie's swimming around the pool, clueless. I shout to him, "You're stone cold!"

He switches direction.

"Getting warmer!" I yell.

I turn back to Angelika. "So was Arnaldo ill for a long time?"

She nods, gravely. "It was a slow end and very unpleasant. And then there was the injustice of their legal situation."

As she tops up our glasses, Angelika explains that Arnaldo wasn't able to register Wilf as his next of kin, as they weren't married. So when Arnaldo had an infection, lost consciousness and was rushed into hospital, Wilf wasn't allowed at his bedside. On that occasion, Arnaldo regained consciousness and Wilf was then allowed to come in during regular visiting hours, but Arnaldo didn't want Wilf showing him affection. "He didn't want Willie to hold his hand and that really upset him. So when Arnaldo recovered—but it became clear he wasn't going to beat the cancer—he stopped the treatment and moved back home."

"Am I warm now?" shouts Archie, treading water next to the filter.

"Red hot!" I shout back.

"After he died, Willie became quite reclusive," Angelika continues. "Then one day—about a month later—I drove down to the house, bundled him in the car and brought him up here. After that I used to tell Edgar to piss off and play golf so Willie and I could sit here drinking. I'd tell him my stories and gradually he started laughing again."

Archie spots the key in the recess, thrusts his hand in and pulls it out. "Got it!"

I trot over to congratulate him, then look for a new hiding place. Callum and Lina are no longer sitting on the side but standing in the pool, and he's trying to impress her by showing how long he can hold his breath underwater. I persuade him to stand with his foot covering the key.

"Right," I say to Archie, "on your marks, get set, go!"

I sit back at the table and take a swig of my drink. "So did Wilf come up here a lot?"

"Every Thursday afternoon at first. Then when Edgar died, we spent more and more time together. During the pandemic, we saw each other pretty much every day. He even moved in for a few months. There were only the two of us so we became like a little family."

I check on Archie and worry I've made his task too hard. I steer him in the right direction, then sit back down. "And did you ever go out?" I ask Angelika. "When it wasn't the pandemic, I mean?"

"Oh, yes. We'd go to Lucca for dinner on the Piazza dell'Anfiteatro. Willie loved it there. Apparently, it's where Arnaldo came to meet him when he arrived in Italy."

I pull my chair closer. "Really? He said something about that in one of his letters."

My heart drops. I didn't intend to tell her I'd read the letters: it just slipped out. I hope she doesn't turn on me for snooping.

Angelika arches an eyebrow. "So you found them, did you?"

"Yeah. Sorry. Should I not have read them?"

She rearranges her bracelets and bangles. "Don't be silly, darling. If Willie left them, I'm sure it's because he wanted you to."

I let out a breath.

"Oh, and we'd sometimes go to opera at the Teatro del Giglio," she continues. "That's also in Lucca. Or the open-air Puccini festival in Torre del Lago. That also brought back his happy memories of Arnaldo."

Seeing that Archie has no idea where the key is, I stand up and approach him. "I'll give you a clue," I say. "It's hiding underneath something beginning with a C."

Archie scrunches up his forehead. "Chair?"

"No. It's in the water."

"Captain America?"

"No, but that's a good guess."

Archie points at Lina. "Curly hair?"

I raise both eyebrows. "No, but you're getting warmer."

I give him an encouraging grin and sit back down, as he swims towards Lina and Callum.

"You know, I was sad to lose Willie," Angelika continues, "but I think he was ready to go. He used to say he and Arnaldo had been apart for too long."

I nod. "Twenty-five years is a long time."

"Absolutely." She takes out another cigarette and lights it. "I've managed five without Edgar and that's bad enough."

"Callum!" Archie shouts, excitedly. He dives down to retrieve the key from under his brother's foot.

"By the way," says Angelika, "now you're in the house, we need to carry out Willie's wishes for his ashes. You know he wanted to have them scattered with Arnaldo's?"

I'm embarrassed to realize I hadn't even thought about this. "Oh, right. Where's that?"

"In the castle, darling." Angelika takes another drag and directs a plume of smoke into the sky. "Well, actually, we stood next to the wall up there and threw the ashes over the side. We weren't allowed to scatter them around the actual castle, as it's a protected building. You have to get permission for these things."

"Shit, how do I go about doing that?"

Archie is hauling himself out of the water and running over to me. "Adam, that wasn't fair!"

"It's fine, I'll do it," says Angelika. "I did it for Arnaldo and Edgar. I know the man in the town hall in Camaiore."

I brace myself as Archie throws himself at me. "Has the same guy been doing the job for twenty-five years?" I ask Angelika, as he starts attacking me with wet slaps.

"And the rest," she answers, stubbing out her cigarette. "You know what small towns are like. But he's divine. And he knew Willie and Arnaldo's story. He was very sympathetic, actually. I've seen him since Willie died and we've spoken about it, so it won't be a problem."

I lift up Archie and shake him, making him giggle and squeal. "Thank you," I say to Angelika.

"Now come on," she commands, standing up. "Let's find this one a treat."

At the sound of the word *treat*, Archie wriggles out of my grasp and onto his feet. "Yes, please!"

Angelika smiles. "I don't think any of the others will be interested."

I look at Mabel and Freya, who are engrossed in devising some kind of synchronized swimming routine. Lina is sitting on Callum's shoulders so he can throw her off and she can scream, loudly.

"No," I agree.

Angelika flips open her lace parasol. "And would you like to see Willie?"

Lina screams again, so loudly it makes me wince. "What do you mean?"

"His ashes?" Angelika replies. "They're in the living room."

"Oh, right, sure."

Her eyes twinkle. "When we pass the kitchen, let's pick up another bottle of Prosecco. If Lina's going to carry on screaming like that, I'm going to need it."

Later, Theo and I make the children pizzas, then leave them to go out on a date night. The idea came up when Callum and Mabel offered to babysit Archie. At first I said thanks but declined: I'm still worried about money and how I'm going to pay Giuseppe for the retaining wall and storm damage—although Angelika gave me an idea on that front. But Theo insisted we should take the kids up on the offer and it would be his treat. So we've come to Lucca, to the Piazza dell'Anfiteatro.

It's a lovely evening and still very warm, but we're bored of wearing shorts and T-shirts so have dressed up in chinos, loafers and linen shirts, which we ironed—joking it was the first time we'd ironed anything in weeks. We stroll around the oval-shaped piazza, admiring the buildings of various heights that are painted lemon, wheat and a gorgeous honeycomb, their upper floors private residences—many of them with balconies—their lower floors occupied by restaurants, most of which have outdoor seating spread out over the paving stones. We find a table at the same restaurant where we ate on our first night in Italy—which we remember wasn't expensive—and order a bottle of house red.

"Here's to your fab A level results, *mio carissimo*," I say, holding up my glass.

"Thanks, *mio tesoro*," says Theo. "Here's to all the students getting good news tomorrow!"

We bring our glasses together and savor our first sip of wine.

On reading the menu, we see that polenta has been translated as "cornmeal mush," which makes us laugh—although, unsurprisingly, neither of us fancies it. Theo orders octopus then roast lamb, while I opt for an *insalata caprese* followed by seabass. Our waitress is skinny, with short hair in a mullet and a tattoo of a paw print on the side of her neck. She begins speaking to us in Italian and we congratulate ourselves on not standing out as much as we used to—before we have to admit defeat and ask her to switch to English. In the center of the piazza, a busker with a sound system is playing a clarinet along to backing tracks of love songs from films—currently "Unchained Melody," from *Ghost*.

I tell Theo that Angelika confirmed Wilf and Arnaldo did indeed meet on this piazza when Wilf came to Italy. We imagine how Wilf must have felt to have given up everything and be alone and terrified, then to come here and finally be reunited with Arnaldo.

"Whatever either of them was feeling," I say, "it must have been awful not to be able to express it."

Theo turns his glass, gazing at the wine as it swirls around. "Can you imagine going through all that and not even being able to hug each other?"

"I just thought," I burst out, "that's the color I'm going to paint their old bedroom!"

"What?"

I nod at a building on the other side of the piazza. "Over there, that gorgeous honeycomb. In honor of their reunion in Italy!"

Theo grins. "Outstanding."

As the light fades and the streetlights flicker on, the busker switches to "My Heart Will Go On" from *Titanic*. Our starters arrive and I tuck into my *caprese*. I find myself thinking about Mum and Gary on their first date in an Italian restaurant. I wonder what Mum ordered. Had she eaten it before?

"You've gone quiet," Theo says. "What are you thinking about?"

I consider telling him about Mum's letter and what I've found out. I probably *should* tell him. And I *want* to tell him.

But this isn't just about me. And I don't want to spoil the evening.

"Just Wilf and Arnaldo," I answer. "Thinking about them makes me appreciate how lucky we are."

"Absolutely. We may have had our challenges, but nothing like what they had to go through."

I nod, solemnly. "Does it make you feel a responsibility to get it right?"

Theo shrugs. "It *would* if I didn't want to get it right anyway. But the commitment's already there."

I smile. "It is for me, too."

Theo puts down his glass and lays his hands flat on the table. "Besides, I feel like we *are* getting it right."

A voice in my head says, *You need to tell him about Mum.*

I dismiss it. "Me too."

I gaze into his dazzling blue eyes, just like I did on our first night on the piazza. And, as the waitress moves in to top up our glasses, I lean forward and kiss him.

Chapter 33

The next day is A level results day, and I'm back on childcare duty. And after spending the day at Angelika's pool, the kids and I have work to do.

In the morning, we move the furniture out of Mabel and Archie's rooms and into the master bedroom of the new family suite. Like the first-floor lounges, this doesn't need replastering, as its walls are made of exposed stone and the electrical wiring runs over them—encased in a steel trunking—which meant it was quick and simple to replace. As the new windows were fitted a few weeks ago, the room is pretty much finished. Callum has already slept in it for a few nights, while the builders were replastering his bedroom, and now they need to do the same to Mabel and Archie's. Once we've hauled in the furniture, we spend a while shifting it around to partition the room and create separate spaces. I'm worried the kids might start falling out, but they seem to like the idea of spending a few nights together. Archie, in particular, views it as an adventure.

After lunch, the priority is moving Theo's and my belongings out of the cottage and into Wilf's old bedroom. The builders have already ripped out the kitchenette that was on the lower floor of the cottage—shortly after they ripped out the kitchen from the main house—in order to do the damp proofing. As we don't need a second kitchen, we're going to transform that level into a flexible space: it will mainly be a private lounge for Theo and me but will also have a sofa bed, so it can become another bedroom, and a table, so it has an added function as a secluded working area for Theo. The builders thought the only big job left was to strip out and refurbish the bathroom, but this morning discovered rotten floorboards that need replacing, pipes that need moving, and blocked, rusty radiators that need both—all of which is going to cost more money. And I've no idea how much I'll be able to generate from the idea I had while talking to Angelika.

More pressingly, all the extra work means Theo and I have to move out. But Theo has back-to-back Zoom and phone meetings so isn't available to help. And the kids were so good this morning, I said they could amuse themselves this afternoon. Thankfully, Giuseppe offers to step in.

Before he arrives, I pile Theo's underwear and mine into a suitcase, then stuff in the boxes of letters and the stone. Then I lug the suitcase through to Wilf's old bedroom and take the boxes out and tuck them under the wardrobe, which is where I originally found them. I've no idea when I'll get a quiet moment to read Mum's second letter. But again, I'm not sure that's a bad thing.

Giuseppe and I drag through racks of clothes, bags of shoes, towels, toiletries and the basket of laundry. Each time we pass through the study, I mouth an apology for disturbing Theo. In return, he mouths an apology for not being able to help.

I make the final few trips alone while Giuseppe stays in the cottage to dismantle the rickety old MDF wardrobe. As I pass Theo one last time, he steps out of his Zoom meeting, puts his arms around my waist and nuzzles my neck.

"Do you have any idea how much I love you?" he whispers.

I smile, coyly. "You might have to show me."

He nibbles on my shoulders. "I will—tonight."

"Dad!" shouts Callum from outside, panic in his voice. "You need to come now!"

Theo's face darkens and he rushes over to the window. "What's the matter?"

"Archie's had an accident!"

My stomach falls away.

Theo excuses himself from his meeting and springs into action. "Where is he?" he shouts, as he flies downstairs.

Callum's face has gone the color of watery porridge and he's yanking frantically at his fringe. "At the castle."

Theo's forehead creases. "The castle? But you're not supposed to go up there on your own."

"Sorry," Callum burbles, as he and Theo rush towards the hill. "Please don't be mad at us."

I rush after them, trailing a few paces behind.

"Never mind that," commands Theo, "just tell me what happened."

Callum's panting. "Archie was looking for the dungeon and started poking at this little hole with a stick," he garbles. "And then the ground just caved in and he fell through."

Theo bolts up the steps, two at a time. "Bloody hell, into what?"

"I don't know, but it looks deep."

"Bloody *hell*!"

When we reach the top of the hill, we pass the equipment from the dig, which the team stack and cover with a plastic sheet each day when they leave. A few meters to the left, Mabel is crouching in the undergrowth, over a hole. She, too, is whey-faced.

"Dad!" she bleats. "He's down here!"

Theo rushes over and kneels down.

"Can you get him out?" Mabel asks, her chin trembling.

"Look, let's all just try to stay calm." Theo activates the torch function on his phone and shines it into the hole. "Archie?"

"Dad," comes a muffled response.

I stand behind Theo and try to peer over his shoulders into the hole.

"Dad, my ankle's killing!" Archie shouts. "Please get me out!"

I can just about make out his little, whimpering face, his glasses gone, his eyes blinking in the light. Fear slices through me, chased by a rush of love.

"I need a ladder," Theo says. "Does anyone know where there's a ladder?"

"I do!" I yelp. "I'll go and get it!"

I dash down the hill so quickly that I trip over a tree root and almost tumble down the steps. I grab onto the handrail and take care as I continue down. When I arrive at the garage, Giuseppe is throwing pieces of the old wardrobe into the skip.

"Everything is alright?" he asks.

I give him a brief summary of what's happened as I grab the ladder.

Giuseppe grabs the other end. "I help."

The two of us carry the ladder up to the castle, my heart pounding.

As soon as we reach the others, we hand it to Theo, and he asks Mabel to shine his torch into the hole. Then he upends the ladder and slowly lowers it, being careful not to hit Archie. He tests that its footing is secure, then straps his phone onto his belt.

"Hold on, squirt! I'm coming down!"

As Theo steps down—soon disappearing from view—I've no idea what to do and don't like to ask in case I get in the way. Thankfully, Giuseppe grabs onto the top of the ladder and holds it firmly in place.

I peer into the hole but, as the light from Theo's torch jerks and sweeps around, it's difficult to tell what's happening. I can hear him talking to Archie and he seems to be examining his ankle. My heart leaps into my throat.

Just as Theo's gathering Archie into his arms, Archie mewls, "Dad, my glasses!"

There's more jerking and sweeping, then the ladder starts squeaking. Moments later, Theo reemerges. Archie is clinging onto his back, his red hair covered in dust, his left cheek smeared with dirt, his green glasses sitting crookedly on his nose.

"Oh my god!" gasps Mabel.

"I'm so glad to see you!" says Callum.

The relief is like nothing I've known.

Theo lays Archie on a patch of grass, away from the diggers' grid system. I notice his T-shirt is grubby, damp with sweat and ripped down one side. He gently presses on Archie's ankle, and Archie screams.

"We need to get him to hospital," Theo declares. He looks at Giuseppe.

Giuseppe nods. "Let's go."

As I stand watching the two of them carry Archie down the hill, his little ankle flopping by Theo's side, all I can think is I was supposed to be looking after him.

However I look at it, this is my fault.

That evening, I pace around the patio, racked with anxiety. I haven't heard from Theo since he messaged to say Archie was about to have an x-ray. What did it show? And how much pain is he in?

With the builders gone, the house is silent. I decide not to put a record on as it wouldn't feel right. Callum and Mabel are sitting at the table, flicking through their phones, barely making a sound, Callum yanking at his fringe. I feel an itch on my calf and look down to see I've been bitten by a mosquito. Shit!

I realize I've forgotten to put on my spray—which means the kids will have, too. I go inside, grab the can, and hand it to Mabel.

"Come on," I say, "there's no point getting eaten alive."

Once they've both had a spray—and I've put antihistamine cream on my bite—I apply it to myself.

Then I go back to pacing. And a new worry enters my mind. Is Theo going to be angry at me? Is he going to be angry that I didn't look after the kids properly?

I decide to water the garden and plug the hosepipe into the tap on the side of the house. But as I walk around the lawn, sprinkling water onto the increasingly dominant patches of green, I feel a spike of shame. I shouldn't have left Archie. I shouldn't have let Callum and Mabel take him up to the castle.

My shame transports me back to the age of thirteen. Every Sunday I used to visit my dad and Debbie in their new house on the other side of Manchester. Dad often didn't know what to do with me, and if it was sunny, used to tell me to play in the street with Trevor and Keith. Once, Trevor got into a fight with a boy around my age. When it became clear he was losing, I ran to get Dad to break it up. He arrived to find Trevor lying on the ground, nursing a broken arm, the other boy running away. As Dad helped Trevor into the car to drive him to hospital, he looked at me and said, "You were bigger than him." I can still remember the anger and disappointment on his face.

More than thirty years later, it occurs to me that Callum and Mabel may be blaming themselves for what happened with Archie. Particularly Callum, as he's the oldest. And he already worries he's a disappointment to his dad.

I turn to face them. "Are you guys alright?"

They respond with grunts that remind me of the start of our holiday—when they were unreachable, their defenses activated.

"Don't worry, Archie's going to be fine," I assure them. "The worst that can happen is he'll have a few broken bones—nothing that can't be mended."

"Are you sure?" asks Callum.

"Absolutely."

He still looks unsettled.

"You know, your dad's not going to be mad at you," I go on. "I'm not saying he won't tell you off for breaking the rules. But he loves you. Don't forget that."

They both smile. I try to do the same but can't, so turn my back on the kids, switch the hose onto the jet function, and water the borders.

I can't escape the thought that Theo won't be mad at them, but he has good reason to be mad at me. And the more I consider it, the more I think he *will* be mad at me. As soon as he found out what had happened, he hardly even looked at me. He didn't address me at all.

I feel a sickness in the pit of my stomach. Is this it, the moment I always suspected would come? The moment Theo's feelings start to fade and our relationship falls apart?

And to think that last night we had a romantic meal in Lucca. To think that just a few hours ago he put his arms around my waist and asked if I had any idea how much he loved me.

My phone pings to tell me I have a message.

"Is that Dad?" asks Callum.

I transfer the hosepipe to my other hand and lift my phone out of my pocket. "Yeah."

"What does he say?"

I'm not sure whether to read the message out loud, till I see it begins with the words *Panic over.*

"The x-rays showed it's only a sprain," I read. "They've given him some painkillers and strapped up his ankle. We'll be back soon."

My relief is instant, as if someone has flicked a switch.

"Thank fuck!" I want to say—then realize I have.

Mabel giggles. "Don't worry, I'm the same."

"And me," says Callum.

Now I do manage a smile.

I retreat to the tap to switch off the water. "Just don't tell your dad I swore!"

Theo carries Archie up to the top floor and gets him ready for bed. He's already given a full report of what happened at the hospital and now wants to make sure Archie gets a good night's sleep.

Theo props up his crutches against the wall and we all gather round the bed. It's brill to see Archie looking so well. His glasses have been straightened and his face is animated by a grin.

"The doctor said I was really brave!" he chirps.

"I bet she did," I say.

"Can you remember the word she used in Italian?" pipes Theo.

"*Coraggioso!*" warbles Archie.

Theo smiles. "Superb! Now, I'm pleased your brother and sister are sharing a room with you tonight: they can keep an eye on you. Isn't that right, Cal? Mabel?"

Mabel nods, several times. "Yeah!"

Callum picks at his braces. "If you like."

I can tell he's still down on himself.

Theo turns back to Archie. "Now, do you want anything?"

Archie puts his finger on his chin and pretends to be thinking. "Can I have some chocolate buttons?"

Theo laughs. "Before you go to sleep?"

Archie nods. "With a glass of milk."

Theo rolls his eyes and smiles.

"I'll come with you," I say.

We set off down the stairs. I'm desperate to apologize but there's something else I have to say first.

"It might be an idea if you had a word with Callum and Mabel," I begin, once we're in the temporary kitchen. "I think they're feeling guilty about what happened, especially Callum."

Theo opens the fridge and pours a glass of milk. "Well, I do want to talk to them about following rules."

"Yeah, and that's fine, obviously—you're their dad. Just do me a favor and make sure Callum knows you love him. He feels bad about letting you down."

Theo closes the fridge door. "OK, understood. And thanks for the tip-off." He puts the glass of milk down. "Now, are you going to tell me what's up with you?"

"Theo, I'm so sorry!" I blurt out.

Theo wrinkles his forehead. "For what?"

"I know you're pissed off with me. And you've every right to be."

"Ads, I don't know what you're talking about. I'm not pissed off with you in the slightest."

"But if I'd been looking after the kids like I was supposed to, they wouldn't have gone up to the castle."

Theo shakes his head. "I ask the older kids to keep an eye on Archie all the time. These things happen. Honestly, it's not an issue. And I think Archie quite enjoyed his adventure. He's feeling like a brave soldier and can't wait to show the builders his crutches."

I draw in a long breath and let it out. I can feel my anxiety clearing. "OK, as long as you're sure."

"I am sure. And I love you." Theo pushes himself off the table and comes closer to kiss me.

A grin splits my face.

"But that'll have to do you for now," Theo says, grabbing a bag of chocolate buttons. "Before Archie goes to sleep, we've got to call Kate."

"It was bad enough when he gave Archie a haircut that made him look like a thug," Kate barks over the speakerphone.

"I *like* that haircut!" I'm about to say.

But Theo intervenes. "Archie loves that haircut. And I'm the one who said he could have it."

Kate scoffs. "Yes, of course. As usual, it's got nothing to do with Adam."

Theo and I are sitting on the patio, as Kate said she wanted to speak to us alone. It's dark so we've switched on the new lights the builders have fitted onto the front of the house. The phone's lying on the table between us.

"Anyway, this has gone far enough," Kate steams on. "I won't stand for it any longer."

"Won't stand for what?" asks Theo.

"Your boyfriend's irresponsible approach to childcare!"

I reach down and scratch my mosquito bite. I tell myself not to get wound up, with a reminder of what Kate's been through.

"*I'm* responsible for the kids," Theo argues, calmly but firmly. "And I had to work today. Just like you've had to work all summer. That's why you couldn't look after them, remember?"

"Yes, well, I didn't think you'd hand them over to someone who'd laze around and let them run riot!"

"Kate, Adam was working on the house." Theo is keeping his voice down, presumably so the kids won't hear. "We're doing a renovation project, remember?"

"As if I could forget that slap in the face!" she blasts on. "Doing up that massive house he inherited from some rich relative, while I'm slaving away doing up someone else's, trying to make ends meet!"

Theo gives a short sigh. "Kate, you're not 'trying to make ends meet.' I gave you every penny you asked for in the divorce. And the calculations you made were based on you not working. Now you are, I'm happy to renegotiate."

I'm surprised to hear Theo standing up to Kate about finances. In the past, he's rolled over and taken whatever she's thrown at him. I wonder if my message about going easier on himself has got through.

"Well, that's just like you," she hisses. "Or should I say the new you, since *Adam* got his claws into you?"

Why can't she say my name in her normal voice, rather than pronouncing it as if it's the name of some hideous flesh-eating disease? Then I find myself wondering if Kate would hate me quite so much if she knew Theo had cheated on her with a man. If she knew their marriage didn't stand a chance—with or without me.

"But of course, now I'm trying to scrape together a little bit of money," she thunders on, "you want to take it away from me."

"I don't want to take anything away from you," Theo hits back. "I'm pleased you're rebuilding your career."

She gives a high-pitched huff. "Well, I might have to give up this job now. First Callum gets wasted, Mabel drives her bike into a car, all three of them get attacked by a snake, and now Adam's supposed to be looking after Archie and lets him fall into a dungeon. As a mother, quite honestly I'm terrified."

Theo runs his hand over his stubble. "Look, I get you're frightened and I'm sorry about that, but I promise you there's no need."

Kate changes tack and addresses me directly. "Adam, I don't expect you to understand this. Everything you do makes it blatantly obvious you're not a parent."

I become aware of a fluttering sound and look up to see two moths dancing around one of the night lights. I keep my eyes on them as I tell myself not to let her get to me.

Before I can respond, Theo cuts in. "Kate, don't say that. Just because Adam hasn't biologically produced a child doesn't mean he isn't capable of looking after them."

Kate gasps. "Theo, what's happened to you? Stop trying to pass off his negligence as some kind of stand for gay rights. It's quite simple: you let your eight-year-old son be looked after by someone who isn't capable."

"No," Theo says, "Adam and I let Archie be looked after by his older brother and sister. Just like you do when you're busy. What's the difference?"

"How many times do I have to say it? I'm their *mother*! Not some skank you picked up online!"

"Mum, don't talk to Adam like that!"

I turn around to see Callum standing in the doorway, Mabel cowering behind him.

"Bloody hell." Theo shoots up out of his seat. "Cal, Mabel, you're supposed to be upstairs."

But Mabel ignores him. "Mum, you're lying!"

Kate sounds like she's got something stuck in her throat. "Shouldn't you be in bed, sweetheart?"

"Lying about what?" Theo says.

"She isn't working!" Mabel shrieks.

"Mabel, sweetheart." Kate's tone has suddenly become much softer, more conciliatory.

But Mabel isn't having any of it. "Mum, I'm not covering up for you anymore! You only said you had a job because you wanted to get rid of us!"

She bursts into tears.

"Mabel, that's not true," Kate insists. "I didn't want to get rid of you at all."

Theo scratches his cheek. "But what about the job, Kate? Does it exist or not?"

There's a pause.

"It did," Kate says, tartly. "But it fell through. I didn't tell you because I didn't want you to gloat."

Theo folds his arms. "And when exactly was this?"

But I don't listen to her answer. Because I'm worried about Mabel, whose crying is becoming louder.

I stand up and go over to put my arms around her. And she crumples into me.

Chapter 34

I've hardly stood still all day.

First thing this morning, I showed Luisa and her team the hole Archie fell down. Part of me worried we might have committed some kind of crime by poking around on what's effectively an archaeological site, but all the diggers were thrilled and went down the ladder to explore. They didn't just find a shaft but a whole chamber, although they've said they need to call in specialized structural engineers to check it's safe before they do any further exploration. Luisa told us they were planning to move onto this section of the site next week, but we didn't mention this to Archie: we told him he was a hero for finding a secret room. He lapped up the glory and loved showing everyone his crutches.

After this, we set up Archie with all his action figures on a rug on a shaded section of the lawn, while I supervised the cleaning of the new kitchen. It's stunning, with maple wood units, paprika red tiles, counter tops in Carrara marble, and a central island with a breakfast bar and three stools. It still has the same stone floors, together with the chestnut beams and big fireplace—although the soot has been blasted off the back and the witch's cauldron relegated to the wine store—but is a much more sociable space, with a much better flow. Not to mention a built-in double oven, a dishwasher, and a fridge freezer with enough space not just for our food and drink, but Mabel's and my skincare products.

Once everything was clean, we dismantled the temporary kitchen and moved down all the crockery, pots, pans and appliances. The four of us chatted as we worked, and Theo did bring up the subject of what we'd found out about Kate, but neither Mabel nor Callum wanted to go there. All they'd say was that Mabel had found out by mistake the day before we flew here and immediately told Callum. Archie had no idea—and still doesn't, which is how we've agreed things will stay.

At four o'clock, our work is done and I switch my attention onto the job I was hoping to do yesterday afternoon, before Archie had his accident: I'm going to Lucca to see if I can find a jeweler that wants to buy Arnaldo's cigarette case.

When I first had the idea of selling something to pay Giuseppe's mounting bills, I ruled out anything of sentimental value. But then Angelika mentioned that Wilf hated Arnaldo smoking—so I decided it would actually be perfectly appropriate to sell his cigarette case. It was quite dirty when I found it, but I cleaned and polished it and it looks like it's in perfect condition. I've no idea how old it is but the clasp still works and the elastic strap to keep the cigarettes in place is—miraculously—still intact. Theo and I did search online for antique gold cigarette cases but found such a wide range—selling for such a range of prices—it was impossible to gauge how much Arnaldo's is worth. There is some kind of hallmark on it but it doesn't mean anything to either of us.

I tell the kids my plan but downplay the extent of my money worries—I just say I'm looking to cover a few unforeseen expenses. Theo needs to stay at the house to look after Archie and is going to teach him how to get better at walking on his crutches. I was going to ask Callum and Mabel if they wanted to come with me but I sense they're still hurting from last night's conversation with Kate. Until, that is, Callum appears in the doorway and swaps his sliders for trainers.

"I'm coming with you," he announces.

My heart gives a little leap. "Oh, fab. But are you sure?"

He fastens his shoelaces and springs onto his feet. "Yeah, in case you need backup. I don't want anyone taking advantage of you."

I grin and Theo pats him on the back. "Thanks, Cal."

During the drive, I tell Callum I've found three jewelers that, according to their websites, buy secondhand gold. The first is situated on Lucca's main shopping street, Via Fillungo. When we arrive outside, we see it has a beautiful old front, with ornate carved wooden display cases and the shop name in gold lettering. I already know the business was established in 1655 and claims to be the oldest jewelry store in Italy. Plus, an ancestor of the family that owns it apparently set the jewels in the crown of the sculpture of Jesus in Lucca's cathedral. But I didn't look up any pictures of the shop and didn't expect it to be so grand. I feel the excitement leak out of me. They're not going to be interested in my little cigarette case. It probably isn't even real gold.

"Come on," says Callum. "Shall we do it?"

I don't have the heart to let him down, so open the door.

We step inside, under vaulted ceilings painted with frescoes and hanging with crystal chandeliers. There's a checked marble floor and more ornately carved display cases, these ones lined with plush blue velvet. In them stands a dazzling array of antique jewels, silver and gold.

"This is going to be embarrassing," I whisper to Callum. "Let's abort mission."

"Buonasera!" calls an elderly man from behind the counter. He has white, receding hair and a moustache and is wearing a plum-colored suit and leaning on an antique silver-topped cane. *"Posso aiutarla?"*

"Go on," says Callum, giving me a nudge in the small of my back. "I'm right behind you."

"Buonasera," I begin. Then I slip into English. "I'm looking to sell something. But you know what, you're probably not interested."

"I am interested in all beautiful things," the man corrects me, as he walks towards us. "Please, show me."

I approach the counter and hand over the case. The man rests his cane on the side and pulls out some kind of big x-ray gun that he presses onto the gold and fires, giving himself a reading. He also weighs it on a set of digital scales and touches a magnet to it. Then he holds it up to the light, turning it a few times and peering in to examine the detail. He does this for so long that my eyes wander to the jewelry in the display cases. I spot an M on a chain that reminds me of the S Mum used to wear and run up and down the chain as she was talking.

I clear my throat. "So what do you think?" I ask the man.

"*Bello,*" he says, approvingly. "*Bellissimo.*" His face may be wrinkled and marked with liver spots but his eyes are bright and engaged.

I lean on the marble counter. "What, so you like it?"

"Yes, very much." He runs his finger over the edges and tests the clasp. "Cases like this were typically given by wealthy families to their sons on important birthdays. In Italy, the eighteenth birthday is more important than the twenty-first."

I winch an eyebrow in interest but my attention has snagged on the word *wealthy*. That sounds promising.

The man takes out a magnifying glass to read the hallmark. "Like all cigarette cases made by this atelier, this is eighteen carat gold."

Callum shoots me a look, as if to say, *Is that good?*

In return, I shrug: I've no experience of dealing with gold. I don't even think I've owned any.

"It was made in 1939," the man goes on. "As you know, that is the year war broke out."

"Of course." I'm about to add that my great-granddad fought in the war but stop myself when I remember he fought on the opposite side. If my great-granddad bore a grudge, maybe this guy does, too.

"These cases were very exclusive and made to commission," the man goes on, not taking his eyes off it. "Only a handful were made each year, but in 1939 people did not want to spend their money as they did not know what was coming. So the atelier made only one."

I push myself up from the counter. "*One*? And this is it?"

The man puts the case down and looks me in the eye. "Yes. I have always wondered where it was. And now it is here."

Behind me, a clock chimes. I can't see it but it sounds old, with cogs and wheels turning. I glance at Callum and he nods, urging me on.

"So how much is it worth?" I ask.

The man takes a pad of headed notepaper and writes down a figure. He rips off the top sheet and slides it across the counter. "This is what I offer you."

"Fuck!" I blurt out. I turn to Callum. "Sorry."

"Fuck!" Callum repeats. "Let's not tell Dad."

The man behind the counter chortles. "Or as we say in Italian, *mamma mia*."

"*Mamma mia*!" Callum and I chime, loudly.

"So you are happy?" asks the man, his eyes moist and sparkling.

"Yes," I almost screech, "we'll take it!"

Callum elbows me. "Wait a minute, we've got an appointment at that other place, remember?"

"Do we?" I'm about to ask. Then I realize he's reminding me to stick to the plan. "Oh, sorry, yes. We're going to shop around, if you don't mind. But we'll be back in touch."

I pick up the case and hurry out of the shop before I can change my mind. "*Arrivederci!*" I call out over my shoulder.

The man shouts something back but the door closes before he can finish.

I stagger to the nearest wall and lean on it. "I can't believe it," I splutter. "I had no idea."

"Me neither," says Callum, his face ablaze. "That is proper mint!"

My heart feels like it's going to burst out of my ribcage and I gulp in some air. As it's the start of the *passeggiata*, the street is thronged with people, buggies and dogs. It's so noisy and colorful it's making me dizzy.

"Are you alright?" asks Callum.

"Yeah, sorry, it's just I really needed it to be good news," I manage, straightening myself up. "But this means I can pay for all the extra building work and can stop worrying about money."

Callum frowns. “I didn’t know you *were* worried about money.”

“Well, yeah,” I say. “But not anymore. That bloke’s offer will pay for everything, with quite a bit leftover. Are you sure we shouldn’t just take it?”

Callum squares his shoulders and stands with his legs apart. “No, we’re doing the right thing. That dude seemed legit and everything but it’s only our first offer: we might get even more from the next place.”

I nod. But I feel a spasm of self-doubt. “Just a minute, can I really sell it?”

Callum pulls at his fringe. “Why do you say that?”

“I don’t know, it just feels like it doesn’t really belong to me. Like I’ve stolen it or something.”

“Who from? Who else could it belong to?”

A blond woman carrying a sausage dog walks past and scowls at us.

“I don’t know,” I answer. “Signor Mancini did say I inherited the house and everything in it. But what if Arnaldo has some younger relatives kicking about?”

Callum shrugs. “So what if he does? That case legally belongs to you. And anyway, why should his family get their hands on it?”

I lean back on the wall. “Well, they paid for it, presumably.”

“But it was a present. And they disowned him, didn’t they?”

I fold my arms. “Yeah. They were total homophobes.”

“Well, it serves them right then.”

I push myself off the wall. “Callum, you are spot on.”

I take out my phone and look up the address of the next jeweler’s.

“Are we off, then?” says Callum.

“Yeah, let’s make some money.”

Chapter 35

After a late night celebrating my unexpected windfall—and christening the new kitchen with a gorgeous meal of seafood gnocchi and chicken *saltimbocca*—I finally get the chance for some time on my own. I know just how I'm going to use it.

It's Saturday, so a day off work—and it's great to have some respite from the builders' banging, plus to know there aren't a group of near-strangers coming and going at the castle. Theo has taken all three kids to the museum in Camaiore, where he's arranged to meet Vito, who's showing them an exhibition on what life was like in a medieval castle. I would have gone with them but spotted the opportunity to read Mum's second letter. Although I still have mixed feelings about this, I need to seize my chance.

I retrieve the shoebox from under the wardrobe, make myself comfortable on Wilf and Arnaldo's old bed, and slide the letter out of the envelope.

Dear Uncle Wilf,

I'm glad you're not annoyed at me and I'm sorry nobody told you about your mum and dad, that's really bad. But it sounds like you'd already made peace with it, or with not having them in your life. Good for you, I say.

I loved hearing about your life in Italy and teaching adults to speak English sounds like a mega interesting job or at least more interesting than mine. I can't believe someone from our family is living such a glamorous life and that Lucca sounds like ~~summat~~ something out of a film. You should be dead proud of yourself moving there and making it work, although I'm sorry to hear about all the crap you've had to put up with. I can't believe you and Arnaldo had to set up a fake bedroom. I hope things are getting better now.

Between us, I think our Adam might be gay. And I'm not just talking about a mother's intuition, although I do think mums know this kind of thing. It's more that he's sensitive and a bit feminine and a real mummy's boy, not that I'm complaining about that because I love it. When he ~~were~~ was little he used to walk around the house in my high heels and I know he's been in my make-up bag a few times and I think he might have tried my clothes on too, but I don't mind. Although I haven't said ~~owt~~ anything in case he's embarrassed. I love him to bits, but I do worry about what'll happen when he grows up, especially with all this AIDS knocking about. One of the girls in the shop had a hairdresser who died of it and it sounds like the worst thing ever and can you believe the same bloke got queer bashed a few years back? That's what I'm saying, there's a lot to worry about. Anyway, I'd love to know if there's any way you think I can make things better for our Adam because if he is gay I just want him to be happy. And it's not as if he can stop being gay, is it? Not that I'd want him to as then he wouldn't be our Adam.

Speaking of being happy, thanks for not thinking I'm a bad person for falling for Gary. And what you said about forbidden love is so true—yes, it is romantic. Mind you, my Gary isn't that romantic, I'd say he's more the strong silent type. But he's very passionate. He can't keep his hands off me sometimes, not that I'd want him to—between us I egg him on. Although please don't think I'm a slag or ~~owt~~ anything because I'm not and this is the first time I've cheated on Mart and that's why I know this is special and not just some fling.

And thanks for your advice. I agree with what you said and I've got to do what feels right and makes me happy. So I've decided I do want to be with Gary and I want to live with him so I'm going to leave Mart. It's a good job I've made that decision as it looks like I'm going to have to get on with it soon. This nosey cow on the reception of the hotel where we go saw my surname and asked if I ~~were~~ was any relation to our Julie. You see we always check in under my maiden name Treadwell and there aren't that many Treadwells, which I'm sure you remember as you're one. Apparently this woman ~~were~~ was at school with our Julie which is just my luck but I pretended I'd never heard of her, even though I could tell she knew I was lying. Flamin eck, she wouldn't stop banging on about it! She kept saying she was sure our Julie had a sister! Anyway, that ~~were~~ was this Friday night and I know she must have said ~~summat~~ something because our Julie's been trying to get hold of me ever since and I can't avoid her forever. I know what she's like, if she can't get me she'll just come into the shop on her dinner break. She won't blab to anyone or ~~owt~~ anything like that but I know she'll try and talk me out of it and I don't want to be talked out of it and I don't want her to make me feel bad. I've no idea if this receptionist will tell anyone else, but I wouldn't put it past her as I can tell she's got a gob on her. So I've spoken to Gary and he went a bit quiet at first but he's come round now and we've decided we're going to take the plunge.

I've found a house for us to rent in Longsight but it's not going to be ready till the middle of May so I've booked two weeks' holiday off work. I got away with it because my boss isn't married and doesn't have kids so she didn't even realise it's not the school holidays and I wouldn't be going away with our Adam. Having said that, I'm sure some of the girls will ask questions once they find out. Anyway, the idea is for me and Gary to get out of the country for a bit, just till everything has calmed down, and come back when the house is free. I'm not good with money but I've been saving up for a while and now I've paid the deposit I reckon I've got just enough left over for our flights and spends. You did invite me to come and stay with you some time and I'm sorry to put this on you so soon when you hardly know me but would you mind if me and Gary came the first weekend in May? That way I can write a letter to Mart explaining what's happened and me and Gary can have some time to ourselves and then come back to Manchester when the dust has settled and move into our new place and get Adam to come and move in with us. I will miss him and I'd love to bring him with us but it wouldn't be fair on him, it'd be too much for him. I'm sure when he's old enough he'll understand why I had to do it and I'm sure one day the three of us will come back to Italy as a family. It seems funny using that word about me, Gary and our Adam but I do think we'll be a family and I'm sure Adam will like Gary once he gets to know him.

But the main thing right now is I've got to make the break and get everything set up for me and Gary. And funnily enough, I ~~were~~ was thinking that we went to an Italian restaurant the first time he took me out so it's actually a nice coincidence if we come to Italy, although now that I've written that I'm not sure coincidence is the right word. But you know what I mean, it's like it was meant to be or ~~summat~~ something and I hope you agree but I think you probably will because it sounds like me and you think the same about a lot of things.

So what do you reckon, Uncle Wilf? Please let me know if you and Arnaldo are up for it as soon as you can. Sorry to put pressure on you but I've got to get a move on and sort all this out before that silly cow in the hotel starts blabbing our secret to anyone else because if she does it'll end up being a right mess all round. Oh and if you say yes please let me know your phone number so I can call you from the shop and we can make arrangements. You are mega and the best uncle in the world.

With lots of love and kisses from,
Suzanne xxx

I realize I've been scratching my mosquito bite and make myself stop.

I feel dizzy and my heart rate is at a canter. I put the letter down and lean back against the headboard, drawing in deep, calming breaths.

So Mum was going to leave Dad and was planning to come here. And not just that but she knew I was gay, she always knew. And she didn't mind. She still loved me.

On the other hand, I'm shocked that she wasn't just going to leave Dad but move in with Gary—and take me with her and make him my stepdad. And by the sounds of it, Wilf encouraged her! Although I've no idea what he said about her plan for the two of them to come to Italy. Did he agree? And what did Arnaldo think about it?

Through the open window, I hear the sound of a siren coming from an ambulance down in the valley. I fill my lungs and let out a long breath.

I look at the date on the letter and confirm it's just a few weeks before Mum died. So what happened? She didn't leave and I don't remember anyone trying to stop her leaving, although it's possible people would have kept that from me. But did Dad know?

Even if we were close, I couldn't ask him. What if he has no idea Mum cheated on him and thinks everything was fine? What if he asks to see the letters and finds out she didn't love him anymore?

And there's another thing: now I know what was going on in

Mum's life, now I know how she felt about me, I can't see any reason why she would have killed herself. So maybe she did have an accident on a night out with Auntie Julie. But just before she was planning to leave?

No, there's something not quite right about this.

And there's only one way for me to get to the bottom of it.

Chapter 36

It's my birthday.

I'm woken up with a kiss and several presents from Theo. He gives me a coffee-table book on Tuscan interiors, a floral-patterned shirt I liked when we saw it in a shop in Pietrasanta, and a black leather man bag—after I noticed several Italians carrying them and commented that they must come in useful.

"I reckon it can fit in my phone, wallet, keys and your reading glasses," I observe.

"Now you're forty-six, you're going to be needing your own reading glasses," Theo quips.

I hit him with a pillow.

At this point, the kids come barreling in. Callum and Mabel sit at the bottom of the bed and Archie climbs in between us—and they all wish me Happy Birthday. They announce they've booked the five of us into a beach club in Viareggio for the day, which Theo helped them plan. I'm delighted.

We arrive mid-morning and have a wonderful day. Archie is allowed to come off his crutches but has to take it easy, so we mainly stay in the pool, playing diving and ball games and making sure he doesn't run too much around the sides. We also go for a walk on the beach—with Theo giving Archie a piggyback—and a little dip in the sea, which is much colder than I expected. But no one complains. No one complains about the sand, either—and there's no mention of jellyfish or sea urchins. When we make it back to the club, I have a read and a nap, much to the amusement of the kids, who rib me about being an old man.

On arriving back at the house, Theo and the kids announce I'm having a night off cooking and they're making me a special birthday dinner. As I shower then get changed in our temporary bedroom, I can hear Theo teaching the kids what we learned on our course back in Manchester, that all Italian sauces are built on a base of chopped onion, carrot and celery—called a *soffritto*—to which they're adding garlic and olive oil.

But when I go downstairs to fix us a drink, I see they're making a mess of the new kitchen. There are vegetable peelings all over the floor, Bolognese sauce splattered on the new tiles, and someone has dropped a bag of spaghetti, which has shattered into hundreds of pieces and rolled everywhere. I don't mind, though. I don't mind in the slightest.

"The best meals come out of the messiest kitchens," I chirp, before leaving them to it.

I sit outside and sip my Prosecco. Our garden is much more colorful and healthier now I've been looking after it and Theo has used a pair of shears to cut the lawn—which is almost completely restored to green. Although these days we don't just have to contend with mosquitoes: as it's the second half of August, there are wasps hovering around the grapes. Actually, I wonder if they might be worker bees, the symbol of Manchester. It would be fitting if they were, but they're very big: could they even be hornets? Whatever they are, they don't seem to be interested in me. So I pay them no attention and catch up on my texts and WhatsApps.

I have two missed calls from Auntie Julie, followed by a text.

"Happy Birthday, chuck!" it reads. "I've got your prezzie but am saving it till you're back. If you don't have something to come home for you might stay there forever!"

"Thanks but don't worry," I reply, "I'll definitely be home. But I'm having a fab day and the kids are cooking me a birthday tea. Can I call you tomorrow? Xx"

Julie hasn't retired yet but recently moved down to part-time hours. I know she isn't working tomorrow but I hope she doesn't have anything planned. After reading Mum's letters, there's a lot I want to ask her.

I check the WhatsApp group I share with my sisters and find several messages, including various memes of naked men with cakes, party poppers and exploding presents. Gloria has created a GIF superimposing my face onto a raunchy video by the Pussycat Dolls, suggesting I recreate the dance routine for Theo later.

"If I do, I'll be celebrating my next birthday alone," I joke.

"You shouldn't get boring in the bedroom just because you're an old lady," Gloria messages back.

"If I try and slut-drop now I'll probably put my back out," I type back.

While reading their irreverent replies, I receive an individual message from Ian.

"How are you feeling, my sister?" he asks.

Ian knows I often miss my mum on my birthday—although I haven't told him what I've found out. This time, I'm definitely going to tell Theo first.

"Good, thanks," I reply. "I'm really enjoying this one."

"And how are you finding being forty-six?" he asks.

"It's not as bad as I thought. Getting older is fine when you're getting it right."

"When you've got what you always wanted," adds Ian.

I'm about to correct him with a reminder that I didn't really know I wanted kids, but stop myself. "Yeah, it's brill."

Then the kids come out with dinner and I have to say goodbye.

As soon as the meal is served, it becomes clear it's rank. The salad is drenched in a dressing that contains way too much balsamic vinegar, the pasta has been overcooked till it's disintegrating, and the Bolognese sauce is unseasoned and so bland it tastes like baby food. But I love it, because the kids have made it. They've made it for me.

"This is fab!" I gush, as I help myself to more. "Thanks a lot, kids."

I watch as all three of their faces are illuminated by grins.

Theo gives me a smile that's more knowing. He turns to the kids. "You've done an outstanding job, gang."

"Woo-woo!" cheeps Archie, directing an overfull spoonful of Bolognese into his mouth and spilling half of it down his shirt.

Theo has opened a bottle of Chianti and fills our glasses.

After dinner, he produces a cake he confesses he and the kids didn't make but bought from the bakery in Camaiore, and the four of them sing "Happy Birthday." As I blow out my candles, they chime in with "*Buon compleanno,*" which Theo must have looked up on his translation app. Callum and Mabel take several pics, with various combinations of subjects, various setups, and various reshoots. But I'm happy to pose for them all. I don't even have to blot my skin as it's less greasy and much clearer since Mabel overhauled my routine. Then we cut into the cake, which is made of sponge and contains rum, custard, chocolate and whipping cream. And it's gorgeous.

I notice Callum posting one of the pics he's taken on Instagram. When the kids go inside to load the dishwasher and Theo follows to supervise them cleaning the kitchen, I have a quick look. It shows the five of us sitting around the cake, with me at the center. And underneath, he's written the caption, *Happy Birthday, Adam!* and has added *#fam.*

I feel like I'm glowing with happiness. I listen to the four of them giggling and am not sure I've ever had a better birthday.

I check the rest of my social media, including liking all the Happy Birthday messages that have been posted on my Facebook page. Then I see I've received an email from my dad.

Something inside me shrinks.

But this time I know I can't ignore it.

I open it and start reading.

Happy birthday, lad! Hope ur having a good un. Sorry to disturb u but just to let u know me and Debbie are going on a last minute holiday to Umbria next Sunday. The doctor Debbie used to work for has a caravan and they've had a cancellation so have given us the week. Isn't that nice? It sounds a bit posher than we're used to but we're looking forward to it. Is Umbria near u?
Dad

Shit. Is he angling to meet up?

"What are you reading?" asks Theo. He takes a seat next to me and retrieves his glass of wine.

"Nothing important," I say.

"Is it from your dad?"

I rear back in my seat. "Why do you say that?"

Theo rubs his stubble. "I can tell from your face. Nobody else makes you look like that."

I reach for my wine. "Like what?"

"Nervous. Ashamed. Unsure of yourself."

I knock back the contents of my glass. "Alright, alright. It's supposed to be my birthday." I hope I don't sound tetchy.

But Theo doesn't seem offended. "What does he say?"

"They're going to Umbria, apparently. Next week." I show him the email.

Theo scratches his ear. "Umbria really isn't far, you know. Well, it depends where they are exactly. But why don't we find out and see if we can meet up?"

Theo has only met Dad once—a few months ago, when Debbie retired from her job as a GP's receptionist and threw a party. It was a big event so we only got to speak for five minutes, which is one of the reasons I'd agreed to go. But he's been suggesting the four of us get together ever since.

He sags back in his chair. "You know, it might be good to spend some time together while we're all relaxed and in holiday mode."

"Dad!" shouts Mabel. "What program do we put the dishwasher on?"

"Coming!"

While Theo's inside, I consider his suggestion. I have been feeling bad about giving Dad such a hard time when he got together with Debbie. Being subjected to Callum and Mabel's hostility at the start of the summer brought back how awful I'd been as a teenager. Well, now I've got the opportunity to make up for it.

And not just that but the news of Mum's affair has made me think. Maybe Dad found out about it and was gutted. If Julie suspected—and even I could tell something was going on—then it's quite likely he did. But would that change anything? It may have made his feelings more complicated when Mum died but it shouldn't have altered the way he felt about me.

I watch two wasps buzzing around a bunch of grapes. They join together and drop down a few inches, suspended in the air. I can't tell if they're playing, mating or fighting. But I suddenly realize how dangerous it is to have them living so close. What if they sting one of the kids? We'll have to set some traps. Mice are one thing—not only are they cute but they run away at the first sight of a human—but wasps are nasty.

As I move to a seat farther away, another thought occurs to me: if Mum knew I was gay, wouldn't she have told Dad? Wouldn't they have discussed it? So why didn't he make things easier for me?

"What do you think, *mio tesoro*?" asks Theo, sliding back into his seat.

I look at him and realize once again just how much I love him. Just how much he loves me.

I'm about to tell him what I've learned about Mum—and how it could have impacted on Dad—but stop myself.

"No, thanks," I say, "I don't want to. I don't want to rake all that up again. I'd rather just let it lie."

There's a pause.

"What is it?" Theo says, his brow furrowed. "What is it you're not telling me?"

I press my hand to my heart. "Nothing, *mio carissimo*. Well, it's not nothing exactly, but I'd rather not talk about it."

"But we're a team, remember? You're not on your own anymore, Ads."

I want to let him in—I really want to—but I can't. Something's holding me back.

"Yeah, I know, I just don't understand it yet. But I will tell you. Just let me get my head around it first."

Theo nods. "Alright, fine."

I shut down my email and put my phone away. "Right, how's that kitchen looking?"

Chapter 37

"A party?"

"Yeah," I say, "a party."

It's the start of our fifth week in Italy and I've had a progress update from Giuseppe, who's assured me that the builders are still on course to finish at the end of the following week—just about. Now that they've replastered Mabel and Archie's bedrooms, they're currently painting them lilac and sky blue: we needed colors the kids liked but that would also be understated enough to work for guests. Archie originally wanted his favorite color green, but he insisted on a bright green and didn't like any of the paler shades I suggested—so we settled on the sky blue of Manchester City's kit. Once the painting was underway, I checked my finances and saw I still have plenty of money left over from the sale of the cigarette case. So I've gathered everyone together in the big lounge—which bears no traces of its former role as a temporary kitchen—and have just suggested throwing a party to celebrate the launch onto the rental market of the Castello Montemagno.

"Only a little one," I elaborate. "Obviously, we don't know that many people in Italy. But we could invite Luisa and Stefano, Angelika, Giuseppe and the builders, everyone on the dig, and even people like Vito and our lawyer, Signor Mancini. We could do drinks and a buffet and make pizzas and show everyone what we've done with the place."

"Can we play games?" asks Archie, Thor in hand.

"Of course," I say. "We can organize them together and you can be our games master!"

"Woo-woo!"

"Can we invite Freya?" asks Mabel, her hair pulled back in a ponytail to show off her newly emerging cheekbones.

"Absolutely," I reply.

"And Lina?" asks Callum, a little bashfully. Since last week, he and Lina have been messaging and have arranged to go for a walk later today, followed by pizza in the village.

"Yeah, it would be brill to see her," I say. "So what do you think?"

Callum smiles. "I think it sounds mint."

"Same," chips in Mabel. "And I've just thought, I could create loads of content for our social media accounts. If we get all the guests to share and tag us in, we could start building up our following."

"Fab!" I turn to Theo. "And what do you think, *mio carissimo*?"

Theo runs a hand over the hairs on his forearm. He breaks into a grin. "It's a superb idea, *mio tesoro*."

I grin back at him.

We decide to throw the party on our last night in Italy—a week on Saturday. And for the rest of the morning, the five of us launch ourselves into planning the guest list, designing a digital invitation, and sending it out. It's almost enough to take my mind off the phone call I've arranged to make later.

But not quite.

Once the builders have left, Theo goes out for a run, Callum goes off to meet Lina—having changed out of his football shirt and asked for a spray of my aftershave—and Mabel goes to meet Freya to show her the kittens. Only Archie's left and I set him up watching a Marvel series on Theo's iPad. Then I go outside, over to the cluster of trees where we've set up the hammocks, where I know he won't hear me. I climb into one of them and lie down, telling myself I need to be as relaxed as possible while I do this.

I call Auntie Julie.

I start by updating her on the holiday and my birthday celebrations, then check in on the Airbnb lettings in Manchester. "And there's something else I want to talk to you about."

I recognize the sound of Julie putting her feet up on the pouffe. "What's that, chuck?"

I fix my eyes on a little cloud, slowly drifting across the sky. "I found Mum's letters. To Uncle Wilf."

There's a pause. I keep my eyes fixed on the cloud.

When Julie eventually speaks, her voice is quieter, more faltering. "And what did they say?"

"They said she was having an affair," I answer, almost shocked to hear the words coming out of my mouth. "With some bloke called Gary. And that she was going to leave Dad and wanted to come to Italy for a bit."

There's a taut silence.

"So you know," Julie says. "I guess there's no point protecting you any longer."

"No." One of my sliders falls over the side of the hammock. "I think you need to tell me everything."

"Are you sure?"

"Yeah. Absolutely."

Julie gives a long sigh, then swallows.

"In the last year of your mum's life," she begins, "I sensed something wasn't right with her, but whenever I asked, she just denied it. Then I got a phone call from this girl Lauren I used to go to school with. Well, she was a woman by then, obviously, and working in a hotel in town. To be honest, I always thought she was a nasty gossip and I didn't like her—I didn't like her one bit. Anyway, she said there was this woman coming into the hotel who she was sure was my sister and did I know she was having an affair?"

I straighten out my legs. "And what did you say?"

"Well, I knew it was our Suzanne, as soon as she said it, I knew it. But I lied through my teeth and said I had no idea what she was on about. But Lauren said she was only trying to look out for me and the bloke your mum was seeing was trouble."

"In what way? What did she mean?"

"I don't know, chuck. I told you, I couldn't stand the woman and I could tell she was enjoying the drama. So I made some excuse and pretended I had to go."

"And then what happened?"

Julie breathes in and out, slowly. "I confronted our Suzanne about it. At least I did when I finally got hold of her. She avoided me for ages and I had to tell my boss I had a dentist's appointment so I could get out of work early and wait for her at the bus stop. The second she clapped eyes on me, I knew what Lauren had said was true. She had a guilty look on her face."

I sit up. "And what did she say?"

"Well, at first she didn't say anything. She pretended she was in a rush and had to get home. But I said if she didn't tell me what was going on, I'd come back every day till she did."

By now the anxiety is screeching through me. "And did she?"

"Yeah. We went and sat on a bench in Piccadilly Gardens and she smoked about ten cigs and told me she'd fallen in love with some fella called Gary and she was going to leave your dad. I begged her not to and she said she knew I wouldn't understand and that's why she hadn't wanted to tell me. She said it was easy for me because I was happy on my own and didn't understand what it was like to be in love."

Suddenly desperate to stretch my legs, I get up out of the hammock and retrieve my slider. "That wasn't very nice of her."

"Well, that's what sisters are like. Brothers, too, I imagine. Our Suzanne was always jealous of me for getting into grammar school and I was always jealous of her for having her pick of the fellas, especially now people had started saying I was on the shelf. At the time, I wanted to get married and have kids but I was starting to face the fact it might never happen. And here was my sister, who had everything I wanted and was chucking it all away. I have to say, I lost my rag with her."

I notice a plant with bright orange flowers, some of which are dead, and start pulling off the heads. "So you had an argument?"

Julie clears her throat. "We did, chuck. Although I didn't tell her what that Lauren had said about her fancy man being trouble. I didn't want to hurt her. Not that it made any difference; she stopped speaking to me anyway."

"And how long was that before she died?"

"Not long. A few weeks?"

I can feel my mouth drying up as I build up to the question I want to ask most. "So how did she die? If you weren't speaking, I take it you two weren't on a night out?"

There's another tense pause. "Well, no, not exactly. But I was there." I get the impression Julie's struggling. "Sorry, this is really difficult."

I toss the dead flowers onto the ground. "I need to know, Auntie Julie. Please don't lie to me anymore."

"I didn't lie to you, Adam. You need to know that. Me and your dad did decide not to tell you certain details, but we never lied to you."

I believe her: the story she's given corroborates exactly what I've read in the letters. "OK, but please stop holding things back. You said you always hated it when older members of the family held things back from you."

"Yeah, but it's not always good to know everything, chuck. There are some things it's better *not* knowing."

I stop still, the anxiety tightening in my chest. I breathe in and out, slowly.

"So did Mum kill herself? Is that it?"

"No," Julie answers, emphatically. "She didn't kill herself."

"Are you sure?"

"Completely sure."

I sink down to the ground, my back coming to rest against the house's bumpy wall. I can feel the lifting of a heavy weight that's been pressing in on me, a heavy weight that's been pressing in on me for so long I'd almost forgotten it was there, that I'd started to think it was part of me, part of who I am. So Mum didn't want to get away from me. I was wrong.

"Look, chuck," Julie breaks in, "it might be better if I sent you an email. It's what we always tell people at work to do when they're getting emotional. And I am getting emotional, and I'm sure you are, too. I need to think straight and not mess this up."

I stare ahead. "But Julie, I really want to know."

"And you will, Adam. You'll just have to hang on a bit longer. Sorry."

I let my head fall back against the wall. "Alright. But please don't take too long."

"So you've found out all that and been keeping it to yourself?" says Theo.

I swallow. "Yeah, I'm sorry."

We're lying in our temporary bedroom, in the room that used to belong to Wilf and Arnaldo, its walls replastered and waiting to be painted. I'm wrapped in Theo's arms and my head's resting on his chest.

"Ads, you don't need to apologize," he says. "I get why it was difficult. I get you had a lot to work out."

I gaze up at the mosquito nets, one of the sides billowing gently as the fan rotates. "And I still am working it out. But now I know Mum didn't take her own life, I feel much better about it."

Theo lets out a breath and I feel it blowing through my hair. "I didn't realize you'd thought that. I didn't realize it had been causing you so much pain."

"Yeah, but it isn't anymore. And I can't tell you how good it feels." I keep my eyes trained on the mosquito net and watch it billow. "Although I still need to get my head around the fact she was going to run off with this Gary. I don't know, I can't believe she was going to make me move house and everything, to move in with some strange bloke. Without the slightest consideration for my feelings."

I feel Theo shifting slightly. "Just a minute, you don't know that. You don't know she didn't torture herself about it."

"I suppose not."

"Try and think about what it must have been like for your mum. It can't have been much fun to be trapped in an unhappy marriage—I can vouch for that. And it sounds like she did her best to make things work."

"Yeah, she stuck it out for a long time, I'll give her that." I reposition myself. "But I need to know what happened in those last few weeks. I need to know how she died."

"Well, when the email comes through, we'll work through it together. And we'll work out a way forward—together."

Happiness rings through me. "Really?"

"Absolutely. We're partners, Ads. Your story is my story."

And he pulls me closer.

Chapter 38

"What do you think, gang?"

We've just entered Pisa's Piazza dei Miracoli and are standing with the Cathedral and Baptistry on our left, the Leaning Tower directly ahead. All the buildings are constructed from the same white marble; every inch of the lawn around them is almost impossibly green, the expanse of sky above uniformly blue. Together, the three elements form a spectacular sight. But the center of attention, drawing crowds of tourists from every direction, is undoubtedly the Tower. And it may be smaller than I expected, but it's much prettier and its lean more pronounced.

"Oh my god," says Mabel. "How does it not fall down?"

"I know," coos Callum. "It's sick."

"So you're glad you came?" Theo teases him.

Callum smiles. "Yeah, I'm glad I came."

Initially, Callum had resisted the idea of spending the day sightseeing, possibly because last night's date with Lina went well and he wanted to see her again. But Giuseppe and the builders told us they'd be fitting the new lights and plug sockets and would need to switch off the electricity. Theo suggested leaving the house and had the idea of visiting Pisa, as it's the only city in the area we haven't seen—and went online to book us tickets for the Leaning Tower.

Walking towards it, we have to weave in and out of tourists chattering away in countless languages, some of them holding up umbrellas to shield their faces from the sun. It's been a long time since I've seen so many people packed so tightly together, and everyone seems so loud, with little awareness of the others around them. I take hold of Archie's hand.

"Let's stick together," I say. "Callum, Mabel, stay close to your dad."

All along the edge of the lawn, tourists are pointing phones and directing friends and family members to interact with the Tower so they can take pictures of them pretending to prop it up, or licking it like an ice cream.

"Can we stop for a minute?" asks Mabel. "I want to take some pics."

"We should probably go inside first," answers Theo. "Our slot's in ten minutes. But don't worry, we'll have plenty of time to do that later."

As we get closer, I notice a group of young men sitting on a section of the marble walkway that curves around the cathedral, so that the Tower rises up like a hard penis between their legs. I remember my sisters joking about Dom's Leaning Tower and think that if they were here, that's exactly what they'd be doing. Although I miss them, it no longer makes my insides drag.

In any case, now isn't the time for grown-up humor: today is about the kids. I gesture to the Tower, before any of them spot the men and their penis.

"Get a load of it in close-up," I say. "It's even more amazing."

"But *why* does it lean?" asks Archie, tilting back so he can take in the length of it.

"I think it's a mistake, squirt," Theo responds, lifting off his Panama and wiping the sweat from his brow. "I read somewhere it was built on soft ground that couldn't take the weight of the marble."

"So it happened naturally?" asks Mabel.

"I think so," says Theo, putting his hat back on.

"Then how can it be a mistake?" Mabel counters.

Theo cocks his head. "Good point."

"And it's proper famous," adds Callum. "If it was straight, nobody would bother coming to see it."

"So maybe it isn't a mistake," I suggest. "More a happy accident."

Everyone nods, satisfied with that assessment.

"What do you think?" says Theo. "Shall we go in?"

On the way back, we call at Viareggio. Theo had the idea of playing a game of football on the beach—mainly to persuade Callum to come on board for the sightseeing—and packed a ball, beach towels and bags for life to use as goal posts.

"It's alright," he says to me, "you just sit at the side and enjoy the sun. Nobody expects you to play."

A few days ago, I told Theo how I feel about football. He was understanding and apologized for trying to persuade me to play on the pitch in Camaiore. I've no idea what he's told the kids, but this time I don't feel any sense of dread.

As it's nearly five o'clock, most people who've spent the day on the beach are leaving and we're able to park the car in one of the side streets just off the front. We find a stretch of sand, Theo sets up the pitch and I make sure everyone's wearing suncream—especially Callum, who's stripped off his shirt. I can't help noticing that the exercise program Dom gave him has started to pay off, and he's filled out ever so slightly—and this has made a big difference to the way he holds himself.

I take the bag, spread out my towel and sit down. But as the kids start discussing teams, I'm surprised to find myself wishing I could join in.

Callum runs over and rummages in the bag for a drink of water. "You know if you change your mind, we'd love you to play," he says. He quickly adds, "But no pressure."

I crinkle my nose. "Thanks, but I'm really crap."

"That doesn't matter," he says, snapping the lid shut on his water bottle, "I'm sick. So if you come on my team, we'll balance each other out." He smiles at me—a wide, uninhibited smile that reveals his braces. And I'm not sure I can resist.

"Go on, then."

I haul myself onto my feet and Callum punches his fist in the air. "Guess what, everyone? Adam's playing!"

The other three cheer loudly and I can't stop a grin spreading across my face. Not for a moment does it occur to me to think back to my schooldays.

"It's me and Adam V," Callum announces. "And we're going to proper batter you!"

"Alright, steady on," I joke. "Don't oversell us."

"Don't worry," chips in Mabel. "I'm not that good but I never let it stop me."

"What's important is we all have a good time," Theo says, smiling. "Ads, I'm over the moon you're playing."

And there he is—my dad.

But the vision isn't given time to linger.

"Give me five," says Archie. He's holding up his arm and I oblige. "I promise I won't tackle you," he says. "But only for the first five minutes."

I chuckle. "Thanks!"

As the sun's low in the sky, we all put on our sunglasses, except Archie, who takes off his green glasses and straps on his sports goggles. As they don't give him any protection against the sun, we decide his team should play with their backs to it, driving the ball in the opposite direction. We run and kick around a bit to warm up but I'm holding onto some tension. Once I've hit the ball a few times, I can feel myself relaxing.

"OK, gang," says Theo. "Shall we kick off?"

Callum quickly takes me to one side to discuss strategy, suggesting that, while we both attack and defend, he should concentrate on driving the ball forward, while I'm the default player to cover goal. I agree but feel a twinge of trepidation.

Like Mabel says, I won't be stopped by self-doubt.

"Right," says Theo, "game on!"

He tosses the ball in the air and, before I know it, I'm running up and down the rectangle of sand. My heart rate rises and the blood starts pumping. By the time I've managed to hit a couple of half-decent crosses to Callum—and even scored my first goal—I'm actually enjoying myself. Before long, I've forgotten I'm a rubbish player—and nobody else seems to notice. Giggles are released, cheers greet each goal, and the adrenaline surges.

A few hours ago, I'd thought the highlight of our day would be the breathtaking views from the top of the Leaning Tower, but this game of football beats it—easily. I watch Archie throwing himself around the pitch, crashing into the sand but bouncing straight up again. Mabel is more authoritative than usual, calling out orders to her dad and brother—and, as she springs around, she doesn't seem remotely conscious of her boobs. And I love seeing Callum looking so confident. When he pulls off a particularly skillful move and his dad compliments him, his face beams with pride. Theo, meanwhile, doesn't stop beaming.

Once again, I'm back on that holiday with Dad, Debbie and my stepbrothers in northern France. But this time it doesn't fill me with negative emotions. It makes me realize that what I'm feeling with Theo and the kids is probably what Dad was trying to instigate: maybe he knew that if I could just get stuck in, it wouldn't matter how bad I was and I'd feel like I belonged. Or maybe he was just in love with Debbie and desperate for his and her sons to bond, the only way he knew how. After all, he must have been devastated when Mum died. He probably just wanted to be happy. And didn't he deserve that?

As the sun slips lower in the sky, I remember something Dad used to say to Mum and me: "Come on, the sun's at half-mast. You'd better hurry up or you'll miss it."

Although he didn't sit with us to watch the sunset, he'd often be the one to tell us it was about to happen. I wonder if he was ever upset that we didn't ask him to join us. I wonder if he ever felt excluded.

To my shock, I find myself thinking that I will get in touch with him. Theo's right: there's no better time than when I'm relaxed and happy.

But I need to read Julie's email first. She promised she'd send it soon.

The ball comes hurtling towards me and I remember what I'm doing. I strike out to kick it, propelling it into the air and towards the opposition's goal.

Chapter 39

On Wednesday, Theo is out of action again, this time to prepare for tomorrow's GCSE results day. I spend the day working on the house, moving Mabel and Archie back into their bedrooms now that the paint on the walls has stopped smelling—or stopped smelling quite so badly. After that, Archie and I empty all the broken and cracked plant pots from the final untouched outhouse—disturbing some enormous beetles, spiders and more lizards—and put them in the skip, while Callum and Mabel go up to Angelika's to hang out by the pool with Lina and Freya. The five of us come together for an early dinner, after which we're expecting a handful of guests. We're gathering to scatter Wilf's ashes.

Angelika is the first to arrive. I know she's left Lina and Freya with their dad, who's landed from Frankfurt and is taking them to Pietrasanta for dinner. I assumed she made this decision because the scattering of Wilf's ashes would be a solemn occasion, but she turns up in full vamp mode, wearing a black trouser suit and boots, a gold studded belt and matching handbag, her nails and lips painted her signature red, a bottle of Prosecco in one hand and the urn containing Wilf's ashes in the other.

"I don't mind admitting, I'm ready to get rid of this," she quips, handing me the urn. "The silver clashes terribly with my jewelry."

I smile.

While we're waiting for Luisa and Stefano, I show Angelika around the house. She loves what we've done with the kitchen, adores the new family suite, and is thrilled to see the pizza oven restored and back in action.

"*Wunderbar!*" she drawls. "You've turned the place into a busy, thriving, welcoming home."

I realize she's right: this has become my home. *Our* home. I wonder if the kids feel the same.

There's a pause that could be classed as solemn when I show Angelika the framed passport photos. But it doesn't last long.

"You know this makes me very happy," she says. "To see Willie and Arnaldo together, expressing such joy. Here, in the heart of your home."

She takes my hand and gives it a tug.

From outside, we hear Theo and the kids greeting Luisa and Stefano.

"Come on," I say, gesturing at the photos, "let's reunite these two."

We step outside and there's a chorus of *buonasera* and some chat between Angelika and the Fiores, who haven't spoken since Wilf's death. While our guests are all dressed in black, Theo, the kids and I don't have enough black clothes, so have just dressed smartly and in dark colors—and I notice that Mabel has put on some light makeup. Once the initial chat is over, I suggest we climb up the hill. While no one's looking I pick up a tote bag I've packed with a little surprise.

Conscious of Angelika's age, I offer to carry the urn so she can hold onto the handrail. She comments on how much easier it is to climb the hill with the new steps—rather than having to scramble.

"That's why I haven't been up for so long," she says, stopping to catch her breath. "*Ach du Scheiße!* I've forgotten how high it is."

"Sometimes I swear I can feel my ears pop," I joke.

Angelika lowers her voice. "It reminds me of my days at the airline. Whenever we were taking off, I used to say to my gay friends, 'Have you got anything to suck on?' And they'd say, 'The pilot's not bad.'"

I roar with laughter.

"What's tickling you?" asks Theo.

"Nothing," I reply, gesturing at the kids. "I'll tell you later."

We reach the top and pass the diggers' equipment on one side, on the other the entrance to the underground chamber, which has been cordoned off. We edge around the grid—each of its squares numbered on little markers in the corners—and over to the wall, and the area Luisa and her team have designated for us. As usual, it's quieter up here, but we can still hear the crickets rubbing their wings together, a few birds chirping, and a light breeze rustling through the trees.

Stefano lets out a groan of pleasure. "The sound of the country breathing!"

We all smile.

I hand the urn to Angelika and take up position next to Theo. We have to stand, as Luisa and her team are in the process of reconstructing the wall, using the stones recovered from the wall that collapsed at the back of the chapel. I take Theo's hand and lace my fingers through his.

The sun is preparing to tuck itself behind the mountain. Again, I notice the imperfection of the view but this time it only seems to add to its beauty. Maybe my time in Italy has made me more romantic, but it strikes me that the rays of the setting sun are skipping over the valley, stroking the surface of the sea, and tickling the underbelly of the little fluffy clouds. I feel an ache of regret that Mum didn't make it here.

Snapping back to the present, I realize I haven't prepared anything to say.

Thankfully, Angelika speaks first. "Willie, I haven't laughed as much since I lost you and I miss you every day. But it's an honor to return you to your happy place, where I hope you'll rest in eternal peace with the great love of your life, Arnaldo."

Again, the mood has tipped into somber.

"Oh and say hello to my Edgar," she tosses in. "Tell him to get lots of golf in because when I arrive all that'll be stopping."

We smile and Theo squeezes my hand.

Angelika gently scatters some of Wilf's gray, finely ground ashes over the hillside, onto the slope along which crawls the vineyard. She passes the urn to Stefano.

Stefano says something in Italian, which Luisa translates as: "You are returning to nature, from where you came. May your energy enrich the earth and give us a bountiful harvest."

Impressed at her vocabulary, I'm now even more worried about what I'm going to say.

"Uncle Wilf," I begin, cradling the urn, "I didn't know you but it's been a privilege to discover your story. Thanks for opening your life up to me. I know yours was sometimes a struggle but I hope it's some consolation to know you got it right. Your bravery and self-belief inspire me every day. And I'm proud to call you uncle."

I tip out some ashes and pass the urn to Theo.

"Wilf, I didn't know you either but you've had a big impact on my life," he says. "Adam and I promise to honor your legacy by making your home our home and filling it with love."

When he hands the urn to Mabel, she looks a little self-conscious. I feel bad that I didn't sit the kids down beforehand and help them come up with something to say. I'm about to tell her she doesn't need to say anything when she starts speaking.

"We love your home," she mumbles. "Thanks for letting us make it ours, too."

"Yeah, it's mint," adds Callum, awkwardly.

But I guess they've answered my question. As they each sprinkle some ashes, I give them a big smile.

Archie takes the urn from his brother, turns around and trots off.

"Archie, where are you going?" I say.

He stops. "I'm putting mine in the dungeon."

"No, darling!" Angelika shouts. "I know it only looks like dust but it's Willie's body and we have to follow strict rules. We only have permission to scatter it over the hill."

Archie frowns and pads back.

"Bye, Uncle Wilf," he says, scattering some ashes over the edge. "I like your castle. And Len and Lionel the lizards. And the pizza oven. But not the snake."

We all smile and pass the urn back down the line to Angelika, who empties out what's left.

"Goodbye, sister," she says.

For a while, we all stand in silence. Thinking about Wilf and savoring the sunset.

"There's one more thing," I throw in.

And from out of my tote bag, I produce the stone inscribed with the names WILF + ARNALDO. I pass it around so everyone can see and explain where I found it. They're all fascinated and the kids run their fingers over the scratched names.

I turn to Luisa. "I was wondering if you and your team could put it back in the wall, with the other stones."

She smiles. "Of course."

Luisa lifts a few stones from the top layer of the wall and slides Wilf and Arnaldo's underneath, explaining that they'll make sure it's secure in the morning. "And their love for each other will always be part of the castle."

Amongst all the buried secrets. I run my hand over the wall.

"Now, I don't know about you," breaks in Angelika, "but I'm desperate for a drink."

I grin. "Come on, let's get down before it goes dark."

I give the wall one last pat and lead everyone back to the path.

"By the way," Luisa says to Archie as we troop down the steps, "that bone we found belonged to a wild boar."

"Oh, no," is his response.

"Don't be disappointed," counters Luisa. "If it had been human, it would have made the dig very complicated."

"Yeah," jumps in Theo. "And you wouldn't want this place to be a crime scene, with police everywhere, would you?" He stops himself. "Actually, don't answer that."

We all laugh.

"And it looks like the underground chamber is safe to explore," Luisa adds. "So we can find out if it really is a dungeon."

Archie's face lights up. "Can I come?"

"We'll definitely make some time to take you down," she says. "After all, you found it!"

I can't see his face but know he'll be beaming.

We reach the bottom of the hill and, just as we're emerging from behind the chapel, I spot a group of wild boars on the patio. I quickly stretch out my arm to hold everyone back.

"Ssssh!"

Stefano is directly behind me. "We must tell them to go," he says.

"Can't we just watch them for a minute?" I protest. "They're not doing any harm."

We all fall silent and watch the boars trotting around the patio, grunting as they sniff at the ground, presumably searching for food. I count seven of them altogether. Three are bigger and darker, with white, bristly hair. The smaller ones are a lighter brown, but gray around the nose and under their bellies.

Theo licks his lips. "I bet they'd taste nice in a pasta sauce," he whispers.

"Dad!" Mabel hisses at him. "Is it a family?" she asks Stefano.

He whispers something to Luisa. "With *cinghiale*, the male does not stay with his mate," she translates. "Groups of females form herds with their young."

Mabel considers this for a moment. "That still counts as a family."

I grin at her. "Absolutely."

One of the smaller boars spots us and the group takes fright, toddling off into the valley.

"Come on," says Angelika, "it's time for that drink."

Chapter 40

The next day, Mabel summons me into the big lounge. Archie's perched in the doorway to the cottage, playing with his figures while also watching the builders, who are creating their usual cacophony of noise. Mabel's sitting with Callum at the dining table, a laptop, iPad and both their phones spread out before them.

"Adam," she declares, "we've got something to show you."

I sit down and they present to me their digital marketing strategy for the Castello Montemagno.

I'm impressed. Callum's website is stylish and slick, and he's worked in the text I gave him about the history of the house—a lot of which came from Luisa—plus information on the village and nearby towns. There are some gorgeous photos that show off the first rooms to be finished, plus plenty of gaps to add more once the refurbishment has progressed. There are some stunning exterior shots of the olive grove, the chapel wall, the castle—viewed from the bottom of the vineyard—and the view from the patio over the valley. Callum's layout, design and graphics are simple but effective, and he's made sure the dominant color is the same turquoise as the front doors. And he's dedicated a whole page to "Instagrammable moments," so far featuring pictures of the hammocks, rope swing and pizza oven. But he doesn't think this is working.

"We need someone *in* the pictures," is his verdict. "Otherwise they just look empty."

"I've got the same problem," chips in Mabel.

She runs through her plans for the social media channels, showing me draft posts on TikTok, Instagram and Facebook. They're nicely shot and do a good job of capturing the look of the property but I agree there's something missing.

"Will you go in them?" she asks.

I rear back. "Me?"

"Yeah," says Callum.

He asks if he can take a pic of me in front of the house and if I'll provide him with a short biography. Although I don't consider myself much of a frontman, I concede that a short section about me and my relationship with the property could help warm it up.

"Alright," I say. "Let's give it a go."

We develop various ideas for social media content and I suggest we start posting on Monday, which is the beginning of our final week in Italy.

"That'll be a good launch day," I say. "The front of the house will be finished tomorrow so we can take pics over the weekend."

The builders have stripped, treated and filled the old front doors so they can repaint them with a color they've had mixed that's exactly the same as the original turquoise. They've just finished ripping up the tiles from the patio—as too many of them were cracked or uneven, not to mention the ones that were dislodged or swept away by the storm—and are about to start relaying it.

Mabel pulls a face. "But Monday's the quietest day of the week on social media."

There's something else I remember from my sisters' WhatsApp chat. "And it's Manchester Pride this weekend, which means Monday's the bank holiday."

"Shall we wait till Tuesday?" suggests Callum.

"That's probs best," agrees Mabel.

I give them a smile. "Fab!"

Behind the closed door to the study, I hear Theo ending a call. It's the day the students get their GCSE results so he has back-to-back meetings again. I fling the door open and grab him before he disappears once more. "Theo, come here for a minute and see what the kids have done."

Mabel shows him her work first and Theo raises his eyebrows. "That's outstanding."

I bring up the website's menu and click through a few pages. "And get a load of this."

Theo nods, slowly. "Cal, I knew you were good but this is bloody amazing."

Callum looks like he's struggling to suppress a smile. "I just used a basic website builder."

"Well, the results are anything but basic," Theo says. "We should definitely talk about you doing that Computer Science A level. It would work really well with PE and Business."

Callum can't suppress his smile any longer. "Yeah, alright."

"You know, Ian was saying he needs a new website," I contribute. "He's not got much money but he's crap at tech. I'm sure he'd appreciate your help."

Callum nods, quickly. "That'd be sick."

I take out my phone. "Let me do a quick email intro."

I open up my app but see an email sitting at the top of my inbox from Auntie Julie.

Fear catches in my throat. What does she say?

I can't read it now. I'll have to make some time later.

After an hour of being unable to concentrate on anything, I slip away to make myself a coffee. Just as I'm flipping the lid of the moka and see it's starting to boil, Theo comes down the stairs.

"Is everything OK?" he asks.

I can tell from the look on his face that there's no point pretending. I switch off the gas. "I got that email from Auntie Julie."

His expression turns grave. "Have you read it?"

"Not yet."

There's a pause.

"I'll cancel my last meeting," says Theo. "You go off and find somewhere quiet."

"I can't," I argue. "This is an important day for you."

Theo frowns. "The next meeting isn't crucial. Honestly, I can cancel it."

I line up two espresso cups and fill them with coffee. "The thing is, I promised Archie we'd make a trap for wasps."

Theo pushes out a breath. "Bloody hell, Ads, forget about that. I'll do it with him."

I lean back against the marble worktop. "But where can I go? It'll be too hot up at the castle."

Theo rubs my shoulder. "You're starting to sound like you're making excuses."

I take a sip of my coffee but find it difficult to swallow. Am I?

"You've got fifty hectares of land," Theo goes on. "There are loads of places you can go."

I blow on my coffee.

"Or would you prefer us to read it together?" suggests Theo.

"No, it's fine," I insist. "I'll do it on my own."

"Look, I can see this is terrifying," Theo continues. "But the only way to even think about dealing with it is to read the email."

I force the rest of my coffee down. "I know."

"We'll sit down and talk about it afterwards," he goes on. "But please remember I love you."

He kisses me and I smile, weakly.

I leave the house, feeling dazed. I walk up to the olive grove, just concentrating on putting one foot in front of the other and breathing in through my nose and out through my mouth.

Once I get there, I find a spot that's set back from the driveway, where no one can see me. And I lean on a knobbly tree trunk.

I take out my phone and open the email.

Dear Adam,

This is an email I didn't want to write. The way your mum died was awful for me, because I was there, and the memory will torment me till the end of my days. But if you already know about the affair, I don't think it'll do you any harm to know the rest of it. If you've been imagining your mum took her own life, it might even set you free.

Your mum died on the night she was supposed to be leaving for Italy. Not that I knew about that at the time. I got another call from that Lauren at the hotel. She said she knew I was lying and the woman she'd told me about was my sister and I'd better come quick because she was sitting in the bar with a suitcase, drinking gin and getting plastered.

Well, I had no idea what our Suzanne was playing at or if she'd even speak to me, but I dropped everything and jumped in a taxi. But when I arrived at the hotel, she'd gone.

That silly cow Lauren was more than happy to fill me in on what had happened. Apparently, your mum had come to meet Gary but he hadn't turned up and hadn't even booked a room. He had left her a note though and Lauren handed it over—with great satisfaction, I'm sure. She'd obviously read it because she told me what it said. It said he was sorry but he only wanted a bit of fun, she'd taken things too far and he was ending it.

Your mum must have been devastated because according to Lauren, as soon as she read the note she went over to the bar and started knocking back the booze. I'm sure Lauren also told her Gary was a rat who'd brought other women to the hotel, because she wasted no time in telling me. 'I did try to warn you,' she kept saying in a smug voice. But I was already halfway out the door.

I had no idea where your mum was but knew I had to find her. So I trudged round Manchester, round all the places where she usually went on a night out. I even went in the ladies loos, banging on the cubicle doors and shouting her name. But I couldn't find her.

Finally, after what felt like hours, I spotted her sitting on her own and clutching her suitcase in some dive on Deansgate. She was so wasted she kept sliding off her seat. I ran over and tried to give her a squeeze, but she wasn't pleased to see me. She just pushed me away, accusing me of wanting to gloat. I knew she'd be feeling humiliated so I didn't have a go at her. I just got her a glass of water and tried to sober her up. Eventually, she calmed down and told me she'd written to Uncle Wilf and her and Gary were supposed to be going and staying with him, although she didn't say anything else, which is why I honestly didn't know Wilf was gay. But then she'd gone to the hotel and Gary had stood her up and written her this note saying he didn't want anything else to do with her.

I did what your mum needed me to do—I told her Gary was a bastard and if that's what he was like, she was well rid. But she started crying. Tears were rolling down her face. She kept saying she loved him and she couldn't believe he just wanted a fling and how could she have been so stupid? I told her we all made mistakes and to look at the state of me with my complete failure of a love life. We had a bit of a laugh at the pair of us and she apologised for being unkind to me and we had a squeeze and I told her to come back to mine and we'd work it all out in the morning. She must have been finally starting to sober up because she agreed.

But then we went outside and there was a big crowd waiting for taxis. It was chucking out time and there were drunks everywhere and people having fights—Deansgate was terrible in those days. Although that wasn't the problem. The problem was your mum spotted Gary across the road. She couldn't believe it. He was going into a bar with some other woman. There was no question they were together—he had his arm around her.

Well, your mum saw red. I've never seen anyone so angry. She shouted Gary's name but he didn't hear her and disappeared into the bar. So she ran after him. I tried running after her but I had to pick up her suitcase so I wasn't very fast. And she ran into the road. Right there, right in front of me, she got hit by a car.

I won't go into the details, Adam. All you need to know is it was quick and she didn't feel any pain. The paramedics said she was dead on impact. And that was that.

Except a few days later, a letter she'd sent arrived at my

house. It said she was leaving for Italy and she hoped I wouldn't hate her but she was in love and just wanted to be happy. The point is, it had another letter in it, which she asked me to give to you. I don't know what it says because I've not opened it. And I've never given it to you because I didn't want you to know your mum was leaving. But now you do, I've posted it to you in Italy. I've sent it recorded delivery so you'll have to be in to sign for it I'm afraid, but I didn't want to run the risk of it getting lost in the post. The woman at the Post Office said it should arrive early next week.

I hope you're not too upset by this, Adam. I know it must be awful for you but hopefully it'll finally bring you some peace.

Make sure you stay close to Theo. He's a good man. You'll need him now more than ever.

Sending you all my love,
Auntie Julie
x

I let the letter fall onto my lap.

I sit, staring straight ahead, my eyes fixed on the lines and bumps of the nearest tree trunk.

I sit like that for a long time.

I've no idea what to think, or what to feel.

I just know that I do want to see Theo.

Chapter 41

I pedal my exercise bike in silence. It's the morning after I read the email from Auntie Julie and I've hardly slept.

Theo and I stayed up late, talking over what she'd told me. Imagining that sickening feeling Mum must have experienced when she realized she'd been used and tossed aside, rather than finding herself at the center of a great, life-changing love affair. Empathizing with her anger as she understood Gary was going to restart the cycle all over again with another woman, having upended her life with little or no regard for her feelings.

From down in the valley comes the sound of a bus tooting its horn. It's seven a.m. and I've already been up for an hour. I decided there was no point lying in bed any longer, twisting and flinging myself from one side to the other, staring at the walls of Wilf and Arnaldo's old bedroom. We've had them painted the same honeycomb as the buildings on the Piazza dell'Anfiteatro—a color I would have enjoyed if I had the slightest capacity for enjoyment.

I grip the handles tighter and pedal a bit faster.

It's as if Julie's email has made me feel a whole new loss: it's only now I know Mum's story that I can actually grieve. It's only now I realize that I didn't grieve properly when she died. I couldn't have: I didn't have a full enough picture of what had happened. I understand why people kept certain details from me but this meant I sensed something didn't add up, so Mum's death didn't seem wholly real. But now it is real—thumpingly, heart-splittingly, gut-wrenchingly real.

I finish my workout, stretch and shower. I don't know what Theo's told the kids but they must understand something's wrong because they all keep a respectful distance and don't bother me. After we've eaten—in the kitchen because the builders are working outside—we toss our squeezed oranges off the hill and I manage to raise the hint of a smile.

At least I still have lots of work to do so can't sink into a pit of despair. I carry the recycling up through the olive grove—today's the day for *multimateriale*, or tin, plastic and polystyrene. I take delivery of a new wardrobe and the sofa bed for the cottage, only for Archie to spill a can of Coke Zero all over the sofa, which I then have to clean up. And I listen to Giuseppe tell me there's a problem with the plaster in the bedroom of the cottage: some of it has started coming away from the wall. I don't understand why, when the plaster everywhere else is perfect. But I don't have the capacity to take in what he's saying so ask him to just do whatever's needed.

And all morning I ache with sadness for my mum. My misguided, impressionable, passionate, romantic Mum. A woman who was still young, just thirty-five when she died. And a woman I finally understand.

"Be careful, gang!" warns Theo.

Once the diggers have left the castle, Luisa takes us down into the underground chamber. I'm still feeling subdued and am much quieter than usual, but I'm surprised to feel a flurry of enthusiasm as I climb down the ladder. The second my head goes underground and I catch sight of the chamber—illuminated by several portable lights Luisa has positioned around the edges—I'm entranced.

It's about twice as high as Theo is tall, and almost as spacious as the wine store or the big lounge in the house. It has a vaulted ceiling and stone walls held together by some kind of mortar. And along these walls are several arrow slits, some of them filled in, some letting through thin slashes of sunlight.

"This slaps!" gushes Callum.

"Oh my god, it's unreal!" squeaks Mabel.

They're not wrong. I can't believe this massive space was lying underground, undiscovered for so long. Hundreds of years, possibly.

"*Is* it a dungeon?" asks Archie.

Luisa screws up her nose. "I'm sorry to say I don't think so. If you look at that wall, you can see what would have been a fireplace and a chimney."

As I move closer, I almost twist my ankle on the uneven ground, but grab onto the wall just in time. "Oh, yeah."

We're all fascinated, but Archie looks disappointed.

"It's also too big for a dungeon," Luisa goes on, tucking a strand of her short hair behind her ear. "Prisoners wouldn't have been given so much space."

"So what was it?" asks Theo.

Luisa runs her hands down her cargo shorts. "I expect it formed part of the main palace. And we need to keep investigating, but the most probable answer is it was some kind of dwelling."

"What's that?" says Archie.

"A living space, a home," answers Luisa.

"For a knight?" asks Archie.

Luisa angles her head. "Well, a chamber this size wouldn't have belonged to anyone insignificant. So it could have been a knight, yes."

Archie gives a satisfied smile.

"Or a princess," points out Mabel, suddenly looking much younger than thirteen.

"Or a king!" throws in Callum, not bothering to disguise his excitement.

"It's unbelievable," I say. "And here we are standing in the same spot a thousand years later."

Luisa gives a half-turn. "And just think, if we've found this chamber, there may be more—lots more. Who knows what we might uncover?"

Theo ruffles Archie's hair. "What do you think, squirt? Are you happy?"

"Yeah," says Archie. And he gives another smile.

I look at him and find myself smiling, too.

When we return to the house, Theo goes to do some work and Archie disappears to play, but I notice Callum and Mabel muttering between themselves, shielding their mouths with their hands. What are they up to?

They approach the cottage and call over Giuseppe. Suspicious, I climb the short wooden ladder into the space above the garage that we call the grain store. I close the door behind me and peer through the ventilation slats. I have a perfect view of Callum, Mabel and Giuseppe standing in the doorway to the cottage.

"We overheard your conversation with Arjan," begins Callum, his feet set apart. "We heard you trying to get him to redo that plaster. So we know he refused to work in the bedroom of two gay men."

Giuseppe twists his wedding ring round his finger. "Yes, he does say that."

"But you let him get away with it," Mabel interjects. "You didn't challenge him."

Giuseppe throws up his arms. "What do you want I say? He is the best plasterer in the area."

"But he wouldn't plaster that room," Callum points out. "And now it's falling off and he won't fix it."

"Yes, this is true," Giuseppe concedes. "I have to ask my other men to do it. But Arjan continues working in all the other rooms of the house."

"Well, I don't feel comfortable seeing him," Callum states, firmly.

"We're not comfortable with him in our home," adds Mabel.

I feel butterflies in my stomach.

Giuseppe shifts his weight from one foot to the other. "Children, thank you for your help. But now I speak to Adam."

Mabel steps forward. "No, we don't want you to do that. Adam's had a lot going on and is sad today."

Giuseppe runs his hand over his jet-black buzz cut. "OK, I speak to your father."

"We don't want you to do that, either," Mabel says. "Dad's already had to handle one lot of homophobia. We don't want him dealing with any more."

"It took him a long time to come out," Callum explains. "He deserves to be happy."

Pride rushes into me, sweeping away my ache for Mum.

Giuseppe, however, frowns. "What do you want I do?"

Callum and Mabel look at each other, as if to bolster their conviction.

"We want you to get rid of Arjan," declares Callum.

"We want you to fire him," confirms Mabel.

"But Arjan is from a different country," Giuseppe argues. "He does not know about these things."

Callum shakes his head, firmly. "It doesn't make any difference. You've got other builders from Tunisia and Egypt and they're not like that. So there's no excuse. Homophobia is unacceptable, wherever you're from."

Atta boy!

"And he's been working here for weeks now," Mabel observes. "He's had plenty of time to change his views."

Atta *girl*!

Giuseppe rocks backwards on the balls of his feet. "Yes, I agree. But the job is nearly finished. We have only one week left."

"Can't you find someone to replace him?" Callum asks. "He isn't doing the work you're paying him for anyway."

Giuseppe runs his hand over his beard. He's starting to look exasperated. "I am sorry but I cannot take orders from children."

"We may be children but we can still write online reviews," says Callum, drawing himself up to his full height. "I'm sure all those customers you're hoping to attract would be interested to hear you employ staff who are homophobic."

I can't help but wince slightly. While I admire the kids' courage—and, of course, their principles—part of me worries that Giuseppe's just going to get annoyed. What if he walks off the job and leaves it unfinished?

There's a pause. Then—to my shock—Giuseppe breaks into laughter. "Children, I like you. You are brave but you are also right. I know another worker who is not available for the first part of the job. I contact him now and see if he can do the last week. And I speak to Arjan: he is not here on Monday."

Callum and Mabel look stunned, as if they can't believe they've succeeded. In an instant, their composure shatters.

"Thank you!" bursts out Mabel.

Callum tugs at his fringe. "Thanks so much!"

"Oh, and sorry, but would you mind not saying anything to Dad or Adam?" Mabel quickly adds. "Could you maybe just tell them Arjan's off sick?"

Giuseppe smiles out of the corner of his mouth. "OK, that is what I say. And well done. You are good kids."

You took the words right out of my mouth.

As I step back from the ventilation slats, I resolve not to mention a word of this to Callum and Mabel. But I can't wait to tell Theo.

Chapter 42

On Saturday I'm still quiet and subdued. But it's time to put the finishing touches to our house renovations, to make the place a bit cozier. As Angelika says, this is the fun part, where our creativity comes in.

Theo and I take the kids shopping in Pietrasanta. We stroll up and down the grid of streets, crisscrossing the main square, popping into shops and picking up pictures, dried grasses and flowers, cushions, tissue-holders, wicker bins and ornaments. Theo buys a leather visitors' book, saying it'll make our guests feel more welcome if we invite them to share their opinions. And I'm drawn back to the Venetian blown-glass vase streaked with the colors of the rainbow that we saw at the start of summer.

"I think you should buy it," pronounces Callum.

"You've changed your tune," I tease him.

"I know," he admits. "But I was wrong: it isn't tacky at all."

I reexamine the vase and notice it's come down in price.

"Don't worry about it," I say, "you saved us some money by making us wait."

While the shop assistant wraps the vase, Callum says that once we've put all the finishing touches to the house, he's going to retake his pictures to capture it at its very best. And Mabel shares with us an idea she has for a social media video in which I'm arranging flowers in the vase while explaining that one of the key values of the castello is a commitment to welcoming guests from all the colors of the rainbow.

"Superb," says Theo.

"I like that!" I chime.

As we move on to the next shop, I pull out my phone to consult the shopping list I've written in my notes. And I see I've received an email. I open the app and see it's from Auntie Julie.

"You guys go ahead," I call out, "I'll catch you up."

"Is everything alright?" asks Theo.

"Yeah," I reply, confident that if I can handle Julie's last email, I can handle anything. "I'll only be a minute."

I spot some stone steps and lower myself down.

Dear Adam,

I hope you're OK and getting your head around what I said in my last email. This is just a short one because I realised I forgot something. I didn't say anything about your dad. And I think you need to know how hard all this was for him.

On the night your mum was planning to leave, she left him a letter, explaining what she was doing and why. One of the reasons she got so panicked when Gary dumped her was because she knew your dad would have read it and she was convinced he wouldn't want her back. He had read it, although I've no idea whether he would have taken her back as I only found out about it when I told him she'd had the accident. By then it didn't matter.

Anyway, I just want you to know your dad had to cope with a lot. It's his story to tell, not mine, and Mart and I aren't as close as we used to be, so I don't even know how much he'd want you to know. But I understand you've always been angry with him so I want you to know he didn't give you up lightly. And I think you should give him another chance. Or at least a chance to explain himself.

Right, that's it. I'll butt out now and leave you to enjoy the rest of your holiday. Please send me more pictures!

With all my love,
Auntie Julie
x

Remorse cuts through me.

So Dad does know Mum cheated on him. And he knows she was leaving. Auntie Julie's right: that must have been awful for him.

I writhe around on the step. *Have* I been too hard on him? What if all this time I've got him wrong?

I've no idea what Julie's hinting at, but I realize I do need to let him tell his story.

I scroll down my inbox until I come to his email. And I compose my reply.

Chapter 43

"Bye!" I shout. "Have a brill time!"

I'm dropping Theo and Callum off at Lucca train station, where they're catching a train to Florence. They're off to watch a football match: Fiorentina, our local team in the Serie A—apparently Italy's equivalent of the Premier League—are playing Lazio at home. It's the first game of the season and Theo surprised Callum by buying tickets from a friend of Stefano's. Seeing the look on Callum's face was pure joy. As it is to watch the two of them bounce into the station, Theo wrapping his arm around Callum's shoulders.

I can't help thinking of my own relationship with my dad. If I've been too hard on him about his response to Mum's death, have I also been too hard on him about his response to having a gay son? What if I've been punishing him all these years and he doesn't deserve it?

Well, I've emailed him now, offering to visit him in Umbria. I'll just have to wait for his reply.

When Mabel, Archie and I arrive back at the house, Mabel and I spend a few hours recording videos for social media. I do tours, share some of the property's history, and even explain that it used to belong to my great-uncle and his Italian partner—although I don't reveal any of the more personal details of their story.

By late afternoon, I'm worried I've neglected Archie, especially as he was upset about not going to the football—although Theo did explain that Stefano's friend only had two tickets, so it would have to be a "big boy" trip. I suggest the three of us go to the beach in Viareggio and he perks up. Then I remember seeing the packaging for Mabel's sanitary towels when I was emptying the bins. I quickly add that I won't be taking my swimming shorts: I just fancy breathing in the sea air while Archie has a run around. I'm delighted when she agrees.

As we arrive, we see the beach is busy with the usual Sunday crowds. We weave our way to the shore and I do have a run around with Archie, but he spots some Welsh boys building an elaborate sandcastle and they invite him to join in. I quickly introduce myself to the boys' mum then spread our towels out a few meters away. Mabel and I sit down, facing the sun but protected by a layer of cream as well as our hats and glasses.

"I'm glad Archie's making friends," I tell her. "I do worry he hasn't been around anyone his own age all summer."

She nods. "Would you think I'm mad if I said I had a dream about being friends with Taylor Swift?"

"No!" I burst out. "I used to dream about being friends with Kylie all the time!"

She smiles. "Really? What happened? In your dreams?"

"Well, we'd be sitting together in my room and talking about school and boys and who we fancied. And it all felt so real. It didn't matter that I was only a kid. I was convinced that if we ever met, we'd be best friends."

Mabel's eyes glitter. "That's exactly like my dream. Oh my god, it was incred. Me and Taylor were talking about skincare and she was looking at my clothes and saying I'm gorgeous and I should have more confidence."

I waggle my eyebrows. "She's right. You *are* gorgeous and you *should* have more confidence."

Mabel looks a little bashful. "Thanks."

I decide not to push the subject.

"I've also been thinking about Sharita and Aurora," she goes on, plunging her hand into the sand. "They flew to Corfu yesterday and snapped some pics of their hotel."

I sit up. "So *that*'s why you had the dream!"

"Probs, yeah." Mabel lifts up a fist and lets the sand slowly fall out of it. "Anyway, Sharita messaged me this morning. Apparently, her and Aurora have fallen out."

"Already?" I say. "That didn't last long. Do you know what it's about?"

"Something to do with a boy. She says she wishes I was there instead of Aurora."

"I bet she does."

Mabel bats the sand from her hands. "I wouldn't want to, though. I'm happy here."

I smile. "Brill."

I watch Archie playing with the two boys. They seem to be digging a moat around the castle and laying a trench that connects it to the sea.

"But I'm not going to fall out with her," Mabel adds. "I've been thinking, and I was probs a bit panicky at the start of summer."

My eyes settle on a kite bobbing in the sky. "We've all been there—or at least I have. You may have been thinking you'd lost your dad and then the whole thing happened with your mum and you were worried about losing her."

I realize I've brought up Kate's lie about having a job. I didn't intend to, especially as Mabel has made a great effort to avoid the subject ever since she told us the truth. I hope it doesn't backfire.

"You know, I was devo about Mum," Mabel confesses, gazing out at the horizon. "About her pretending to have another job and going away without us."

I'm pleased she's confiding in me but am aware that what I say next is very important.

"Mabel, I don't know your mum very well," I begin. "But I do know breakups can be very difficult. Especially when it's not what you want."

She plunges her hand back in the sand. "I suppose so."

Into my head flashes an image of my mum, spotting Gary with another woman and bolting into the road.

"People can behave irrationally when they're emotional," I continue. "But we shouldn't judge them because we can never really know what's going on in their head—even when we're very close to them. The important thing is it wouldn't have been about you: your mum wouldn't have lied because she wanted to leave you. She'd have been angry and wanting to get at your dad. That doesn't change the way she feels about you."

I pause as I remember the one thing Mabel needs to hear most.

"Your mum loves you."

Mabel pulls out her hand and lets the sand fall from her fist. "That's what she says."

"And . . . ? Have you forgiven her?"

"Not yet."

I watch the sea rush into the trench Archie and the boys have dug, filling the moat around the castle. The three of them cheer and Archie looks up to check I've seen. I give him a wave.

I turn back to Mabel. "Take it from me, keeping resentment inside you is like storing rotting fruit in the fridge: it'll only go on rotting and the badness will just spread."

I wonder if my metaphor could be applied to my feelings about my dad.

I check my phone to see if I've received a reply: I have.

"Sorry," I say to Mabel, "I just need to read this."

I shield my screen from the sun and give the email a quick scan.

> Great news, lad! Wud love to see u. We arrived today but the campsite is quieter than we're used to. Why don't u come tomorrow? Our address is . . . Dad.

I feel a jangle of anxiety.

But I know the answer has to be yes.

Chapter 44

It's Monday and the start of our final week in Italy. I'm on my way to visit Dad and Debbie in Umbria. My breathing is shallow and my shoulders are around my ears.

At least I've got used to driving on the right-hand side of the road—and am not fazed by a ninety-minute journey, including a long stretch on the motorway and several toll roads. The only thing that does make me uncomfortable is having to navigate around the cyclists—and, even worse, clusters of cyclists—darting down the country lanes. I don't think I'll ever get used to them.

When the satnav directs me down a tree-lined road that leads into the campsite, fear creeps up my spine. I try to concentrate on the instructions Dad gave me to get to their caravan. *Take the first left, right at the clubhouse and follow the shore of the lake. . . .*

Very quickly, it becomes clear this isn't anything like the campsites we stayed on when I was young. First of all, there are hardly any children: the people staying here are mainly middle-aged or retirement age, and mainly couples. I see a spa and massage center, the equipment for all kinds of watersports, and something called a "floating sauna." Plus, there are signs and posters for language classes, a nature trail, and an exhibition by an artist-in-residence. The accommodation seems to be largely in static caravans that look more like luxury chalets. Outside each are high-end cars, many of them electric, many with their own charging points.

I spot a much more modest car I think belongs to Dad and stop to look closer. In the rear window, I recognize a Manchester United sticker. Yeah, that's it. . . .

My heartbeat races as I pull up alongside it and switch off my engine.

Dad and Debbie must have been listening, because they open the door and step out of the caravan. Dad's wearing sports shorts and trainers, with a blue-striped polo shirt that's a little too tight for his belly. His hair is still thick and predominantly the color of milk chocolate, with only patches of gray at the front and sides. Debbie's dressed in pink sandals, gray shorts and an eggplant-colored sleeveless top that complements her—presumably dyed—brunette hair. Their skin is still pale, although Dad's already managed to get sunburnt on his nose.

"Alreet, lad," he says.

We exchange bright smiles and awkward hugs, and I realize my forehead has broken into a stress sweat. I wipe it with my forearm.

"After all these weeks, I still haven't got used to the heat," I lie.

"I'm not surprised," says Dad. "It's crackin' flags."

"I'm t' same, love," offers Debbie. "I'm sweatin' cobs." She suggests we go inside, where it's cooler.

The caravan has several high-tech air-conditioning units that are mounted on the walls, plus real wood floors, an enormous flat-screen TV, and patio doors leading onto a terrace equipped with sun loungers and a hot tub.

"Well, this is nice," I coo.

"It's dead posh, i'n't it?" says Debbie.

Scattered around are framed photos of a family, at the center of them a woman in her fifties who I recognize from Debbie's retirement party as her former boss.

Dad sits on the L-shaped sofa, taking up most of one side with his huge frame. I perch across from him.

Debbie starts fussing over the drinks, running through a list of the cans and bottles in the fridge. "Or I'm brewin' up," she says. "We always bring our own PG Tips."

I'm about to say no, thanks, and ask for something cold, but stop myself and say yes.

Debbie fills the kettle and drops tea bags into three mugs. She's a sturdy woman with thick arms, but agile and still sprightly. She's always been eager to please but today she seems nervous. "Sorry, love, I can't remember if you take sugar," she says.

"No, thanks."

In her flustered state, she puts a teaspoon of it in my mug. As I watch her tip the contents down the sink and start again, I feel a stab of guilt for the hostility I used to show her. I'm not surprised I make her nervous.

I overcompensate by being wildly cheerful. "The campsite looks fab!"

Debbie seems relieved to be on safe ground. "I know! You want to see t' clubhouse—it's like bein' in a five-star hotel."

Dad flashes her a cheeky grin. "They don't have beer on draft, though. Only bottles."

Debbie gasps. "Mart! I don't know how I put up wi' you!" But her tone is affectionate. "Finally, we get the chance to come somewhere classy and all you can do is moan about t' beer."

"Not just t' beer," Dad teases. "They also don't have anywhere to watch t' football."

"What are you like?" Debbie rolls her eyes and brings the tea over. She sits down next to Dad and he shuffles to one side.

"How's Theo, love?" she asks.

I feel a twinge of discomfort. I haven't officially told them Theo's my boyfriend, although they obviously know.

"Does he still support Man City?" pipes Dad.

My discomfort doubles. Why does Dad always have to make it about football?

But I tell myself I don't need to feel inadequate anymore. I don't need to be upset by football.

I reveal that Theo and Callum went to the match yesterday and share Theo's comments and observations. Dad's fascinated, his eyebrows raised.

"And how's it goin' wi' the house you're doin' up?" asks Debbie, blowing on her tea.

"Yeah, brill, thanks." I give them a rundown of the improvements, making special mention of the windows for Dad.

"It sounds fantastic," Debbie comments, sipping from her mug. "Did you say it belonged to your mum's uncle?"

"Yeah. He was called Wilf."

Dad runs his hand through his hair, leaving it even more tousled than usual. "You know, I've thought about it and I can't remember her mentionin' him. Or anyone else in t' family."

I fill them in with a summary of Wilf's story. "So nobody had spoken to him since Mum was very little. But she got in touch with him a few months before she died. I actually found her letters."

Something shifts in the atmosphere, as if the air has sharpened.

But I'm not backing out now.

I finish my tea and set it down on the little glass-topped table. "Actually, that's what I wanted to talk to you about, Dad."

Debbie stands up and says she'll nip out.

"You don't need to," I insist.

"No, I need a pint o' milk from t' shop," she says. "It won't take long. And it'll give you and your dad a bit of time on your own."

Dad smiles but I can tell he's concerned.

"I know how Mum died," I blurt out, as soon as Debbie's out of the door. "I read her letters and found out she was seeing another bloke. I phoned Auntie Julie and asked her about it."

Dad frowns. "We always said we'd protect you from that."

"To be honest, I didn't give her much choice. And I'd already found out most of it from the letters."

I spot what looks like shame scudder across Dad's face. "Yeah, well, I could tell summat were up. But I didn't realize it were as bad as that. I didn't realize she were going to leave me."

I give a little cough. "Apparently, Mum and this bloke were going to stay with Uncle Wilf."

Dad tilts his head. "Well, I didn't know that. Although now you mention it, I do remember she were goin' to Italy." He finishes his tea and puts down his mug. "What else did Julie say?"

I draw in a ragged breath. "She told me about the night Mum died. She told me how it happened."

Dad looks out of the window. "I hope you didn't find it too upsettin'."

"I'm glad I found out," I say, nodding, firmly.

There's a beat.

I tighten my jaw. "But it must have been upsetting for you."

Dad's eyes take him somewhere else. "It were, lad, yeah."

I don't want to be cruel but need to push him a little further. "Auntie Julie said you took it hard."

Dad turns to face me. "Well, if you want to get everything out in t' open, yeah, I couldn't cope. I had a breakdown."

I squeeze my eyes shut and snap them open again. I'm so stunned I can't think of anything to say. Surely not? Surely not my big, strong, manly dad?

"In them days, men didn't have breakdowns," Dad goes on. "Or posh, clever men might have done—not men like me. If they did, they didn't talk about it. So I were ashamed and didn't want anyone to know."

"Oh, Dad," is all I manage to say.

"Obviously, I were grievin'," Dad continues. "And whatever 'appened, I did love your mum. But I were also gutted she'd cheated on me. And I thought it were my fault."

"How do you mean?"

"Well, I could have paid her more attention, told her she looked nice and that, taken her out, told her I loved her." He lets out a shaky sigh. "If I had, maybe she wouldn't have started messin' about with that other bloke. Maybe she wouldn't have walked into that car. Maybe you wouldn't have lost your mum."

I'm flabbergasted. I had no idea he was thinking all this. All I manage to say is, "Dad, don't think like that."

He leans forward and clasps his hands. "I don't anymore. But I did at t' time."

"And how did you get over it?"

"Your Auntie Julie marched me down to see t' doctor. She wanted me to see some counselor an' all, but I couldn't be doing with that."

I rub my collarbone. "And what did the doctor do?"

"He put me on antidepressants and said I should get someone

to look after you for a while. That's when you went and lived with her. By the time I were back on my feet, you didn't want to come back wi' me."

I'm still reeling. "What, so it wasn't because I was gay?"

I realize that's the first time I've actually told Dad I'm gay. I realize I've just come out to him.

He looks confused. "You what? Why would it be because of that?"

"I don't know. I just thought you were disappointed, with the way I turned out."

After so long, I can't believe we're having this conversation—and both of us speaking so openly, much more openly than we've ever spoken to each other before. In a way, it's like I've detached from it and am watching two actors play our roles. At the same time, I'm so engaged I can feel every muscle in my body clenched, every nerve on edge.

"I thought you wanted to start again with Trevor and Keith," I go on. "I thought you liked them more than me."

Dad shakes his head. "Give over, lad! I'll admit I knew what to do wi' them but that's not t' same thing. I didn't know owt about gays. I hadn't met any till you. You have to remember I grew up in t' fifties, on a council estate in Wigan."

I feel a pique of annoyance. "Dad, I'm sure there were gays on council estates in Wigan."

"Well, not any who admitted it. It were another world back then."

I stiffen in expectation of the question I need to ask next. "You did know I was gay, then?"

Dad runs his hand along his jaw. "Your mum said she thought you might be, but I didn't really know what it meant. I just thought it meant you'd be lonely and hang around public toilets and get beaten up and die of AIDS. And I wanted to stop that 'appening to you. So I tried to get you interested in football. I tried to steer you towards things normal boys liked."

He spots me flinch at the word *normal.*

"Sorry, lad. Even now I don't know t' right words."

I slide my hands under my thighs. "But you can't change someone, Dad. You can't *make* someone fancy girls, just like no one could have made you fancy boys."

He scratches his cheek. "Yeah, well, obviously I know that now. But I didn't at t' time. Nobody talked about that kind of thing in them days. The only thing you heard about gays were horrible things you read in t' paper. It's not like now, when you can go online and find out about anything you want and there are gays in *Corrie* and *Emmerdale*. They even 'ave 'em on quiz shows, you know. Debbie saw a lesbian on *The Chase* the other day. I'n't that great?"

I smile. "Yeah, it is."

But I'm realizing how little I know of Dad's story. And there's so much overlap between our lives, so many ways in which his life has influenced mine. In a way, his story is my story. If I can't understand him, I can't understand myself.

"Anyway, I didn't know what to do about it," he goes on. "And I didn't know how to talk to you. I just felt like I'd failed you as a dad."

I lower my eyes to the floor. "I felt like I'd failed you as a son."

There's a heavy silence.

I look up. "Dad, why have we never talked about this?"

"I always thought you weren't comfortable with it," he says. "You never wanted to see me at t' best of times. I were frightened if I pushed it, I'd lose you completely."

I feel dragged down by guilt. Because he's right: I do feel uncomfortable around him. I do struggle with his masculinity—his deep voice, his slightly earthy scent, his love of beer and football, even the way he calls me "lad." As Ian would say, I find it triggering, because it reminds me of what I'm not. So I pushed him away. To protect myself, I shut him out completely.

I swallow. "Sorry, Dad. I think I misunderstood you. I didn't give you a fair chance."

He inches forward. "Don't be daft, lad. You've nowt to apologize for. *I'm* sorry I weren't always sensitive. I'm sorry I didn't know how to talk about things."

"It's OK," I manage to say. But I can feel myself collapsing inwards. Because all this time I've been thinking I was abandoned by both parents, I've been thinking that neither of them loved me. And it turns out I was wrong on both counts.

I can feel the tears rushing to my eyes. But I don't want to break down here. I don't want Dad to see me crying.

I stand up and make for the door. "Sorry, Dad, I've got to go."

"You what, lad?"

I grasp the handle. "Sorry. I will be able to talk about this. Just not yet."

Chapter 45

The day after my conversation with Dad, I'm still feeling winded.

After I left the campsite, I had to pull over in a dirt track at the side of the road and surrender to the tears I'd been holding in. I wasn't sure who I was crying for—myself or Dad—or if I was just crying with regret. But I cried hard, until spasms racked my body and my face was raw. And I cried for a long time, until I saw a tractor approaching and decided I'd better move before I was asked questions in a language I didn't understand.

Later that evening, I recounted what Dad and I had talked about to Theo and he put his arms around me and told me he loved me. I sobbed into his chest and he kissed my head and told me it was alright and I hadn't known the whole story so shouldn't blame myself. I felt comforted and forgiven. This morning, I've no more tears to cry.

That's just as well, as I don't have the time to sit around crying. It's the launch day for the castello's website and Airbnb entry, plus its social media accounts. At ten a.m. UK time, Mabel starts posting our photos and videos on TikTok, Instagram and Facebook. She interacts with all the comments, explaining this will boost engagement and push the post up people's feeds. Over the course of the day, Callum monitors how many people are clicking through from the social media platforms to the website. The numbers are good but we expect they'll be inflated by all the friends and acquaintances who'll be looking out of curiosity. Our theory is backed up by the number of texts and messages we receive. But it's good to get feedback—and everyone is impressed.

There are just four days till the party and we throw ourselves into preparations. Mabel and Callum put together a playlist of music that will be pumped through some speakers Angelika has lent us. The list is heavy on Harry Styles, Taylor Swift, Oasis and the Stone Roses, but I persuade the kids to let me slot in a few songs by Kylie, Madonna and various girl bands.

For drinks, we create two cocktails, which we'll pre-mix in jugs—and I message my sisters for tips on ingredients and twists on classic recipes. One of them we name the Montemagno Margarita, the other the Castello Cosmo. When the kids point out that we should also have a non-alcoholic option, we create a third—the Virgin Versilia.

We spend a long time planning the food for the buffet and Theo has the idea of setting up a build-your-own pizza station. We compile a list of the toppings we want to offer, from peppers to mushrooms, from cooked meats to tuna. To my disbelief, the kids even agree to have olives on the table—but only if we make a sign telling people to avoid cross-contamination. We also make signs encouraging people to post about the castello on their social media and tag our accounts, which we're going to place on the buffet table.

Next, we turn our attention to the games. As our designated games master, Archie's principal idea is to set up a mammoth Top Trumps tournament. Thinking this may not be the best way to create a party atmosphere, Theo and I tactfully persuade him to scale it back and add a few other options. An obvious one is an orange-throwing competition, and we calculate that, if we save all our orange halves between now and Saturday, this should give us enough for each guest to have several throws.

"And how about a competition to see who can do the longest keepy-uppy?" I suggest, much to my own surprise. After our game of football on the beach in Viareggio, Theo and the boys spent an hour taking it in turns to keep up the ball using their feet, legs and knees, the others hollering and howling when it hit the ground. "That should appeal to the football fans."

Callum and Archie think this is an excellent idea.

"How about a treasure hunt around the house?" chips in Mabel. "We could come up with clues based on all the history we've learnt."

"That's a superb idea," says Theo. He suggests the treasure should be little replicas of the Leaning Tower, which he's seen for sale in a shop in Camaiore.

"Oh my god, perfect!" chirrups Mabel.

It's fab to see everyone so enthusiastic and eager to make the party a success. And everyone we've invited has replied to say they can make it—including some who've asked if they can bring partners. Theo suggested I invite my dad and Debbie, and I do feel really bad about bolting at the climax of our heart-to-heart. But I'm also feeling rotten about the way I've treated them over the years. And if they do come to the party, I don't think I'll be able to enjoy myself. I make an excuse about not wanting the numbers to spiral out of control—although Theo's expression tells me he can see through this. I promise him I'll work out what to do about Dad once I'm back in Manchester.

Just before lunch, Stefano comes barreling through the olive grove and down the gravel driveway. He's wearing his work overalls and clutching the *macchinetta* he uses to spray the olive trees with insecticide.

"Adam," he calls out, "I have a letter for you!"

There's only one letter it could be: the one I've been expecting since I read the email from Auntie Julie. Although I'm excited to read it, right now dread wins through.

"I think it is important," he expands. "The postman make me sign a document."

I take it from him and slot it into my back pocket. "*Grazie*, Stefano."

Stefano's eyes stand out. "But Adam, you must read!"

"It's OK," I say. "I know what it is. I'll read it later."

It was written thirty-four years ago, I'm tempted to add. *A few more hours won't make a difference.*

* * *

As the sun sets, I sit on the castle wall. Theo's promised me I won't be disturbed for as long as I need. I take a moment to savor the peace.

When I'm ready, I open the envelope and take out a second, smaller envelope. On it, Mum has written my name. Her handwriting is instantly familiar, but rather than feeling fear or excitement, I feel a sense of calm. It's as if I'm confronting something much bigger than me, something I'm powerless to resist.

I pull out the letter. Mum's written it in the same standard blue biro and on the same basic notepaper as the letters she wrote to Wilf. Once again, I can see the pressure she exerted on the page, except this time, as she wrote every word, she was thinking of me.

I run my hand over the lines, trying to feel a connection. And I may be kidding myself but I'm convinced I can feel her presence.

I start to read.

Dear Adam,

When you get this I'll have gone away but don't panic because it's only for a couple of weeks while I sort myself out.

There's something I need to tell you and I'm dead nervous so I'm just going to come out with it before I bottle it. I've fallen in love with a man called Gary. I tried my hardest not to, I want you to know that but when you get older you'll understand we don't always have control over who we fall in love with. And I did try to keep loving your dad but I couldn't do that either. So I'm leaving him to set up a new home with Gary but I'm not leaving you and as soon as I can I'm coming back to fetch you so you can live with us.

I know this might come as a shock and I'm sorry about that and you might also think I'm being selfish but I haven't been happy at home for a while now, although you might not even have noticed because I'm always happy when I'm with you but I want to be happy all the time and Gary makes me happy. I'm sorry if that upsets you, Adam.

Anyway I'm not very good at letter writing and I had to practise this one three times to get it right but I just want you to know that your dad will look after you and I've also written to Auntie Julie and asked her to call in and check on you both. Your dad's a good man but housework isn't his strong point and I don't think he even knows how to use the hoover, I'm not even sure he knows where it is. I've also asked Auntie Julie to cook you some meals and you may be glad of that because let's be honest I'm a dead loss in the kitchen. Now that I think of it you probably won't miss me at all!

When I come back I'll tell you the whole story and I'll introduce you to Gary and I'll also tell you about getting to know an uncle I haven't seen for ages but I won't do that now as I'll do a much better job of it when I can speak to you. I just don't want you to think I've forgotten you because I could never forget you. And if you need to remember that please sit on our bench in the back garden and look at the sunset like we do when we say goodbye to the day and know that I'll be looking at the same sunset in Italy and I'll be thinking of you because I love you. I love every bit of you, Adam. Never forget that.

With lots of love and kisses from,
Mum xxx

I breathe in and out slowly. And thirty-four years later, I do as Mum said. I look at the sunset and think of her.

I feel so calm and contented and so *right*—after years of feeling wrong—that it's almost as if I've entered some new dimension. I wonder if this is what people feel when they meditate or have a spiritual experience. I feel very small, like a tiny part of a big wide world. But that's good. It makes me feel secure, like I'm where I'm supposed to be.

I smile.

And I say out loud, "I love you, Mum."

Chapter 46

"I just wanted to say thank you."

"Thank you?" echoes Auntie Julie. "For what, chuck?"

"For everything you've done for me. For letting me come and live with you. For looking after me for so long."

I'm in the olive grove, but not sitting down: I'm feeling too driven to keep still. The phone's on speaker and I'm pacing between the trees, or as much as I'm able to pace without tripping over the uneven ground and knobbly roots. Now that I've told Julie about my conversation with Dad, I've switched the focus onto her.

"It's only recently I've started to understand the sacrifice you made," I elaborate. "And I don't know what I would have done without you. So thank you. A big, big thank you."

I can hear Julie sitting up and rearranging her cushions. "That's lovely, chuck, but honestly, there's no need. When you came to live with me, I was lonely. I was desperate to meet someone and have a family but for whatever reason, it just wasn't happening. You rescued me from that."

"How do you mean?"

"Well, we formed a little family of our own, didn't we? So I stopped aching for the thing I was missing. And then Jason came along. And he's my soulmate: he was always going to be the one for me. But if it weren't for you, I'm not sure I'd have seen that."

I lift up my sunglasses and press my eyes with my thumbs. "Why not?"

"Well, he didn't want to get married and he didn't want to have kids so I would probably have knocked him back; time was running out. But you helped me realize that idea in my head wouldn't have been right for me at all."

I drop my sunglasses back down over my eyes. "Do you not think so?"

She sighs. "No, chuck. I definitely had the urge to look after someone, maternal feelings or whatever you want to call them. But I probably would have got ground down by little kids—all those early mornings, sleepless nights, nagging them to eat their veg, all that baby talk and singing nursery rhymes over and over again and letting your brain go to mush. But when you came to live with me, I learned there were other ways to express my maternal feelings. And I loved being an auntie, an involved, hands-on auntie. So if we're saying thanks, thanks to you, too."

I insist there's no need, but feel my contentment growing.

Once we've said our goodbyes, I pull down a branch and examine a few olives. We're still a couple of months off the harvest but they've grown much bigger, although I've no way of telling which have been attacked by the flesh-eating flies, and which will be good enough to make into oil.

I try to sit down but am still feeling driven, like I'm on a mission. And I know there's another communication I need to deliver. I write an email to my dad.

Since visiting him in Umbria, I've accepted it may take a while for me to truly relax in Dad's company, but the only way to combat my regrets about our relationship is by getting it on track for the future. And all Dad wants is to be let into my life. What better way than inviting him and Debbie to this celebration of what I've been doing over the summer—with the people I've been doing it with?

Hi Dad, I'm sorry I ran off the other day. It was rude and there's no excuse but it was all just a lot for me to get my head around.

> Having said that, I'm really glad we had the conversation and I've been thinking about it a lot. I was wondering if you and Debbie would like to come to Montemagno for a party we're having on Saturday. Theo's kids will be here and I'd really like you to meet them. And you can see what we've done with the house. Please say yes—I'd love you to come.
> Adam x

I reread the email to check it captures what I want to say. And, just as I'm hitting Send, Giuseppe calls my name.

Chapter 47

As I follow Giuseppe to the cottage, he tells me there's a last-minute problem with the renovations.

He dismisses his men—including the Syrian plasterer who's replaced Arjan—with an instruction to take a quick break. He turns their radio off but the silence only adds to my anxiety, as does Giuseppe's order to wear a hard hat. This must be serious.

He takes me upstairs and indicates a corner of the ceiling that has caved in—at the back of the bedroom—sending a cloud of dust and plaster everywhere. It's beneath a section of the roof Giuseppe and his men left, as it seemed OK: in general, they thought the roof of the cottage was in a much better state than that of the main house. But it's now become clear it isn't OK.

Giuseppe scratches the back of his head. "Sorry, we judge it bad. Now we look at that part of the roof. We see if we can fix one part or if we need to replace the whole roof of the cottage."

"The whole roof?" I'm aware that my voice has risen a few octaves. "But that'll take ages."

Giuseppe frowns. "Yes. Sorry. I think one extra week, maybe more. We also need to hire scaffolding again. And we need extra money for the scaffolding and labor."

Oh, for fuck's sake. "How much?" I ask.

Giuseppe tells me.

My throat tightens. Even with what's left over from the cigarette case, I don't have enough. "But where am I supposed to find that? And we're supposed to be throwing a party on Saturday. We're supposed to be showing everyone the finished house."

"And I've just invited Dad and Debbie," I want to add—but keep this to myself; it isn't relevant to Giuseppe.

"Yes, but it is possible the house is not finished," he reasons. "And it is possible it is not safe for the party."

"Not safe? What, even if we were to cordon off the cottage?"

Giuseppe looks puzzled. I search around for a way to rephrase my question.

"Actually, scrap that," I toss in. "Let's forget about it for now. You investigate, see if you can fix that section of the roof. And when you know, let's talk."

Giuseppe strokes his beard and nods, gravely. "OK, Adam. We do our best."

"Dad," Mabel says, "you'd better speak to Mum."

Theo lowers his eyebrows. "What is it?"

The sun has gone down, we've just put Archie to bed, and Theo and I are sitting on the patio, drinking a glass of wine as we discuss the potential hitch in the renovations—and how we'll respond if the worst really does come to the worst. But from the look on Mabel's face, there's another problem. A flash of dread passes through me. Especially as Mabel doesn't answer Theo's question—and nor does Callum, who's standing beside her.

"Mum," says Mabel, "we're with Dad and Adam now. Can you tell them?"

She passes the phone to Theo and I see Kate's on video call. Theo holds the handset out so the camera captures both of us and I come face-to-face with his ex-wife for the first time in weeks—for the first time since she started attacking me. She's wearing a candy-floss pink, lightweight hoodie, and her honey-blond hair is as immaculately styled as the last—and only other—time I saw her, when she dropped the kids off at Theo's flat. Theo notices something else.

"Kate, you're at home," he comments, before any of us can say hello.

She nods, but seems a little unsure of herself. "I was just telling the kids I've missed them so much I've come back early."

"I don't get it," says Theo. "What's going on?"

Kate gives a shaky smile. "It didn't cost me anything to change my flight so I thought I'd come and make things up to the kids—for not seeing them all summer."

A bolt of panic shoots through me. What's she building up to?

"OK . . ." says Theo, sounding equally wary.

"I've looked online and there's a flight I can get to Pisa tomorrow," Kate continues, tucking the longer side of her bob behind her ear. "I can bring the kids back to Manchester on Friday so we can spend the last weekend of the summer together."

But I don't want them to go! I have to stop myself from wailing. What I manage to say is, "But we've got things planned this weekend."

Kate's mouth tightens and I sense a crackle of irritation. "I'm sorry, Adam, but I do, too—and you've had them all summer."

Whose decision was that? I want to fire back. But I notice Mabel is hiding behind her hair again and Callum is pulling at his fringe. I keep my objection to myself.

"Look, I'm only asking for one weekend," Kate goes on. "I don't think that's unreasonable. Obviously, there's been some bad feeling and I want to work through it before the kids go back to school."

I can't tell if she's causing trouble again and trying to spoil our party or if she's genuinely remorseful—but something tells me it's the latter. The nasty edge to her voice has disappeared, replaced by sadness. It reminds me of the sadness on Dad's face when he commented that I didn't seem comfortable around him. I'm surprised to find myself feeling sorry for her.

"What do you think, Cal? Mabel?" she asks.

Theo turns the camera onto them, but not before Mabel can flash him a pleading look and Callum signals his thoughts by shaking his head.

"Wouldn't that be great?" Kate presses, with a touch of desperation.

"Yeah," they mumble. Clearly, they don't want to upset their mum.

"Whatever works best," says Callum.

"Look, I'm really sorry, Kate," Theo says, turning the phone back onto us, "but we're having a party on Saturday and the idea is to celebrate finishing the house and thank everyone who's helped. The kids have been working really hard on the preparations. I'm not sure it would be fair on them to miss it."

Kate's mouth stiffens. "From what I hear, the party's probably going to be cancelled anyway."

I can feel myself bristling, but it doesn't sound like she's gloating.

"We don't know that yet," I say, making sure there's no trace of animosity in my voice. "We're still hoping it isn't."

Kate pulls on the sleeves of her hoodie. "When will you find out?"

"Tomorrow apparently, late morning," I reply. "That's when our head builder says he'll know if he can patch up the roof or if the whole thing will need replacing." I realize this is probably the longest exchange I've ever had with Kate.

Theo picks up the box of matches I used to light the citronella candles and turns it around and around in his hand. "When's your flight?" he asks.

"Three-thirty. So I'd need to set off for the airport at about one."

Theo nods. "Have you booked your ticket?"

"Not yet," says Kate. "I wanted to speak to you and the kids first. But there's decent availability—I just had another look."

Theo puts down the box of matches. "Alright, well, how about we see what the builders say? And if the party's happening, the kids stay here. If not, you come and take them back with you."

I feel a tug of sadness as I think about them leaving before the end of our summer. But it's only fair. And if the kids do resent Kate for lying to them, it'll be better if they can work through that. What was it I said about rotting fruit?

Theo looks up at Mabel and Callum. "What do you think? Cal? Mabel?"

"Alright," they both say. But they've brightened up considerably. They're clearly relieved we've found a resolution and another argument hasn't erupted.

I'm also proud that I managed to contain my annoyance. "Brill," I chirp.

"Great," says Kate, with a smile that seems authentic.

We say goodbye.

But now I'm even more desperate for the party to happen.

Chapter 48

"How's it going, Giuseppe? Any news?"

Our head builder is looking hot and bothered. "Adam, I tell you again," he says, wiping his brow with a muscled arm, "I find you when we know."

"Sorry, sorry!"

I'm waiting to discover if the roof of the cottage can be patched up and can hardly contain myself. Neither can Theo. Already this morning, he's done two loads of laundry and hung it out to dry, while I gave the kitchen a deep clean—ready for the party that may or may not happen.

It doesn't help that Callum and Mabel are also on edge, scrolling through their phones, their earphones jammed in. Archie, however, knows nothing about the drama. We've decided we'll only tell him if it's bad news and will affect him. Blissfully unaware of the tension, he asks Theo if they can check on the wasp traps.

"I'll come too!" I almost shriek.

"Woo-woo!" says Archie, jumping up and down.

Theo and Archie take me around the three traps they created, using plastic water bottles with their tops cut off and inverted, their rims smeared with jam to attract the wasps, and their insides filled with vinegar to poison and drown them. When we check the first trap, we find the bodies of several dead wasps floating in the vinegar. Theo and Archie use an old wooden spoon to fish them out.

"Dad, what do wasps *do*?" asks Archie.

"I think they spread pollen, like bees," answers Theo. "And they eat little insects that attack our crops, so they're part of the food chain."

Archie frowns. "I don't like them."

I smile and tilt my head. "I don't think anybody does. But that doesn't mean they're bad."

"So why are we killing them?" he says.

Theo takes the dead wasps and tosses them over the hillside. "Good point."

But it's a point neither of us knows how to answer.

By the time we're emptying the third trap, it's become clear that however many wasps we catch, we're never going to get rid of them completely: everywhere we look, they're still buzzing around flowers or grapes.

"They must have a nest somewhere," says Theo.

Archie stands up, his eyes bulging. "Can we find it?"

Theo contorts his face. "I don't think that's a good idea, squirt."

Once again, I remember Angelika saying Wilf embraced all aspects of nature, good and bad. And once again, I think that living here, there isn't really any alternative. Besides, as soon as we've gone, nature will just resume its advance.

"I've got an idea," I say. "Why don't we stop killing them and leave them alone?"

Theo pauses, his spoon plunged in the vinegar. "I suppose they haven't actually stung any of us. What do you think, squirt?"

Archie blinks a few times as he considers the proposition. "Yeah, OK."

We set about dismantling the traps and throwing them away.

When we return to the patio to rejoin Callum and Mabel, they're still on their phones—and looking increasingly agitated.

"Do we still not know what's going on?" asks Callum, removing his earphones. "This is proper unbearable."

"I'm afraid not," I reply. "And I can't nag Giuseppe any more."

Mabel puts her phone down and suggests recording more social media content. "In case we do have to go home," she says to me under her breath. "That way, I can keep posting from Manchester."

She reports that over the last few days, engagement on our various channels has held up well but still comes mainly from already existing friends and connections: we're struggling to widen our network. She did post a video of me playing with the kittens—introducing each of them by name—to which she added several cat hashtags. This attracted a lot of attention from largely female cat owners in the Midwest of America—but our clickthroughs to the website actually went down. "We should probs try something different," says Mabel.

She suggests doing a post in which I appear with Theo—until Theo reminds her that, as a headteacher, he can't generate content himself. "It's fine if I happen to stray into someone else's post, but I can't be seen to promote a business."

Archie must have overheard the conversation as he erupts. "I know! I can do a dance! The one where I wiggle my bum!"

He demonstrates and this raises a giggle.

"That's superb," says Theo. "But we couldn't really have you in the videos unless your mum agreed."

"Let's phone her!" Archie suggests.

Theo rakes his hand through his hair. "Now's not really the time, squirt."

Actually, what *is* the time? I look at my watch and see it's eleven o'clock. What's taking Giuseppe so long?

Desperate to keep myself occupied, I come up with ideas for some TikTok videos. First, I suggest introducing our followers to Len and Lionel the gay lizards, then realize this might actually backfire. "Not everyone wants to share their home with reptiles, whatever their sexuality."

"Why don't you do something in the kitchen?" suggests Mabel.

Theo proposes a demonstration of how to make Italian coffee in a traditional moka, but we decide this isn't fun enough—and too many people will know, anyway.

"You should cook something," pipes Callum. "You love cooking."

"But it needs to be something quick," cautions Mabel. "What was that thing you made us on the first day?"

"I can't remember." Already the start of summer seems a lifetime ago, as if it happened to someone else. "Oh, a *frittata*! But you all thought that was rank!"

Mabel gives a sardonic grin. "We didn't really. Surely you've learned that by now?"

Reasoning we can eat it for lunch, I agree.

As I fry an onion and spinach, crack and whisk the eggs, and fold in the ricotta cheese, I give a commentary to the camera. Just after I've slid my *frittata* into the oven, I hear a shout from Giuseppe.

"Adam! Adam! Where are you?"

Finally!

Mabel and I rush out onto the patio, where Theo and Callum have stood up, eager to hear what he has to say.

"I have good news," booms Giuseppe. "The repair works!"

My stomach gives a little flip. "So we don't have to do the whole roof?"

"No, we do not do the whole roof," Giuseppe confirms.

Theo, Callum and Mabel cheer. Archie joins in, even though he has no idea why he's cheering. And I find myself hugging a shirtless, slippery Giuseppe.

"Thank you!" I gush. "Thank you, thank you, thank you!"

"I am pleased you are happy," Giuseppe says, looking a little stunned.

"Why are we celebrating?" asks Archie.

"We're having a party!" I sing-song.

"I know that!" But he jumps up and down and wiggles his bum anyway.

"Right, I need to call your mum," says Theo, scouting around for his phone.

"Can I speak to her too?" I ask.

Theo looks at me with a confused expression.

"I'll explain on the way," I say, urging him towards the olive grove.

Then I remember. "Hang on a minute; I need to take out my *frittata*!"

Chapter 49

On Friday, the builders put the finishing touches to the cottage, including applying a second coat of paint to the bedroom. We didn't want a color that would be too overpowering so opted for a soft ivory. The bathroom, on the other hand, has walls that are painted an oyster gray, which complements its new ivory suite. The whole cottage looks stunning. If it weren't for the smell of paint, I'd be tearful.

I go outside to water the garden for what I realize will be the last time this summer—before Stefano takes over. It's the first day of September, so the season will be changing soon. Already, there are noticeably fewer flowers and less color than just a few weeks ago, although there's still just as much greenery. The grapes on the vine twisting through the pergola are almost ready to harvest—I know this because Stefano has examined them and said they're "OK," which Luisa joked means the same as "excellent" from anyone else. The cycle of nature will indeed continue without us. Again, it's enough to make me tearful.

Towards the end of the morning, Theo and I take the kids up to the castle to see Luisa and her team of diggers. They're supposed to be packing away, as today is their last day before Luisa, a couple of other middle-aged teachers and the young student start the new academic year. I expect everyone to be in a downbeat mood but there's excitement in the air, overlaid with loud chatter in Italian.

"We've found another wall!" Luisa trills.

"It's at the back of the castle," adds Vito, equally upbeat. "And it looks well-preserved."

"Amazing!" I say.

"Superb!" chimes Theo.

"Can we see it?" asks Archie.

Luisa and Vito lead the five of us through the site and indicate the very top of a stone wall peeping through the earth.

"It's a shame we don't have time to excavate it properly," comments Vito.

"But at least we've got something to look forward to," Luisa adds.

We discuss when the dig can be resumed. Although the dates will be dictated by academic holidays, I no longer feel the need to be present when the team are on site. On the other hand, if we get any bookings for the house, they'll have to work around those. But this still hasn't happened—and I'm starting to think I may have to tout myself around for some contract work in HR when I'm back in Manchester. It's a grim thought and one I'm keen to suppress, at least until the end of our holiday.

I break into a smile. "Well, it seems to have been a successful dig. I had no idea you'd find so much."

"I know," says Luisa. "And who knows what's to come?"

We leave the diggers to pack up their tools, trowels and rolls of tape and load up their trolleys.

When we arrive back at the house, the builders have finished in the cottage and are in the process of vacating it. The five of us move inside to clean everything, install the furniture and ornaments, and hang a few of Wilf's watercolors on the downstairs walls, discussing what we'll do with the upstairs walls after they've dried. Theo and I had intended to move back into the cottage for our last few nights but the delay put paid to this—and now the smell of paint is too strong. But we work as if we are moving in, as we want to show off the place to our guests tomorrow. And all this we do to the sound of Wilf and Arnaldo's opera records, which I tell myself is probably the last time we'll hear them this summer. But I'm determined not to feel sad.

Outside, the builders switch focus onto loading their workbenches, wheelbarrows, dust sheets and boxes of tools into the van. The skip has already been collected for the last time but they have plenty of unused materials—half-full bags of plaster, sand and cement, piles of stones and tiles, plus lengths of piping, trunking and electric cabling—that also need transporting away. As it's clear they won't be able to take everything today, I agree they can stash what's left in the garage and collect it next week.

"Just as long as it doesn't get in the way of the party!" I tell Giuseppe.

"Don't worry," he says, "nobody sees anything."

Talking about the party reminds me that we still need to finalize our outfits. Towards the end of the afternoon, Theo drives me and the kids into Lucca to buy a few items of clothing to supplement what we already have. As we drive down the tree-lined main road, through village after village, over the two baffling junctions, I realize this is something else we're doing for the last time this summer. Again, I feel a dip of sadness.

Pull yourself together, Adam. You'll be back soon!

Theo drops us off just outside the city walls.

"Are you not coming, Dad?" asks Archie, putting on his cap.

"Sorry, I've got to go and pick up the spare chairs," Theo says. He gives me a wink. "I'll see you back here in a couple of hours!"

And, with another wink, he drives off.

We set off down Via Fillungo—Archie's hand in mine—and call into several clothes shops. Many of them have discounted their summer stock, so we try on tops, shirts and T-shirts. As I slip on a pair of silver mesh espadrilles, I can't remember the last time I wore socks. I realize I'll have to get used to that again as soon as I'm home.

I grab some more clothes and take them into a fitting room. When I step out wearing them, Callum says, "Nice drip."

We all laugh.

As well as buying a few clothes for myself, I pick up a patterned linen shirt for Theo and treat Callum to a double-pocketed utilitarian shirt in gray, Archie to a bright green T-shirt emblazoned with the word *Ciao!*, and Mabel to a lilac crop top that shows off her newly flat stomach, a metallic purple lip gloss, and a bead-making kit she spotted.

"Why do you want that?" I ask.

She shrugs. "I'm going to make something to match my outfit."

Just as we're leaving the shop, my phone vibrates to tell me I have a message. It's from Theo.

All it says is, "Passenger on board."

We drive through the olive grove and park in front of the garage. As we get out of the car and grab the bags of shopping from the boot, my heart does a cartwheel. What are the kids going to say when they see who Theo's picked up from the airport?

We reach the patio, where our guest is waiting.

It's Kate.

As soon as they spot their mum, the kids drop their bags and rush towards her. In an instant, I know we've done the right thing.

"Wait a minute," says Callum, breaking out of what's become a group hug, "this doesn't mean we're going home, does it?"

Kate squeezes his shoulder. "No, sweetheart. Adam invited me to your party." Her voice cracks and she pretends she has to clear her throat. "Isn't that nice?"

Callum stretches up onto his tiptoes. "Yeah, it's sick!"

Mabel gives a little squeak. "It's incred!"

Archie throws his hands around Kate again. "I love you, Mum!"

I had the idea of inviting Kate after she seemed genuinely remorseful for lying about the job and keen to make amends to the kids. I figured I could handle her company for a couple of days—even if she does take the odd swipe at me—as I'll be so caught up in the party. I also figured it would be good for Theo to have the chance to tell her the truth about that time he cheated on her. I wasn't expecting him to do it straight away but he messaged me before picking us up to say they'd already had the conversation and he was glad he'd got it off his chest. But I couldn't find out any more, as when we met I was with the kids—so I've no idea how she responded.

As I step towards Kate, I can't help my spine stiffening. I hold out my hand. "It's nice to see you."

She smiles and shakes my hand. As she does, I sense a tremble coming from hers.

"Your house is beautiful!" she burbles. "Theo gave me a quick tour—I love what you've done with it. Very understated and classy."

I force out a wobbly smile. "Thanks."

I thrust my hands into my pockets and start playing with a chewing gum wrapper.

"And look at you kids!" Kate gabbles on. "Cal and Mabel, you've gone so blond! Look at your golden tans! Archie, look at all your freckles!"

She bends down and kisses him several times on the head and cheeks, and he squeals with delight.

"You're so gorgeous I could gobble you up!" she says.

Archie leans against her and gives her a nuzzle. "You're gorgeous too, Mum!"

He isn't wrong: Kate's taller than I remember, her features less sharp, her skin enviably smooth and clear, even with a light tan. She's wearing a coral blue, patterned, flowing sundress, with three-quarter-length sleeves.

Spotting her suitcase, Mabel asks, "Are you staying with us?"

Theo sucks in a breath. "I'm afraid there's no room. Giuseppe says no one's allowed to sleep in the cottage for a few days."

"I'm staying in an *agriturismo* just at the bottom of the hill," Kate explains. "I'm not quite sure what that means but I guess I'll find out when I check in."

"It's very nice, apparently," I say, a little too chirpily. It was Angelika who recommended it, telling me she often uses it when she has an overspill of guests.

"Well, thanks for making the booking," Kate says, with a tight smile.

"My pleasure." I realize I've rolled the chewing gum wrapper into a tight ball.

It's obvious that Kate feels as uncomfortable as I do, so I excuse myself, saying that I have to make a start on dinner—which isn't a lie. As I pick up all the bags and take them inside, she unzips her suitcase and starts handing the kids presents she bought them in Atlanta.

Once I've put the shopping away and hung up our new clothes, I set about making an *insalata caprese* and a seafood risotto, which keeps me out of Kate's way for a while. By the time she and I are sitting at the table, we've each had a glass of wine and our discomfort is fading. Even so, I make sure to position myself a few seats away from her and also a few seats away from Theo: I don't want to rub her nose in our happiness.

Over dinner, I don't have to say much as the kids are still excited to see Kate and can hardly stop talking—even Callum, who in between sentences grins so widely I can see pretty much all his brace. I've no idea what happened while I was inside—or what was discussed—but he and Mabel have clearly forgiven her.

After we've eaten, Theo shows Kate the digital marketing Callum and Mabel have done for the castello.

"You're both very talented," she gushes. "You've just got yourself a new follower!"

"Mum, can I be in a video?" Archie asks.

She takes a sip of wine. "What do you mean, sweetheart?"

Archie sits up. "I want to go on my swing, with Adam pushing it. And put it on TikTok!"

"I said they needed to ask your permission first," clarifies Theo.

There's a pause. All three kids look at their mum, expectantly.

"Yes, of course," answers Kate. She tips back the rest of her wine.

"So can we *all* be on the social media?" checks Mabel.

Kate puts down her glass and smiles. "Fine by me. In fact, why don't we do the video now? Is it still light enough?"

We look out at the skyline and see the sun is slipping towards the mountain.

"Just about," judges Mabel. She jumps up out of her seat. "We'll have to be quick!"

Theo and Callum stay back to clear the table, while the rest of us walk over to the rope swing. Mabel films me pushing Archie, and Kate stands behind her, watching.

When Mabel decides we've got enough footage, she and Archie dash back to the table, where there's a better Wi-Fi signal. "I'm posting this right now!" she declares.

Kate and I find ourselves alone. A tense silence sets in.

"Sorry I was such a cow," she blurts out. "Clearly, I got you wrong."

Kate's apology—and its directness—take me by surprise. "Oh, thanks, I—"

"—Look, I don't know what came over me," she goes on, almost rushing through what she's got to say before she can talk herself out of it. "But I want you to know I'm not some hysterical desperado. I think I just felt aggrieved by the whole thing. I was hurt. And I was probably a bit jealous."

"That's OK," I say. "I get it. As long as you know I never wanted to replace you."

"Well, you have in a way," she snaps back. Then she looks surprised. "Sorry, I mean, you have got Theo."

I'm not sure how to respond to that. Why did I wind her up by saying something so stupid?

Thankfully, Kate continues. "But I could never have made him happy. I know that now."

There's another silence.

I look down at the grass. "No. But I know you've had it hard."

She gives the empty swing a little push. "I have to admit, it's slightly less hard now I know the truth about his little affair." She grabs onto the swing and stops it.

I'm not brave enough to face her so look back at the patio, where Mabel and Archie are tapping away on her phone. "If it's any consolation, I understand why you'd have found it confusing."

Kate folds her arms. "Well, I'm not confused anymore, am I? Now I just need to stop myself from looking back over our entire relationship and thinking it was a sham. Every intimate moment, every romantic gesture, every happy memory." Her chin trembles and she squeezes her eyes shut. She reopens them. "But I'll get there. And I guess I'm not the only woman who's found herself in this position."

"No." I look up at the side of the house—the side of what would have been the watchtower for the castle. I realize I hadn't considered the women, all those wives and girlfriends who ended up heartbroken and hurt simply for falling in love with the wrong men, men who could never have loved them in return. And if the stories of all the men who suffered from prejudice in the past have been forgotten, the stories of the women who suffered in their shadow are possibly buried even deeper.

Kate gives a little kick to a tree root. "Anyway, you'll be pleased to know you're no longer the focus of my anger. I can hardly go on blaming you."

I rock backwards on my heels. "I appreciate that. But I apologize in advance if I do anything insensitive."

She waves away my comment. "Don't worry about that. Theo's all yours. I don't hold your happiness against you."

"Thank you."

She takes a seat on the swing and pushes herself off the ground. "You know, it actually helps seeing how much the kids like you. Even if I was hoping for the opposite—at first, anyway. Clearly, they adore you."

I smile, realizing this is the best compliment she could have paid me. "Thanks. I adore them, too. They're fab kids. You've done a great job."

Kate smiles, as if this is the best compliment I could have paid her. "Thanks."

There's another pause but this time it isn't awkward.

"What I meant to say earlier was, I wasn't trying to replace you in the eyes of the kids," I comment. "You're their mum. You're irreplaceable." I don't add how I know that. I don't explain how I'm able to deliver the line with such conviction.

I don't have to: Kate is happy to accept it. "Yeah, I can see that now. And it looks like there's room for both of us."

"Yeah."

"Mum! Adam!" Mabel shouts from the table. "Have a look at this before I post it!"

Kate stops the swing. "Just a minute, sweetheart!"

"Coming!" I shout.

She looks at me and frowns. "Anyway, I hope you can accept my apology."

"Absolutely. Let's move on."

She lets out a breath and straightens her sleeves. "I think I deserve another glass of wine."

She flashes me a smile that's ever so slightly sassy, ever so slightly playful. And something about it makes me think that one day, the two of us might just be friends.

Chapter 50

There's half an hour to go until the party starts. The kids are upstairs, getting ready. Theo and I are already dressed, in our new, freshly ironed shirts, our reliable, regularly worn chinos, and the Panamas we've commented will remind us of this summer forever. We've been working hard all morning, although Theo has been whistling and humming jaunty tunes. Since his conversation with Kate, it's like he's had an added spring in his step. And now that our work is done, it's time to inspect the results.

On the island in the kitchen, we've laid out a buffet of bruschetta and *crostini*, polenta chips, *arancini* balls, *caprese* and *tricolore* salads, spinach and ricotta pastries—all of which I've made—plus cooked meats, olives and artichokes that Theo picked up from the deli in Camaiore. The only food we haven't set out are the ingredients for the build-your-own-pizza bar that we'll take out later and arrange on a table next to the wood-fired oven.

We've converted the larder into a bar, the centerpiece of which are the jugs of our pre-mixed cocktails—with refills in the fridge. There are also bottles of beer, white wine and Prosecco standing in ice buckets, plus spirits and mixers and a bowl full of lemons and limes. Outside, the patio is dotted with extra tables and chairs we've borrowed from Angelika and the Fiores, and we've decorated the front of the house with bunches of balloons and strings of Italian flags, plus we've hung from the pergola a disco ball that Mabel spotted in the window of a gift shop in Lucca.

All the elements for a fab party are present. The only thing missing is guests.

Normally, I'd be apprehensive before a party, especially one that's going to bring together groups of people who don't know one another—some who won't know anyone, other than us. And I am worried about Dad and Debbie: will they feel like they don't fit in or be able to relax and enjoy themselves? But other than that, I feel under much less pressure than I normally would. And that's because I'm not hosting this party alone: I'm hosting it with Theo.

The two of us stand in the entrance to the house—the turquoise doors propped open behind us—and gaze out onto the patio, behind it the Freddana valley stretching out in all its late-summer glory.

"We did it, *mio carissimo*," I say.

"*You* did it, *mio tesoro*," Theo replies.

I shake my head. "This is a joint project—I couldn't have done it without you."

"I'm not sure I agree with that but I'll take it," Theo concedes. "And whatever happens now—even if the heavens open and nobody turns up—we can be proud of ourselves."

"Yeah." I draw in a long breath and let it out, slowly. And I *am* proud of myself.

"Do you remember what this place was like when we first saw it?" Theo says.

"How can I forget?" The two of us sat on the patio, looking out over the spring landscape. I struggled to believe the property belonged to me and was clueless about Uncle Wilf, but enchanted by the romance of the place. "I think I fell in love at first sight."

"I think we both did."

I frown. "I also remember being frightened I wouldn't be able to pay the inheritance tax and keep it."

Theo nods. "And I remember being daunted by all the work that needed doing."

"But it was so beautiful." I sigh. "And now we've done all the work, I think it's even more beautiful."

There's a beat.

"I tell you what else is beautiful," says Theo.

"What?" A smile lifts the corners of my mouth: I hope he's going to say me.

A wolfish glint appears in his eye. "Your bum in those chinos. Bloody hell, Ads, what are you doing to me?"

He starts grabbing at me and growling, and I burst into giggles.

"Shall we just cancel the party and go upstairs?" he says, kissing my neck, hungrily.

I give a little scream and slap him away.

Just then, the kids come clattering downstairs.

Theo and I jump back from each other, straighten out our shirts, and turn to face them.

"We're ready!" announces Archie.

Mabel gives a little twirl. To my surprise, she isn't wearing the crop top I bought her yesterday but the lilac jumpsuit her mum brought from Atlanta. There's no sign of the bracelet she was going to make, either. But I'm not remotely offended. She *is* wearing the lip gloss I bought—and her hair is off her face, revealing the false eyelashes and more makeup than I've seen her wearing since Gloria was here. But it isn't over the top, and she's done a great job.

Callum, meanwhile, is wearing black shorts, his new gray shirt and freshly cleaned white trainers—and he's had a spritz of my aftershave, which he's started doing whenever he sees Lina. Next to him, Archie is dressed in denim shorts and his new *Ciao!* T-shirt, clutching a jar of hair product.

"Will you put some wax in for me?" he asks.

I do, and I also clean his glasses. When he smiles his thanks, I notice his new adult teeth have almost completely come through and nearly fill the gap at the front of his mouth.

"You look fab," I tell him. "You all do."

"Yeah," says Theo, "I can't wait for everyone to see you."

I quickly run through the kids' jobs and remind them what they're supposed to be doing. I don't want Callum to get distracted by Lina, Mabel by Freya, or Archie by anyone who's charmed by his cuteness—which I imagine will be the entire guest list.

I think how nice it is for the five of us to have a moment to take stock before the guests arrive. Because I'm not just hosting the party with Theo: I'm also hosting it with the kids. We're all doing it together. But, just as I'm about to ask the kids how they feel, the sound of voices—and a very theatrical laugh—drifts over from the driveway.

"I hate it when people arrive early." I turn to Theo and pout.

Theo's eyes glisten. "Yeah, but would you say that about *everyone*?"

Before I can answer, bursting from behind the garage comes Gloria, resplendent in a rainbow lamé body stocking, a gold wig and matching beard glitter, stack heels that make him look like a giant, and wafting around an oversized rainbow fan. He's followed by Ian, who's customized one of his signature gingham shirts with a sunflower pinned to his left breast, and is clutching four bottles of Prosecco—two in each hand—that clink together. Then there's Dom, who's showing much less flesh than usual, in shorts that almost reach his knees and a long-sleeved shirt, albeit one that's too small for him and clings to his arms and chest.

I feel a rush of emotion. My sisters!

"Don't panic, everyone!" trills Gloria. "We're here! The party can start!"

Theo grins.

The kids whoop.

And I burst out crying.

Gloria, Ian and Dom rush over and put their arms around me.

"Adam, what's the matter?" says Ian.

"I've never had that effect before," jokes Gloria. "Not since I went to see my ex to tell him I had chlamydia."

I laugh so hard I let out some snot.

"What's chlamydia?" asks Archie.

"Never you mind!" chorus all the adults.

"Sorry," I splutter, wiping my nose, "I'm just really happy to see you. And you've come all this way!"

"We could hardly let a party happen without us," comments Dom.

Gloria clicks open his fan. "It wouldn't be fair on our sister!"

"And what's a couple of hours on a plane when you're family?" adds Ian.

I turn to Theo. "I take it you were behind this."

He holds up his hands. "Guilty as charged."

"Oh, Theo, I love you!" I burst out. "And I love my sisters!"

"And I love your makeup," says Gloria, spotting Mabel. "That lip gloss is gorge!"

Her face splits into a smile. "Thanks."

Dom nods at Callum's physique. "Nice rig, mate. You've really packed on the muscle."

Callum beams and holds his chest a little prouder.

And Ian says to Archie, "I hope you've got your Top Trumps, because I'm dying for a game."

Archie produces a pack from his back pocket and does a little wiggle. "Woo-woo!"

"Now, never mind the games, who's in charge of the playlist?" interrupts Gloria. "I'm going to need some input!"

"More importantly, who's running the bar?" chips in Dom. "Because if we're getting into party mode, we're going to need some pre's!"

Chapter 51

A few hours later, the party's in full swing. While Theo slips around the back of the house to set up the pizza bar, I mingle with the guests to check everyone's happy.

I'm pleased to see various builders and diggers engrossed in conversation. It turns out they didn't get much chance to talk to one another while they were working, as one group was at the top of the hill while the other was at the bottom—but they're making up for it now. One older digger is sipping from a Castello Cosmo as he tells the Syrian builder about the pottery they found. And the student has struck up a conversation with a builder from Hungary, ostensibly to ask for advice about her upcoming trip to Budapest, but it looks like her real objective is to flirt—and she's succeeding.

Signor Mancini is one of the people I was worried wouldn't know anyone, but he seems perfectly relaxed. This is the first time I've seen him out of a formal suit and smart leather shoes, although he's still doused himself in aftershave. He's come with his wife, a raven-haired, statuesque woman who recognized Luisa as their children's history teacher and is chatting to her over Montemagno Margaritas. They're joined by Vito, who tells them he's moving out of town and asks the Fiores how they like living in the village—in a break from cuddling and pawing Dom. Dom steps away to get the two of them more drinks, and I take the chance to grab him and steer him to one side.

"I can't get over you and Vito," I say. "I didn't even know you'd stayed in touch."

"Yeah, we've been messaging ever since I got home," he reveals. "I think this might be it, Adam."

"Well, I'm really happy for you." I take a sip of my Prosecco. "It may have come as a surprise but I'm loving the plot twist."

"Me too. I've learnt that just because something was my story before, it doesn't mean it has to be forever."

I raise an eyebrow. "It sounds like you've been talking to Ian."

"Why, did he tell you the same thing?"

"Yeah!"

We laugh.

"Well, he's right," says Dom. "I also think part of the problem was I only ever saw basic, boring relationships. But you inspired me, my sister. You showed me it's possible to create something different."

"Oh, Dom, that's a lovely thing to say."

His thoughtful expression gives way to a mischievous smirk. "Speaking of relationships, has Theo proposed yet?"

I move to elbow him but he holds up his glasses to defend himself.

"No!" I yelp. But now he's mentioned it, I realize I would quite like Theo to propose. "I'm not going to let you tease me. Go and get those drinks!"

I hug him and move on to find Ian. I spot him sitting in a hammock, next to Kate. When she arrived from her *agriturismo*, I worried my sisters wouldn't be very welcoming, but I managed to take them to one side and tell them about our reconciliation. After that, Ian made a special effort and it looks like he's now switched into coaching mode: as I edge closer, I hear him and Kate discussing her career plans.

I decide not to disturb them and look around for Gloria, who towers over most of the guests so is easy to find. He's chatting to

Giuseppe and his wife, a ginger-haired woman called Judith, who has a strong Geordie accent.

"You know what I like most about this place?" Gloria asks her, Montemagno Margarita in hand.

"What's that, pet?" says Judith.

"Your husband's arms!"

Giuseppe laughs but Judith almost chokes on her polenta chip. I hope Gloria hasn't overstepped the mark.

"Don't get me wrong," he goes on, swigging his drink. "The house is nice and everything but those muscles are something else."

Judith breaks into a naughty grin. "The rest of him isn't bad, either."

The two of them cackle with laughter.

Gloria spots Angelika and excuses himself to rush over and launch himself at her. "I've been dying to meet you!" he erupts. "I've heard all your stories! I swear down, you are iconic!"

Angelika looks slightly overwhelmed and twists her rings round her fingers. "Well, thank you."

"Go on," says Gloria, "ask me if I've got anything to suck on."

There's a second before Angelika understands what he's getting at, then a twinkle appears in her eye. "Have you got anything to suck on, darling?"

Gloria snaps open his fan. "Those builders aren't bad!"

The two of them hoot with laughter and I decide it's safe to leave them.

I look around for Dad and Debbie. When they arrived, they looked nervous, and I noticed Dad tipping back his first beer. At first, he clung to Debbie's side, apart from chatting to Giuseppe and some of the other builders, complimenting them on their windows. Then Theo joined them and they struck up some banter about City versus United. That's something my younger self could never have imagined—seeing my football-obsessed dad chatting to my football-loving boyfriend. But I liked it, and I think Dad did, too.

I spot him with Debbie, the two of them standing in front of the grain store, sharing one of the first pizzas to come out of the oven. They're chatting to Callum, who's holding hands with Lina, and Mabel, who's standing next to Freya, the two of them sipping Virgin Versilias. I lean in to check they're all getting on.

"We were horrible to Adam at first," Callum is saying. "We pretended his food was minging."

"One time I scrubbed the toilet with his toothbrush," adds Mabel.

Debbie chuckles. "I wouldn't worry about that. When Adam were your age, I saw him wipin' my toast on t' kitchen floor."

"I didn't know you saw that!" I break in.

Debbie looks at me and rolls her eyes. "'Course I did, love. I just didn't say owt because you chickened out and chucked it in t' bin. I don't mind admittin', part of me were disappointed."

"*I* weren't disappointed!" Dad pipes up. "But we had a right laugh about it, didn't we, Debbie?"

The three of us have another laugh now and I'm relieved to see that everyone has loosened up.

Gloria moves in. "Addy, you didn't tell me your dad was so handsome!"

I feel flummoxed and take a swig of my Prosecco. "Oh, urm, well . . ."

"Move over, Theo!" Gloria shouts out. "Mart, you're my new favorite zaddy!"

Dad furrows his brow. "What's a zaddy?"

"A hot daddy," Gloria answers, with a snap of his fan.

Dad grins. "In that case, ta very much."

Gloria turns to Debbie. "Respect, girl. What's your secret?"

Debbie giggles bashfully. But before she can answer, Dad jumps in. "As if she needs a secret! Look at her—she's beltin' lookin'!"

Debbie continues giggling.

"Now I fancy him even more," declares Gloria. "There's nothing hotter than a man who appreciates his woman!"

That comment seems to delight both Dad and Debbie. And Callum pulls Lina closer and kisses her on the side of the head.

When Debbie asks Gloria to teach her how to throw a fan, I slip away.

I find Theo and he tells me Stefano has relieved him of his pizza-making duties. But I don't have the chance to commandeer him, as Mabel grabs him to announce the start of the treasure hunt. Those who don't want to play are invited to have a look around the house—and, while they're at it, sign the visitors' book.

I go into the larder to fill up my glass as everyone troops inside and up the stairs. Then I follow them, drifting from room to room, listening to what they're saying, happy to lap up their compliments. While lots of people praise the renovations and décor, it's Wilf and Arnaldo's photos that attract the most attention.

"They're absolutely lovely," says Ian.

"And so moving," adds Vito, wrapping his arm around Dom.

"I hope you're listening, Willie!" drawls Angelika, glancing up at the ceiling. She turns to me. "You know, he'd love being at the center of a party. And Arnaldo could be a bit grumpy but I'm sure he would, too."

She gives me a beam and I feel a rush of happiness.

When Angelika totters downstairs to pour herself another Castello Cosmo, I open the visitors' book to read more compliments.

"To a wonderful couple," Kate has written. "You've created a beautiful home and I wish you a long and happy future in it—all five of you."

My happiness blossoms.

Just as I'm closing the book, Theo and Mabel announce that the treasure hunt is over and anyone who's found any little Leaning Towers should come outside and hand them over. When they've calculated the scores, Freya is declared the winner. Freya and Mabel squeak with glee and treat themselves to another round of Virgin Versilias.

Next on the agenda is the orange-throwing competition, coordinated by Archie, who I quickly grab to wipe a smudge of tomato sauce off his face. He hands out the oranges and directs each contestant to stand behind the line of stones he's arranged along the ridge of the hill. As each contestant throws, he judges how far the oranges travel by studying their impact on the tops of the trees. The builders become very competitive, then unite in opposition to the diggers. Signor Mancini must have drunk too many Montemagno Margaritas, as he loses his balance and his wife has to grab onto him before he totters over the hill. And Callum draws his arm back as far as possible and flexes his bicep to impress a besotted-looking Lina. When his orange arches through the air, clearing the top of the tallest tree, Archie declares him the winner. Lina rewards him with a kiss.

As the keepy-uppy competition is declared open, all those who didn't win the orange throwing are keen to take another shot at glory. Theo's attempt to keep the ball up is admirable—not to mention sexy—but it's Dom who manages to keep it up for the longest, as Vito watches, possibly even more besotted than Lina was with Callum. That is, until my dad steps up.

Dad starts by saying he's had too many beers to do his best, then stuns the party with an incredible run of 423 bounces, to some extremely enthusiastic cheerleading from Debbie, Gloria and—once he passes 300—pretty much everyone. Afterwards, my sisters lift him up onto their shoulders and parade him around like a hero. Seeing this gives me an unexpected thrill.

When the games are over, Gloria takes charge of the playlist. The introduction to Bananarama's "Venus" blasts out of the speakers and he lip-synchs along, directing an energetic, physically expressive performance at Angelika. She stands watching, sipping on her cocktail and smoking a cigarette from her extravagant holder, then declares herself honored to be his goddess.

After kissing her hand to riotous applause, Gloria asks everyone to clear away the chairs and tables and transforms the patio into a dance floor. Under the disco ball, he teaches the guests a simple routine to "Mambo Italiano," in a deliciously camp version by Bette Midler.

Theo asks Kate if she'll dance with him, and she accepts. I watch the two of them laughing as they mess up the moves and feel another unexpected thrill.

I find myself dancing with Mabel and Archie—and Callum breaks away from Lina to join us. When Kate and Theo spot us, Kate takes out her phone to film it.

"That was great," she says, once the song's over. She hands her phone to Mabel. "Why don't you post it online?"

As Mabel steps away to open her TikTok, I remain on the dance floor. And, finally, I manage to commandeer Theo. The two of us dance to song after song, enormous smiles on our faces, buoyed up by the party atmosphere but at the same time almost unaware of everyone else, our eyes fixed firmly on each other.

I dance closer to him and say into his ear, "We did this, Theo—you and me."

He puts his arms around my neck. "I love you, Ads."

"I love you, Theo."

After a few more songs, we decide to switch off the music so I can make a short speech. I tidy up my hair, wipe my forehead, and take up position on the edge of the lawn, the valley behind me. I start by thanking everyone for coming and remind them to please post about the castello on their social media.

"But the main reason we're throwing this party isn't to launch the castello," I go on. "It's to thank you for all your help. Some of the jobs we've done we knew absolutely nothing about, so we've had to rely heavily on you all. And I'm embarrassed to say I still can't speak a word of Italian."

Stefano shouts something that fittingly, I don't understand. Those that do, laugh.

"But I must say a special thank you to my gorgeous, brilliant, attentive, romantic boyfriend." I turn to face him and take his hands. "Theo, on our first night in Italy I hoped it would be the start of a special adventure—and it really was. Thanks for being at my side and for promising you always will be."

He leans in to kiss me on the lips, to the sound of cheers from the crowd. As I turn back to them, I catch sight of Dad and he shoots me a grin.

"I also want to say a special thank you to our main helpers Callum, Mabel and Archie," I continue. "I think it's fair to say we got off to a bit of a shaky start, but we soon hit our stride, and looking back I wouldn't have had it any other way. Callum, Mabel, Archie, I'm so happy to have you in my life."

As the three of them run over to hug me, I hear a female voice hollering and I can't be sure but I think it may be Kate's.

"And everyone else," I say, "this may be the end of our summer but it's definitely not a goodbye. We'll be back soon. And I may be crap at Italian but I did ask Luisa how to say that. *Alla prossima!*"

Chapter 52

By early evening, the social media post of the kids and me dancing is generating high levels of engagement across all platforms.

"That's what we needed to do differently," asserts Mabel, her face flushed. "People love it!"

I wonder what exactly she means but study our accounts and see she's altered the bios and captions to present the castello as a family home.

"You're right," I say. "And look at all the lovely comments!"

Theo beams. "You've done a superb job, Mabel!"

Callum joins our huddle. "Do you want some more good news?"

"Yes!" I yelp.

"We've just had our first booking!"

I give a little leap on the spot. "Amazing!"

"It's for two weeks in October," Callum elaborates. "I've just had a notification on my phone."

Theo puts his arm around his son and gives him a squeeze. I don't think I've ever seen Callum so happy.

He shows me his phone and I notice that the customer has asked some questions I need to answer, but I've had several glasses of Prosecco, so am not going to do it now. Instead, I pause the music and relay the news to the party. It's greeted by a rowdy cheer, followed by the sound of a balloon popping—which generates another, even rowdier, cheer.

By this stage, most of the guests have been drinking for hours. The Hungarian builder is leaning against the garage, straddling and kissing the student digger. Dom has a string of Italian flags draped around his shoulders, his shirt crumpled up by his feet, and Vito wrapped around his waist. And Gloria has opened Grindr and is showing it to Angelika—until he spots the profile of a man he's sure is our Egyptian builder. I watch him take a few drags on his vape, top up his lip gloss, and stagger off in the builder's direction.

Ian moves in mine. "Is now a good time to whisk you away for a few minutes?"

I look around for Theo and see he's dancing with the kids. "It probably is, yeah."

We find a quiet seat on the doorstep to the cottage.

"It was great to meet your dad," Ian says, taking out his lip balm and running it over his lips. "And great to see him getting on so well with Theo."

I swivel to face him. "I know. I hadn't realized but in some ways they're very similar."

Ian corrugates his brow. "Had you *seriously* not realized? I always thought that was obvious."

"Ian, I'm not going there," I say, smirking. "You can have your abandonment issues, but I'm not going near any daddy issues."

"Alright, alright!"

I roll my eyes. "Anyway, how about *your* love life? When you see Dom with Vito, are you not tempted to give it another go?"

Ian pushes his glasses up his nose. "No, thanks. Greg and I would have been together for twenty years this summer. And in some ways it feels like we still are. He's with me all the time, even when I'm not thinking about him."

"That's lovely." I think the same is true of me and my mum, or at least it is now I've got to know her better, now I understand what she did and why.

"I don't want to find love again," Ian goes on. "I've done that and I couldn't possibly improve on the experience. I'd rather do something different."

I narrow my eyes. "Oh yeah? It sounds like you know what that is."

"That's what I wanted to talk to you about." He runs his hands down his legs. "You know I've been doing these group coaching workshops in Manchester?"

"Yeah. . . ."

"I was wondering about doing something similar here. You and me running them together."

I cock my head. "Tell me more."

Ian gestures to the party. "Well, you're great at hosting. You like creating a warm, welcoming atmosphere and bringing people together."

We're distracted by the sound of someone throwing up and scan the crowd to see Signor Mancini bent over a hydrangea bush, his wife rubbing his back.

"Most of the time," I joke.

Ian chuckles. "Well, one of the things that keeps coming up in the sessions I've done is the importance of knowing your own story so you can understand who you are. I think I'm going to focus on that more and more."

I stretch out my legs and consider this for a moment. "It's not a million miles away from what I've been doing this summer."

"Exactly. That's why I think you and me could do a great job of encouraging other people to do it, facilitating it. Especially queer people who are detached from their stories or denying them in some way."

The excitement stirs within me. "It does sound interesting. So is it like group therapy?"

Ian bounces a fist on his thigh. "Yes, but it's also about creating a permanent record. So that other people can understand us too—even after we've gone."

I screw up my nose. "But how would we do that? I don't want to be a writer."

"It's not about being a writer: it's more about sharing your story, your emotional truth, the experiences that have defined you. And you can do that in different ways—yes, by writing it down, but also through extended interviews, in audio or video recordings."

I nod. "OK, I get it."

"And what better place to do it than here? The castle where stories were lost but have also been found."

I can feel my excitement building. "Very clever."

The music changes and I look down to see Luisa and Stefano coming together for a slow dance. They snuggle into each other and gently sway from side to side, Luisa resting her head on Stefano's shoulder.

"We could start small," Ian suggests, "maybe running a week-long workshop in the spring and another in the autumn."

I nod. "That could work."

"Fantastic."

I stand up. "The only thing is, my story isn't quite finished yet."

"Oh no?"

"You've just reminded me of one more thing I need to do."

Chapter 53

I find Dad and Debbie sitting on the sofa in the big lounge, sipping mugs of tea.

"Alreet, lad," says Dad when he sees me.

"We're just havin' a breather, love," explains Debbie. "We weren't sure if you'd have tea bags, so we brought our own."

"We're not as young as we used to be," jokes Dad. "And we're jiggered after all that dancin'."

I sit in the armchair facing them. "I thought you did well. You kept up with most of the kids."

Debbie smiles. "Yeah, but we're payin' for it now."

I'm suddenly compelled to tell them what I came to say. With no preamble, I bark, "Debbie, I'm sorry."

There's a pause. She brushes some imaginary fluff from her lap. "What for, love?"

"For wiping your toast on the floor and all the other grim things I did."

She waves away my concern. "That's alright, love. You don't need to apologize."

"No, I do," I insist. "It's important. And Dad, I've already apologized to you, but please, can we not keep anything from each other again?"

Dad looks thrown. " 'Course not, lad."

"Fab." I shuffle forward so I'm perched on the edge of the chair. "In this new spirit of openness, I'm going to share the way I feel about you."

Dad rests his tea on the side. "Oh yeah?"

"I love you, Dad."

He looks shocked. "Really?"

"Yeah. Even if I haven't always shown it."

A smile sweeps across his face and into his eyes. "I love you, too, Adam."

"I know," I reply. "Or at least I do now."

"I always have," Dad goes on. "I never stopped loving you."

I stand up and hold out my arms but Dad struggles to get to his feet. I lower a hand and he grabs onto it. Once he's standing up, I draw him into a hug. He feels warm and his back is slightly damp, but I hold onto him tightly and breathe in his familiar earthy scent, overlaid with deodorant and beer.

"I may not have understood you properly in the past," I say. "But I do understand you now and I'm looking forward to understanding you even better in the future."

I pat him on the back and he pats mine several times. "Same 'ere, lad."

We come out of the hug and he wipes a tear from his eye.

"That's beltin' that is," says Debbie. "Seein' you two have a hug."

Dad sits down again and she links her arm through his.

"Well, get used to it because it'll be happening a lot more often," I say.

Dad wipes another tear from his eye. "Good. I'd like that."

"Me too."

As I step outside, I notice that the sun has started setting. I wonder if I can slip away and go up to the castle to watch it.

Theo slides in next to me. "Come on, let's get up there," he says.

I smile. "I was just thinking the same thing. But where are the kids?"

The last time I saw Archie, he was playing with Giuseppe—riding him like a horse; Mabel was lying in a hammock with Freya, monitoring our likes on TikTok; while Callum was leading Lina into the grain store. I don't like to think what for.

"Don't worry about the kids," Theo says. "Kate will keep an eye on them. There's something I want to talk to you about."

My breath stops in my chest. Maybe Dom's right; maybe Theo *is* going to propose. Come to think of it, Gloria's been teasing me about it, too. Do they know something I don't?

I swallow and nod. I follow Theo around the edge of the dance floor, behind the chapel wall and over to the bottom of the hill, my heart galloping.

As we walk up the steps, I notice the blackberries on the brambles are now perfectly ripe. I pick one, put it in my mouth and lick the juice off my fingers. I grab another for Theo and when we make it to the top, pop it in his mouth. We look into each other's eyes and I realize I've nothing to be nervous about.

"Surprise!"

I almost jump back in shock, then turn around to see Callum, Mabel and Archie.

"I thought you were with your mum," I splutter.

"I just said that to get you up here," admits Theo. "Come on, come over here and sit down."

I follow them past the entrance to the underground chamber and through the ruins of the castle. I may no longer be nervous but I'm even more intrigued to find out what's going on.

Then again, I'm obviously not going to get a proposal if the kids are here. My spirits plunge as I realize just how much I did want that. Part of me was holding out for Theo to do the traditional thing and get down on one knee.

When we reach the stone wall, we sit down, facing a glorious pumpkin and peach sunset.

"Right," says Theo, "there's something the kids and I want to ask you."

He, Callum and Mabel turn to face Archie as if to give him his cue. Clearly, they've rehearsed this.

Archie stands up. "Adam, will you be part of our family?"

"We were going to ask you to be our stepdad," pitches in Callum, excitedly. "But we're not sure we like that word. And we're not sure it describes you."

Wait a minute, so *is* this a proposal or not?

"Then we realized we already had the perfect word," Mabel runs on. "We just didn't realize it at the time."

I crinkle my face. "What's that?"

Archie takes a deep breath. "Will you be our Dadam?"

Mabel hands me a bracelet she's made from the bead kit I bought her in Lucca. I see they're all wearing them.

"We made this specially for you," she says, proudly.

I turn it around in my hands, seeing that it's lilac, sky blue and bright green.

"We all did it," says Archie, grinning. "I did the green."

"I love it," I say, turning it around in my hands. But I'm also confused. Is this instead of a ring? What's it supposed to mean?

Mabel must have read my expression. "We wanted to do something different because we're a different kind of family. And we like it like that."

"Being the same as everyone else is proper boring," elaborates Callum.

Theo picks up their explanation. "When I talked to the kids, we realized they like being part of a family we've invented ourselves. It makes them feel they're not restricted by having to conform to expectations."

"Yeah, what Dad said," quips Callum.

We all laugh.

"And they've realized it's a privilege," adds Theo.

"Actually, we didn't say that," Mabel corrects him.

"We said it's a *superpower*!" chirps Archie.

"Oh, yeah," says Theo. "They said it's a superpower to be able to express our uniqueness in the shape of our family."

I'm so touched. What they're saying has been carefully thought out and is so intelligent and wise. But I also feel embarrassed for expecting a traditional proposal. After spending the summer creating something so special, how could I be so basic as to want Theo to get down on one knee and pull out a ring? The kids have asked me to be part of their family—their alternative, unique family—

and the way they've asked is much more meaningful than if Theo had followed any kind of template.

But part of me can't help wondering if Theo's going to say anything. The kids have had their say: is he going to express *his* feelings?

I tell myself to keep quiet: Theo loves me. He tells me that all the time. The last time he told me was less than an hour ago.

I tug in a breath. "Yes, of course I will. Thanks a lot, guys." I slide the bracelet onto my wrist and give them my brightest smile.

Everyone cheers. I feel a powerful sense of belonging, of being in exactly the right place with exactly the right people. Then I realize it's this I've been looking for all along.

"While we're on the subject," says Theo, his face glowing pink from the sun's last rays, "I want to ask if you'll share the rest of your life with me. As your partner, your soulmate, your other half, your husband—whichever word you prefer. Or we can invent our own word."

All of a sudden, I feel choked up.

"I don't know," I stutter. "I . . ."

The kids' faces drop.

Theo looks crestfallen.

"Sorry, the answer's yes!" I shout. "Of course that's what I want! That's what I've always wanted!"

"So what's the problem?" asks Theo.

"I don't *know* the right word," I say. "I don't know which word I prefer."

"That's OK," he reassures me, taking hold of my hand. "We've got plenty of time to work it out. We can spend the rest of our lives working it out."

I squeeze his hand. "There's nothing I'd like more."

I look up at the sunset and remember that somewhere beneath me is the stone inscribed with the names WILF + ARNALDO.

And the sun slips behind the mountain.

Acknowledgments

All my books come from the heart but this one was a real passion project, a true labor of love. I want to thank all my writer friends who kept me sane not just while I was writing it but when it took me to a turning point in my career and I had to battle to stay on course. Freya North, Alexandra Potter, Chrissie Manby, Ruth Hogan, Imogen Parker and Tasmina Perry, I couldn't have done it without you. An equally big thank you goes to my agent, Lisa Highton, who fought as hard as she could for it at every step of the way.

Thanks to all the team at Kensington, my long-term publishing family in the U.S.: Lorraine Freeney, Jackie Dinas, cover designer Kris Noble, production editor Carly Sommerstein, publicists Michelle Addo and Vida Engstrand, and the big boss, Steve Zacharius. Extra-special thanks goes to my editor, John Scognamiglio, who believes so fervently in the message of my work and is my biggest cheerleader and champion.

Thanks to my nephews Jayden and Freddy for answering my research questions on the life, likes and especially the favored slang of teenage boys. And to my friends Amy Rynehart, Laetitia Clapton and Bianca Sainty for helping with my research on teenage girls, including giving me all the detail on the Harry Styles concert. An extra-special thanks goes to Bianca for checking and correcting my dodgy, largely computer-generated Italian.

But the most important thanks I have to give for this book doesn't go to a person but a property—the real-life Castello Montemagno, with its chapel and farmhouse in Tuscany. Yes, the house and grounds described in this book exist and are every bit as romantic, atmospheric and beautiful as they are on the page—if not more so. My husband, Harry Glasstone, inherited it from his dad's cousin a few years before we met and it was this that gave me the inspiration for the book. But much as we love the place, the cost of maintaining buildings that are up to a thousand years old is so high that we just can't afford to keep it. At the time of writing, we're selling the castello. I'm heartbroken to be losing a place that's been so special to me but also feel incredibly privileged to have had it in my life for more than six years. I consider this book a means of keeping it alive in my heart.

Grazie to all the loved ones who've visited Harry and me at the castello and helped us create the many happy memories that inspired *The Castle of Stories.* Another even bigger *grazie* goes to our Italian friends, especially Massimo and Carla Montemagno—yes, they are named after the village!—who've always done such a good job of looking after our house and its grounds. And *grazie mille* to Harry for bringing this very special place into my life.

But *The Castle of Stories* isn't just about the setting, however beautiful it may be. I also wrote it to provoke thought and challenge traditional beliefs about the nature of family. I've been very moved by the stories and struggles of various people close to me who've become step-parents and I wanted to write a book that provided some positive representation of their role and experiences. To all step-parents and anyone who's trying to make a success of a blended family, you have my utmost respect. As do all queer parents, who these days can find themselves on the frontline of the ongoing battle against homophobia and the prejudice directed at our community. Please see this book as an expression of my solidarity.

And to everyone in a found, nontraditional family—the kind of family represented by Adam and his sisters—please know that the bonds you've created and nurtured are equally valid. More than anyone, this book is for you!

A READING GROUP GUIDE

The Castle of Stories

ABOUT THIS GUIDE

The suggested questions are included to enhance your group's reading of Matt Cain's *The Castle of Stories*!

DISCUSSION QUESTIONS

1. How much do you think Adam's approach to romantic relationships both in the present and the past has been affected by his childhood experiences?

2. What do you make of Adam's initial struggle to be himself around the kids? Is his suppression of his sexual attraction—and even affection—towards Theo evidence of internalized homophobia?

3. Step-parents are often demonized in literature and other narrative arts. Why do you think this is? How does Adam's journey compare to the usual representation?

4. Do you see any metaphorical value in the ruined castle? How might it comment on the action and relationships unfolding in the house and on the content of the letters discovered there?

5. Do you see any parallels or echoes between the past-tense love stories related in the letters from Wilf and Suzanne and the present-tense love story between Adam and Theo?

6. What do you make of the interaction between the characters in the house and the natural world around them? How does this comment on the way Adam and Wilf have been made to feel about their sexuality and on the nontraditional family unit the book ultimately celebrates?

7. What do you think of Adam's relationship with his 'sisters' and the found family this represents? How does this relate to the family unit Adam and Theo are struggling to create with Theo's biological children?

8. What's your take on the struggle Theo experiences at the start of the novel between, on one hand, making his kids happy—which he sees as his responsibility as a parent—and on the other, his responsibility to himself and his own happiness?

9. To what extent was your sympathy for Theo affected by the revelation of his one-night stand? Did this change when you found out the one-night stand was with a man?

10. How do you feel about Kate? Did you understand the lie she told the children and her hostility towards Adam? Did you feel any sympathy for her?

11. What's your response to the book's message about the importance of understanding and telling our stories as they make us who we are? What about the stories of those close to us?

12. What did you make of the book's ending and Theo and the children's nontraditional proposal? Were you hoping for something more conventional? If so, did the ending make you reexamine your beliefs?